Murder So Rash

Penrose & Pyke Mysteries, Book 5

Rose Pascoe

Published by Flax Bay Books, 2023

Copyright

MURDER SO RASH

Written by Rose Pascoe
First edition November 10, 2023.

ISBN: 978-1991181350 (Softcover POD)
978-1991181343 (Epub)
Publisher: Flax Bay Books, New Zealand

Cover design: Rose Pascoe
Cover images from Shutterstock and Adobe Stock

Contents

Unwelcome News

Chattering voices and childish squeals drifted down the train carriage. Grace Penrose sat in silence, as dread pricked her nerve endings and churned her innards into a gurgling mush.

The view from the train window did nothing to calm her anxiety. Dark waves rolled towards the shore, sprouting white tips as they surged onto the rocks. Across the harbour, Otago Peninsula hid under a blanket of ill-tempered cloud. Not the day for a sea voyage, however short.

But it was not the thought of the boat trip to Quarantine Island that worried Grace – it was what they would find at their destination.

Two weeks ago, a ship had steamed into Port Chalmers carrying a dozen cases of measles. Fortunately, the captain had raised the yellow flag and the harbour master had put the ship under quarantine orders. Today, Grace was part of a small medical team sent out to make a final examination of the passengers and crew. If there were no more cases of measles, the passengers would be released from quarantine.

The consequences of making the wrong decision were unthinkable. If measles got into the community, the death toll amongst vulnerable children would be devastating. Although the life and death decision would be made by wiser heads than Grace, she felt the burden weighing heavily on her conscience. Of all the deadly diseases in the age of Queen Victoria – plague, cholera, typhoid, scarlet fever, smallpox and many others – measles was the one Grace feared the most, from bitter experience.

Her great-aunt, Anne Macmillan, was also a member of the medical team, but appeared untroubled by the day ahead. Anne sat opposite Grace, engrossed in the latest issue of the *Dunedin Ladies' Journal*.

Grace did not read the *Ladies' Journal* as a rule. She dipped into the pages only when in need of a frivolous diversion after a gruelling day. The earnest enthusiasm of the articles rarely failed to bring a wry smile to her face. ("Ostrich feathers are *de rigueur* for every lady of distinction this season!" … "Whether toque or bonnet, spring hats simply must perch daintily upon the head, angled just so, and sprigged with an abundance of nature's bounty!!").

On rare occasions, Grace envied the path chosen by other women, but mostly she relished the challenges of being the first female medical student in New Zealand. If other ladies were aghast that Grace also chose to assist the police surgeon, she simply replied that the work was fascinating and she needed the job to support her studies. As her mother often lamented, perhaps recalling the agonies of childbirth, Grace had been born with a stethoscope in one hand and a scalpel in the other.

Besides, dabbling in the malodorous art of autopsy had brought Charlie Pyke into her life. She had known Charlie was the man for her from the first moment they bumped heads over a corpse. Back then, he had been a lowly police constable. Now, he was a detective in the only private investigation agency in the country, in partnership with his former commanding officer.

Grace was never happier than when she was working by Charlie's side, using her medical skills to help bring criminals to justice. Not that there had been much of that lately. Since the Southern Investigations Agency's dramatic first case, Charlie had spent his time chasing lost dogs and missing valuables, with not a single corpse in sight.

Grace's musings were cut short by an unladylike splutter from her great-aunt.

"Why the snort, Auntie?" Grace asked. "Has the *Ladies' Journal* finally roused itself to outrage over the appalling failure of our parliament to allow women the vote? Or is it something truly important, such as the rise to fashion of a mauve chiffon bow so large as to obscure the entire bosom?"

Grace held out little hope of the former. Despite the largest ever petition presented to parliament, the Franchise Bill of 1892 had recently been scuppered by last gasp trickery. Yet another reason for her uncharacteristic despondency.

Anne's lips pinched to a thin line at the reminder of the women's suffrage defeat. Now in her mid-seventies, Anne Macmillan had spent her entire life fighting for women's rights. With her rapier-sharp wits and fearsome determination, Anne Macmillan was a force to be reckoned with. Woe betide the man or woman who dismissed her as an addled-headed old lady.

"Grace, dear, you simply must keep up with the significant events of the day." Anne tapped a page of the *Ladies' Journal* and began to read out loud. "A new arrival in Dunedin, Mrs Fendalton-Dabney, dazzled the assembled company at last week's Mayoral tea party, in a gown of ruched green velveteen, with cuffs of crème corded silk, braided in gold."

"How enthralling," Grace muttered. She recognised Anne's tactics as a diversion from the terrifying duty they were about to undertake. Grace had no wish to be churlish, but it would take more than Mrs Fendalton-Dabney and her ruched green gown to distract Grace from a potential epidemic of measles.

Anne looked over the spectacles perched on the bridge of her nose. "I take it you have no wish to hear more of the Mayoral tea party? The pink bows, silver spotted gowns, shot-silk parasols … oh, and an entire column on the very latest fashion in footwear, made from crocodile skin. You should go out at once and purchase all of the above, Grace, before the stock sells out."

Now it was Grace's turn to snort. "The only place I wish to see a crocodile is on the floor of the parliamentary debating chamber. But, do go on, Auntie. What occasion was being celebrated? The presentation of an award for the most fatuous comment by a local politician?"

"A visiting trade delegation from Australia," Anne replied, with a smirk. "You will be fascinated to hear that they are looking forward to making a tour of our frozen meat export plant. In truth, the reporter wastes few words upon the marvels of refrigeration and many, many words upon the fashion choices of the ladies present."

"Perhaps a wise choice, if the delegation's interests range no further than frozen legs of lamb. I couldn't imagine anything worse than attending such an event."

Anne turned the page. "Grace dear, if you insist on mimicking the face of a constipated bulldog –"

"A constipated bulldog? Really Auntie, of all the breeds of dog, I would claim the least resemblance to the bulldog. And my bowel movements are perfectly regular, thank you very much."

"Perhaps not a bulldog in looks, at this point in your life, but in character there is a certain resemblance." Anne forestalled Grace's rejoinder with a raised hand. "Very well, point taken. If you insist on mimicking the face of a disgruntled whippet, no man will wish to take you to anything half so exciting as a reception for frozen meat devotees, regardless of the number of pink bows upon your bonnet. The point is, Mrs Fendalton-Dabney is obviously attempting to establish herself as a new presence in town. I must hasten to inform her that the path to social acceptance passes through the gates of charitable works."

Anne considered it her duty to know the who, why, what and how of every citizen of their city. As the director of a free medical clinic and refuge for the women of Dunedin's poorer areas, Anne relied on them for the little titbits of information that helped her target wealthy folk for donations. Without women like Mrs Fendalton-Dabney, Lavender House would fall to rot and rust. Anne's intimate knowledge of the populace was also a boon to the detective agency. Their "society spy", as she had dubbed herself.

"Does the *Ladies' Journal* say nothing about the terrifying consequences of measles reaching our shores?" Grace queried. "Or anything at all remotely important?"

Anne arched an incredulous eyebrow. "Hardly likely, Grace. Let's see what the Lady Detective has to say in her column. She has quite the nose for a story, that one …"

Anne's mouth formed a tiny puckered circle as her sentence trailed off. Grace diagnosed a particularly titillating bit of scandal. To her surprise, Anne closed the *Ladies' Journal* and rolled it tightly, declaring it was a load of horse manure and they were almost at Port Chalmers station anyway.

Grace hadn't got to where she was today without a stubborn streak that would put a mule to shame. With a lightning lunge, she snatched the *Ladies' Journal*.

"Grace, no," Anne pleaded. "Please don't read it. It's nothing but foolish gossip."

Grace skimmed the pages until her eyes froze on a headline. "Has Dunedin's Dashing Detective Met His Match?" The *Ladies' Journal*, via the wiles of the reporter who called herself the Lady Detective, had hounded Charlie Pyke in recent weeks. Since their discovery of the existence of a private detective agency in Dunedin, privacy and discretion had been blown to oblivion. Charlie could scarcely venture from his lodgings for fear of eager ladies accosting him in the street.

On seeing the headline, Grace was certain her own name would be exposed as Charlie's faithful companion. She read on. The reality was far worse. Dunedin's dashing detective, Mr Charles Pyke, the article said, was observed with Miss Caroline Davenport, "loitering companionably" outside a jewellery shop, which featured a window display of diamond rings. After several lines of feverish innuendo, the article ended with a suggestion that readers should not be surprised if an engagement notice appeared in this paper in the near future.

Grace ripped the page out of the paper and tucked it into her satchel. Charlie Pyke was not a reader of the *Dunedin Ladies' Journal*, but someone would show him the article sooner or later. She would rather do it herself.

Anne eyed her great-niece warily, as one might a whippet with rabies. "Surely you trust Charlie, Grace. Anyone with eyes in her head can see the way he looks at you and only you."

“I’m not concerned in the least about Charlie’s choice of companions, Auntie,” Grace lied. “I’m only worried about the effect of this ongoing campaign of falsehoods on the Southern Investigations Agency. Charlie’s ability to solve cases discreetly has been hopelessly compromised by this woman calling herself the Lady Detective.”

“I have one or two acquaintances in the newspaper industry,” Anne said. “I could try to find out who she is and have her admonished. Perhaps I could persuade her editor to change her by-line to ‘Miss-Informed’?”

Grace knew she ought to brush the matter aside as the foolishness it was. But, as Anne had told her more than once, Lady Detective had a finely tuned nose for scandal. Lady Detective’s literary style might tend to the exuberant when it came to the use of adjectives and was positively gravid with hints of intrigue, but there was always a nub of truth behind every story. The article wouldn’t say that Charlie Pyke had been seen outside a jewellery shop with the divine Miss Caroline Davenport, eldest daughter of the Davenport sheep-farming empire, if it was entirely untrue.

Charlie knew the lady, as he had recently been employed by Caroline Davenport to find a stolen set of diamond jewellery – a parure of perfectly matched diamond necklace, earrings and brooch. After an initial burst of activity, Charlie had become tight-lipped about the case. As far as Grace knew, the case was over. Or, at least, he had not mentioned Miss Davenport or her fabulous diamonds again.

With the potential for a measles outbreak hovering over their heads, Charlie Pyke ought to be the least of Grace’s problems. But, the truth was, he had been behaving oddly in recent days. When he dined with them on Friday evening, he had changed the subject when asked about his day and affected the face of a poker player when asked why. As soon as he thought Grace had looked away, he had reverted to an expression somewhere between naughty schoolboy and unrepentant sinner. Most telling of all, he had toyed with his food and refused a second helping of dessert, an unheard-of departure from normality.

Grace hadn't seen Charlie since Friday night. He hadn't even offered to see her and Anne to the railway station this morning, despite knowing how nervous Grace was feeling about going out to Quarantine Island.

Charlie Pyke was hiding something. Grace knew it in her bones.

Emerson & Son

Charlie Pyke arrived at Emerson & Son, Watchmakers & Jewellers, a full fifteen minutes before opening time on Monday morning. The "closed" sign on the door mocked his eagerness. By now, the proprietor should have been downstairs to turn on the gaslights and prepare for the day.

Through a gap in the shutters, Charlie could see nothing but the looming shapes of cabinets, whose contents were rendered invisible by the feeble light.

Charlie paced the empty lane to keep his toes from freezing, pulling his thick overcoat close against the chilly southerly wind. Halfway through spring it may be, but winter had a nasty habit of making an encore appearance in the southern city of Dunedin. In his pocket, the roll of banknotes felt crisp and portentous to his nervous fingers. Charlie glanced around to ensure no loitering footpad was waiting to relieve him of the money, which represented a not insignificant portion of his life savings.

He had found Emerson & Son's jewellery shop quite by chance, after a rapid retreat through a series of dingy alleys and quiet lanes the preceding Friday. Charlie had been escaping from a persistent woman called Caroline Davenport, who had developed an annoying habit of appearing when he least expected it. On Friday, it had been in Princes Street, outside another jewellery shop.

Miss Davenport's presence had been particularly unwelcome, because Charlie was searching for a gift for his beloved Grace Penrose. Grace's spirits had been low after a difficult year – being implicated in one death and injured in another tragedy, seeing months of effort to gain women the vote fail at the last hurdle, and now the threat of a measles epidemic weighing heavily on her mind.

The rapid approach of end-of-year examinations at medical school was not helping either.

Once Charlie had escaped Miss Davenport, fate had intervened in the form of Emerson & Son's, an Aladdin's cave of glittering gems and expensive watches. Inside the tiny, out of the way shop, Charlie had seen a piece of jewellery that would send Grace into raptures. By the time he had gone to the bank to get enough funds, the shop had closed. Hence, his nervous wait until Monday morning to make his purchase. Grace had commented on his distraction and accused him of being secretive. Sometimes he wondered if she was a better detective than he was.

Charlie risked the biting wind to reach for the watch in his waistcoat pocket. Two minutes to nine o'clock. Still no signs of movement in the shop. He glanced down the lane, worried that Miss Davenport would appear again and attempt to invite him to an intimate supper party. The woman was a menace.

As he peered into the shop again, Charlie wondered if he had made the right decision. He had seen a pretty locket too – a far safer choice as a token of his affection. The canny shopkeeper, Mr Emerson, had talked him into the riskier and more expensive choice. With deep-set blue eyes sparkling within a wrinkled face, the elderly jeweller had looked into Charlie's soul and shown him perfection. Charlie had hesitated. How would Grace react? Was it too much? But the hesitation was short-lived. It was meant to be.

A grandfather clock chimed the hour within the shop. Charlie tried the door again. Locked, as it had been the previous three times he had tried it. He glanced upstairs, but the curtains were still drawn. The only light shone out from the attic, which seemed odd. Perhaps Mr Emerson was stocktaking upstairs and had forgotten the time. Unlikely, as a dozen clocks within the shop were now chiming the hour.

Charlie peered through the crack in the shutters again. The changing angle of the sun reflected on shiny fragments on the floor. Broken glass, by the look of it. Instincts aroused, Charlie circled the block of buildings, looking for a rear entrance. The gate to the little courtyard at the rear of the jewellery shop was easy to spot, as it was hanging open. The back door beyond the gate banged in the wind.

The door had been levered open by force, breaking the old lock. Charlie entered the shop, quietly at first, in case the intruder was still there. Inside, every one of the glass-topped cabinets was smashed. The rows of expensive watches and exquisite necklaces, rings, lockets and other valuables were gone. Including the one he had his heart set on for Grace.

"Hello? Mr Emerson?" Charlie called up the stairs. He ought to call for a policeman, but his gut told him to waste no more time.

Charlie ran up the stairs, calling the proprietor's name with increasing alarm. Upstairs, in one of the two bedrooms, he found Mr Emerson tied to a chair. A gag bound his mouth and nose so tightly, breathing must have been near impossible. Bruises marred Emerson's kindly, shrivelled face. A thin trail of dried blood ran down the side of his head, underneath his nightcap. Charlie searched for a pulse on the cold skin, knowing it was far too late.

Not content with the riches from the display cabinets in the shop, the robber must have come upstairs looking for more. Presumably, Mr Emerson had been bound and assaulted to force him to disclose the location of the shop's safe. A decent, honest man, needlessly murdered for a sack of glittering baubles. For how could one old man, whose rasping breath had indicated a weakness of the lungs, stop a determined villain?

Charlie touched Mr Emerson's cold, battered face and swore he would find the man responsible for this outrage.

Setting his anger aside, Charlie stepped back to the doorway, surveying the scene of the struggle slowly and thoroughly. The trail of destruction told a simple, tragic story. The robber had pulled Emerson out of his bed, casting his blankets aside and knocking over the items on the bedside table. Splayed pages of a novel, thin spectacles trampled to splinters, a water glass shattered on the wooden floorboards. The chair had been dragged into the centre of the room, leaving scratches in the polished floor. A mantelpiece clock lay on its side, miraculously undamaged and still ticking, its back panel gaping open to reveal the inner workings.

As far as Charlie could see, the robber had left nothing behind but the victim and the ropes and gag that bound him.

Victim. The word recalled that there were two bedrooms and a sign saying "Emerson & Son" above the front door. Charlie reluctantly left Mr Emerson's body and searched the rest of the residence. He got as far as the deserted cubicle that served as a kitchen, when he heard banging and scraping from above.

Charlie climbed the steeply angled steps to the attic, a heavy pot grasped in his hand. A second body lay on the floor of the attic, but this man was alive. Although thoroughly trussed, blindfolded and gagged, the man was banging his bare feet on the rough floorboards in a desperate attempt to call for help. Dressed only in a nightshirt, after enduring a freezing night, it was a wonder he managed that much. Beyond the man, a large iron safe stood open and empty within a cavity in the wall.

"Help is here, Mr Emerson," Charlie called as he hurried across the room. "I'll have you untied in a minute. I'm a customer. Charlie Pyke. The robber has gone."

Charlie eased off the gag and blindfold first, revealing a middle-aged man with a shock of greying red hair. Blood matted the hair behind his right ear, but the wound did not appear too serious. The rope was cutting off the man's circulation, so Charlie ignored the knots and cut the bindings with his pocketknife in the interests of speed.

"Don't try to move just yet, sir. Best to get the blood flowing first." Charlie draped his overcoat over the man and gently rubbed his wrists and ankles to restore circulation. Emerson must be in agony. "How's that head injury?"

"Aches like the devil, but I'll live." Emerson's voice was little more than a croak. With obvious effort, he pushed himself to his elbows.

Charlie kept a small flask of brandy in his jacket pocket. Not for his own use, but to revive clients in times of distress. He held it to Emerson's lips. The jeweller's son sipped and paused, before taking a larger gulp. He shuddered, but a little colour returned to his cheeks.

Woozy eyes locked on his rescuer. "Daniel Emerson, at your service. You're a welcome sight, Mr Pyke. Can I ask you to see to my father, please? The robber hit him."

Charlie helped him to sit up. "I'm very sorry, Mr Emerson, but I regret to inform you that your father didn't survive his injuries."

The sharp cry of anguish his words elicited cut straight to Charlie's heart. For all the satisfaction detective work brought him, the pain of imparting tragic news never grew easier. He replaced the overcoat, which had fallen to the floor, on Emerson's shaking shoulders.

Emerson clamped a hand on Charlie's arm. "Those villains killed my father? Two of them against one frail old man. I'll see those devils hang, if it's the last thing I do."

"I promise to help you, Mr Emerson. But, right now, you need to rest awhile after your ordeal. I'll summon the police and return as quickly as I can."

"Wait. You're the customer who came in on Friday, aren't you? My father said you are a private detective."

Charlie nodded. Mr Emerson Senior had subtly interrogated him during his first visit. Without realising it, Charlie had divulged much of his life story in the face of the man's persuasive questioning. His determination to forge a living as a private detective, after being forced out of the police force. His adoration for a certain young lady. His plan to work hard, so that someday, in the distant future, he could afford to give her the life she deserved. Her insistence that she would not marry until she qualified as a doctor, even if he could afford to ask for her hand.

"I've no doubt you have thought your situation through with commendable logic," Mr Emerson Senior had observed on Friday afternoon, with a twinkle in his eye, "but it doesn't mean you cannot declare your intentions to the lady. Life is short, young man, and love is precious. My advice is to leave your beloved in no doubt of your true feelings. As I always say, better a long engagement than a lifetime of regret."

Charlie had tried to tell the elderly jeweller that his lady was in no doubt of his love.

Mr Emerson Senior had ignored his protestations and cut to the chase. "What type of jewellery does the young lady prefer? Does she have a birth stone she favours? Silver or gold? Simple or ornate?"

"I'm not sure," Charlie replied. "Grace does not wear rings because of her work. The only time I have heard her talk with enthusiasm about an item of jewellery was when she told me about a beautiful sapphire and diamond necklace her grandmother wore. They keep a portrait of her grandmother wearing the necklace in the drawing room."

"Ah, in that case ..." Mr Emerson Senior beckoned him along the counter to another display case. He removed a tray of exquisite sapphire and diamond rings and slid it in front of his customer with a knowing twitch of his lips.

Nestled in the exact centre of the tray was a ring with a lustrous blue sapphire, surrounded by tiny diamonds. Charlie's fingers plucked it from the tray of their own accord. The ring might have been made to match the sapphire necklace treasured by Grace's grandmother. It was perfect. He had to have it. Grace had to have it. Whatever the cost. And Mr Emerson Senior had known it.

Charlie hadn't been able to put the ring down. He'd stared at the twinkling diamonds and deep blue of the sapphire. The discreet little numbers on the tiny tag made the price look less shocking, but it would still take a hefty chunk out of his hard-earned savings, which he had set aside for more sensible expenditure. A horse, a home (eventually), rainy day savings. On the other hand, there was nothing he wanted more than Grace Penrose. The old jeweller was right. Secure an engagement now, even if they married later.

Mr Emerson Senior had watched Charlie closely. "You seem a worthy young man. I'll make you an offer. A ten percent discount on the price, as long as you return with the young lady. I confess, nothing makes me happier than seeing the perfect ring adorning the hand of a blissful recipient."

Reluctantly, Charlie placed the ring back on the tray. "Unfortunately, I do not have sufficient funds on me at present."

"Don't you worry, young man. I'm about to close up for the day. This ring will be safe here, awaiting your return on Monday." Emerson settled the tray back into its spot with a flourish. "We have a payment plan, if required."

Charlie found himself assuring Mr Emerson that he would be back with the full amount as soon as he could and pleading with him not to sell Grace's ring to anyone else. He distinctly recalled the satisfaction on the old man's face. Without a doubt, Mr Emerson Senior had taken pride in finding the perfect item for each customer. He had certainly been good at his work.

Now, only three days later, Grace's ring was gone and so was the jeweller who made it. And the man's son was in front of Charlie, struggling to control his grief.

"You seem a worthy young man, Mr Pyke," the younger Mr Emerson said, unconsciously mimicking his father's words and tone. "Father was delighted to find you the perfect ring. He always knows exactly what a customer needs. Please, I beg of you, find the men who killed my father and the sapphire ring is yours."

Charlie didn't mention that the ring had been stolen, along with all the rest of the stock. "I promise you that I will do everything in my power to find the men who did this, Mr Emerson, ring or no ring. Your father was a fine gentleman. He deserved better. But I must also inform the police without delay."

"Will you help me down the stairs first, Mr Pyke? I want to see my father, before they take him away."

The man ought to be tucked up in a bed, preferably in hospital, in Charlie's opinion. However, he didn't look to be in imminent danger and, once the police arrived, there would be little chance of a last moment to be alone with his father.

"Of course, if you feel able," Charlie replied. "But I must ask you to refrain from touching anything, even your father's body. It is a lot to ask, I understand, but there might be clues as to who did this."

Quarantine Island

The arrival of the train at Port Chalmers, with the usual cacophony of screeching brakes and billowing steam, gave Grace a moment to collect her thoughts. Doctor Osborne, Dunedin's medical specialist in public health, was waiting for them on the platform. He helped Anne down from the train, while Grace collected their belongings, leaving the *Dunedin Ladies Journal* behind.

Grace nodded at Osborne's assistant, Doctor Carrington, who relieved her of the bags and escorted them to a hired hackney coach.

As they rattled down the rough road to the wharf, Grace was determined to put aside thoughts of Detective Charlie Pyke. It was hardly his fault that he drew admiring glances from women of all stations in life. His size was enough for a second glance. Once seen, the attention was held by his air of authority. Closer yet, and many a fan was sent aflutter by Charlie's emerald green eyes, flecked with gold and intriguingly shaped, thanks to his Chinese ancestry.

The hackney pulled up alongside a long wooden wharf, which seemed to reach right into the low, thunderous clouds beyond, reflecting her own mood. Time to focus on the work at hand. Nothing was more important than stopping measles from reaching Dunedin city and starting an unstoppable epidemic.

Grace breathed a sigh of relief at the sight of the robust boat tied up beside the wharf. It rocked gently, deflecting the bucking waves that pummelled its sides, one after another. Common sense told Grace she ought to be more afraid of exposure to a deadly disease than a short trip in a perfectly seaworthy vessel, but she had little experience of sea travel. The thought of going overboard in her heavy wool skirt and thick overcoat sent her pulse on a merry dance.

As she helped to unload their baggage from the coach, the deckhand yelled, "Last call for Portobello." Grace looked around frantically, but the other members of the team seemed unconcerned. The boat let out a blast on her whistle and chugged away from the wharf.

Anne settled her woollen hat more firmly on her braided grey hair. "That was the Port Chalmers to Portobello ferry, Grace." She jabbed her walking cane at a dismal little bathtub bobbing in the ferry's wake like a child's toy in a tempest. "This one's our vessel. Come along. Since you insisted on joining us, you can help me aboard."

Grace contemplated a word of protest, but what would be the point? She had wanted to join the medical team, both for the work experience and to assist her elderly great-aunt. Too late to have a failure of courage now. She wondered what it would be like to drown, but nipped that thought firmly in the bud.

Anne walked the gangplank as if she was strolling along Princes Street. The boat man helped Anne down with a cheery, "Lovely morning for it, ma'am", despite the bitter wind and glowering clouds.

"Indeed it is, Skipper," Anne replied heartily.

The skipper turned a weather-beaten face to Grace, who was eying up the narrow gangplank with misgiving, perched as it was above the blue-green swell of freezing water. He sprang up beside her and extended a hand. "Nowt to worry about, lass. I've been navigating these waters all my life, and my father before me. Never lost a passenger yet and don't aim to start today."

Once on board, Grace tried to head for the shelter of the tiny cabin, but Anne called her to the side of the boat to see a pair of blue penguins ducking and diving. Before Grace got her fill of the marvellous swimming birds, the mooring lines were cast off and they were heading for open water. To her surprise, the smooth surge of the toy boat through the waves felt exhilarating rather than stomach-churning.

The voyage was a short one. Otago Harbour cut a long, narrow channel between the hills on either side. Thus, the distance between the port, on the north side of the harbour, and the Portobello headland on the far side, was not much more than a mile as the royal albatross flies. Goat Island and the larger Quarantine Island formed two giant's stepping stones between the two settlements.

Doctor Carrington wobbled his way across the rolling deck to join Anne and Grace at the rails. Grace hadn't had much to do with him before, but she knew he had graduated as a doctor the previous year and was now undertaking a year of public health work under Doctor Osborne. Thus, Carrington was only three years older than herself, although he treated her with lordly condescension.

"May I escort you into the cabin, Mrs Macmillan? It's a mite rough out on deck for you ladies."

"Thank you for the offer," Anne replied, "but I love the feel of sea spray on my wrinkles. Does an old lady good. Tell me, young man, what prompted you to volunteer for the thankless task of visiting sick people in quarantine?"

Carrington gripped the lapels of his coat, preparing to pontificate, but a rogue wave forced him to clutch the rail instead. "One must take every opportunity to gain experience, Mrs Macmillan. I intend to apply for a residency at St George's Hospital in London, specialising in infectious diseases. I hope to enter the new scientific field of immune therapy. Edward Jenner himself was apprenticed there, not that his name will mean much to you, I expect."

Anne Macmillan twirled the end of her walking cane against the salt-crusted decking. Grace watched with interest to see how her great-aunt would rebuke Carrington's low expectations of her knowledge. Like Grace, Anne had been fascinated by medicine since she was a young girl. With the encouragement of her family and her husband, and the experience forged amongst Dunedin's poorest and sickest inhabitants, Anne had accumulated more medical knowledge that most qualified doctors.

"Edward Jenner, creator of the smallpox vaccine," Anne said. "His work is said to have saved more lives than any other man. No great overstatement, when as many as one in ten people died of smallpox in Jenner's time, and a third from infectious diseases as a whole. You are embarking on a worthy career, Doctor Carrington. Let us hope you achieve as much good in the world as Edward Jenner did. Perhaps soon we shall have a measles vaccine to ward off such tragedies as await us today."

Carrington examined Anne with new respect. "I feel most fortunate, Mrs Macmillan. This measles outbreak could not have been better timed for me. One requires field experience of such diseases, you see, to have the best chance of securing a position in a prestigious hospital or research institution."

"How thoughtful of those children to die of measles in order to advance your career." Anne's glare would have felled a more sensitive man, but Carrington was now gazing out to sea, perhaps dreaming of his future acceptance as a Fellow of the Royal Society. Anne's gaze fixed on his back, which leaned over the rail, presenting a tempting target. Anne resisted, although her grip on the walking cane tightened momentarily.

The boat turned across the wind as they rounded the end of Quarantine Island. The Portobello coast was not much more than a stone's throw from the island, for someone with a sturdy slingshot and a strong arm.

"Look for seals on the rocks," the skipper called to them. "If you're lucky, you'll see spoonbills too, once the tide turns and the sandbar on the other side of the island is covered."

Grace shielded her eyes with her hand and scanned the trees and cliff. Seagulls filled the sky and shag nests dotted the trees, but she saw no sign of elegant white spoonbills or the enormous royal albatrosses that nested by the ocean at the far tip of Otago Peninsula. She moved to the shelter of the wheelhouse to ask the skipper about the buildings she could see on the island. The main building seemed ridiculously out of scale with the rugged little upthrust of land, as if it had been dropped there by mistake.

"The big two-storey building, above the scarp, houses the dormitories," the skipper said. "The structure jutting out from it is the dining hall. The smaller cottage to the left is where the keeper's family lives. Grew up here, did Will Dougall. His father was the keeper before him until he died back in '90. Buried in the cemetery on the far side of the island, along with three of his children and the poor souls who perished before ever making it to the mainland."

Grace shivered at the thought of those lonely graves. How many more had been dug of late, for the quarantined passengers off the SS *Australis*?

The skipper raised a hand to the man waiting on the jetty. He manoeuvred the little boat expertly alongside with no more than a gentle bump. Carrington threw a mooring line across. Within seconds, they were passing supplies across to a broad, dark man, who looked as if it would take nothing short of a hurricane to perturb him.

"Morning, Mr Dougall," Doctor Osborne called. "What news?"

Dougall finished hoisting a sack of flour onto a handcart, before turning a sombre face to their group. "Had to dig two more wee graves not long after you left, Doctor Osborne. But no more new infections, according to the nurse. With luck, you'll be able to clear the ship's passengers to leave, so my family can have the island to ourselves again."

Osborne was clearly relieved at the news, tragic though it was. Measles spread with alarming ease amongst anyone in contact with an infected person, days before the rash signalled their infection. Ships from Australia were the most risk, as the voyage time coincided with the infectious period for measles. The nurses must have done an outstanding job of keeping the infected families isolated and the dormitories disinfected and ventilated, to have kept the death toll so low.

Anne had told Grace about her first visit to the island with Osborne, a day after the SS *Australis* had been quarantined. The children of one family had been in a bad way. Inflamed eyes and blotchy red rash, rapidly spreading from face to toes, were only the outward signs of measles. The real killer was the fever and pneumonia that followed, with young children making up four out of every five deaths. Most adults were immune, having been exposed to periodic outbreaks of measles during their lifetimes.

Mr Dougall swept Anne from the boat with a brawny arm and set her down on the jetty. "Welcome back, Mrs Macmillan."

Grace was determined not to disgrace herself again. She leapt over the narrow gap onto the jetty, holding her long skirt bunched in her hand. Oddly, her legs were a little wobbly, even though the jetty was stable. The keeper watched her with a raised eyebrow and a suppressed grin.

Anne glanced up from scraping seagull droppings off her boots. "My great-niece, Miss Grace Penrose. She's a medical student, here to assist. Are the infected patients still up at the hospital, Mr Dougall?"

"Aye. The nurse will bring them down when you are ready. The remaining hospital patients are well, she said, but she thought it best to keep them apart from the others as long as possible. All the other passengers are gathered in the dormitories, eagerly awaiting their release."

"Excellent," Anne replied. "I won't have to walk up the hill to the hospital again."

They left Mr Dougall to his supplies and walked the track up to the buildings.

Doctor Osborne outlined the plan. They would set up in the dining hall, with Osborne checking the men at one end of the room and Anne checking the women at the other end. Doctor Carrington and Grace would be responsible for recording the results and ensuring that every person was examined.

"We cannot let a single case of measles off this island," Osborne reminded them. "As you are aware, measles is one of the most highly contagious diseases known to man. Miss Penrose and Doctor Carrington, I want you two to stay as far away from the patients as you are able. Wash your hands thoroughly before and after the visit and cover your mouth and nose with the linen cloth provided."

Grace nodded. The risk of catching measles was low, as the passengers had now completed their full quarantine period. Nevertheless, she intended to follow instructions to the letter. Grace and Carrington had only been accepted as part of the team because they had had measles as children, during the last epidemic in 1874. Their natural immunity, plus the precautions Osborne had just outlined, ought to see them safe.

Osborne had been reluctant to have a young woman on the team, as the effect of measles on fertility was still unclear. He had – with a red face and profuse apologies – asked her if there was any chance she could be with child. Grace, equally red-faced, had thanked him for his needless concern. The question was a critical one, overruling the usual proprieties. Measles was known to have serious consequences for pregnant women and their unborn babies.

The nurse was ready for them. Grace spent the rest of the morning at a table, placed well away from the curtained-off examination area, with the window open behind her. As each person was shepherded through, Grace checked their name against the passenger list and recorded Anne's comments. The passengers were a stoic group, who generally managed to hide the boredom and frustration that must have been their lot over the last two weeks. One or two beseeched Anne to release them from quarantine, but the rest awaiting their fate in nervous, but hopeful, silence.

As the morning drew on, the tight knots in Grace's intestines eased. Her report was blessedly monotonous. A few runny noses and coughs, but no fever, no signs of developing rashes, no ominous symptoms of any kind.

At noon, when they took a break, the atmosphere bordered on jovial. The storm clouds had rolled back, allowing the sun her due. A typical spring day, lurching between winter and summer within a matter of hours. The four of them ate outside in a sheltered spot, surrounded by flax bushes and serenaded by bellbirds. A steady stream of boats fought the tidal rip of the narrow channel with puffs of steam, taunt sails and muscular oarsmanship. Shrieks of laughter from a group of children floated across the water from the Portobello ferry.

Osborne smiled. "It's good to know those little ones will be safe from the devastation of measles. I'm sure the passengers will be delighted to be off this island too, just as soon as I can get the Harbourmaster and Resident Magistrate to sign the official release papers."

"Thank the Lord, and all those willing to adhere to the Quarantine Act," Carrington added, as he threw a crust of bread to a solitary, hovering seagull.

Within seconds, a flock of squawking, scuffling gulls descended on their idyllic picnic. Grace hoped it wasn't a forewarning of the perils of complacency.

First Response

Charlie hurried out of Emerson & Son's jewellery shop into the everyday bustle of central Dunedin. A couple strolled past, arm in arm and blissfully unaware of the tragedy so close at hand. Charlie didn't waste time looking for a constable walking the streets. The police station was nearby and he knew the man he needed to deal with the serious crimes of murder and robbery.

He found Detective Inspector Wallace at his desk, scowling behind a pile of papers, which featured columns of figures and scrawls of red ink. Charlie diagnosed a new round of cost-cutting, no doubt directed by the overlords of the police hierarchy and the government ministers who ruled them. Charlie had to stifle a surge of glee at his own independence, for the sake of Wallace's temper. Robbie Wallace could face a gang of gun-wielding criminals with calm, calculated confidence, but give him paperwork and his patience fizzled out as fast as the lit fuse of a bomb.

Charlie was not about to test that patience. For one thing, news of a major crime would come as a welcome relief to his old boss. For another, Charlie had great respect for the man. He wouldn't be where he was today without the guidance and support of DI Wallace and Charlie's previous boss, Alistair Stewart, who was now Charlie's partner in the private detective agency.

Wallace flicked a bushy grey eyebrow toward the vacant chair in front of his desk. "I hope you've brought me news of murder and mayhem, Pyke. Tell me the government minister in charge of resourcing the police force has been assassinated and you'll make my day. The Chief Inspector has ordered me to slash the station's costs, again. Can't afford so much as a police whistle without going down on my knees and begging."

Charlie remained standing. "A murder and a robbery, sir, but not a politician. Two robbers cleared out Emerson & Son, Watchmakers & Jewellers, last night and killed Mr Emerson Senior in the process. I've left his son, Mr Daniel Emerson, at the scene, as he was in no state to go anywhere. He was hit on the head during the robbery. I suggested he go to the hospital, but he refused to leave his father."

Wallace was out of his chair and at the door faster than the swish of a baton. "Elliot! My office, now. Bring Weston."

Detective Sergeant Elliot and Detective Constable Weston would not have been Charlie's first choice, but Wallace must have had his reasons for choosing them.

"I'm bogged down with this," Wallace explained, waving a hand at the stack of papers on his desk. "DC Kelly is assisting Customs and Excise with an investigation into illegal liquor imports. Waste of Kelly's talents, of course, but the government needs the tax income from imported liquor more than they need to apprehend real criminals. Besides, this will be Elliot's last case before he retires. It's only right to give the man a decent shot at a final bit of glory by solving a robbery and murder."

As far as Charlie was concerned, Elliot could have all the glory. All Charlie wanted was to find the killer and to retrieve Grace's ring. He'd have preferred to work alongside Detective Constable Declan Kelly, who was a personal friend as well as a fine detective, but it was Wallace's call. DS Elliot had decades of experience and was a good copper, but he was no friend of Charlie's. He would have to tread carefully to stay on the right side of Elliot.

Elliot shuffled into Wallace's domain, wiping egg from his whiskers. His sharp eyes narrowed at the sight of Charlie, before passing on to Wallace. "You wanted me, sir?"

Weston bounced in behind him, the eager pup at the heels of his grizzled master.

"Murder and robbery at Emerson & Son's Jewellers last night," Wallace said. "Pyke will tell you about it on the way."

"I know where the shop is," Elliot replied. "No need for Pyke to come."

Wallace gave his retiring detective sergeant a hard stare. "Don't make me order you, Elliot. Mr Emerson was a fine man. Sold me the perfect engagement ring thirty years ago. Without his encouragement, I would never have had the courage to ask Mrs Wallace to marry a penniless policeman. I want Mr Emerson's killer brought to rights without delay. If Pyke has information to assist the case, don't ignore it." Wallace turned to the younger man. "Weston, fetch the police surgeon immediately."

Charlie briefed Elliot on the robbery on the way back to the shop.

When they reached the busted door, Elliot turned to block his way. "You can go now, Pyke. This is not your business any longer. And if I see a single newspaper reporter sniffing around, I'll know who to blame. Your attempts to gain fame do not impress me."

Charlie had no idea what Elliot was talking about. He and Alistair Stewart, and everyone else associated with the Southern Investigations Agency, had done everything in their power to keep their services discreet. They hadn't been able to avoid some coverage in the newspapers, including a certain degree of notoriety because of exaggerated stories in a minor publication called the *Dunedin Ladies' Journal*, but none of it had been sought or welcomed. Besides, that was weeks ago.

He did not want to get on Elliot's bad side, but Charlie had a job to do too. "As a matter of fact, Detective Sergeant Elliot, it is my business. Mr Daniel Emerson has engaged my services to find his father's killers." He stepped past Elliot into the shop and adopted his professionals-working-together demeanour. "The display cabinets have been looted, as you can see. Mr Emerson's body is in a bedroom on the first floor. The safe is in the attic."

Daniel Emerson was in the corner of the bedroom where Charlie had left him, still huddled in Charlie's overcoat. He was on his knees, praying. He lifted his head, his emotions writ upon his face in exhaustion and tears. "I've touched nothing, as you requested, Mr Pyke."

Having already undertaken a cursory examination of the room for evidence, Charlie assisted Daniel Emerson to his feet. "Detective Sergeant Elliot, may I take Mr Emerson to his bedroom? With your permission, I can ascertain the required family information."

Elliot continued his examination of the older Mr Emerson's body, but grunted his approval.

The second bedroom was the larger of the two, with a wide bed and a cot. Mr Emerson took a baby's blanket from the cot and held it to his face. "Thanks be to the Lord, my wife and baby are away, visiting her family."

"Do you have other family in Dunedin, Mr Emerson?" Charlie asked.

"A married daughter and son, both in Dunedin, and another son undertaking his apprenticeship in Christchurch. The baby was rather a late-life surprise. The children used to have rooms in the attic. I hate to think …"

"Best not to dwell on it, Mr Emerson, except to give thanks that they are safe. When the police have finished here, I will take you to stay with your daughter or son. Perhaps your son can arrange for a new lock."

"Not that there is anything left to steal." Emerson sighed. He shrugged out of Charlie's overcoat, handing it back. Charlie turned his back while Emerson changed from his nightshirt to his clothes.

"Thank you for your kindness, Mr Pyke. I am recovered enough to answer questions, if you have any. I will grieve once the killers are caught." Emerson found a scrap of paper and scrawled the name and address of his son. "I would be much obliged if you would send my son to me here to help me set the shop to rights."

Light footsteps on the stairs announced the arrival of the police surgeon.

Charlie's time alone with Daniel Emerson was almost at an end. "You will have to go over it with the police, but if there was anything particular you recall that would help me to track down the killers quickly, I'd like to hear it."

Emerson sat down on the bed, cradling his head in the baby's blanket. "I'm not sure I can help. I was awoken by a noise from my father's room. A crashing sound, as if my father had knocked over a chair. When I went to check, I saw that a man – all in black – had pulled my father out of his bed. He was hitting papa, demanding the key for the safe. I shouted for him to stop. I told him where the key was. When the scoundrel went for the key, I was going to tackle him, but that is all I recall. A second robber knocked me out."

"Did you get a glimpse of either of their faces?" Charlie asked. "Or any distinctive items of clothing?"

"I saw nothing of the man who hit me, Mr Pyke, as he approached from behind. The man who was attacking my father had an ordinary black hat, a black scarf covering his face and a dark overcoat. That's all I saw. When I came to, I was blindfolded and my arms were tied. They dragged me upstairs to show them where the safe was. After that, they gagged me and tied my feet. I heard them clearing out the safe, then leaving. I suppose I must have passed out after that." Daniel Emerson reached a tentative hand up to the wound on his head, wincing from the pain. "It is impossible. I cannot imagine how you will find them, with so little to go on."

From experience, Charlie was sure the victim would remember more details if he was taken slowly and methodically through the events of that terrible night, once the initial shock had worn off, but voices in the corridor prevented further questioning.

The police surgeon strode into the room, nodding to Charlie, as he went to Daniel Emerson. "I'm Doctor Cranston-Hartfield," he said. He ran an experienced eye over the second victim. "You took a blow to the head, I understand, Mr Emerson. Any blurred vision, dizziness, nausea?"

Emerson turned his head to the side to show the site of the wound. "Nothing too serious. A thumping headache, a little dizziness. Still stiff from being tied up." He held his wrists out. The ropes had left deep, weeping welts and angry contusions. "My father … did he …"

"I believe your father died of suffocation, or a combination of suffocation and heart failure," the police surgeon said gently. "The cloth around his mouth and nose was tied tightly. Did your father have any medical conditions?"

"Papa was an old man with a weak chest, congested lungs and a faltering heart." Emerson's voice wavered as he struggled to control his grief. "The scoundrel kept hitting him."

"The bruising on your father's face was minimal," the police surgeon said. "I believe the robber used only enough force to extract the information he needed. I'm sorry, Mr Emerson. I have no wish to make excuses for the appalling behaviour of the perpetrators, but I believe your father did not suffer as much as you might fear."

Emerson's face caved in, his eyes shut tight against the tears. "A small blessing, I suppose. What will happen now, Doctor?"

"I will take you to the hospital, sir, as a precaution. The wounds on your head and arms need to be cleaned and bandaged to prevent infection. You need to rest. I will have your father's body taken to the hospital mortuary for a full examination. I hope we can release his body to you and your family within a day or two."

"I need to interview the witness," Elliot protested. He turned to Charlie. "And I want you gone, Pyke."

"Do you not want me to give a formal statement, Detective Sergeant Elliot?" Charlie asked.

"Submit a written statement at the police station, Pyke. But, mark my words, I'll get my hands on the culprits soon enough. A couple of vicious local thugs, I don't doubt. My sources will cough up their names soon enough, don't you worry."

Charlie exchanged a glance and a quick nod with his client, and another with Doctor Cranston-Hartfield. As he left, the police surgeon was quietly, but assertively, informing Elliot that Mr Emerson would answer questions at the hospital, after his injuries had been attended to. Charlie and the police surgeon hadn't started off on the best of terms, because of a rivalry of the heart, but they had reached a point of firm professional respect, edging towards camaraderie.

As for Elliot, if he did not wish to interview a witness about what he had seen when he entered the shop this morning, that was his loss. Charlie counted himself fortunate that Elliot hadn't arrested him as a suspect. The detective sergeant was of the firm opinion that Charlie and Grace became entangled in murder investigations rather too often for his liking. True enough, Charlie conceded, but not because of any wrongdoing or desire for notoriety on their part.

Charlie clattered down the stairs at speed, relieved to be free to pursue his own investigation. He took another quick look in the ring cabinet, in case Grace's sapphire and diamond ring had miraculously been spared the pillaging, but today was not the day for miracles.

Out in the fresh air again, Charlie went to fulfil his promise to Daniel Emerson to inform his son of his father's injury and his grandfather's death.

As he walked, Charlie considered Elliot's view that the criminals were vicious thugs. He thought it unlikely. The robbers had not been overly violent and probably hadn't intended to kill the elder Mr Emerson. Perhaps the appearance of the younger Mr Emerson had startled them. No doubt they had scouted the shop before the robbery. If Mr Emerson Senior had been the only one in the shop, as had been the case when Charlie had first visited, they might have seen him as an easy, single target.

When Mr Daniel Emerson had recovered from his ordeal, a further interview was definitely in order.

If Elliot had bothered to interview Charlie, he would have found out that there was another reason to believe that vicious thugs were not to blame. Charlie had been hired by three separate women over the past few weeks, all of whom had had expensive jewellery stolen from their homes.

In each case, the burglar had been both brazen and careful. The first burglary scene yielded only two clues - a single blond hair and a man's boot-print in the garden. In the other two cases, there had not been a single clue, beyond an open window and a single empty jewellery box in the ladies' dressing rooms. Only the most expensive item had been stolen in each case – a set of diamond jewellery, a pearl necklace, and a ruby bracelet – suggesting a targeted theft, and thus a thief with inside knowledge. The stolen items had eye-wateringly high valuations, although the victims had seemed remarkably calm about their losses.

Without any other evidence, besides the open windows, Charlie was not entirely convinced that the thefts were the result of a break-in. He had looked into guests attending social events, family members and servants. He remained baffled, to his embarrassment. All three women had been adamant that the police must not be informed, while pestering him constantly for progress reports. Frankly, he wished he had never agreed to investigate for them. Miss Caroline Davenport had been the first and most persistent victim.

With a sigh, Charlie realised he would have to talk to the three women victims again, as there was a chance all the cases were linked. While it was true the methods used differed, it was also possible that the criminals had become greedy, switching from burglary to robbery with menaces. An entire shop full of expensive items would certainly be an enticing target, and no riskier than entering a home.

Charlie would have to go back to his informants too, to see if there were any rumours of stolen goods coming up for sale. Given the value and uniqueness of the items stolen in the first three burglaries, he wasn't too surprised that the local pawn shops hadn't been approached. But he had expected to glean a rumour or two from the streets. In his experience, it was rare for a successful thief to seal their lips so completely. A few celebratory drinks usually led to careless whispers, if not outright bragging. Charlie's group of informants, coordinated by a lad called Johnny Todd, had not heard a peep.

The thought of Johnny Todd brought a smile to his lips. Not three years ago, Johnny had been a skinny little boy selling kindling sticks on the street. Anne Macmillan and Grace Penrose had taken him under their wings and secured his family's future by giving his father work as a gardener. Everyone had gained from the deal. Mr Todd was an exceptional gardener with a knowledge of natural remedies, passed down from his grandmother, who was a Māori healer. This had inadvertently resulted in DS Elliot suspecting Grace of murder a few months ago, which hadn't improved the relationship between Charlie and Elliot.

Johnny Todd was now a strapping young lad with an eye for making his way in the world. He had established a delivery and transport business with old carriage parts and sheer determination. Now, Johnny's team of messenger boys doubled as Charlie's ears on the street.

Somebody, somewhere, must know something. Charlie would not rest until he had the killers in irons and the sapphire and diamond ring where it belonged – on the ring finger of his beloved Grace Penrose.

Measles Misery

After the abandoned picnic on Quarantine Island, Grace sat down again at her table in the dining hall. According to her list, they still had to examine the passengers who had been infected with measles, who were being brought down from the hospital at the top of the island. After that, they would check the first-class passengers, none of whom had been infected. It struck her that this was probably the first time in their lives that the wealthy first-class passengers had been left until last. They would be fuming at the enforced stay on this windswept dot of land, far from the comforts and amusements of the city.

The nurse announced the arrival of the hospital patients. Two miserable little girls entered the dining room first, their hands firmly clasped by a weary-eyed mother. Grace didn't need her three years of medical training to identify them as the first of the infected children. The rash was fading from the girls' faces, leaving peeling skin, but their lower legs were still a blotchy red below their rumpled pinafores. The girls, each clutching a worn ragdoll to a fragile chest, coughed with every step.

If this was what the post-infectious stage looked like, Grace was grateful not to have been present to witness the measles infection at its worst. Her own memories of suffering measles as a four-year-old remained vivid, if hazy. Sodden sheets, a racking cough, her family hovering like ghosts over her bed.

Nevertheless, Anne declared her satisfaction with their state of health, and the line of thin children and harried adults who followed. Only three families and two single adults, fortunately, and every last one of them was now free from infection.

By mid-afternoon, the nurse declared they had examined the last of the patients.

Anne washed her hands, then came over to Grace's table. "Has every female passenger on the list been checked off, Grace?"

"All but the first-class passengers," Grace confirmed. "There were only three women in first class, so we are almost finished."

The nurse joined them. "No, Miss Penrose, you've seen them all. The first-class passengers left the island last week."

"That cannot be right," Anne said, in a tone of voice that had the nurse taking a step back. "Doctor Osborne did not give permission for anyone to leave quarantine early."

"It wasn't Doctor Osborne who let them go, Mrs Macmillan. A government official came over with a release order signed by the Premier himself. Special circumstances, he said, due to there being an important trade delegation travelling in first class." The nurse shrank another step back at the sight of Anne's rising anger. "The doctor who came questioned the first-class passengers and declared there had been no contact with the infected passengers. The classes are kept separate onboard ship, ma'am. They needed to release the cargo early too, there being perishables on board. Melons and sugar…"

The nurse's voice trailed away as Anne vented her fury.

"This idiot doctor took the word of the first-class passengers as sufficient? And since when does our Premier put melons over the lives of our vulnerable children?" Anne let out a sharp huff of breath and grasped the edge of the table to steady herself. "My apologies. You nurses have done a splendid job here. I ought not to have taken out my wrath on you."

"I was as angry as you, Mrs Macmillan," the nurse said. "Unfortunately, I did not have the authority to stop them, not with a signed order. None of the first-class passengers had a rash when they left, although more than one had a cough and red eyes. It was a dreadful crossing from Sydney by all accounts, so the doctor put the symptoms down to common colds. Likely he was right, but I'd wager he didn't have your experience, Mrs Macmillan, though he was a qualified physician."

Grace felt sorry for the nurse, who had been put in an impossible position. Had she been present, Anne's opinion would certainly have been discounted as well, because she had no formal medical training. Yet her half century of medical experience, at the side of her husband, Doctor Macmillan, had been spent in service to the impoverished folk of Dunedin, who bore the brunt of the regular waves of deadly infectious diseases. A doctor practicing amongst the well-to-do would have a framed certificate nailed to his wall, but he wouldn't have seen a fraction of the cases Anne had experienced.

Even Doctor Osborne, an acknowledged public health expert from the Otago Medical School, had no special authority. The role of medical officer for public health had been dispensed with as a cost-saving measure after the last outbreak of scarlet fever had ended. A dangerously short-sighted economy, in Grace's opinion, as the next outbreak was always just around the corner. However, money was short and memories even shorter.

"Well, no harm done, with God's grace," Anne replied. "All the same, we need to talk to the infected patients again. If you would be so kind as to bring them back into the dining hall, Nurse, while I have a word with Doctor Osborne."

Grace studiously ignored the eruption of anger that soon rent the air from the men's side of the room. She found it hard to believe that the mild-mannered Doctor Osborne knew so many curse words, let alone uttered them in mixed company.

The nurse brought in the three families and two single women who had been infected with measles.

Doctor Osborne sat them at one of the dining tables. "First, the good news. You will all be cleared to make landfall, probably tomorrow morning."

A spontaneous cheer rose from the passengers, tempered with the sense that bad news might follow.

"I assure you that what I am about to say will have no bearing whatsoever on your release," Osborne continued. "It has come to my attention that the first-class passengers were released a week ago. You have all experienced the dire consequences of measles, and

I am sure you will join with me in ensuring that the disease does not enter our community here in Dunedin. Therefore, I implore you to be forthcoming when I ask whether any of you had any contact whatsoever with anyone from first class."

Nobody spoke. A small boy with a shock of blond hair shrank into his chair and slid behind his mother's arm.

Grace sent him her sweetest smile. "Mathew, isn't it? You're the lad with the tin whistle, aren't you?"

The lad nodded. He wasn't much more than six or seven years old, but he had an ear for a tune.

"Were you clever enough to sneak onto the first-class deck, Mathew?" Grace asked. "We won't be the least cross, I promise you."

Mathew glanced at his mother, who put her arm around him and told him to tell the truth.

"I only went over the barrier because the lady wanted to hear me play, Miss. She had ever such a nice voice and pretty clothes. Taught me a tune, she did. It were only a few minutes, I swear. I were that fed up with lying in bed feeling sick. I hardly had any spots when I went out, honest, Miss. She was right nice to me, but I don't know her name or nothing."

"Thank you for your honesty, Mathew," Osborne said gently. His smile didn't waver, but anyone who knew him well could hear the tension underlying the kind words. "Anyone else?"

One of the single women raised her hand. Her heart-shaped face and soft skin lent her the appearance of a young girl, but her eyes held the look of a woman who had seen her share of life. The woman beside her tried to pull her hand down, but the first shook the warning hand away. "After seeing those wee ones die, we got a duty to tell the truth, Flo."

"Your honesty is appreciated, Miss," Osborne said.

"Some of the single men in first class had a knees-up on the first night of the voyage. Me and Florence went along to listen to the music and they asked us to join them. After a rum or two, we showed them how to dance. We're part of a group of performers from Sydney, come to join a revue in New Zealand. They were short in the chorus line, what with some of their own dancers out with influenza, so they paid our fares. We didn't see the harm in having a little fun along the way, or so we thought at the time."

"Did the men you danced with tell you their names, by any chance?" Osborne asked.

"Not so as I recall. I'd had a bit to drink and the lights were dim. There were about five of them, a couple of them rather too free with their hands. Pretty much ordinary fellas as far as I could see. Average height, brownish hair, too much rum and not enough clean laundry. To own the truth, I was happy to leave early, as I was feeling a bit out of sorts. Came down with the spots two days later."

"That is very helpful, thank you," Osborne said. His smile was definitely ragged around the edges now, knowing the infectious period for measles started several days before the rash appeared. "Anyone else?"

Silence.

Grace could feel the knot back in her intestines, tighter than before. She did the calculations in her head. A five-day voyage, followed by seven days of quarantine, meant any first-class passenger exposed to measles on the first night of the voyage would have been in the early stage of infection when they left quarantine. Perhaps a mild fever and cough – the cold-like symptoms the doctor noted before signing the release form – but probably not yet showing the characteristic measles rash.

If one or more of them had been infected, the consequences could be dire. The released passengers would have been infectious for most of the week they had spent at large in Dunedin, when they should have been in quarantine. Goodness knows how far they might have spread the disease. If the trade delegation was the same one mentioned in the *Dunedin Ladies' Journal* article, the Mayor of Dunedin and half the society ladies in the city could have been exposed to measles. If measles took hold, it would pass to their children, maids, visitors, and then on to the friends of their children, and so on.

Grace could only pray that the first-class passengers had all had measles as children and thus were less likely to transmit the disease to others. The medical team would have to track down the exposed passengers without delay. By now, the worst symptoms would likely have passed, leaving them with a fading rash and residual cough.

It was a sombre medical team who took the path back to the jetty that afternoon. The same boat was waiting for them. The skipper must have sensed the mood, for he handed the ladies aboard without a word and set the little bathtub on course for Port Chalmers. None of the medical team would have noticed if a troupe of friendly penguins, a score of seals, or a sky-full of spoonbills and albatrosses had cavorted around them.

Anne whispered the words they were all thinking. "Please let them stay abed if they are ill. And please, please, dear Lord, do not let them come within a mile of any children or pregnant women, especially those who live cheek by jowl in the poorest areas of our city."

Grace added another prayer of her own. Her best friend, Molly Sugden, had married Rory Ravenwood earlier this year. Molly was now six months pregnant with their first child. And Rory was the doctor at Lavender House, Anne's refuge and medical clinic, located in the heart of one of the poorest areas of Dunedin.

Boots And All

Charlie returned to Emerson & Son, Watchmakers & Jewellers, after delivering the tragic news of his grandfather's death to Daniel Emerson's son. The son hadn't wasted words. He downed tools and hastened to his father's side.

Charlie had made a couple of stops on his way back. First, he wanted to ensure that he didn't lose the money he had withdrawn to buy the ring. He set his mind at ease by leaving it secure in the detective agency's safe. After that, he went to see Johnny Todd, to ask him and his team of messenger boys to keep an ear out for any new talk on the street of valuable jewels for sale.

Johnny assured him that his informants had not heard so much as a whisper. Not a single lowlife had been bragging about pilfering a trinket or two, let alone pulling off a lucrative job. It seemed the criminal classes of Dunedin were content to dabble in nothing more than a little illegal betting between drunken brawls.

To Charlie's surprise, Daniel Emerson was already back at his shop, working to clean up broken glass alongside his son.

Emerson greeted Charlie like an old friend, although he winced as Charlie gently shook his bandaged hand. "Don't take to hospitals, if I can avoid them," he said. His ashen face and red eyes belied the superficial heartiness of his welcome. "Come through to the parlour, Mr Pyke."

Daniel Emerson insisted on acting as host. When he had poured Charlie a cup of tea strong enough to tan an ox hide, he waved Charlie to a chair. "Ask whatever you wish. I want these murderers caught."

Charlie started with the less distressing questions. He ascertained that there had been no suspicious customers in the shop over the past couple of weeks. Men shopping for rings and trinkets, women browsing for the perfect adornment for a special occasion, servants bringing in broken items for mending, a few watch sales – much as usual. One or two salesmen attempting to sell them cheap tat, who were given short shrift.

"In fact, as I recall, only two new clients came into the shop last week," Emerson said. "One man had had his watch stolen on board a ship. The theft had been particularly aggravating as the watch had been a gift from his father on the occasion of reaching his majority. I can't recall much about him, other than that he was here as part of a small trade delegation from Australia. The other man was a camera salesman from out of town, who was trying to interest us in stocking his wares. Not our area of expertise, but certain of the larger shops in our trade do stock optical devices as well as watches, clocks and costume jewellery. At Emerson's, we prefer to specialise in the craft of exquisite jewellery, as you know, Mr Pyke. We sell only the best and therefore our customers are relatively few in number and tend to be well known to us."

"May I ask if the young ladies of the Davenport, Fothergill and Nesbitt families are customers?"

Mr Emerson paused, presumably deciding whether his customer's privacy superseded the need for full disclosure.

"In strictest confidence," Charlie added. "I only ask because I have been hired by each of them in recent weeks to investigate the theft of valuable items of jewellery. You'll appreciate that jewellery theft is rare, so there is a chance the crimes are all linked."

"Miss Caroline Davenport and the other Davenport ladies are amongst our most loyal customers, Mr Pyke. The Fothergill ladies and gentlemen purchase their jewellery and timepieces here too. I had their lady's maid in recently, asking me to fix a broken clasp on a pearl necklace. I must send a reminder for her to pick it up. Miss Nesbitt? Perhaps on occasion. My father usually serves the customers, while I tend to the watchmaking and repairs upstairs. I will look in our sales register."

Mr Emerson went out to the serving area of the shop, but failed to find the sales register in its usual place under the counter. The robbers had been extremely thorough, leaving only a cabinet of cheaper trinkets and the row of grandfather clocks lining the far wall. The constant ticking and chiming would have driven Charlie mad before the day was out, but the Emerson men seemed oblivious.

"I cannot imagine why they would wish to steal our sales register," Emerson said.

Charlie had that sinking feeling that comes with imparting bad news. "Did the register contain names and addresses of your customers, and specifics of the items purchased?"

Emerson's already grim expression dropped a notch further. "You're thinking that the robbers will use the information to target their next victims. If so, our reputation will be ruined."

"That may have been their intention, Mr Emerson, but if the robbers have any sense, they will lie low or leave town." Charlie hoped his reassuring words were true. Facing a murder charge would be enough to make most criminals flee. But these two might be feeling safe, knowing they had left no clues behind, aside from the briefest of glimpses of a covered face. If the robbers were careful about selling the stolen jewellery, the chances of catching them were not good.

The next stage of the interview would be a challenge. Given Daniel Emerson's injury and grief, Charlie was unsure whether or not to proceed. Emerson gestured for him to go upstairs, leading Charlie back to his father's bedroom, which was now unnaturally tidy and empty of life.

"You wish me to recall the events of last night," Emerson stated.

The man had obviously inherited his father's ability to read customers and detectives. "If you are willing, I find the best way is to recreate the scene in as much detail as possible. Close your eyes and imagine it, if that helps. Not only what you saw, but what you heard, what you smelled. Even the smallest glimpse or fleeting impression – whatever comes to mind." Charlie touched Emerson's shoulder. "It will be distressing, I'm afraid, but with so little to go on, any tiny clue might help. Take it slowly."

Daniel Emerson retreated to his own bedroom, re-enacting the scene from the point the noise first woke him up the previous night. Nothing fresh came to mind until he stood in the doorway of his father's bedroom. He closed his eyes and paused for several seconds, before describing the man hitting his father. "The gaslight was on. I saw a man dressed in black from head to toe. A dark overcoat, thick and bulky, but the man was slim. Medium height, I suppose, more or less."

"Excellent work, Mr Emerson," Charlie said. "Focus on the details."

Emerson scrunched up his eyes and took a long, slow breath. "I recall the sound as he slapped my father's face. A slap, not a punch, muted with gloves. Leather gloves." He took a step forward, his fists curling and lifting, as they must have last night. "He wore a dark cloth cap of a cheap type, but the black scarf over his face was fine wool or cashmere. He was speaking in a low voice, but full of aggression, with an odd twang. English but different. When I entered this room, he was demanding to know where the key to the safe was hidden."

"Did your father tell him?" Charlie asked.

"Papa saw me in the doorway, I'm sure of it. He had been refusing to tell the robber where the key for the safe was, but when I came in, he told the scoundrel what he wanted to know. 'The key is the Delander,' papa said. The robber obviously didn't understand. I yelled at him to stop hitting papa. I told him the key was hidden in the Delander clock on the mantlepiece."

Charlie glanced at the mantelpiece. The clock was still there, tipped over with the rear panel hanging open – a clever place to hide the key to the safe. "And then?"

"The robber turned to get the key, so I decided to try and tackle him. But there was a rasping cough behind me. I ducked to the side. Felt an instant of pain. That's all I recall." He opened his eyes and turned to Charlie. "If the second robber hadn't coughed before he attacked me, I might have been killed too. I can't have been unconscious for long. When I came to, I was bound and blindfolded.

Dripping wet too. They must have thrown cold water in my face to revive me."

Emerson was breathing heavily at the terrible recollections. Charlie patted his shoulder. "You're doing brilliantly, Mr Emerson. Take a rest if you need to."

The jeweller shook his head. "They demanded to know where the safe was. I told them the safe was hidden behind a fake wall in the attic, so they dragged me up there to show them. As soon as I showed them where it was, they gagged me and bound my feet."

"I'm sorry to ask, but could we go up to the attic again?"

"Yes, yes, it's coming back to me now …" Emerson hurried up the steep steps into the attic and crossed to the safe.

To Charlie's surprise, Emerson got down on the floor, with his hands behind his back and his feet together, his eyes closed so tightly that every part of his face was creased. Charlie had never had a witness who was so intent on recalling unpleasant memories. The pain of his father's loss must have shaken him to the core and given him the strength to do all in his power to help.

"I was blindfolded," Emerson continued, using both words and gestures to convey the scene. "I could see a little of the floor in front of me. I rubbed the blindfold against the floor to push it up, to see better. When I lifted my head, I saw one of the robbers crouched beside the safe. The second robber was dressed in the same type of clothes as the man who killed my father – all in black. I heard items being pulled from the safe. Rustling and tinkling – the banknotes and the jewellery, I presume. I could see a large sack. He was kneeling, so his trousers had ridden up to show his shoes – no – ankle boots. New, leather. Odd pattern, like cobblestones."

Emerson squirmed on the floor, as if his hands were really tied. Then, he reached out towards the safe. "His arm. I could see it as he stretched for the safe in the light of his lantern. Fine-boned, and a strange colour. Blotchy, discoloured." His mouth turned down in distaste. "Peeling skin. A rash of some sort. Black gloves too."

Suddenly, Emerson curled into a ball and lay still. Charlie held his breath. Emerson's re-enactment was so realistic, Charlie could feel the blood pulsing through his veins just watching him. He hoped the jeweller had a stronger heart than his father.

"The robber took everything and pulled the drawstring on the sack. I didn't want the robber to see me watching him, so I pretended to have passed out. The other robber was already downstairs, stripping the shop of valuables. I heard glass smashing." Daniel Emerson sat on the floor, trembling like an old man with palsy. "That's all I recall."

"Papa!" Daniel's son was staring at them from the top of the stairs. He rushed to his father's side, his face ashen. "That's enough!"

Charlie nodded his agreement. "You have an extraordinary memory for detail, Mr Emerson. Thanks to you, I have a great deal more to go on."

Emerson dug his knuckles into his eyes. "It is you who are due thanks, Mr Pyke. I never would have remembered any of it, but for your prompting."

Charlie wanted to ask for one more impression, about the least appreciated of the senses recalled by witnesses, but he could see the man's son would not allow further questioning. Instead, he made a general observation, hoping it would trigger a further memory.

"It's often the smallest things that help. Even a distinctive smell, such as tobacco or coal or wood, can tell us much about the type of man we are seeking."

Emerson's nose twitched as he drew in air. "I recall nothing of the sort, I'm afraid. The only smell about the robber was a pleasant waft of fresh soap as he hit me, although it might have been a delicate eau-de-cologne, I suppose. I may have imagined it."

Charlie could have hugged him. He had never met a single lowlife thug who smelled pleasant. Almost all of them reeked of something – mostly tobacco, ale, and stale sweat, but often some hint of their trade as well. Coal for a coalman or sweep, dung and straw for a stableman, hops for a brewer, and so on. Put alongside the new leather boots and fine cashmere scarf, and the picture was clear – Charlie was seeking a better class of criminal that the average smash and grab crook.

A trivial detail, one might think, but it ruled out the vast majority of the robbers and burglars he had dealt with in his career. The fact that the robber was fine-boned and suffered from some type of skin condition, eczema perhaps, would also help, once he had a suspect in hand. The only problem was in finding such a man, who would operate outside the usual haunts open to Johnny Todd and his informants.

Charlie wondered again about the type of men who might be known to the three ladies who had had jewellery stolen. Gentleman thieves or indoor servants were beginning to look like the most likely prospects. Yet another reason to revisit the three lady victims.

Daniel Emerson was still sitting on the floor, all traces of energy having drained from his body with the effort of recall.

"My father needs to lie down now," his son said.

Daniel Emerson pushed himself off the floor with a determined thrust. "Actually, a little fresh air would do me the world of good. Perhaps I could accompany Mr Pyke for a short way. I promise I shall come back and take my rest once I have done all I can to assist the detective's inquiries."

The son tried to argue, but Daniel Emerson put on his overcoat and chivvied Charlie to the door. The son shook his head and went back to tidying up the mess. They passed a locksmith on their way out, here to put a stout new lock on the damaged door.

Daniel Emerson led Charlie down to Princes Street and turned right. After another hundred yards, they stood outside a shop selling high-quality footwear.

"You've the makings of a fine detective, Mr Emerson," Charlie said.

Emerson smiled. "I want to see that ring on your fiancée's finger almost as much as you do, Mr Pyke." He approached the owner of the shoe shop and described the odd, cobblestone-patterned leather of the robber's boots.

"I know the very ones, sir," the shop owner declared. "A fine choice, sir. All our most discerning clientele want crocodile skin boots, after the *Dunedin Ladies' Journal* featured them in the latest edition." He took a pair of ankle boots from one of a pile of boxes behind the counter.

"Yes, exactly the type," Emerson exclaimed. "Crocodile skin. Well, I never. I suppose that explains the unusual pattern in the leather, although I cannot imagine why anyone would care to take the skin from a crocodile."

"I assure you, sir," the shopkeeper said, "the skin gives a superb leather, when combined with the finest touch of the cobbler's artistry. Not cheap, mind, but superior in quality. Newly arrived in New Zealand, so I can guarantee you will be amongst the first to own a pair. Suitable for both ladies and gentlemen, wonderfully robust yet pliable. You will find they make an exceptional walking boot, as well as a fine boot for everyday wear about town."

"Where did you purchase the boots?" Charlie asked the salesman, when he could get a word in.

"A gentleman from Sydney, Australia, came into my establishment last week. Tuesday, as I recall. He wanted to find a superior purveyor of footwear to expand his distribution to this country. I admit I was unsure that ladies and gentlemen would wish to wear a reptile upon their feet, so I called in the fashion expert from the *Dunedin Ladies' Journal* for her opinion. Miss Davenport met with Mr Thornton, who not only showed the lady his selection, but offered her a pair of the boots for her to try."

"Miss Davenport?" Charlie queried. "Miss *Caroline* Davenport?"

"The very lady, sir. The fashion correspondent for the *Dunedin Ladies' Journal*, although she writes under a nom de plume to protect her reputation amongst society's elite. Miss Davenport was most impressed with the design and comfort, with the happy result that she promised a feature article. True to her word, the article appeared on Saturday."

Charlie struggled to tamp down a flare of anger. Darn it, that woman was tormenting him with her presence at every turn. But, at this point, Caroline Davenport was not his main concern. He needed to know how many men had bought the crocodile skin boots by the Sunday night of the robbery. "When did you have the crocodile skin boots in your shop, for sale to the public?"

"By opening time this morning," the shop owner replied, with a wide smile. "After the *Ladies' Journal* article, we cannot keep up with demand. You have caught me in the only quiet period since I opened the doors today."

"You did not sell any last week? Or give any pairs away? Or see them for sale anywhere else?"

"No. I told the salesman that I would want an exclusive deal to stock them, if I chose to stock them at all. Naturally, with all the interest, I shall be signing the contract with all haste."

The shopkeeper's response had Charlie stumped. The boots must have come from elsewhere for the robber to have worn them on Sunday night. Yet they had not been available until today, Monday. "Do you know where the Australian shoe importer is staying in Dunedin?"

The shopkeeper looked sharply at Charlie. "You wouldn't be in the shoe business, sir? As I indicated, I have the option of an exclusive deal with the gentleman."

Charlie pulled out his identification. "The boots may provide a clue to the perpetrator of a dreadful crime. I need to speak to the man who sold you the boots."

The shopkeeper reluctantly withdrew a card from a drawer. "Mr Bernard Thornton. I do not know where he is staying, but he said he would come back tomorrow to hear my final decision on stocking his line of footwear."

"Can you describe him?"

"Ordinary looking. Average height, brown hair, youngish, but very professional. Rather a charming character. He knows his footwear, I can tell you that. I thought I knew everything there was to know about lasts and linings, but Mr Thornton taught me a thing or two."

Charlie thanked the shop owner. Out in the street again, Mr Emerson looked ready to crumple. The traumatic events of the last twelve hours had taken a heavy toll on the jeweller.

Charlie offered his arm. "I'll see you to back to your shop, sir, before I take this vital information to the police. With your help, I expect we'll get the robbers sooner rather than later. If the public did not have access to the crocodile skin boots until after the robbery, I must conclude the robber was an associate of the shoe salesman from Australia, or a visiting Australian who brought the boots with him."

Mr Emerson shuffled along beside Charlie, leaning heavily on him, his reserves of willpower having run dry. "Without you, Mr Pyke, I might still be in the attic, bound and gagged. I might not have made it. I hope you will come to my father's funeral. Father was a fine judge of character. He took a liking to you. I can't tell you how delighted he was that he was able to match you to the perfect engagement ring. He can – could – spot a man in love at a thousand paces."

"I would be honoured to come to his funeral, Mr Emerson. I'll bring my lady friend too."

"Your fiancée," Emerson corrected.

"If she accepts my proposal," Charlie said.

Mr Emerson smiled his father's knowing smile. "She will. We must cling to what is truly precious, as life can be short."

When they reached the jewellery shop, Charlie handed Mr Emerson into the care of his son. Charlie was relieved to see that Mr Emerson now gave in to his son's demands that he rest in bed.

Charlie walked away with renewed determination. He had a sudden longing to see Grace Penrose, but he knew he had a duty to pass the fresh evidence to the police first. With any luck, he could pass the information directly to Detective Inspector Wallace or Detective Constable Weston.

As fate would have it, he ran into his old friend, Detective Constable Declan Kelly, outside the police station.

"Charlie Pyke. It's been too long." Declan scrutinised him with wary eyes. "May I ask if everything is all right between you and Grace?"

The smile slipped from Charlie's lips. "Why wouldn't it be, Declan?"

Declan Kelly – a tough, unflappable, seen-it-all policeman – was as flustered as a debutante at her first ball. "Ah, I take it you haven't seen the latest edition of the *Dunedin Ladies' Journal*. My wife reads it. I wasn't sure whether to warn you or stay out of the path of the inevitable explosion."

Charlie felt his blood pressure rising. "What did that deplorable Lady Detective say about me this time?"

Declan took a step backwards, his hands upturned in a not-my-fault gesture. "Um, well, they rather implied that you and Miss Caroline Davenport were about to announce your engagement."

Charlie let out a rare curse and sprinted to the railway station, detouring past a newspaper vendor on the way. Grace would be coming back from Quarantine Island soon. With luck, she wouldn't have been told about the article yet. He would meet her at the wharf and fall at her feet. Whatever it took to get her to believe the article was nothing but a lie.

He made the Port Chalmers train by the skin of his teeth, a copy of the damnable *Ladies' Journal* flapping in his hand as he hurled himself aboard the moving passenger carriage.

Crossroads

On the return trip from Quarantine Island, the boat cut through the light swell with ease. Before long, the wharf at Port Chalmers came into view. Grace longed to be home, with a nice cup of tea in one hand and a piece of rich shortbread in the other. Better yet, curled up against the warmth of Charlie Pyke's chest, with the clock wound back to a time before measles and the latest edition of the *Dunedin Ladies' Journal*.

Grace craved Charlie's company so intensely, she could almost see him in the lone figure standing on the end of the wharf, picked out by a ray of light between the gathering clouds. The closer she got, the more she began to believe the hallucination was real.

The moment the boat touched the wharf, Charlie swung her off the deck and enfolded her in a tight embrace. Grace wrapped her arms around his neck and pulled his head down to her level.

"Grace, we're in public," Charlie whispered.

"I don't care," she breathed, with her lips against his. She felt his smile as he responded.

A loud throat-clearing behind them broke the spell. Charlie let go of Grace and went to assist Anne Macmillan across the gangplank. He stayed to help unload the boat, while Anne went over to Grace, rapping her walking cane so firmly upon the boards of the wharf that Grace knew she was about to be given a stern talking to.

Grace attempted to get in first. "I apologise for the excessive public display of affection, Auntie. The trials of the day seem to have overwhelmed my sense of propriety."

"Propriety is the least of my concerns, Grace Penrose," Anne retorted. "You are training to be a doctor. Did you not stop to think about the consequences of potential exposure to measles? Have you even asked Charlie if he has ever had measles? He comes from a small town, which may have escaped the ravages of measles in the last epidemic."

Grace's vertebral column turned to blancmange as shock, shame and fear fought for ascendency. If her carelessness caused Charlie to become ill, or worse, how could she ever live with herself? The risk was miniscule – she had taken every precaution and they were confident that none of the ship's passengers were contagious. And yet …

Anne huffed. "Just as well I am aware of your unseemly enthusiasm for close contact with that young man. I sent a telegram to Charlie's mother. He had measles as a child. A lesson well learned, I trust?"

Knees still trembling, Grace nodded.

Anne put an arm around Grace's shoulders. "Come now, my dear. No need to look quite so dejected. I rather think your delightful young man is just the person we need to cheer you up."

Doctor Osborne, Doctor Carrington and Charlie joined them. As they walked down the wharf together, Anne apprised them of her plan.

"Gentlemen, may I introduce Mr Charlie Pyke, who is a private detective. I propose to engage Charlie's services to track down the first-class passengers, to ensure that none of them has been spreading measles over the past week. Let us pray they have not yet dispersed far and wide across the countryside. Charlie, the matter is of the utmost urgency. Eleven passengers were allowed out of quarantine a week early, after several were exposed to the disease."

"Why on earth were they released early?" Charlie asked.

Anne swatted at a discarded apple core with her walking cane, sending it arcing into the waves. "The powers that be decreed that a trade delegation from Australia was of more importance than the children of New Zealand."

The five of them arrived at the waiting coach, which had four seats. Carrington offered to sit with the coachman, so the others could continue their discussion.

Grace settled at the far side, to allow for Charlie's breadth. "I will go with Charlie. He'll need someone who knows what the late-stage symptoms of measles look like. Doctor Osborne, perhaps you could give me an official letter to allow me to examine the passengers."

"Excellent idea, Grace," Anne said. "The rash clears first from the face, but lingers in the extremities, especially the lower legs. I imagine the first-class gentlemen will be reluctant to lower their stockings in your presence without official authorisation. But what about your medical studies?"

Osborne came to Grace's rescue. "Given the circumstances, I can arrange a credit for Miss Penrose in the Public Health and Medical Jurisprudence examination, in the event of her falling behind in her studies. I will convene the infectious diseases response team, to spread the word to doctors, and so forth. A private detective would be a great asset to our cause, if you are available, Mr Pyke."

"Unfortunately, I am fully engaged already," Charlie replied. "A jeweller was robbed and murdered last night. I was first on the scene and pledged my assistance to the victim's son."

"Dreadful as that is, Charlie," Grace pleaded, "we are talking about a potential epidemic of measles, which could kill dozens or even hundreds of people, mostly children."

"I have given my word, Grace," Charlie said. "However, our cases may have a point in common. Did the quarantined ship come from Sydney?"

"It did," Osborne replied. "The SS *Australis*, to be specific."

"A shoe salesman from Sydney offered expensive crocodile skin boots to a footwear shop on Princes Street last Tuesday."

"The day after the release of the first-class passengers from quarantine," Osborne said.

"The point is," Charlie continued, "One of the robbers was wearing crocodile skin boots last night, before they were generally available in Dunedin. The accent the witness described is consistent with an Australian too. In addition to that, the robber had a skin rash, described as blotchy, discoloured and peeling. Could that be measles?"

"It most certainly could," Anne said. "Measles is more than a rash, it is a respiratory disease. Did the robber have a cough?"

"He did. It seems we might both be looking for the same men," Charlie said. "How would the disease progress?"

"If the robber had measles," Anne explained, "he would have been incubating the disease on board the ship, before becoming infectious for most of the week after the first-class passengers were released. On release, he would be showing the first, mild symptoms. The rash and the worst of the fever would have set in soon after, during his week in Dunedin. By the end of the week, the fever would likely be gone and the rash would be starting to fade. If he had some natural immunity from a previous infection, the symptoms may not have been so marked."

"Thus, by Sunday night," Charlie said, "he would be well enough to commit the robbery, while still having the remnants of a rash and a persistent cough?"

"Correct," Anne replied.

Grace turned it over in her mind. "Does it not strike you as odd that the robbers would come all the way from Australia, travelling first class, to commit a robbery?"

"Perhaps," Charlie replied. "However, the robbers targeted the most exclusive jewellery shop in Dunedin. The items they stole were not only highly valuable, they were also unique, hand-crafted pieces. My guess is that such items would be hard to sell in a country as small as New Zealand. But in a large, distant city such as Sydney, they could be sold without risk. If so, the robbers might have a legitimate reason for their travel to this country, using it as cover for their offending. Or, they are here to steal as much as they can, to make the journey worthwhile. Leaving again quickly would reduce their risk of capture, especially as they would be unknown to the authorities here."

"The link still seems a tenuous one," Grace said, "albeit worthy of further investigation."

"I agree, Grace," Charlie replied. "However, there is a complication. I have also been investigating three previous jewellery thefts, involving burglaries of family homes. I had been wondering if the thefts and robbery were related, as crimes specifically targeting expensive items of jewellery are rare. However, the first thefts occurred before the ship arrived, which rules out any connection to the passengers."

"Could the thefts and robbery be unrelated crimes?" Grace asked. "A violent robbery, causing a shopkeeper's death, is a step beyond common larceny."

Charlie paused and appraised her closely before replying. "I have my suspicions about the thefts. The first victim, Miss Caroline Davenport, has been rather too inquisitive for my liking. A most annoying woman. I suspect her of following me. Today, I found out that she writes fashion articles for the *Dunedin Ladies' Journal*. I am beginning to wonder if she has made up the story of a theft as a ruse to follow me, so she can pass information about my investigation to her fellow writer, the Lady Detective."

Heat rose in Grace's cheeks. Clearly, Charlie knew of the *Ladies' Journal* article and wanted her to know that his relationship with Miss Davenport was professional and far from amiable. "Rest assured, Charlie, ladies of good sense do not believe the ridiculous gossip they read in that rag."

The tension dropped away from Charlie's broad shoulders. "If there is a link between the ship and the robbery, which I am determined to investigate as a priority, then the odds have shifted in our favour. If there were only eleven passengers released early, that narrows the suspect pool considerably. If some were woman and children, then the number of suspects may be smaller yet."

Osborne did not share Charlie's positive assessment of the situation. "The robber's rash also means one of those passengers was almost certainly infected with measles. After a week at large, the disease may already be spreading in the community. If we don't find the source and his contacts immediately, we may be too late to stop an outbreak."

Tears pricked at the corner of Grace's eyes. She clenched her jaw and tried not to think of the young lives at risk. Fortunately, they had arrived at the station and found a train about to leave. The bustle of switching from coach to train carriage provided a sufficient distraction to cover her distress. They opted for an empty compartment, where they could maintain a level of isolation from the other passengers.

Charlie took Grace's arm and diverted her into a separate compartment. "I can see you are deeply upset, Grace. Is it over the article in the *Dunedin Ladies' Journal*? I assure you, there is nothing whatsoever between Miss Davenport and me. It is you I love. No one else comes close."

"It's not that, Charlie," Grace replied, although his assurance was welcome. "I trust you. The truth is, the thought of a measles epidemic is terrifying. I don't think I have ever told you, but I lost my younger sisters in the last outbreak."

Charlie grasped her hand to his chest. "I didn't know you had sisters, only five brothers."

"Rosemary was a newborn. Lily was only one and a half years old. I was four, so I can only recall how sick we all were and how affected I was by my parents' grief when my baby sisters died. I didn't understand at the time how dreadful it was for my mother, having her infant child taken while she was still recovering from the birth. My father and grandfather, being doctors, were working around the clock to care for their patients, and no doubt blaming themselves for bringing the disease home from the surgery. I might have brought it into the house myself, as I was too young and stupid to obey my mother's instructions to keep away from other children. I'll never forgive myself for putting the family at risk."

Charlie's arm snaked around her shoulder, acknowledging the hurt. "Dearest Grace, you were four years old. You cannot blame yourself. In a large and busy household, there was never any chance of keeping the family isolated."

Grace nestled her head into the soft spot under his clavicle, drawing strength from his warmth through the soft wool of his overcoat. "Fortunately, my grandma was there to hold our family together. I think that's why I had such a strong bond with my grandma. She used to sing to me in French. She told me she was singing my spots away. I believed her."

He pulled her closer. "I wish I could have met your grandmother. From what your great-aunt tells me, she was a lot like you."

Grace was silent for a long time. The train was in sight of Dunedin station when she sat upright and looked him in the eyes. "We must stop this disease from spreading, Charlie. We simply must."

He bent and kissed her cheek. "My darling Grace, measles and murderers are no match for you and me working together."

No Stone Unturned

As soon as the train reached Dunedin station, Doctor Osborne led the medical team back to the Otago Medical School for a council of war.

Charlie's respect for Anne Macmillan and Doctor Osborne moved up a notch at their rapid response to the crisis. Within an hour, Osborne had alerted the group of medical experts who would work together to avert the spread of measles, dubbing them the Measles Response Team. He also recruited a team of medical students to make copies of a letter warning of the potential for a measles outbreak. Anne called upon Johnny Todd's band of messenger boys to take the letters to all corners of the city, spreading the news to everyone from doctors, to hoteliers, to brothels, and beyond.

Before dusk drew a curtain over the city, they had a plan in place, with messages dispersed far and wide, including one to the head steward of the SS *Australis* to obtain further information on the first-class passengers.

As twilight turned to night, Charlie escorted Grace and Anne home, tired but secure in the knowledge they were doing everything they could. Anne went straight indoors, closing the door behind her, leaving Charlie and Grace on the path. The scent of spring flowers rose up around them, the fragrance accentuated by the night air.

"Tomorrow morning, I'll apprise the police team of developments," Charlie murmured, his lips grazing Grace's ear lobe. He forgot the other point he had been about to make, as her fingers ran up his spine and through his hair.

"Don't forget the Measles Response Team meeting Doctor Osborne has called for ten o'clock tomorrow morning," Grace whispered, her skin soft against the stubble on his cheek.

"Grace, if you keep doing that, I'll forget my own name."

"Sweet dreams," she murmured. "It's going to be a busy week."

With that, she kissed his cheek and disappeared, with a rustle of skirts and a soft click of the door latch. The suddenness of her departure left him feeling bereft. The night the latch clicked with them both on the same side of the door could not come soon enough.

The following morning, Charlie arrived at the police station early. He passed through the building without being stopped. He was well known here and generally accepted, especially as his partner in the detective agency, Alistair Stewart, was revered within the police force.

Alistair was a former detective inspector with a formidable reputation. Charlie could have used his experience on this case. With so much at stake, he wanted to leave no clue missed and no stone unturned. Unfortunately, Alistair and his wife, Charlie's Aunt Lily, were out of town investigating a fraud case. Truth be told, it was Alistair Stewart's growing reputation for unravelling complex frauds that was keeping their detective agency solvent. After a spectacular success in his first case, Charlie's own work had fluctuated between ladies who had lost items of value (more often than not, later found down the back of a sofa) and lost or stolen animals. Of the two, he far preferred the animals.

Detective Sergeant Elliot should have been his contact for this case. Charlie thought it over for at least half a second, before heading towards Detective Inspector Wallace's office. He hoped the potential seriousness of the situation might outweigh the breach of protocol. He consoled himself with the thought that Elliot was about to retire, hopefully to make way for the promotion of Charlie's friend, DC Declan Kelly.

Kelly intercepted him in the corridor. "Charlie Pyke. You keep turning up like a bad penny. I hope you sorted out the … er, Davenport situation … with Grace."

“My apologies for the hasty retreat yesterday, Declan.” Charlie slapped his friend on the back. “Grace remains true. She’s one in a million.”

Declan punched him on the shoulder with a meaty fist. “That she is. Far too good for the likes of you, Charlie me lad. If you ask me, you’re a lunatic for not slipping a ring on Grace’s finger before she comes to her senses.”

“Thanks for the sympathy, Declan. Believe me, I’d have proposed long ago if I had the funds to support Grace properly. Besides, she has vowed not to marry until she has finished her medical training.”

“Doesn’t mean you can’t make the offer, you dolt.”

Charlie leaned in and lowered his voice. “As misfortune would have it, the ring I chose for Grace last Friday was stolen in the Emerson robbery.”

“Darn it, Pyke, what rotten luck,” Declan replied. “Now I really do feel sorry for you. I suppose you’re coming to see me to ask a favour.”

“I’m here to brief your colleagues on new information in the Emerson case. But, now you mention it, it would be useful to have a man on the inside, Declan, my old pal. Elliot is trying to shut me out of the case.”

“Oh, no, Charlie. Don’t ask me to get between you and DS Elliot. I’m planning to put my name forward for the detective sergeant position when Elliot retires. I can’t afford to put a foot out of place. Besides, I’m busy chasing my tail on the customs case. If anyone knows who is importing illegal booze, they ain’t talking. Even the infamous network of Kelly relatives hasn’t turned up a half-baked rumour, let alone an actual clue. I’ll never get that promotion at this rate.”

Charlie understood his friend’s need to follow the rules better than most, having falling foul of the police hierarchy himself. It had cost him his job. He covered his disappointment with another back-slap and a jest. “Visiting taverns, on the hunt for illicit alcohol.

Sounds right up your alley, DC Kelly. Send me a message if you need someone to carry you home."

Charlie was moving on when Declan called him back. "If I hear anything, I'll let you know. Wouldn't want Grace to miss out on that ring now, would we?"

Detective Inspector Wallace, predictably, followed the rules and called Elliot into his office to hear what Charlie had to say. Elliot listened without comment or apparent interest, as Charlie outlined the evidence he had gathered and the possible link between the Emerson robbery and the quarantined ship. Wallace spent most of the meeting scrawling on a piece of paper, leaving Charlie wondering why he had bothered to share his information. Still, the police had to be made aware of the seriousness of the situation.

Elliot, needless to say, had not been convinced that a first-class passenger from Australia could have any part to play in a fatal robbery. The detective sergeant got up to leave as soon as Charlie had said his piece.

Wallace opened his mouth for the first time. "Pyke, I agree with Elliot that you might be barking up the wrong tree." Elliot greeted this with a smirk. "Nevertheless," Wallace continued, "you have an annoying habit of being right. I would ask you to bear that possibility in mind, Elliot. I'm sure I don't need to remind you, Mr Pyke, that DS Elliot is in charge of the police operation, and therefore, you will do as he commands."

Wallace waved Elliot out. Charlie got up too, but Wallace gestured for him to stay. "I've instructed our records clerk to search the files for similar robberies. I'll get him to send you a copy if he finds anything relevant. I will also put out an urgent bulletin regarding the measles situation. Do you have a list of the ship's passengers?"

"Thank you, sir. I'm picking up the list after I leave here. I'll have them send a copy to you." Charlie noted the tightening of his old commander's jaw. "I mean, I'll have it sent to DS Elliot. No matter who solves the case, sir, I want Elliot to get the credit. He may not be my greatest admirer, but he deserves to finish his long career with a win."

The ends of Wallace's mouth tweaked up, which was as close to a smile as he usually allowed himself during work hours. "Well said, Pyke. Off with you now, lad. I'm a busy man." Wallace handed Charlie the letter he had been writing during their meeting. "Close the door when you leave, Pyke, in case I am tempted to set this paperwork alight and follow you out."

Charlie didn't open the letter until he reached the street. The letter was a "To whom it may concern", authorising Mr Charles Pyke to undertake such investigations as he deemed appropriate into the robbery and murder of Mr Emerson, with the full authorisation of the police. Charlie sent Wallace a silent vote of thanks and heard his old commander's equally silent admonition to use the document sparingly and wisely.

Charlie strode down the street with a renewed bounce in his step, in good time for the ten o'clock meeting of the Measles Response Team.

A porter stood guard at the entrance to the medical school building, steadfastly refusing entry to a skinny lad with a mop of black hair under a jaunty cap. Language unsuitable for minors featured in their exchange.

"Copper Charlie," the lad said, extending a grubby hand and a cheeky grin. "Can you explain to this man that I am on a mission from Mrs Macmillan to see Doctor Osborne?"

"It's Detective Charlie these days, as you well know, Johnny Todd." Charlie turned to the porter. "Please excuse this young man, sir. He has forgotten his manners in his eagerness to see Doctor Osborne. He and his team of messenger boys have been engaged to run errands for the Measles Response Team." Charlie handed over the public health authorisation letter that Doctor Osborne had written him yesterday evening. "I'm Charlie Pyke, the detective and liaison with the police for the team. I'm afraid you'll be seeing a great deal of me as well."

"A grim day, when measles darkens our shores again." The porter stepped aside. "Godspeed, sir. I have grandchildren myself, so I'll not stand in your way a moment longer."

"No need for me to go in, now that Detective Charlie is here," Johnny said. "I was only delivering three messages. First, my lads have delivered all the letters and are standing by for further orders. One of us will wait here at all times." Johnny pointed out a boy sitting on a nearby step, who seemed to have a greater expanse of hand-me-down dungaree than body to put in it. "That's Grubber."

The porter nodded. A grandfatherly kind of nod, rather than the official kind of nod that usually preceded an order to cease loitering and move on, or risk a boot in the rear.

"And the other messages?" Charlie asked Johnny.

"Mrs Macmillan said to tell you that she has alerted the medical team at Lavender House. The ladies of the St Andrew's Church Friendly Aid Society have been out since dawn, going from door to door to warn folks to be on the lookout for fevers and rashes and coughs."

Anne Macmillan had wasted no time, as expected. St Andrew's Church served one of the poorest areas of Dunedin, known as the Devil's Half Acre. Along with South Dunedin, it would be the most likely breeding ground for any serious outbreak, given the crowded, often insanitary living conditions.

"And third," Johnny Todd continued, with a widening grin, "Miss Penrose says she is unavoidably detained. She will be here as soon as she can."

"Do you know the reason for her delay, Johnny?" Charlie had a sneaking suspicion he would not like the answer. He had, of necessity, developed a sixth sense to warn him of Grace's propensity for trouble.

Johnny's grin turned into a throaty chuckle. "Your Miss Penrose is visiting a house of ill repute. Seems they reported a sighting of spots where no man would want them to be." Johnny laughed so hard he could hardly mount his bicycle, before riding off with a two-arm wave.

The porter stood, open-mouthed. Charlie shrugged and went inside. Nobody could accuse his beloved Grace of living a sheltered life. He had long since given up worrying about her, he told himself, knowing it wasn't true and never would be.

Spotted Clue

Grace would have left early that morning if it hadn't been for the row of empty pegs by the door. Her hat, coat and satchel had mysteriously vanished from the location she always left them, so that she wouldn't have to waste half of each morning looking for them.

She mentally retraced her steps from last night and quickly isolated the source of the problem. The enormity of yesterday's events, combined with the bliss of Charlie's fond farewell last night, had left her in such a fluster, she had walked right past the pegs and straight up the stairs to her bedroom. The hat, satchel and coat would be exactly where she had left them – in a pile on the floor, under the chair she had flung them at. Probably covered by her clothes from yesterday, also flung haphazardly, before Grace had flopped into bed and dreamed of a dashing detective covered in deadly spots.

A piercing shriek and an ominous series of thumps cast all thoughts from Grace's head. Her heart did a backflip around her aorta as she turned tail and ran. Anne lay in a tangle of limbs and walking cane at the bottom of the stairs, frightening in her stillness. Grace would have given anything in the world at that precise moment, to hear her great-aunt utter an outlandish curse or tell Grace off for fussing.

"Auntie!" she shrieked. So much for Grace's medical training, where the first rule was to stay calm and assess the situation with rational detachment.

Anne's groan was feeble, but welcome. "Don't screech, Grace. I'm not deaf, only winded."

"Stay still, so I can check you for broken bones."

"By the plague of Saint Gertrude, there's no call to fuss, girl. It was only the last three steps." But Anne didn't move as Grace dropped to her knees and examined her patient.

Mrs Brown, their housekeeper, rushed out of the kitchen, with soapy hands and apron askew. "Oh, Mrs Macmillan! Not again. Are you hurt?"

Grace put aside the implications of "not again", for the moment. "Nothing broken, this time, but you'll have some painful bruises. You need to rest." Grace helped Anne to sit up, noting that her great-aunt was showing no signs of dizziness, but also no sign of leaping up by herself. "I don't think it's safe for you to be upstairs until you recover, Auntie."

"Lily's old room will be fine. Help me up, Grace, I'm not an invalid."

Anne was soon settled in the downstairs bedroom, with pillows plumped, and Mrs Brown off to arrange a reviving cup of tea, that panacea of all ills.

"You've fallen before," Grace said.

"A couple of times," Anne admitted. "Not down the stairs. Nothing more than a stumble, when I am distracted by my thoughts or tired after a long day. I'm sure you do the same, Grace Penrose, when your head is in the clouds after seeing that young man of yours."

Grace refrained from mentioning that her many distractions had never resulted in falls and she was not in her seventies, using a walking cane. "I'm visiting Lavender House before I go to the meeting of the Measles Response Team. I'll let everyone know that you need to have a few days of complete rest. Rory Ravenwood can take over the organisation of your team of ladies."

Anne crossed her arms over her chest, wincing at the pain. "When did you learn to order your elders about?"

"When I moved in with you, Auntie, and learned from the best teacher in the world." Grace took her great-aunt's arms and moved them to a more comfortable position. "And I'm very grateful for the lessons. I do love you, Auntie, even if I don't say it enough."

"Don't get all sentimental on me, girl." Anne attempted a glare, but the effect was undone by the crinkles of a smile around her eyes. "I will agree to rest for one day. Perhaps two, if necessary. I sent messages to the St Andrew's ladies last night. They will already be out, spreading the word about measles. Johnny Todd is taking any important information to the measles team. Tell him to report to me here."

"Yes, Auntie." Grace knew better than to argue with such a firm decree. Besides, she was relieved that her great-aunt had consented to a day of rest. "I'll come back as soon as I can to check on you."

"You most certainly will not. You have work to do and Mrs Brown is perfectly capable of pampering me far more than I deserve. And don't you go sending a telegram to Kenneth. I'll not have him cutting his trip short on account of a minor mishap."

"I won't, if you promise to rest for at least two days." Kenneth Drummond, Anne's suitor, was out of town seeing his daughter and grandchildren. He would dash back in an instant if needed, although he knew better than most how Anne hated to be fussed over.

"Extortion now, is it?" Anne grumbled. "I suppose I can manage two days of rest without going mad. Off with you, girl, before I change my mind."

Grace paused at the door. "No dancing a jig on the stairs while I'm gone."

Anne rolled her eyes. "Nothing more than a waltz to the water closet."

Mrs Brown passed Grace in the hallway, bearing a tea-tray. "I've put some shortbread and apples in your satchel, Miss Penrose. Happen you'll need a little something, if you're rushing hither and thither all day. I've hung the satchel back on the peg by the door, next to your hat and coat. And don't you be worrying about Mrs Macmillan. I'll keep her in bed, even if I have to dose her with laudanum to achieve it."

Grace arrived at Lavender House to find a crowd spilling out onto the street. At first, she assumed it must be one of the periodic protests they had become used to. It struck Grace as irrational that men would want to protest against a medical clinic providing free healthcare to their womenfolk. But some men did not trust anything that happened to their women behind closed doors, especially as Lavender House provided refuge and medical help for beaten wives and abused daughters. So far, the protesters hadn't resorted to anything beyond harsh words and aggressive blocking of the entrance.

As Grace got closer, she realised it was not a protest, but a queue. Most of the patients recognised her, allowing her to enter Lavender House ahead of them. Grace found Doctor Rory Ravenwood and his two medical assistants working frantically to calm worried patients with runny noses and minor skin rashes. She signalled Rory to come to the office, where she could maintain her distance from patients and doctor alike.

Rory arrived a few minutes later and stood in the doorway. "It'll have to be a quick word, Grace. Anne sent a note to me yesterday evening. This morning, her ladies have been out door-knocking from dawn. News about measles has spread like wildfire, as you can see from the queue. No actual cases of measles so far, I'm relieved to say."

"I'm afraid my great-aunt won't be in to help today, Rory. She had a fall on the stairs this morning and is resting up with minor bruising."

"I'll send Mrs Macmillan home if she turns up here," Rory promised. "Do pass on our best wishes."

"I also wanted to check on Molly." Grace didn't need to remind a doctor of Rory's experience to take extra care with his wife, who was six months pregnant, but she still wanted to make sure that her best friend had got the message.

"I sent Molly off early this morning to stay with her aunt," Rory confirmed. "Her aunt and uncle live in an isolated fishing community out beyond Port Chalmers, so she ought to be safe there. Even so, I've given her strict orders not to mix with other people until I send confirmation that measles are not spreading in the community."

"Good." Grace knew Molly would hate to be so far away from her husband, as well as her business and friends, but it was a relief to know she and her baby were safe from the risk of infection.

Rory must have thought the same, but worry still etched lines on his forehead. "I miss Molly already. I hope she isn't away for too long. Not that I'm likely to get much time at home with so many patients to examine."

"There were only eleven passengers released early from the ship and none of them were children," Grace said. "They only had a brief exposure to measles, so I hope luck may be on our side."

"I'm afraid our luck has run out already, Miss Penrose," a youthful voice said. Rory stepped aside to reveal Johnny Todd, the leader of the messenger boys. His usual cheeky grin was absent. "A case has been reported in a brothel."

"Who else have you told, Johnny?" Grace asked.

"The madam sent me straight here. She don't trust any other doctors."

Rory was already reaching for his coat. Grace stopped him. "I'll see to it myself, Rory. You're run off your feet here, and I will be reporting to the Measles Response Team later, anyway. Johnny, can you go down to the medical school and warn Charlie Pyke that I might be late? He'll be there at ten o'clock for the meeting. Tell Doctor Osborne, if Charlie's not there. Mrs Macmillan is resting at home today. Can you report to her there, as well as to the medical school?"

Johnny flipped his cap back on and tugged the brim. "Right you are, Miss. I will escort you to the brothel, before I deliver the rest of Mrs Macmillan's messages."

Once outside Lavender House, Johnny darted through the crowd and headed down the street at deceptive speed. Grace called for him to stop. "Your ma will have my guts for garters if I let you escort me to a brothel, Johnny. Who reported the case?"

"It were Fanny Snoot, Miss Penrose," Johnny said. "You'd not be wanting to go to that knock house on your tod."

"I've been there before," Grace said. "I'll be fine. I'd rather you spent your time delivering messages."

Johnny hovered, kicking his boot against the gutter. "You sure you'll be safe on your own, Miss?"

"I'm armed and dangerous, as well you know, young man." Grace had learned the basics of how to defend herself after previous encounters with ruffians. Johnny and a friend of his, a former bouncer at a gambling den, had been her teachers. Breaking holds, unbalancing an attacker, weak spots to hit for maximum impact – just enough to get free and run like the blazes. Grace had also taken to carrying a knife, which she kept hidden from friends and foe alike.

"Right you are, Miss." Johnny grinned and touched the brim of his cap again. Then he was gone, over a fence and down a hidden by-way, his satchel banging against his skinny frame.

Grace walked around the corner and down the hill to the seedy alley that housed the most notorious brothel in town. It was stretching the truth to say she had been there before, as she had only been to the street end of the alley, not inside the brothel. The murder victim in Charlie and Grace's first case had been found in the alley, so the place evoked mixed emotions.

However, the women who worked in the brothel were known to Grace, as they relied on the free medical care at Lavender House. Notorious as the area was, the brothel was run by a madam who maintained strict rules around the safety and health of the workers. Grace had never met her. Presumably, the madam had sufficient means to consult a private physician.

The door was locked – nine o'clock in the morning being out of hours for the type of entertainment provided. Grace hammered until she was let in by a rumple-haired woman wearing a tattered woollen shawl over a gorgeous silk wrap.

"You'd better not be one of those Bible-bashing do-gooders," the madam said, "because I don't take kindly to being woken from my beauty sleep for a lecture on the evils of sin."

"I'm not …"

"Well, you ain't come for a job, I reckon." The madam ran an eye down Grace. "Although, with a bit of titivating, you might do well enough. Some men prefer a bit of prim and proper."

"I'm Grace Penrose, from Lavender House," Grace explained, before the woman could make any further comment on her suitability or otherwise. "Fanny Snoot sent word that she was visited by a man with measles last night. I'm very sorry to wake you so early, but the matter is urgent. Can I speak to Fanny?"

The madam held the door open for her to come in. "You're the one they call Miss Bones?"

Grace nodded. She'd gained the local nickname after a minor emergency surgery to fingers caught in a machine, soon after she arrived in Dunedin.

"Fanny stayed over in case someone came calling about the measles. Whatever you need, you've only to ask. I remember the last time we had an outbreak of measles and I'd not want to go through that again."

"You must have been no more than a child," Grace said, with a straight face. The madam was knocking on the door of forty, if not through the door and out the other side.

The creased skin around the woman's eyes wrinkled even further as she smiled. "I like you already. You've the touch of Mrs Macmillan about you."

"She's my great-aunt," Grace replied.

"Then you're welcome here anytime, Miss Penrose. Fanny is upstairs, last door on the left."

Fanny Snoot was bleary-eyed when she let Grace into a room decorated in red satin and black lace. Grace tried not to be distracted by the unfamiliar items and erotic art on the walls. Instead, she apologised for the early hour, before getting down to the business of recording Fanny's observations. From her detailed description of the customer's fading rash and cough, Grace was certain that it was measles.

The tension in Fanny's face drained away, when Grace told her the symptoms indicated that the man had passed the infectious stage. "Thank the Lord for that. I was too scared to go home, in case I infected my young nieces and nephews. Seven of us living in a two-bedroom cottage, and only me with a decent wage, since my husband died. I can't afford to have time off work."

"You can keep working. We're grateful you took the time to contact us." Grace didn't envy Fanny's life, but she admired her spirit. "Can you tell me about the man, Fanny? What he looked like, where he was staying – anything at all that might help us track him down?"

Fanny leaned back into the blood-red pillows on the bed. "He was a sad-sack, I reckon, not that we got that far. I sent him packing as soon as he dropped his drawers."

"A sad-sack?" Grace queried.

"Most men want nothing more than rough and tumble, but some want to talk first. Sad-sacks are all talk and no action. This one droned on about how lonely he was after his wife left him and how he had never done this before. They all say that, but I think this one meant it."

"You felt sorry for him," Grace said.

Fanny shrugged. "Maybe. I hate it when they get weepy. Makes it harder to pretend they're not a person."

"Can you describe the man for me?"

"Ordinary. Brown hair, skinny, sad face. No scars or nothing. Dressed like a gentleman, but worn down, as if life had turned sour on him. Smelled a bit whiffy too, though I think the worst of it was coming from the bag he was carrying. A large canvas bag."

"What was the smell like?"

"I'm not sure I can describe it," Fanny said, wrinkling her nose. "Like old rags gone musty, but sharper. Put me right off, it did. If he hadn't been dressed as a gentleman and lacking in muscles, I'd have pegged him as a sailor. Said he'd just arrived in Dunedin and couldn't wait to leave again. Complained about how cold it was compared to some place in Australia. They all do that. Don't know why they come to Dunedin if they're going to whine about the weather."

"Thank you, Fanny, that is exactly what we needed to know." Grace crossed her fingers for the last critical question. "Did he say where he was staying?"

"Not so's I recall. They never do. Worried we'll follow them, I expect, and people will find out what they've been up to. Sorry, love, that's all I remember. He wasn't here long and the light ain't good in these rooms. Madam don't want them to see that some of us are past our first flush of youth." Fanny grinned, baring a row of rotten teeth. She looked Grace up and down. "So, you're still Miss Penrose, then? Thought that handsome copper had his eye on you. If you don't want him, you can send him my way anytime. Was he not good enough for you?"

"He's more than good enough for me," Grace replied. "I want to finish my medical training before we get married." She wasn't sure why she'd told Fanny something she normally kept to herself. Fanny was a good listener. The sad-sacks must flock to her, which must make a pleasant change from the physical demands of the usual run of customers.

"Why ever would you keep the poor man dangling like that, girl? Don't they let married women go to medical school?" Fanny watched as Grace failed to form an adequate answer. "You're afraid you'll get knocked up and booted out, aren't you? I know that feeling. Nothing worse for us working girls than a bairn on the way and no way to earn a shilling."

Grace smiled to be included as a working girl, but Fanny had hit the nail on the head.

"Don't they teach you about womanly matters at medical school?" Fanny leaned forward with genuine interest.

"We're taught obstetrics and gynaecology as part of our course."

"Hmph. I'll bet I could teach those fancy medical gents a thing or two about what women really need to know."

Grace didn't doubt it for a second.

Grace arrived at the medical school late, flustered and much better informed. Not the ideal way to meet the experienced doctors who were already discussing important matters in the meeting room.

She paused by the door to set herself to rights. Inside the room, Grace could hear Charlie outlining the possible link to the robbery and the outcome of his meeting with the police.

Doctor Osborne followed with a summary of what had been done so far. "I hope I have not been premature in my response to the situation, gentlemen," Osborne concluded. "All we know for a fact is that a few of the first-class passengers were exposed to measles and let ashore early. There are no confirmed cases yet, other than a suspicious rash glimpsed during the robbery. Hopefully, it amounts to nothing."

"You've done the right thing, Osborne," Doctor Harvey said. Harvey was a local general practitioner and a close friend of the Macmillan family. "Word has spread rapidly, after the *Otago Daily Times* printed a 'Stop Press' warning the populace to watch for fever and rashes. I had patients queuing at my door this morning. All to the good. Better safe than sorry. I'd not want to relive the 1874 outbreak."

"You ought to have waited, Osborne," a walrus-moustached man grumbled. Another local doctor, but not one Grace knew. "The doctors of Dunedin are busy enough without the additional strain of a queue of anxious patients suffering flea bites, nettle stings and laundry rash. I vote we take no further action until there is a confirmed case."

Grace knew a cue when she heard one. She took a deep breath and stepped into the room. "I believe we now have a confirmed case, gentlemen."

All eyes turned to the door. Grace tried to ignore the stares of the assembled men, whose expressions ranged from interest to indignation at her intrusion. She stifled her nerves and continued in a firm voice. "One of the local brothels reported a probable case of measles to Lavender House this morning."

Doctor Osborne gestured her forward. "May I introduce Miss Penrose to those who don't know her. She is a medical student and a valued member of the Measles Response Team. Please proceed, Miss Penrose."

"When I went to the brothel to investigate–"

"You what?" the walrus-moustached doctor gasped. "I must protest, Osborne. Have you descended to such depths of desperation that you are sending innocent young girls into houses of ill repute?"

"I went of my own volition," Grace replied. "The situation is too serious to brook unnecessary delay."

Doctor Carrington rose to his feet, his outrage blooming in crimson on his cheeks. "I must add my objections. A fully qualified medical practitioner ought to have been sent, not a half-trained girl."

Charlie's deep voice rose from the rear of the group of assembled doctors. "Miss Penrose has worked as a medical assistant at Lavender House for some years, treating women patients, regardless of their backgrounds. She knows these prostitutes personally. Do you know them as well, Doctor Carrington?"

He paused for a ripple of laughter. Carrington sat down, with cheeks hot enough to fry an egg. Grace kept a straight face, but inside she was blowing kisses to her defender.

Chalie continued speaking. "Perhaps we might move on to the more important question of what Miss Penrose discovered."

The walrus-moustached doctor got to his feet. "This is outrageous, Osborne. I will be sending a sharply worded letter to –"

Doctor Osborne, who was well acquainted with Grace's unorthodox tendencies, cut off the rest of the sentence. "By all means, send a letter. But Mr Pyke is correct, gentlemen. I fear we have no time to discuss matters of propriety. Miss Penrose, please go ahead and state the relevant facts."

Grace fixed her gaze on a spot above the heads of the assembled men. "Mrs Fanny Snoot, a prostitute, was approached by a customer last night. When he dropped his drawers, she noted a fading rash on his body. Notably, the lower half of his body. Mrs Snoot refused to serve the man."

Murmurs of disquiet and embarrassment filled the room. Charlie, on the other hand, was trying to stifle a grin.

"I questioned Mrs Snoot regarding the characteristics of the rash and associated respiratory symptoms," Grace continued. "She was very clear and specific in her observations. There is little doubt that the man had measles, with a late-stage presentation."

Charlie raised a hand. "Miss Penrose, may I ask if Fanny Snoot was able to provide any information on the man's identity or current location?"

"Unfortunately not, Mr Pyke," Grace replied. "However, there is reason to believe the man came from the quarantined ship. He specifically referred to his recent arrival, the dreadful cold of this country, and his desire to return to Australia soon. Our information indicates the first-class gentlemen on the ship were exposed to the disease on the first night of the voyage, which tallies with the fading rash, peeling skin and residual cough that Mrs Snoot described. In which case, he is past the infectious stage now, but has likely been infectious all or most of last week."

"Thank you, Miss Penrose," Doctor Osborne said. "Gentlemen, you know your tasks, which are now more urgent than ever. Please notify me of any developments."

Osborne took Grace and Charlie aside. "The head steward from the SS *Australis* has promised to deliver the passenger details this morning. I'll leave the tracking of the ship's passengers in your capable hands, Mr Pyke, with the able assistance of Miss Penrose, of course. I suggest you both take the chance of refreshment while you can. Excuse me, I must go."

Osborne hurried from the meeting room, with a stack of papers clutched in his hands and a grim expression on his face.

Grace turned to Charlie. "As your able assistant, may I offer to get you a cup of tea, Mr Pyke? It's the least I can do, after your support. I've never seen Carrington so effectively silenced."

"I couldn't resist," Charlie said. "Not that you needed any help. Osborne is so impressed by your talents that he delayed the start of the meeting for you."

"He did? In that case, I shall offer not only tea, but a piece of Mrs Brown's shortbread to go with it."

Charlie took her arm. "I rather enjoy having my own personal tea lady."

"Don't get used to it, Pyke."

Passengers

Soon they were alone, with a cup of tannin-heavy institutional tea in front of them and the shortbread but a memory on the tongue.

Charlie leaned closer to Grace, a golden glint in his green eyes. "I fear my reputation might be put at risk by associating with you, Miss Penrose, as a frequenter of houses of ill repute."

Grace choked on her tea, sending bubbles up her nose. "As I recall, your reputation was already sullied by your earlier meeting with Fanny Snoot. Or should I call her Lady Victoria? She specifically asked after you. You obviously made quite the impression on her when you clambered into her boudoir."

"Fanny is no friend of mine, as you well know." Charlie had first met Fanny during his first case with Grace, when he was a raw recruit with no experience of brothels. He hadn't lived it down. "Could you give me a detailed account of your interview?"

Grace repeated everything Fanny had told her about the man and nothing of the other matters that had been discussed.

Charlie tapped his fingers on the table. "Setting aside the rather shocking familiarity with which you engaged with a prostitute, Grace, it seems we have little to go on, in terms of locating the man. I must say, the man Fanny described doesn't strike me as a likely suspect for a brazen robbery."

"Fanny did say he appeared to be a gentleman fallen on hard times. He might have been desperate for funds."

"His low spirits might have another cause," Charlie said. "If he was recruited as an accomplice for a simple burglary, he may not have been expecting to confront the shopkeeper, let alone to find himself becoming an accessory to murder. I doubt Mr Emerson's death was intentional, although the man who killed him was certainly culpable, due to his callous actions."

"Whether or not he is the robber," Grace said, "we must find the man with the measles rash without delay. Let us hope he was too sick to leave his lodgings while he was at the infectious stage of the disease."

"Agreed. We need to get that list of first-class passengers from the ship's steward as soon as possible."

No sooner had Charlie said the words, than Carrington knocked and entered. "Osborne said you wanted the passenger list as soon as it arrived, Mr Pyke. I've taken a copy. I'll see that the list is circulated."

A sun-browned man of military bearing entered the room as Carrington left. He doffed his cap. "Banbury, Head Steward of the SS *Australis*, at your service. Doctor Osborne said you wanted to speak to me in person."

Charlie rose to shake his hand. "We appreciate you coming in, Mr Banbury. I'm Mr Pyke, the detective responsible for tracking down the first-class passengers from the ship. And this is Miss Penrose, a medical expert working with the Measles Response Team."

Banbury swung slate-blue eyes in Grace's direction, but made no comment.

"Captain Souter wishes it to be on record that the decision to release the first-class passengers was made by your government officials," Banbury stated, with a note of apology in his deep voice.

"We accept that was the case, sir," Charlie replied. "There is no question of blame, only the urgent need to find these passengers and assess their medical status."

Banbury nodded. He produced a list from his pocket. "As requested, the list of first-class passengers, along with their stated addresses in Dunedin. Eleven, including three women."

Charlie ran a finger down the list and passed it to Grace.

Mr Nicholas Applegate, trade envoy, and his secretary, Mr Geoffrey Farley, staying at the Grand Hotel. Both residing in Melbourne, travelling by way of Sydney. Three men of business from Sydney – Mr Bernard Thornton, shoe salesman, Mr John Vaughan, camera salesman, and Mr Tobias Barlow, sales agent, staying at other central city hotels. Another two men, Lester and Lionel Smith, visiting family, but with a local hotel as the contact address. One couple, Mr and Mrs Quinn, with a local business address. Two single ladies, Miss Elsie Walsh and Miss Lucy Labelle, who were listed as artistes, with a contact address at a local theatre.

Thankfully, no children.

"It would be most helpful if you could describe each of the passengers to us, Mr Banbury," Charlie said. "Please be forthright in your impressions. Anything you say will be in confidence."

"It wasn't a long voyage," the head steward replied, "and a rough one at that, so I could not claim to know any of them well. To be honest, I'm not sure I gained much impression of the men, as they kept to themselves for the most part. In appearance, they were ordinary men, with not much to make any one stand out from the others. Medium height and build, more or less, brown hair of various shades, all reasonably well turned out, as one would expect of first class. Men of business, rather than idle rich, if you know what I mean."

"What of their characters?" Charlie asked. "Their demeanour and behaviour? Both good and bad."

"Oh, aye, they differed in character, for sure." Banbury glanced at Charlie. "You'll not be repeating anything I say, will you, Mr Pyke? Not even to the Captain? A head steward who speaks ill of passengers is a man who will be looking for a new position before the sun is over the yardarm."

"Strictly in confidence," Charlie confirmed.

"In that case," Banbury said, with a hint of relish at the opportunity to let loose his opinions, "the Smith brothers were fond of a drink. I kept an eye on them, as that type can be quick to show their temper when in their cups. A tough look about them, as if they had pulled themselves up to first class the hard way. One of the first-class passengers reported he had an expensive pocket watch stolen during the journey and I overheard another passenger, Mr Quinn, complaining about lost cufflinks. If I was a betting man, I'd lay odds on the brothers being the culprits. But, with no proof, the items might have been mislaid rather than stolen."

Charlie's senses quivered at the scent of potentially suspicious characters. Not that he wanted to jump to conclusions so hastily. He would look at each and every passenger with a suspicious eye, but perhaps the Smith brothers most of all.

"Naturally, Mr Applegate, the trade envoy, was quite the opposite," Banbury continued. "More of your silver spoon gentleman, who thought the rest of us beneath him. But pleasant enough, if a little brusque if his needs were not attended to promptly. A hard worker, always busy in his cabin with his secretary. The secretary, Farley, bustled around, trying to look important. He had the demeanour of a man who is put upon, but is too afraid to complain. Rather a poor specimen, physically, the secretary, but courteous and no trouble. He was the one who lost the pocket watch. Angry about it, as it was a present from his father."

An official trade delegation did not sit high on Charlie's priority list as potential robbers, but he did not dismiss them. Greed could run hot through the veins of all types of men, regardless of class and position. "What of the salesmen?"

"Mr Barlow was a little like Farley. An easy man to overlook. Rather a gloomy outlook on life. The two of them struck up an acquaintance. I've nothing against Barlow, you understand, but I didn't much take to him. Kept to his room a great deal and not much of a talker. To be fair to the man, I suspect he was not a good sailor. As I say, it was a rough sailing for a day or two. More than one passenger was seasick."

Charlie and Grace exchanged a glance. The gloomy Barlow sounded a fair match to Fanny Snoot's customer.

"This man Barlow," Grace said, "was he unwell towards the end of the voyage? Or Farley?"

Banbury paused. "I can't say I noticed. The cold weather affected most of the passengers. Several were sniffing and coughing by the end of the trip and none ventured onto deck without thick coats and woollen scarves."

"What about the other two salesmen?" Charlie asked.

"I'm afraid I tried to avoid Mr Thornton, the shoe salesman, after the first encounter," Banbury said. "A genial fellow, charming at first acquaintance, but rather over-enthusiastic on the subject of footwear. Mr Vaughan, the camera salesman, was the same, but somehow he had the opposite effect. His enthusiasm was infectious. A most interesting and entertaining fellow. So much so, I almost bought one of his cameras. Quite marvellous they were, small enough to be held in the hand. Had to have a stern word to myself about wasting my meagre wages."

Charlie perked up at the thought of a camera salesman on board. "I don't suppose Mr Vaughan took photographs of his shipmates, Mr Banbury?"

"I believe he may have, Mr Pyke, although I couldn't say which of the passengers he photographed. Probably the ladies, who were a pretty subject for a picture, if I may be permitted to say so."

Grace leaned forward intently. "We were told one of the ladies had contact with a sick child from third class."

"Contact between classes is not allowed," the head steward replied. After a pause, he relented. "But, of course, it is impossible to stop contact entirely. Some of those lads in third were little ratbags. All three of the first-class ladies were delightful, but I expect it would have been Mrs Quinn who was with the lad. She must be good with children, as she told me all about the Sunday School classes she teaches. Her husband, Mr Quinn, was a respectable gentleman with an importing business. They were the only two New Zealanders in first class."

Acid rose in Charlie's gullet. A Sunday School teacher exposed to measles – a worse prospect could hardly be imagined. Grace's anguish was written into every muscle of her body. He could see she wanted to leave immediately, but the chance to interview the head steward would come only once.

"And the two single ladies?" Charlie prompted, ignoring Grace, who was squirming in the seat beside him.

"Miss Elsie Walsh," Banbury said, with more than a hint of awe in his tone. "A powerful voice and commanding presence, although she was no more imposing in build than Miss Penrose. The entire company was enraptured when she consented to entertain in the first-class saloon. The first evening of the voyage it was, when the sea was still calm. Unfortunately, Miss Elsie later came down with mild bronchial catarrh, which robbed us of a repeat performance. She was engaged to perform as top billing for a travelling musical revue. A terrible shame for the New Zealand public when she was forced to miss the first week of the tour because of quarantine."

Grace winced at being relegated to unimposing. Or perhaps she was wincing at Banbury's flattery of the singer. Grace could hardly fail to notice that the divine Miss Walsh was afflicted with the grand-sounding bronchial catarrh, while the rest of the passengers were dismissed by Banbury as having sniffles and coughs. Evidently, nothing so common as the common cold would be good enough for a star like Miss Elsie Walsh.

"And the other single woman? Miss Lucy Labelle?"

"A charming voice and pretty too," Banbury conceded. "A devoted assistant to Miss Elsie. I believe Miss Labelle may have been engaged by the revue as a substitute singer. What do they call it in the theatre? An understudy? Miss Elsie referred to Miss Labelle as her dresser. A perfectly amiable young lady, but without the striking qualities of her mistress. Oh, you should have seen Miss Elsie's gowns and fripperies. She positively sparkled. She had the loveliest pair of peacock hair ornaments, with stones the exact shade of her eyes."

Banbury stopped and cleared his throat, a trace of pink highlighting his prominent cheekbones at straying into unnecessary excesses of enthusiasm. "But you do not to need to know that. Was there any other information you required, Mr Pyke?"

"We have been informed that there was another point of contact, between the first-class men and two young dancers from third class, who later came down with measles." Charlie noted the shutters dropping down over Banbury's face. "I assure you this is of the utmost importance, Mr Banbury, as all the passengers in contact with these two young women were exposed to measles. We must find them with utmost urgency."

"I'm afraid it's true, although you didn't hear it from me," Banbury said. "Those troublesome Smith brothers again. I had left the saloon to see to a request from Mr Applegate, the trade envoy. When I returned, the Smiths had the two young women at their table, plying them with rum. Bundaberg rum, which is a potent drop. They must have known it was against the rules. I tried to remove the women for the sake of decorum, and for their own safety, but ... well, the two brothers weren't having it."

"Who else was there?" Charlie asked.

"Let me see ... Mr Thornton, for sure. He and one of the Smiths were dancing with the girls, rather too intimately in my view. I was about to step in, but the girls seemed to know how to handle themselves when the gentlemen's hands strayed too far. Mr Vaughan was there too, but he was dancing with Miss Elsie. Mr Quinn had been playing the piano earlier, but his wife made him leave when the dancing became too indecorous. Miss Labelle took over the piano for a short time, but Mr Vaughan saw her and Miss Elsie back to their cabins when the amount of rum drunk became excessive. I was grateful for his help. I had to find two other crew members to end the evening's entertainment."

Charlie consulted the list. "What about the other three men – Applegate, Farley, and Barlow?"

"Applegate had retired early to read. I took a glass of port to his cabin. Farley and Barlow were in the first-class saloon, but mostly watching on. One of the Smiths pressed some rum on them and one of the girls tried to get them up to dance. Barlow joined in for a short while, without much enthusiasm, before he and Farley retired to their cabins." Banbury slid a pocket watch out of his waistcoat pocket and consulted it. "If there is nothing more?"

"We are extremely grateful for your insights, Mr Banbury," Charlie said. "I expect you will be wanting to return to your ship."

"I'm afraid so, sir. No shore leave, this trip, with two weeks wasted in quarantine. Fortunately, we were granted permission to unload the cargo, which included perishable items. We sail again on the evening tide."

When Banbury departed, Charlie bent over his notebook to record the head steward's observations while they were fresh in his mind.

"Can't that wait, Charlie?" Grace pleaded. "We must find Mrs Quinn as soon as possible."

Charlie glanced up. Grace was standing by the door, practically pawing the ground.

"Can we take a moment to consider our priorities, Grace?" Charlie suggested. "We're not certain it was Mrs Quinn who was exposed to measles, and she's definitely not high on the list of the robbery suspects. Or her husband, for that matter, the respectable local businessman. We have at least one man and perhaps two who almost certainly had measles. The man who went to the brothel and the robber's accomplice. We need to talk to the shoe salesman, Thornton, to find out who bought the crocodile skin boots that the robber wore. And track down Barlow, the morose man."

"Damn the crocodile skin boots, Charlie! I couldn't give a fig about the robber. Mrs Quinn is a *Sunday School teacher*. Measles could be spreading amongst the children of Dunedin as we waste time pursuing a robber."

Charlie kept his voice calm. "A man was murdered, Grace."

"What is one man's death, compared to the multitude of innocent children who could die?" Grace wrenched the door open.

Charlie ran for the door, before it slammed closed again with Grace on the other side. He came close to losing his fingers, but managed to stop her from fleeing. "Grace, please wait. I'm sorry. You're right, children's lives come first."

Grace came back into the meeting room and sank into a chair. "You're right too, Charlie. I apologise for my outburst. I don't mind admitting, this measles situation has me on edge."

With Grace's experience of two sisters taken by the deadly disease, Charlie had no problem understanding why. "You have my full commitment to the task, Grace. But I do need to fulfil my commitment to Mr Emerson as well. And you know me – ever the dull policeman – writing up my notes before I forget all the details of what the witness said."

"Dearest Charlie, you may be methodical and thorough, but you are never, ever dull. And not one to hold back when action is needed. It's what makes you a good detective. Unlike me, plunging in where angels fear to tread."

Charlie took the seat beside her. "Perhaps if people gave your abilities due credit, you wouldn't have to plunge in without telling anyone. Besides, I've seen you going about your medical work in the same methodical manner you accuse me of – calmly assessing a patient and asking the right questions until you reach a diagnosis. We're not so different."

She leaned her head against his shoulder. "Perhaps in this instance, it would be more efficient if we each go our own way. I understand your client is your first priority. And I agree that the man or men with measles must be found urgently. But I insist on seeing Mrs Quinn as my first priority."

"Agreed." Charlie flicked her an uncertain glance. "I hate to mention it, but there is one slight problem."

"What?"

"The only address we have is Quinn's business premises. No matter how assertive you are, I doubt Mr Quinn would agree to be examined by a woman alone." He could see her frustration flaring again. "I know it's unfair on you, Grace, and I applaud your desire to change the world. But can we please not do it today, when we need to find all these passengers as fast as possible."

“I can see your point, Charlie, even if I don’t like the reason,” Grace grumbled. “Perhaps I ought to send someone who will command Mr Quinn’s attention, such as the talented Miss Elsie Walsh or the beautiful Miss Caroline Davenport.”

Charlie punched her on the shoulder with feather lightness. “I think the talented and beautiful Miss Penrose will do just fine. Maybe you could take Carrington along for the ride, to show him how a real doctor works.”

Grace caught his hand and brought it to her lips. “Go catch me a murderer with measles, Detective Pyke. After you have written up your notes in a calm and orderly fashion, of course.”

Sunday School

Grace left the meeting room with her heart still racing, after coming close to slamming a door on Charlie's hand. Frustration had got the better of her, but she had no excuse for taking it out on him. Fortunately, his calm understanding had steadied her, as always.

The last few days had affected her more than she cared to admit. Grace found a quiet spot and closed her eyes. When challenges proved daunting, she sought strength from her great-aunt's tales of battles past. Anne Macmillan was both St George and the dragon – equal parts fearless and feared. When Grace sallied forth again, her armour was back in place, the fire-breathing fury tamped down for another day.

Doctor Osborne was in his office, seated behind a stack of papers and maps. Doctor Carrington and the departmental secretary were present too – the latter reading names of people and hotels off a list, while Carrington marked locations on a map of Dunedin. The pins clustered around central Dunedin. Tacked up along the side of the map were notes about each team member's tasks and movements, as well as a list of tasks not yet allocated.

Grace imagined that this was what an army general's office looked like during wartime. Her own name was up there. Her square of paper read, "Help Pyke". Not exactly dragon-slaying, but a step up from "Make tea". Charlie's read, "Track down ship pax. Murder/robbery – measles? Liaise police."

Carrington's note read, "Strategic Command Centre. Medical emergency response." Grace imagined sneaking in late at night and changing it to "Paper-pusher", but banished the thought as unworthy, especially as efficient organisation would be critical to the team's success.

“Do these pins represent the hotels where the ship’s passengers are staying?” she asked.

“Listed hotel locations are the pins with the blue tags,” Carrington said. “We’ll switch to green tags when the passengers have been examined and their measles status is confirmed as negative. The two red tags mark the positive sightings so far. Yellow tags for any transmission within the community, black for deaths. None of those yet, of course, but it is rather thrilling, isn’t it? I shall publish an article on it when the dust settles.”

Grace failed to express just how thrilled she would be to see the first black tag go up. She visualised St George instead.

Osborne looked up. “Miss Penrose, what news from the ship’s steward?”

“The bad news is that Mrs Quinn, the woman who may have had contact with the sick boy, is a Sunday School teacher.”

All three men reacted with a sharp intake of breath. Charlie might not have recognised the seriousness of the situation, but these medical men certainly did.

“Mrs Quinn must be our top priority,” Osborne said. “Has Mr Pyke gone to find her?”

“I volunteered to find Mrs Quinn,” Grace replied. “Mr Pyke is tracking down the male passengers, with the aim of finding the man or men with measles.”

Doctor Carrington was already putting on his coat. “The only address we have is Mr Quinn’s business premises. He will need to be checked for measles too, of course. A male doctor must go. Miss Penrose can send out the copies of the passenger list.”

“You should both go,” Osborne said. “Any differences you have, put them aside for the greater goal. It is vital we get a complete list of Mrs Quinn’s contacts. She may be more willing to disclose anything of a personal nature to Miss Penrose.”

Grace and Doctor Carrington arrived at the Bond Street warehouse owned by Mr Quinn within ten minutes, thanks to one of the waiting hansom cabs, which had been engaged to provide transport to the Measles Response Team.

The sign above Quinn's premises read: "Tropical Trading Company". They opened the door on raised voices, coming from an interior office. Or rather, one raised and irate voice, the other calm and apologetic.

"This is the third time the cargo delivered has been short of what I paid for, Herbert. I'll not have it!"

"Yes, Mr Quinn. It's only a few dozen sacks of sugar, sir. Might be a miscount."

"Get the storeman to check the inventory again. If I'm a single pound short on the sugar I paid good money for, I'll be demanding compensation and changing suppliers. I'm scarcely making a profit as it is, without the supplier trying to cheat me. What about the melons?"

"All present and correct, Mr Quinn. Riper than usual, because of the delay in offloading the cargo, but orders have been brisk. Not a lot of other fruit available at the moment."

"Of course not, man. That's why I import the melons at such expense at this time of the year. And next time, find me a ship direct from Queensland."

"But, sir, the primary shipping route goes via Sydney and …"

"Just do it, Herbert."

A man in dungarees and a flat cap exited the office, throwing a surly glance at the visitors without greeting them. A gentleman of some thirty years of age followed, adjusting his tie under a tomato-red face. Grace gave him another decade or two before apoplexy or heart problems ensued.

The gentleman stopped short on seeing them. "My apologies. I did not hear you enter. How may I be of assistance to you, sir?"

Doctor Carrington stepped forward. "Are you Mr Quinn, recently arrived from Sydney on the SS *Australis*?"

"I am." Quinn shook his hand. "Is this about the problem with my sugar shipment?"

"No, sir. I am Doctor Carrington from the Otago Medical School. We have reason to believe that the first-class passengers on the ship were inadvertently given permission to disembark, despite exposure to measles."

"Nonsense," Quinn barked. "We had no exposure to the lower-class passengers. And, might I remind you, we spent a miserable week imprisoned on that appalling island. You can see that I am perfectly well."

"Nevertheless, sir, I am required to conduct a brief examination of each passenger." Carrington retrieved his authorisation from an inner pocket. "A quick look at your legs and arms will suffice, as I can see you have no visible symptoms." Carrington advanced towards the office. "In the privacy of your office would be most convenient."

Quinn opened his mouth to protest, but thought better of it in the face of Carrington's authority. He followed the doctor into the office, closing the door on Grace.

Having seen how disagreeable the man was, Grace had to concede that Charlie had been correct. She was glad she hadn't had to deal with Quinn on her own. He would certainly have refused to let her examine him.

Instead, she paced the outer room, venting her frustration internally. Would there ever be a time in the future when male patients came to her willingly? Somehow she doubted it. It did not cause her sleepless nights. When she finally qualified, as the first female doctor in the country, she hoped to have women patients queuing at the door.

Grace longed for the day she would graduate for more than one reason. The joy of achieving her lifelong goal was the major reason, naturally. She had also, rather foolishly as it turned out, vowed not to marry before becoming the third generation Doctor Penrose. For all her best-laid plans, she had not expected to fall in love so completely that it was a relentless ache inside her.

Love had been on her life checklist, as if it was an examination she could study for and pass when the time was right. How naïve she was. Love was not a logical tick in a box, it was an uncontrollable and incurable contagion that took over the body and mind. What if the man she wanted became tired of her unladylike ambitions and obsession with medicine? What if another woman came along – an attractive, talented, wealthy woman such as Caroline Davenport, for instance – and the wait no longer seemed worth it?

Grace cut short her drifting thoughts, in favour of more urgent matters. She owed it to Charlie to consider the passengers as robbery suspects, as well as potential carriers of measles. She was ready by Quinn's office door when Carrington came out, setting his hat back on his neatly trimmed hair and thanking Mr Quinn for his cooperation.

She stepped inside the office, startling Mr Quinn, who was gazing out the window with his hands clasped behind his back. "Excuse me, Mr Quinn, we have one further question. Did you, perchance, purchase a pair of crocodile skin boots on board the ship?"

Quinn stared at Grace as if she was something nasty on the bottom of his boot. "Who are you and why the devil do you wish to know that, girl?"

"Miss Penrose is a medical student, who is assisting me," Carrington said. "We have what we need, sir."

Grace ignored the pull of Carrington's hand on her arm. "I would not ask if it was not important, Mr Quinn. A witness noted a measles-like rash on a person wearing such boots. We are obliged to investigate."

"It wasn't me the witness saw, I assure you. I bought the boots for my wife, who had been complaining that she had no boots comfortable enough for walking. I have not yet given them to her, as I wished to surprise her on her birthday."

"And where were you last Sunday night, Mr Quinn?" Grace inquired.

"How dare you?" Quinn spluttered.

"Grace, I don't think –" Carrington said.

Grace refused to be put off. "If you could answer the question, sir. All part of our authorised duty under the quarantine legislation."

"Where else would I be but my own home, on the Lord's day?" Quinn replied. "After attending church, of course."

"Thank you, sir. Good day." Before she left, Grace took a mental note of Quinn's description. Light brown hair, brown eyes, thick lips, medium height, and a slim build, showing the first hints of a portly middle age to come. A description that might apply to a fair proportion of the male population of Dunedin, including the robber of Emerson's jewellery shop.

Grace and Doctor Carrington showed themselves out to the waiting cab.

The coachman gathered up the horse's water bucket, receiving a nudge in the back in return. The horse kept his head lowered, as the coachman scratched his ears and forelock. "Me and this old fellow have been together a long while," the man explained. "Where to now, Doctor Carrington?"

Carrington gave him an address in Maryhill. They mounted up, and the horse headed off without so much as a touch of the reins, as if the old fellow had overheard the direction and knew exactly where he was going.

"May I ask what you found out from Mr Quinn, Doctor Carrington?" Grace asked.

Carrington gazed at the passing trams, carts, and pedestrians for some time, as if they held the answer to her question. Finally, he deigned to speak. "Your alarm was unfounded, Miss Penrose. Mrs Quinn gave up teaching Sunday School after she married Mr Quinn five months ago. Quinn said that she has not mentioned having a skin rash."

"That's marvellous!" Grace noted Carrington was not as cheered by the news as he ought to have been. "Is there more?"

“Quinn did mention that his wife took to her bed two days after leaving Quarantine Island. He left it to her maid to look after her, believing her only to have a lingering chill from the voyage and the week in quarantine. I gather he has hardly seen her, such have been the pressing demands of his business interests. The risk is slight, but I will not feel completely at ease until I have checked the lady myself. I questioned Mr Quinn about their household arrangements. Their maid lives out and comes from a large family.”

“Oh.” What else was there to say? Grace sat back and fiddled with her gloves. That was the problem with a highly infectious disease like measles. The web of human contacts meant it spread out across the community quickly, taking hold before the symptoms showed. One infected maid from a large family might spark a wave of infections.

The maid appeared perfectly rosy-cheeked as she showed them into a stuffy sitting room. Mrs Quinn lay on a chaise longue, surrounded by cushions and blankets. A large bowl sat close at hand. “Edna, I told you, I am not well enough to receive visitors.”

“I’m afraid I must impose upon your good will, Mrs Quinn.” Carrington went through the preliminaries of their visit, explaining about measles and securing the reluctant consent of their hostess to an interview. “We are trying to find the lady on the ship who was seen with a young boy from third class.”

Mrs Quinn looked at Carrington as if he had implied she was a woman of ill repute. “You cannot believe it was me, doctor. I wouldn’t go near a boy like that, for fear of catching fleas or lice. I suspect the brat of thievery too. My husband lost the expensive pair of cufflinks I gave him for his birthday and now I cannot find the precious locket my mother gave me before she died. I know I had it on the ship. Lower-class children have no moral standards – none at all.”

“I would not have asked if it was not for the fact that we were told you taught Sunday School, Mrs Quinn.”

Her hand fluttered with a dismissive wave. “Mama’s idea. It is important for a young lady to show a charitable nature, in order to secure a husband. Once one is married, naturally, one does not have time for such activities."

"So you didn't teach Sunday School last Sunday, Mrs Quinn?" Grace asked.

"I did not."

"May I ask how you and your husband did spend Sunday?" Grace continued. "I am sorry to have to intrude on your private life, but it is of utmost importance."

Mrs Quinn bit back her annoyance, probably to hasten the end of the interview. "If you must know, we went to church and spent the rest of the day at home. My husband was busy in his study in the evening, so I retired early. I was feeling tired and unwell."

Carrington took over again. "May I inquire as to the nature of your current illness, Mrs Quinn?"

"What haven't I suffered over the past few weeks?" Mrs Quinn sighed like a much-afflicted lady of advanced years, although she was no more than Grace's age of twenty-three. "*Mal de mer*, a dreadful chill, constant exhaustion and nausea." At the last, she fluttered her fingers toward the spotless enamel bowl.

"I am sorry to hear it," Carrington said. "I am sure your malaise will pass now that you are home from your voyage. Nevertheless, I am required to examine your legs and arms, Mrs Quinn, to establish beyond doubt that you have no trace of a rash that might indicate a measles infection."

"You most certainly will not examine my person, young man," Mrs Quinn retorted. "Why, you're hardly old enough to put up a shingle. I will not allow any man other than my own doctor to examine me. He has been my family physician for decades and his father before him."

"Perhaps I might be permitted, Mrs Quinn?" Grace asked. "I am a medical student, with particular experience with lady patients. We would not ask if it was not essential."

Mrs Quinn sniffed. "I suppose so, if you must."

Grace quickly ascertained that the lady showed no sign of a rash. "Mrs Quinn, have you noticed any other symptoms? Changes in your appetite perhaps, or a corset that seems tighter than usual? The absence of your monthlies?"

"Why yes, now you mention it. I am entirely unable to stomach my usual cup of coffee in the morning. Indeed, I struggle to eat at all. No wonder I feel so weak." Mrs Quinn crossed her arms over her chest, in case the unusual swelling of her bosoms was clear for all to see. She leaned forward to Grace and whispered, "I cannot imagine how you knew I also suffer the other unmentionable symptoms you mentioned. Does that mean I have been infected with measles from that ghastly ship?"

Grace despaired at the ignorance and ridiculous delicacy that shrouded any sensible discussion of female medical conditions. Give her Fanny Snoot any day. Fanny's work was dangerous and despised, but she knew what was what. Retreating to a chaise longue was not an option for her, with an extended family to feed, yet she still retained a sense of humour and a certain tough-shelled dignity.

"Mrs Quinn," Grace continued with calm reassurance, "I am sure you do not have measles. Indeed, I suspect you are not ill at all. May I suggest you seek an appointment with your physician? I believe you may be with child."

After a brief interlude involving shrieks (joy? shock? both?) and the application of smelling salts by a thoroughly experienced maid, Grace and Doctor Carrington took their leave.

Carrington ordered the coachman to return to the medical school, then lapsed into silence.

Grace kept her thoughts to herself. Her first thought was relief that Mrs Quinn did not have measles, especially as her baby would have enough to contend with, without birth complications from the disease. Her second thought was that their task was not over, as they knew one of the ladies on the ship had had contact with the sick boy. The only other candidates were the two single ladies who had given a local theatre as their address. Grace hoped their performances did not involve contact with a cast of children.

"I have to get back to the medical school to attend to my other duties," Carrington said, when they reached the outskirts of the central city. "Am I correct in presuming you will wish to return to your lectures? You cannot afford to slip behind in your studies, Miss Penrose, if you truly wish to become a doctor."

His condescending tone ran sharp nails down her spine. His emphasis on "truly" was particularly aggravating, as if she was merely pretending an interest in medicine. "Of course I wish to become a doctor. Why else would I have sacrificed so much to enter medical school?"

Carrington turned away, but not before Grace detected a smirk.

"If you have something on your mind, Doctor Carrington, please have the decency to share your opinion with me, rather than laughing at my expense."

"Miss Penrose, I have no wish to make an enemy of you, or to have my eyes scratched out. I was merely taking a position of logic. As a woman, it is obvious you cannot hope to practice medicine."

"And why is that, Doctor Carrington?" Grace said, with claws reluctantly retracted.

"Because you will marry and have a family, of course. That being so, the only logical explanation of your attendance at medical school is to find yourself a husband. I can only assume that your dalliance with the policeman is a fleeting diversion from the greater goal."

Grace thumped on the ceiling of the cab with her fist, causing the coachman to rein in his horse sharply. "You are wrong on every count, Doctor Carrington. I have every intention of practicing medicine and none whatsoever of marrying a doctor. Now, if you will excuse me, I have important business to attend to."

She jumped down, narrowly avoiding a steaming pile of horse droppings, which rather summed up her mood.

Footwear Fanatic

Charlie sat in the meeting room after Grace left to visit Mrs Quinn, writing up his notes from the interview with the ship's head steward. When he was finished, he tucked his notebook into his pocket and set out to find a critical witness – the man who had sold the rash-suffering robber his crocodile skin boots.

Luck turned in Charlie's favour when he found the shoe salesman, Mr Bernard Thornton, in his hotel room. The man who answered the door greeted Charlie like an old friend, pumping his hand and flashing a set of perfectly white teeth. Neatly dressed in a good quality dark-coloured suit, his collar bleached and starched until it sat as a solid white underscore to a tanned, handsome face. His good looks and charm had no doubt caused susceptible ladies to purchase more footwear than necessity dictated.

More importantly, Thornton fitted the general description of the robber glimpsed by Daniel Emerson. Average height, slim build, fine-boned wrists. A trace of pleasant eau-de-cologne wafted in Charlie's direction as he shook the man's hand. And Thornton had danced intimately with a measles victim. Charlie had high hopes, although Thornton looked a healthy specimen, with no trace of a rash on his face.

"Come in, come in. If you are here to purchase my fine footwear, sir, I must warn you I am down to my last few pairs of the crocodile skin boots. Quite the sensation they have been! Can't think why nobody else has thought to sell them in New Zealand. I had hopes of them being well received, for it is my experience that discerning buyers, such as yourself, seek quality above price. But I'll own I never expected such excellent sales. I've had to wire to Sydney for more stock. Of course, I cannot take all the credit for sales. An extraordinary young lady, who writes for a well-regarded ladies' journal, wrote a flattering piece about my wares." Thornton paused for a long overdue breath. "Please excuse my enthusiasm, sir. What do you require? Are you buying on behalf of a footwear retailer or has word of my location reached an eager public?"

"Neither, Mr Thornton." Charlie rushed out the words to prevent another torrent of sales patter. "My name is Mr Pyke. I am here on an entirely different matter, of much greater importance."

Thornton tipped his head to one side, allowing a slightly raised eyebrow to highlight his disbelief. "Come now, Mr Pyke, I'm sure you would agree that few things in life are more important than top quality footwear. We must guard the welfare of our feet, must we not, for we cannot manage without them. I could tell you many, many stories, sir, of everything from painful bunions to gentlemen literally crippled by poor quality shoes and boots. And how much worse for the ladies, who suffer blisters and pinched–"

Charlie was forced to interrupt rather abruptly, as time was of the essence. "Mr Thornton, I am investigating a potential outbreak of measles, which could have devastating consequences for the children of Dunedin. I do not wish to hear any more of bunions and blisters."

Thornton took a step backwards at Charlie's outburst. "My apologies, Mr Pyke. Please, take a seat."

Charlie lifted half a dozen boxes of shoes off the nearest chair. "Can I confirm that the ship you arrived on was the SS *Australis*, which was quarantined with several cases of measles?"

The shoe salesman nodded. "We spend over a week on a miserable island to avoid spreading the disease."

"Unfortunately, quarantine ought to have been at least two weeks. Have you noticed any rashes on your skin or experienced any fever or coughing?"

"Never a sick day in my life. I put it down to –" Thornton must have finally realised the seriousness of the situation, for he cut the sentence short. "No, neither rash nor coughing. Not like some of the other passengers. Farley coughed all the way through a wonderful medley of songs from our very talented lady passengers. Vaughan and Quinn had decent voices too. Miss Elsie and Vaughan received the loudest applause for a boisterous duet from one of the Gibert and Sullivan abominations. For my money, Miss Lucy Labelle and Mr Quinn gave a far superior performance with a beautiful duet from *La Traviata.* Altogether a better class of music than that served up by music halls, in my opinion, but then … Forgive me, I am digressing, again."

"Would that be the same night the two dancers from third class came to the first-class saloon?" Charlie asked. If he expected Thornton to deny contact with them, he was mistaken.

"That's right. After the singing, the Smith brothers smuggled the girls and rum into the saloon while the steward was absent. A lively pair of girls they were too. Showed us one of their stage dances, with legs flying in all directions most provocatively. That stiff upper lip fellow, Quinn, had to reel his eyeballs back in. His wife dragged him off to an early bedtime."

Charlie couldn't blame Mrs Quinn. The Smith brothers did not sound like gentlemen at all. "But you stayed, Mr Thornton?"

"Yes, but not for the reason you appear to be implying, Mr Pyke. While it could have been an entertaining evening, the Smith brothers were knocking back their rum a little too quickly for my liking. I was sure they had been drinking on the deck with the girls before they came into the saloon. To be frank, I was worried about the girls. In fact, I asked one to dance, so I could discreetly offer to escort them back. She said she could handle herself. I did my best to keep them dancing with anyone but the Smiths, with limited success. It was a relief when the steward intervened."

"Unfortunately, both dancers were infected with measles and thus you and the other men have been exposed to the disease," Charlie said. "I will have to ask you to show me your arms and lower legs, Mr Thornton. I have a letter of authorisation, if you wish to see it."

Charlie hardly dared hope he could get so close to the man's boots without receiving a lecture on the workmanship and exceptional features. However, Thornton did as he was asked in miraculous silence. The man appeared to be in rude good health, with not a trace of a rash or peeling skin. He was, however, wearing a pair of his own boots. If Mr Emerson had been mistaken about the presence of a rash, then Thornton was still on the suspect list.

"Thank you, Mr Thornton. I also need to inquire whether you sold any of your footwear to the other first-class passengers on the ship. Specifically, the crocodile skin boots."

Thornton perked up again. "Indeed, I did. Several pairs, in fact." The smile was back, but rueful this time. "Rather a captive audience. I admit I can be something of an enthusiast when it comes to my occupation."

"The world would be a better place if everyone enjoyed their jobs as much as you do," Charlie said.

"Quite so, Mr Pyke. Let me think now. I sold a pair to Mr Quinn for his wife. The boots are of such a fine cut they make an excellent ladies' walking boot. Mr Smith bought a pair of the boots too. I'm not sure I could tell you which Smith, as I never did fix in my mind which brother was which, and I did not care to further our acquaintance by asking. The shorter and slimmer of the two brothers – Mr Lionel Smith, I think."

"Did you talk to the Smith brothers at all?" Charlie asked. "About their reasons for travelling, where they were headed, perhaps?"

"We passed the time of day, as one does on a voyage, but not at length. I do recall that they were visiting family in Dunedin. Had rather an interesting discussion about the sugar trade in Queensland too, which is their line of business. Must pay well, because their tailor knew quality, even if the men themselves were a little rough around the edges. I'm no teetotaller, but those boys made me look like a choirboy when it came to hard drinking."

Well-off but rough-mannered, in keeping with many successful men who strayed onto the wrong side of the law. Charlie was looking forward to making the acquaintance of the Smith brothers. "Any other boot sales, Mr Thornton?"

Thornton paused to consider. "Mr Applegate's secretary purchased a pair too. I would rather Mr Applegate had bought them, for a trade envoy would have been a perfect advertisement. But, as I always say, any sale is a good sale. I can't recall the secretary's name. Mousy little fellow. Handshake like a cheap pair of insoles."

Charlie consulted his list. "Mr Geoffrey Farley?"

"Oh, yes, Farley, that was his name. His friend tried a pair on too, but just between ourselves, I don't think he could afford them. Rather down at heel, if you will excuse a double entendre. I do hate to see a pair of boots almost worn through."

Charlie looked at his list again. "Would that be Mr Tobias Barlow, sales agent? Strange that he should be travelling first class if he is short of funds."

"Farley told me that Barlow had been engaged to work for a wealthy man in Sydney, who paid his fare. I don't think Barlow himself had two brass farthings to rub together."

"Do you know what line of business Barlow is in, Mr Thornton?"

Thornton crossed a leg over his other knee, stroking the heel of his boot idly as he tried to recall. "It was something odd. Quite the oddball himself, Mr Barlow. Very quiet in company, although I'd hazard a guess that he was not feeling well. A rough trip. Poor man developed rather a nasty cough while we were in quarantine. Darned cold, that island, despite all the blankets they gave us."

Thornton barrelled on before Charlie could interrupt his flow. "I shan't be sorry to return to Sydney, although I have some weeks ahead of me, travelling up the country. The company I work for wishes to establish a retail agency to stock our footwear in each major city. That is the primary goal of my journey. I flatter myself that I have achieved far more than I expected here in Dunedin, despite the delay in quarantine. Arriving alongside the Australian trade delegation has been fortuitous. I have been invited to a formal reception for the delegation on Thursday evening, along with the other passengers engaged in trade between our countries. A great honour, as I am sure you will agree. I intend to gift a pair of boots to the host, Mr Davenport, who is said to be a man of great distinction. If I have any boots left!" Thornton chuckled. "I say, I have rather rattled on. My apologies."

Charlie had quite lost the thread of his questioning, but he didn't dare let a gap in the conversation open up. "Getting back to the boots. You sold three pairs to passengers – Mr Farley, Mr Quinn, and Mr Lionel Smith. I believe you also gifted a pair to Miss Caroline Davenport, in exchange for an article in the *Dunedin Ladies' Journal*?"

"Yes, that's right," Thornton said. "Quite the detective, aren't you? What a charming lady Miss Davenport is. If I may be so bold, she is a woman who appreciates a fine pair of boots. I cannot bestow higher praise. I only wish I sold pretty ladies' slippers as well. Perhaps on my next trip –"

"Mr Thornton," Charlie interjected. "Where were you last Sunday night?"

"Birds!"

"I beg your pardon?" Charlie was beginning to wonder at the man's grasp on sanity, at least as it pertained to matters other than footwear.

Thornton chuckled at Charlie's puzzled frown. "Sorry, bit of a non sequitur. My mouth runs faster than my brain sometimes. I have just remembered that Barlow was here to buy birds. Stuffed and mounted, that is. He works as an agent for a collector of rare species in Sydney."

"Oh, I see." Charlie resisted the urge to check his pocket watch. "Getting back to Sunday night?"

"I dined at my hotel, then went to the Evensong service alone. I'm partial to choral music. Afterwards, I went for a stroll, before turning in. Busy week ahead."

"So, you would have been in bed before ten o'clock or thereabouts?"

Thornton inspected his manicured fingernails. "Somewhat later than that, I imagine. I walked all around the city, looking in the shop windows. Lost track of the time."

Possibly due to stopping at all the shops selling shoes, to compare notes on every last detail from heels to laces. Or, more likely, in Charlie's opinion, lying through his pearly white teeth. This was the first time Thornton had been unwilling to look Charlie in the eye. For a man who tried to give the impression of genial sincerity, the change in manner jarred. A word to the desk clerk of the hotel was in order, to confirm what time Thornton arrived back on Sunday night.

Charlie couldn't think of anything else to ask. He would have liked to search the hotel room from skirting board to ceiling, but he had no probable cause for a search at this point, especially as he was here under the guise of being a health inspector. The room was of modest size, with little more than a bed, a chair, a washstand and a coat rack. The pile of shoe boxes in the corner took up most of the spare space.

Charlie rose from his chair and thanked Thornton, ducking out the door before he was talked into spending his hard-earned savings on a new pair of boots.

The desk clerk at the hotel had been on duty on Sunday night. He recalled the shoe salesman (who had engaged him in a baffling one-way discussion of insoles and eyelets) and confirmed his departure shortly before eight o'clock on Sunday night, having asked the way to the nearest church. "The man was wrapped in a thick coat and black scarf," the desk clerk said, "as if it was mid-winter, rather than a mild spring. I gave him a pass key to the rear entrance, so he could return after reception closed for the evening at ten o'clock. I was not here when he returned, so I presume he used the key."

Charlie was delighted to get back to the fresh air of Princes Street. Outdoor air, he corrected himself, as he stepped over a pile of horse droppings and a rotten cabbage.

The next hotel on his list proved less successful. The Smith brothers had given the name of a shabby hotel on the outskirts of the city, near the railway station. The desk clerk did not recall them. Indeed, he had no record of two male guests called Smith or two brothers of any description. Both the head steward and the shoe salesman had indicated the brothers were unsavoury characters, for all they could afford to travel first class. Thus, Charlie was not surprised to learn that they had either used a false name or given a false address.

The name Smith was so common, it would prove difficult to track the men down, especially if they were travelling under that name to hide their real identities. Charlie would have to leave it to the police to use their greater resources to find the pair, unless he could find out more about them from the other passengers. Perhaps the man who was selling cameras? If Mr Vaughan had taken photographs of the Smith brothers, that might help to unmask them.

Charlie checked his list again. Barlow, the stuffed bird man, was nearest. The New Provincial Hotel on Stafford Street. The less than flattering descriptions of the man given by the head steward and the shoe salesman suggested a match to the morose man with measles who had visited Fanny Snoot at the brothel. Barlow had moved to the top of his Most-Wanted list as the potential robber with measles, with the Smith brothers a close second.

Charlie was tempted to stop for a bite to eat and a pint of ale, after a challenging morning. But he didn't want Grace to stumble across him coming out of a tavern smelling of mutton stew and beer when there was important work to be done. Instead, he bought a pie and devoured it on his way to the hotel.

Marvellous Musicale

Grace made her escape from the hansom cab before Doctor Carrington could call her back. They had stopped close to the central city, so it did not take Grace long to make her way to the corner of Princes Street and High Street.

Tempting though it was to return to her home further up High Street, she had a different plan in mind. The Princess Theatre also graced that street and was the address given by the two singers from the ship. Whatever men like Carrington thought of her motives for studying medicine, Grace was determined not to let them get in the way of what really mattered – stopping a measles outbreak.

When Grace reached the Princess Theatre, she found a man and a boy outside, stripping off one set of playbills ("Marvin's Marvellous Musicale direct from Sydney Australia") and pasting up another ("Virtuoso Piano Recital").

Grace approached the man. "Has the musical revue finished?"

"Aye. Moved on this morning to Christchurch, by way of Oamaru and Timaru. A merry show it was, Miss. A shame you missed it."

"Did you meet Miss Elsie Walsh or Miss Lucy Labelle, by any chance?" Grace asked.

"Never had the honour." The man continued with his work, but seemed happy to talk. "The famous Miss Walsh arrived a week late, because of being detained in quarantine. Then she was too ill to perform. Mr Marvin was furious, after paying for her to come all the way from Australia. With half the performers out with influenza, he had to hire locals to fill the gap. One of the lasses he found wasn't much to look at, but, my word, could she sing. Marvin was cock-a-hoop. A lucky escape, if you ask me. Just between us, I heard Miss Walsh could be rather a handful."

"Do you happen to know what illness Miss Walsh had and where she is staying, if she is still in Dunedin?"

"I wouldn't know, Miss. You could ask at the New Provincial Hotel, just around the corner. Many of the performers were staying there, being so handy to the theatre."

The boy wandered over, slopping soapy water from his bucket. "Miss Walsh done gone back to Sydney. I heard Mr Marvin say so. Waste o' his hard-earned money, he reckoned, bringing 'em both over, only to have 'em leave without stepping foot on the stage. I heard Miss Walsh had such a bad cough she couldn't sing a note, but it didn't stop her tearing a strip off Mr Marvin when he tried to hold back their wages."

"Thank you for your assistance." Grace stepped around the puddle of soapy water and hurried around the corner to Stafford Street. It would be good news indeed, if the two ladies had departed before exposing the local populace to measles.

She rang the bell on the desk of the New Provincial Hotel and showed her authorisation to the man who appeared from a back room, wiping crumbs from an extravagant moustache. He introduced himself as the proprietor.

He flipped back through the hotel register. "Miss Walsh and Miss Labelle arrived a week after their booked dates. I was here when they arrived. Those poor ladies were so hoarse they could hardly speak, let alone sing. Wrapped in scarves and coats they were, as if it was the middle of winter, not a glorious spring day."

"Do you know what was wrong with their voices?" Grace asked. "Were they ill?"

"I don't know, but I expect it was a chill, for I heard a lot of coughing coming from their room. They never called a doctor. As far as I know, they never left their room. They asked not to be disturbed. I arranged for soup to be taken up and that's the last I saw of them. Miss Walsh was not pleased to be sharing a room, but it was what Mr Marvin had reserved. The two ladies only stayed here for two nights, before returning to Sydney early."

"Did anyone visit them while they were staying here?"

"Not that I recall. Wait a minute." The hotel proprietor disappeared up the stairs and came back with a girl in a chambermaid's uniform. "This is my daughter. Dora, this lady needs to know about Miss Walsh and Miss Labelle, who shared room seven. Did anyone come to see them?"

"Only Mr Marvin," Dora replied. "He came in when I was there, making a linseed poultice for Miss Walsh's back. Miss Walsh had caught a nasty chill and thought it might turn to pneumonia. Only a cold, if you ask me, but she was worried about losing her voice." Dora looked up at Grace with stars in her eyes and a mop in her hand. "Miss Walsh is ever such a famous singer, Miss. She told me about all the places she'd been. I saw the show, you know. Marvin's Marvellous Musicale. I don't think Miss Walsh was best pleased when I told her how marvellous the show was, especially when I said how good Miss Moana was. She was the new singer."

Grace smiled at the girl's enthusiasm. "Did you notice if either of the ladies had spots or a rash on their skin?"

"They was both wrapped up in blankets when I saw them," Dora said. "Miss Walsh was not so ill that she didn't take the time to powder her face, but I expect that I would have noticed a rash even so. I put the poultice on Miss Walsh's back when Mr Marvin left. No spots there. Lovely skin she had, like a proper lady. You should have seen their costumes. Hanging up around the room like something a duchess might wear in a romantic novel."

Which left Grace with only one possible contender as the lady who was exposed to measles. "What about the other lady, Miss Labelle?"

"Tucked up in her bed in the far corner of the room, shivering, despite the extra blankets she asked for. Coughing fit to bust, poor lass. If you ask me, she was the sicker of the two, but not such a one to fuss. Can't speak to spots and rashes, as she never lifted her head from the pillow and I didn't want to get close enough to see."

"They didn't go out, or to the hotel dining room?"

"I don't believe so, Miss," Dora said. "They arranged to have meals taken up to their room, not that they ate much, from what I saw when I cleared the trays. After the argument with Mr Marvin, they up and left, back to Sydney. Only stayed two nights and never stepped foot outside."

Unfortunate for the poor singers, Grace thought, but wonderful news for the city's inhabitants. "What was the argument about, Dora?"

Dora composed her face, but her eyes were alight with the thrill of being a star witness. "Mr Marvin was ever so cross that they couldn't perform, especially as he had paid both their fares, first class. Miss Walsh had insisted on him providing an assistant for her, so Mr Marvin had gone to the trouble of hiring the new girl, Miss Labelle, on the understanding she should be able to sing in the chorus as well as attend to Miss Walsh. He was put out that Miss Labelle was too ill to perform as well. Told them both they were no use to him and they could forget about their wages and jolly well go home. His language was not what you'd call properly respectful, if you know what I mean. Quite the ding-dong they had, with Miss Walsh giving as good as she got and Miss Labelle quiet as a mouse."

Grace slipped a coin into the girl's hand. "Thank you, Dora. You have been most helpful. Would you promise me one thing? If you feel ill – even just a sniffle or a cough – I beg you to take to your bed and not have contact with anyone else. If you start to get a rash, send a message to any doctor or the medical school without delay."

"Yes, Miss. My mother has already had a visit from two St Andrew's ladies, warning her of the measles. Ma says I had the measles when I was a baby, so I should be right."

Grace headed for the hotel exit, feeling a great deal lighter in spirit, knowing that the women from the ship were unlikely to have spread measles into the community during their brief stay in Dunedin. She only hoped the two singers kept to themselves on their voyage home. But that was not her problem. Grace was looking forward to checking on her great-aunt and giving her the good news.

The feeling of relief passed quickly. The threat of measles still lurked from the male passengers, a murderer roamed free, and then there was the worry over the increasing frailty of her great-aunt. As if those problems weren't enough, Charlie Pyke loomed large in Grace's thoughts. She had her head down, trying to decide whether she had offended him with her earlier outburst of temper, when she ran into a six-foot wall of muscle.

Precious Gift

Charlie grabbed Grace by the arm to prevent her from falling. "Pardon me, Miss. I was so dazzled by your presence that I misjudged your speed."

Grace recovered her wits quickly. "Very amusing. Is that a line you use on all the ladies, when you run them down like a stampeding bullock?"

"Not at all," Charlie replied, "as no other lady would be courageous enough to throw herself into the path of such a beast."

"With charm like that, I'm tempted to invite you home with me, sir."

Charlie leaned close to Grace's ear. "What temptation did you have in mind, my angel?"

"Sustenance, Charlie. The noon hour has passed and my stomach is rumbling." Grace brushed a solitary pastry crumb from his lapel. "I see you have eaten already."

"One small pie eaten on the run does not a luncheon make. Will you allow me a minute or two? I have a suspect to track down." Charlie took her arm and guided her back into the New Provincial Hotel.

"Back again, Miss Penrose," the hotel proprietor said.

"This is my associate, Mr Pyke. He wishes to ask you about another visitor from the same ship as Miss Walsh."

"Mr Tobias Barlow," Charlie added.

"I do not recall a gentleman of that name, sir." The hotelier checked the register. "We had been holding the room for Miss Walsh and her companion, and several other performers who were coming out on the same ship. All the other rooms were full. No, wait, here it is. Mr Barlow reserved a room for a single night but failed to show up. It was rather chaotic, with the ship quarantined and substitute performers for the musical revue being brought in at the last minute."

Another dead end. Charlie thanked the clerk for his time and escorted Grace from the hotel.

They exchanged information on the way back to Anne's house, which was a short trudge up the steep incline of High Street. News of the early return to Sydney of the two singers had Charlie smiling. Nevertheless, he made a note to check with the shipping company to be sure they had left.

Charlie opened the gate to Anne's house and held it for Grace. "You've done an exceptional morning's work, Grace. Ruled out all three of the women from the ship as a measles risk and found a lead on another measles case, albeit in a place no lady ought to be seen."

"No gentleman ought to be seen in a brothel either, Charlie, least of all you. Fanny Snoot has set her sights on you."

"She ought to know I am a one-woman kind of man."

Grace stopped on the doorstep. "I cannot believe I have found a man who so readily praises me for investigating a potentially deadly disease inside a brothel. Promise you'll never leave me, my love."

Charlie stopped on the step below. He took her hand and brought it to his lips. "Or what, Grace? You'll chase after me with a rusty scalpel and surgically remove my heart in the middle of High Street?"

Grace used her elevation to look him straight in the eye. "You offend my professional sensibilities, sir. I would never condone cardiac surgery under such unsterile conditions, without anaesthetic."

He held her gaze. "If I promise never to leave you, will you promise to desist from unnecessary surgical procedures on my anatomy?"

"With pleasure. I might even promise not to cause you too much trouble."

"I ask only for your love, Grace, not a miracle." Charlie brushed her cheek with his lips, then stepped back. "Now, where's that food you promised me? I haven't got time to be distracted by a cheeky assistant, when I have vital work to attend to."

"Yes, sir." Grace saluted. "Mustn't keep an important detective waiting." She paused with her hand on the door latch. "Charlie, I should warn you that my great-aunt had a fall on the stairs this morning. Hopefully, she's in bed, resting."

"You should have told me before, Grace. I wouldn't have been so frivolous if I'd known. Was Mrs Macmillan badly hurt?"

"Only bruises. I think yesterday tired her out more than she admitted."

Mrs Brown, their housekeeper, intercepted them in the hall. "Mrs Macmillan is sleeping," she whispered. "She finally admitted that the bruising was causing her discomfort and agreed to a dose of laudanum. You're not to worry, Miss Penrose. She's not got a fever or any swelling. Simply exhausted from her exertions, if you ask me." The housekeeper handed Charlie a basket and a blanket. "I knew you'd be home to see her, so I packed you both a bite to eat. 'Tis a lovely day for a picnic in the garden."

Charlie thanked Mrs Brown for her thoughtfulness and took the basket outside, while Grace went to look in on her great-aunt.

The day had grown remarkably warm, without so much as a breeze. A picnic amongst the spring flowers would be a welcome, if brief, respite from a hectic day. Charlie was dozing in the sun when Grace joined him on the blanket. After Grace relayed the news that Anne was indeed sleeping peacefully, they ate in silence.

When the basket was empty, Charlie brushed the crumbs from his waistcoat and lay back on the blanket. A bee buzzed erratically above him, its legs heavy with pollen from the mass of spring flowers. "Is it not astonishing that bees can fly, with such small wings and heavy loads?"

"Perhaps it is a lesson to us, that we can carry on, no matter the burden." Grace plucked a sprig of thyme and held it to her nose.

"I'm glad we took this moment of rest, Charlie. I have a feeling that this case has burdened you more than most. Or is it the scrutiny of the *Ladies' Journal*?"

"Not the latter, although the unwanted attention has been a thorn in my side. The three thefts of jewellery from society ladies are causing me disquiet, because they occurred before the ship's passengers were released from quarantine. The dreadful prospect of a measles outbreak has loomed so large that I wonder if I have wrongly convinced myself of a link between the passengers and the robbery. The jeweller's son caught no more than a glimpse of a rash, after all. Even the crocodile skin boots might have come from a source other than the shoe salesman from the ship, although I have never seen their like before."

Grace moved the picnic basket so she could sit beside him. "We have a horde of doctors and volunteers working to prevent the spread of measles. You should feel under no obligation to help, Charlie, when you have an important case to investigate."

"I want to do both." Charlie picked up her hand and stroked her fingers. "I feel a strong obligation to ensure justice for Mr Emerson, the jeweller who was murdered. He was a good man, Grace. He helped me see what was truly important in my life."

"I was not aware you knew him so well."

Charlie sat up, still holding on to her hand. "The elder Mr Emerson helped me to find the perfect gift for you, to show you how I feel. His exact words remain etched in my mind: 'Life is short and love is precious. Leave your beloved in no doubt of your true feelings'. The next time I saw Mr Emerson, he was dead."

"Oh, Charlie, I'm so sorry. Mr Emerson was a wise man indeed. You must find his killer." Grace reached out her free hand and touched his cheek. "And Charlie, I need no gift to know your true feelings, or my own."

"Just as well, as the robber took the gift, along with everything else precious in the shop."

"Trust you to visit the day of a robbery, Charlie. But surely, losing the item you had chosen is a small matter, compared to murder and measles."

Charlie slipped back into silence, fighting an inner battle between the urge to say more and the logic that the timing was not right. Grace settled into his arms, her hair warm upon his chin. He decided logic was overrated when it came to matters of the heart. Mr Emerson was right – what was he waiting for?

"It was an engagement ring, Grace. I want us to be married, when you are ready. While I wait for that day, however long it takes, I want you and the rest of the world to know that we are promised to each other. If that is what you want too."

Grace twisted around in his arms, until they were face to face, inches apart. "It's all I want, Charlie. What if I told you that I cannot bear to wait much longer to be your wife?"

"Darling Grace, I would marry you tomorrow if I could." Charlie ran his fingers through her hair, dislodging hair pins, and kissed his newly betrothed with a passion.

Grace emerged from the embrace, eventually, delightfully dishevelled and pink in the cheeks. "Tomorrow might be a little soon, my love. Imagine what Lady Detective would read into such a hasty marriage. Unconventional we might be, but I would prefer a proper wedding. We need time to make the arrangements."

"I have waited for two and a half years. I suppose I can wait a little longer. Perhaps between Christmas and the start of the new term?" Charlie hadn't known what to expect when he made the spur-of-the-moment proposal, but he hadn't expected to be setting a wedding date only three months away. As he brushed the loose strands of dark hair off his future wife's face, he had a sudden vision of sitting here in half a century, brushing strands of white hair aside. A burst of pure happiness overwhelmed him.

"A January wedding would be wonderful." Grace was still looking into his eyes, her smile a little lopsided. "I cannot believe I just said that. You'll have to ask me again tomorrow, otherwise I will think I have dreamed it. My parents are going to be delighted."

Charlie took a deep breath to regain control of his emotions. "I have already asked your parents for permission." He had sent a telegram on Friday, after seeing the ring.

"My parents adore you, Charlie. I don't doubt they will give their permission. They will probably beg you to take me off their hands. In fact, they are probably sitting at the kitchen table right now, working out how much they need to sweeten my dowry for you to follow through on your proposal."

"Your parents have already given their consent. But, now you mention it, they did reply to my telegram with startling speed. The reply read, 'Delighted. Permission granted. You are a brave man.' Wasting pennies on the last sentence does have me slightly worried. Is there something you are not telling me, Grace?"

Grace burrowed deeper into his embrace. "You know the worst. I am stubborn, obsessive and reckless. I cannot cook or sew or arrange flowers. I will argue with you and demand to be heard. Not one man in a million would put up with me."

"Fortunately, I am that man. Whilst we are confessing the worst, I should remind you that I cannot afford to keep you in the comfort you deserve. We may have to live in a cramped cottage, eating stale bread and cheese, with holes in our stockings, at least until you qualify as a doctor." Charlie was pleased to see Grace didn't flinch. "Does that not cause you to reconsider?"

Grace planted a kiss on his nose. "You cannot think me so shallow. I would be content to live anywhere, as long as I am with you. We'll manage, with regular visits to the Macmillan and Stewart households for decent meals." She extracted herself from his arms and twisted her wayward hair into a tidy knot.

He pulled her back into his arms, with his lips against her earlobe. "Need we leave so soon?"

Grace closed her eyes and sank back into his embrace. But only for a moment. "No time for dilly-dallying, my love. We have a robbery to solve as a matter of urgency. I want my engagement ring back, preferably before the police seize it as evidence. And once we get the ring, I want a proper proposal, Charlie Pyke, down on one knee."

"Whatever you desire." Charlie sprang to his feet, pulling Grace up after him. "Let's pay Miss Caroline Davenport a visit. I need to know for sure whether there is a link between the three jewellery thefts and the robbery at Emerson & Son's."

"And whether Miss Davenport has fabricated the theft as a ruse to get close to you," Grace added.

"Indeed," Charlie replied. "Not for personal reasons, but in the interests of advancing her gossip column. I suspect Caroline Davenport of being one and the same as the Lady Detective, now that I know for sure that she is associated with the *Dunedin Ladies' Journal*. However, there were also two other unrelated thefts, which I cannot ignore. The three victims told me that were not well acquainted, which does support the notion that a professional jewel thief is targeting Dunedin. Time to find out."

Confessions

Charlie doubted he would be welcomed into the Davenport residence after the *Dunedin Ladies' Journal* article linking him to Caroline Davenport. He would not have been surprised if her outraged parents had circulated his description to the household staff, with instructions to bar to door and prepare the shotguns. Thus, when the door opened, he stepped inside quickly, to avoid the door being slammed in his face.

The Davenports' housekeeper used her ample proportions to block the hallway. "Miss Caroline is unable to see any callers, because of a prior engagement."

The sound of ladies' laughter drifted down the oak-panelled hallway. Charlie handed over his calling card. "It is vital I talk to Miss Davenport on an urgent matter. A few minutes of her time will be sufficient." He stood his ground, regarding the housekeeper with a steady gaze, to give her the message that he was not willing to accept a refusal.

The housekeeper yielded. "One moment. I will inquire."

Charlie followed her down the hall on soft feet, with Grace creeping along behind.

The sight that greeted him in the drawing room raised his suspicions still further. The three supposed victims of the jewellery thefts were seated together, chatting merrily. All three young ladies were wearing crocodile skin boots. Unless they intended to go out walking, the footwear seemed unsuitable for afternoon tea. Then again, who was he to question the whims of a new fashion, when such things came and went with the regularity of tides?

The ladies ceased their chatter at the sound of the housekeeper protesting the intrusion. The trio reacted with shock at the sight of Charlie in the doorway. Miss Fothergill went red, Miss Nesbitt went white, and Miss Davenport glared at him, with lips pursed and cheekbones as sharp as knives.

Charlie pushed past the housekeeper. "Good afternoon, Miss Davenport. And Miss Fothergill and Miss Nesbitt. Please excuse my interruption of your little party. How very unexpected that the three victims of jewellery thefts should be gathered in one place, when you have told me you scarcely know each other."

"Sir," the housekeeper spluttered, "I must ask you to leave immediately. My apologies, Miss Davenport, this man forced his way in. Shall I call for assistance?"

Caroline Davenport waved the housekeeper away. "Mr Pyke may stay. We are eager to hear if he has caught the thief yet. After weeks of investigation, we were all beginning to have our doubts as to your detecting skills, sir." Caroline caught sight of Grace, standing behind Charlie. She smiled. "I see you have brought a bodyguard. I assure you, there was no need."

Charlie plopped down on an empty chaise longue without an invitation, a most provocative move. He gestured for Grace to take her place beside him. His gaze travelled between the three theft victims, lingering on each in turn. "May I introduce my associate at the detective agency, Miss Grace Penrose."

Caroline Davenport showed her class by making no comment on Charlie's brash behaviour. She was of average height and slim, but made up for her lack of imposing stature with the inbred sense of superiority that marks a natural leader. Her light brown hair, tinged with auburn, had not a strand out of place. Her slim neck was a pale canvas for a subtle, but exquisite, necklace, while her gown rustled with silk in the most fashionable colour of the season.

In short, Charlie knew he would have to provoke Caroline to crack her shell. He hoped Grace would not be intimidated.

Grace wasn't. She didn't wait for the ladies to utter the little niceties that ought to accompany an introduction. "You must forgive Mr Pyke his directness. He has been inconsolable since his name was linked to yours, Miss Davenport, because of the distress felt by Mr Pyke's lady friend. I cannot imagine where the reporter got her information. Lady Detective, she calls herself. I imagine you must be furious too, Miss Davenport, to have your name besmirched by the unfounded gossip linking the names of the two of you."

Caroline Davenport, who had been observing Charlie up to this point as she would a beetle under a magnifying glass, had the grace to blush. "I have informed the *Dunedin Ladies' Journal* of their error, Miss Penrose. A retraction will be printed on Saturday. More than a retraction, in fact. An engagement announcement between myself and my own true gentleman friend." Caroline glanced between Grace and Charlie, leaving an extended pause before she added. "Perhaps Mr Pyke will also be making an announcement when his heartbroken lady is informed of the unfortunate mistake."

Miss Nesbitt giggled. "As soon as Caroline's gentleman was told of the article, he dashed to Dunedin to propose to her. About time! Some men do drag their feet when it comes to matrimony. A subtle hint of a potential rival never goes astray."

Miss Fothergill didn't care to be left out of the conversation. "Especially a man such as Jasper, always busy with important dignitaries and their elegant entourages. So many glittering receptions and exciting travels are wont to turn a man's head from what truly matters. He needed to know that Caroline is more than a society lady who loves gorgeous shoes and pretty gowns."

Caroline shot her friends a glare that would have felled them on the spot, had it been a dagger. But she couldn't resist a quick glance at her left hand, where an enormous diamond obscured the knuckle of her ring finger. Even the extravagant ruffles at the end of her long sleeves could not hide the sparkle.

"Wonderful what a little fictitious rivalry will achieve," Grace agreed. "But do not expect me to applaud you for your successful manipulation of your betrothed, at the expense of Mr Pyke's reputation. It is inconceivable that Lady Detective reported an association between you and Mr Pyke in error, as she must be well known to you, Miss Davenport, as a fellow correspondent to the *Dunedin Ladies' Journal*."

Caroline declined to reply, but looked chastened. Charlie allowed her a moment to confess. She said nothing, so he took up the conversational baton again.

"In answer to your earlier query, Miss Davenport, I have not yet apprehended the jewellery thief or thieves." Charlie allowed an uncomfortable pause to stretch their disquiet. "There were no substantive clues at the scene of each crime, no neighbours or servants who witnessed anything suspicious. I have inquired of every jeweller, pawnbroker, purveyor of stolen goods and back-alley informant – with not a single ounce of success. Most extraordinary. In fact, unprecedented, in my experience. Why, it's almost as if the thefts never happened."

Miss Davenport began to speak, but Charlie raised a hand to stop her. From the curl of her lip, no man had ever dared to insult her by interrupting so rudely. Charlie continued, "You have each assured me that no servant is to be considered a suspect, but I must tell you that there is no other avenue to explore. Indeed, Miss Fothergill's maid delivered a pearl necklace to one of the jewellers I spoke to, shortly before the theft was reported to me. A necklace matching the description of the one stolen. I suggest we refer the matter to the police, so the maid can be officially questioned."

Miss Fothergill's teacup rattled in its saucer. Her face would have done a tomato proud. "I asked my maid to get a necklace fixed. She is no thief, I assure you, Mr Pyke."

Charlie was relentless. "I must apologise for being so forthright in my quest for answers, Miss Fothergill. The fact is, that same jewellery shop was robbed two nights ago, on Sunday, and the jeweller was brutally slain. A charming gentleman called Mr Emerson, who is known to you all. You will, naturally, understand the urgency of the situation. Your thefts may be linked to the Emerson's robbery and murder. If you, or any of your servants, are withholding any information – however slight – a murderer may get away with a heinous crime."

"Perchance I have mistaken the necklace being stolen, when it was simply in for repair," Miss Fothergill stammered. "An easy mistake to make. Pray, consider the matter settled. It can have no bearing whatsoever on Mr Emerson's tragic death."

"And your ruby bracelet, Miss Nesbitt?" Charlie inquired. "Could it perhaps be located if another thorough search was made?"

"Given the gravity of the situation, I will overlook your insult, sir," Miss Nesbitt said quietly, not meeting Charlie's eye. "I concede it is possible, as my maid can be rather careless about where she puts my valuables. Now I think on it, I ought to have ordered a thorough search before reporting it to you as stolen. I assure you, the matter is entirely unrelated to the fatal robbery."

Charlie turned his attention to Caroline Davenport. "I presume your maid would not be so careless with a valuable set of diamonds, Miss Davenport," he said. "I must insist you refer the matter to the police. I know you asked me to investigate discreetly, but the circumstances have changed, with a vicious robber and murderer at large in the community."

Caroline placed her teacup on the side table with exaggerated care. "And I insist you do not tell the police, Mr Pyke, as you agreed while I engaged your services. The diamonds are a family heirloom, and I do not wish their loss to become known. I feel the best option is for you to cease your investigation, forthwith. Please send the bill for the work you have already undertaken and I will see that it is paid without delay."

"Perhaps your associate, the Lady Detective, would care to take over the investigation?" Charlie suggested. "I confess I would be happy to see her distracted, as she has caused me considerable distress."

Caroline Davenport did not so much as blink. "She has also made you famous in Dunedin, Mr Pyke. Your fledgling detective agency must have reaped the benefit of the interest the articles have stirred amongst the ladies of Dunedin."

"On the contrary, Miss Davenport," Charlie said. "The only persons who have gained from the articles are the writer herself and the owners of the *Ladies' Journal*, who have benefitted from an increase in sales. My ability to investigate important cases has been seriously compromised by the distraction of mindless gawkers and time-wasters. If I was still a policeman, I would have Lady Detective and her associates arrested for obstruction of justice. A little time behind bars might help her understand that unfounded gossip has consequences."

Caroline Davenport did not reply, but she looked as if she had swallowed a particularly unsavoury rat.

Charlie rose from the sofa, holding out his hand to Grace to assist her up. "Our business is concluded. We have taken too much of your valuable time, Miss Davenport. I wish you well in your new endeavours."

"Whatever do you mean, Mr Pyke?"

"Your marriage, of course. Perhaps when you are married, you will not have quite so much time for your diverse writing interests. What a shame." Charlie bowed to the three ladies, took Grace's arm, and sauntered from the room.

Caroline caught up with them in the hall. "If I may take a further few minutes of your time, Mr Pyke?" She ushered them across an enormous reception room and into an adjacent small sitting room. When the door was firmly closed behind her, Caroline said, "I owe you an apology, Mr Pyke. The diamonds were never stolen, as you have correctly surmised."

Charlie let silence judge her confession. His gaze swept the room, which was less an ordinary sitting room than a space to display wealth and refinement. The walls dripped with fine paintings and shelves of exquisite porcelain, music boxes, clocks, and other collectors' items. His eye was caught by a display case, prominently sited to draw attention. To Charlie's shock, the display case held a parure of necklace, earrings and brooch, set with perfectly matching diamonds – the very items that Caroline Davenport had hired him to find.

"Full marks for audacity, Miss Davenport," Charlie said. "To engage my services to find a stolen diamond parure, whilst freely displaying it in your home, indicates how little you thought of my skills. No wonder you refused to allow me to interview the household and conduct a thorough search."

Caroline waved her hand dismissively. "You are mistaken, Mr Pyke. Real as they appear, these jewels are merely paste replicas, which my father had crafted so they could be permanently on display. One must not only *be* wealthy, one must be *seen* to be wealthy, in Father's view. The real diamonds are safely secured under lock and key, naturally."

"Why did you come to me with this false tale of theft, Miss Davenport? I find it hard to believe it was merely to call attention to yourself so that your gentleman friend would propose."

Caroline Davenport allowed seconds to pass as she decided how to respond. She locked her sharp eyes on Charlie, daring him to look away first. "You are correct. I will admit that my aim was to expose your detective agency as the sham I believed it to be. I could see no point to it, other than as a scheme to separate vulnerable victims from their money – people who were desperate but unable to seek the help of the proper authorities. I thought I was doing the people of Dunedin a service."

Charlie was completely taken aback. Of all the motives he had considered, this one had never occurred to him. "I am shocked you could think so ill of our work, Miss Davenport. Our aim is to help people, not swindle them."

"I accept I was wrong. I have underestimated your skills and I am truly sorry if I impeded your investigation into the death of Mr Emerson. An honest and talented man, who deserved better. I ask for your forgiveness, both for myself, and for my friends. Miss Fothergill and Miss Nesbitt wished only to have the thrill of meeting a detective and seeing you at work."

Grace wasn't about to let her off too lightly. "And do you apologise for using Mr Pyke so cruelly in your attempt to compel your gentleman friend to propose to you?"

"That too was wrong of me, I admit, but I doubt the falsehood has caused any damage to Mr Pyke's reputation. Indeed, being linked to me will enhance his business prospects amongst the elite."

Caroline looked down her nose at Grace again – quite a feat as they were much the same height. "I doubt Mr Pyke's lady friend would be so easy to fool, or so quick to withdraw her favour at the merest hint of gossip. Nevertheless, I shall add a generous donation to Lavender House to the full payment for Mr Pyke's services to demonstrate my remorse."

Charlie was lost for words at both the sincerity of Caroline's apology and her knowledge of his interests.

"Do not look so surprised," Caroline said. "I have my sources of information. I know all about you and Miss Penrose, including her work at Lavender House. I sometimes wish I had had the courage to rebel against my upbringing and do something useful in the world, as you have, Miss Penrose."

Grace refused to rise to the ill-advised praise. "I needed no courage, as my family supported my ambitions. As for you, Miss Davenport, I think you have succeeded admirably at carving yourself a career in print, whether or not it is widely known. I don't doubt you will assist your husband to rise through the ranks of his career too."

"You see through me, Miss Penrose," Caroline replied. "My fiancé is a junior government trade official. His background is impeccable, naturally, but his career has not yet reached its potential. He has an unfortunate tendency to favour his enthusiasm for the tedious game of cricket over his work on trade policy. Once I am by his side in Wellington, I will see that his attention does not stray too far."

"We offer you our congratulations on your engagement, Miss Davenport," Charlie said. "I presume your fiancé must have visited Dunedin recently to have proposed to you. Did he arrive on or before this past Sunday, by any chance?"

The momentary tightening of the muscles in Caroline's face would only have been noted by a person watching closely. She recovered quickly. "Indeed not. He arrived on Monday." Caroline cast another glance at the diamond gracing her finger. "He was coming to Dunedin anyway to attend a dreadfully boring reception for a visiting trade delegation, which my father is hosting here on Thursday evening. He arrived early in order to make his intentions clear to me, after being told of the *Ladies' Journal* article."

"How fortuitous," Grace said. "May I ask the gentleman's name?"

"My fiancé, you mean? Mr Jasper Newton. His father established one of the country's largest shipping companies. An old and dear acquaintance of my own father."

"You must have been awaiting his arrival with eager anticipation," Charlie said. "May I ask how you spent Sunday, Miss Davenport? Perhaps an outing to take your mind off Mr Newton's impending arrival?"

"I was at home and church, as usual," Caroline snapped, "not that it is any of your business. Now, I expect you will wish to take your leave, because none of us will rest easy until Mr Emerson's murderer is apprehended." Caroline waved towards the door, emphasising the hint that the interview was over. "If I can be of any service to you in that investigation, please do not hesitate to ask, both for the sake of my conscience and justice for Mr Emerson."

Charlie ignored the hint to leave. "Will the reception for the trade delegation be a small affair, Miss Davenport?"

"Evidently you are not acquainted with my father, Mr Pyke. The word 'small' does not have a place in the Davenport vocabulary. Aside from the members of the Australian and New Zealand delegations, there will be representatives of business, as well as everyone who is anyone in Dunedin social circles. The Minister of Agriculture and Trade himself will be in attendance."

"Would your offer to be of service to our investigation extend to an invitation to the reception?" Charlie noted her hesitation, diagnosing it as doubt that a private detective could be safely let loose amongst the elite. "I assure you, we would wear the correct formal attire and be on our best behaviour, Miss Davenport. I promise not to hawk my services like a street vendor."

Caroline allowed a small smile to cross her lips. "I cannot deny the pair of you would liven up a dull affair." She gestured for them to follow her across the reception room to a pier table, from which she took an invitation. "All I ask is that you do not liven up the evening too much. Father would not care for any unseemly incidents at so important an event."

Without waiting for a reply, Caroline Davenport led them through the entrance foyer to the main door. Her farewell was perfunctory, but at least she hadn't had Charlie and Grace booted out the tradesman's entrance.

When they reached the end of the long sweep of driveway, Grace broke her silence. "I presume you have good reason to commit us to a scintillating evening of discussions about frozen meat exports and society gossip?"

"I have," Charlie replied. "Mr Thornton, the shoe salesman, mentioned that he and other first-class passengers have been invited to the reception. We won't get a better chance to meet the potential suspects from the ship, some of whom are proving difficult to track down."

"Do you think the robbers would dare to show their faces?" Grace asked.

"I'm counting on it," Charlie replied. "They do not know we have made the link between the robbery and the ship. As far as the suspects know, we are questioning them only in relation to their exposure to measles, so there is no reason for them to lie low. Besides, the invitation specifically lists a viewing of the famous Davenport diamonds amongst the evening's attractions. What could be more enticing to our gentlemen thieves than an extremely valuable set of diamond jewellery?"

As they continued their walk home, Charlie considered what he had learned. Grace gave him the time he needed to think, not talking until he was ready. Fate had certainly been on his side the day he met her. A more perfect partner, he could not imagine. He would not swap places with Mr Jasper Newton for all the diamonds in the world. His thoughts drifted to his future with Grace.

"You appear full of the joys of spring, Charlie," Grace said after a long silence. "Are you not cross with Miss Davenport for tormenting you with fake thefts and false gossip?"

"Nothing can dent my happiness today, my darling Grace, since you have agreed to be mine forever. I care not for Caroline Davenport's silly intrigues. Besides, Miss Davenport's apology was honourable, she has agreed to pay my fee, and she has provided us with the perfect opportunity to gather the suspects in one place. Furthermore, I am mightily relieved that I can now rule out any link between the three supposed thefts before the ship arrived and the Emerson robbery."

That much was true, but Charlie still harboured doubts about Miss Davenport. She was a potent combination – intelligent, determined, bored and unscrupulous. Without doubt, she would act in her own best interests. Her knowledge of his relationship with Grace wasn't the only part of her testimony that had unsettled him. One thing was certain – he would not be trusting her to assist in the investigation, unless he had a compelling reason to do so.

"I can tell your detective instincts are roused, Charlie," Grace said. "Have your suspicions been stirred by the much-travelled fiancé and the crocodile skin boots of Miss Davenport? If so, I commend you for allowing that a woman could be bold enough to commit robbery."

"Our thoughts are walking the same twisted path, Grace. I admit it crossed my mind to wonder if the second robber was a woman as soon as I heard of the fine wrist-bones and pleasant scent of the accomplice. Improbable, given the violence of the crime, but not impossible."

"As Sherlock Holmes said, 'when you have eliminated the impossible, whatever remains, however improbable, must be the truth'."

Charlie groaned. "I begged my father not to send you copies of those Conan Doyle stories. I am surprised you are not following me around with a magnifying glass and a deer-stalker hat."

"At least you have not presumed to relegate me to the dim-witted Doctor Watson role," Grace said.

"As if I would dare," Charlie replied. "In all honesty, I cannot see a wealthy socialite such as Caroline Davenport stooping to such a dreadful crime, even for the sake of a sensational article in the infamous *Dunedin Ladies' Journal*. It is a far cry from orchestrating a series of fake thefts to committing a violent robbery. Although I would like to know why she was so reluctant to answer the question about Jasper Newton's date of arrival and her own whereabouts on the Sunday night of the robbery."

"We could ask her lady's maid, although I doubt she would tell us if she values her position."

"I'll go down to the police station after I see you home," Charlie said. "The police need to hear what we have found out, and they are better placed than me to check the alibis of Newton and Davenport. However devoted the lady's maid is, she wouldn't dare lie to a policeman investigating a capital offence."

"I beg to differ," Grace said. "The lady's maid is probably terrified of Caroline Davenport. If Caroline did have any involvement in a criminal act, I'd wager my pin money that she would be the mastermind. She is far too intelligent and ambitious to waste away her life playing the subservient wife role. I hope Mr Jasper Newton knows what he is letting himself in for."

Charlie loosened his grip on Grace's arm. "Not unlike someone else I know. Perhaps I should withdraw my offer of marriage, for my own safety."

Grace secured his arm again and smiled sweetly. "Too late, Pyke. If you withdraw from our betrothal now, I shall have to reconsider the option of surgery with a rusty scalpel."

Candid Camera

Grace had invited Charlie to join her for breakfast on Wednesday morning, to plan their day of suspect hunting. Grace hardly slept the previous night, as her mind was awhirl with thoughts of their engagement and future together, but Charlie looked as sharp as ever when he arrived at the appointed hour, with a bunch of wildflowers and his usual healthy appetite.

As Grace watched him wolf down porridge, boiled eggs and toast, two thoughts came to mind. First, that soon she would be watching this scene every day for the rest of her life. For all her joy at their engagement, the everyday realities of married life struck her at odd moments like an unexpected blast of shotgun pellets across a meadow of daffodils.

Her second thought was that she ought to increase her hours as an assistant to the police surgeon, in order to afford the food bill they would incur. This thought inevitably led to other patches of financial quicksand, if they married before she qualified as a doctor. The detective business was still new and untested. A few lucrative cases kept the business in profit, but with worrying stretches of lean times in between. With Charlie paying for his room and board by way of labour rather than cash, and Grace living with her great-aunt, money had not been an issue before. Living together, there would be rent and other expenses to cover. Hard enough with two uncertain incomes. What if, despite her newly gained knowledge, she became pregnant and was forced to end her medical studies? How would they survive?

And then there was the impossibility of leaving her elderly great-aunt on her own, with only Mrs Brown and a single maid to look out for her. Anne Macmillan was fiercely independent, but there was no denying she was also increasingly frail.

Charlie paused between swallows. "You have that rusty-scalpel look in your eye again, Grace. Have I done something wrong? You haven't changed your mind, I hope? I was awake all night, unable to believe my good fortune."

"No chance of that, Charlie," Grace said. "You are stuck with me forever. I was merely wondering how we will be able to afford to buy enough food to fill you."

He put his spoon down and took up her hand. "I'll take on only the more lucrative investigations, and I have savings put aside to cover lean times. If we can find a small cottage to rent with a patch of garden, we could raise chickens and grow vegetables. It will have to be close to this house, of course, so we can keep an eye on Mrs Macmillan."

Typical of Charlie to consider Anne's welfare, Grace thought. Perhaps he was right. If they lived nearby, leaving her great-aunt would not be such an insurmountable problem. "If we're close enough, we might convince Mrs Brown to cook for both households, so I don't poison you with my cooking."

At the tap of a walking cane behind them, Charlie leapt from his chair. "Good morning, Mrs Macmillan. If you overheard, Grace was jesting about luring Mrs Brown to our household."

Anne prodded him gently in the chest with her cane. "You can have Grace, with my blessings, but don't think for a minute that you can steal my housekeeper. Congratulations and welcome to our family, by the way, Charlie. About time you two made it official, if only to save me the effort of looking the other way every time you breech the established conventions of courtship. Which seems to be every five minutes."

Charlie pulled out a seat for Anne and poured her a cup of tea. He had long since become used to Anne's teasing. "You have been a saint, Mrs Macmillan, from the moment you rescued me and Aunt Lily. How are you feeling this morning?"

"Much better," Anne said. "Don't give me that scolding pout, Grace. I intend to rest today, but I cannot stand another minute lying in bed." Anne held out her bowl. "That is, if I am not weakened by lack of food."

Apart from a livid bruise on her face, Anne appeared remarkably well after yesterday's long rest. Grace removed the scolding pout from her face and dished a bowl of porridge for her great-aunt.

"Besides," Anne continued, "I have a better proposition for you two than a draughty, freezing cottage. The stairs here are getting a little difficult for me. Now that Lily has moved next door with Alistair, I have decided to move into her old room on the ground floor permanently. It would be a shame to leave the upstairs rooms unused, and I could do with a bit of lively company. I expect Mrs Brown would be delighted to have an appreciative audience for her culinary skills too, not to mention a strong pair of arms to help with the heavier household chores. That is, if you two young lovebirds can stomach the idea of indulging an old lady's whims."

Grace and Charlie exchanged glances, reading each other's delight at the suggestion without need for words. Simultaneously, they rose and kissed Anne's cheeks. There would be heated discussions to follow about paying their way, but that could wait.

"Good, I'll be glad that is settled," Anne said. "I hope you two will not be one of those annoying couples who can read each other's minds. I insist on knowing everything that is going on. Everything medical and criminal, that is. I wouldn't wish to pry into your private lives. Speaking of the former, what news of your investigations?"

Grace refrained from mentioning how happy she was to stay in the house and look after her elderly great-aunt. Anne didn't like anyone to fuss. "We've all but ruled out the women from the ship as a measles risk to Dunedin. What about you, Auntie? Any news from your web of informants?"

"No more measles cases reported," Anne replied, "but then we wouldn't necessarily expect the symptoms to show up this soon. The next few days will be critical, to see if the disease has spread from the ship to the community. What of the male passengers?"

"The male passenger with measles who went to the brothel is the main target of our search, assuming he is also the robbery suspect," Grace said, "but we need to rule out the others too, as most of them were exposed to the disease."

"I've only found one of the male passengers so far," Charlie added, "so today will be crucial. The most likely suspects for measles and the robbery – the Smith brothers and Barlow – never arrived at the hotels they listed as their contact address."

"Which is grounds for suspicion, even without their dubious characters," Grace added. "What are your plans for today, Charlie?"

"My priority is to find Mr Vaughan, the camera salesman, who may have taken photographs of his fellow passengers and probably visited the Emerson's shop in the week before the robbery. Unless you have another plan, Grace?"

"Vaughan is a good start," Grace agreed, "unless the police have a better lead on the other suspects."

"I went to see DI Wallace yesterday evening," Charlie said. "The police have had no success finding the Smiths and Barlow, either. Wallace also told me that there have been other similar jewellery robberies around the country, although none involving the death of the shop proprietor. The robberies have not previously been linked, as they have been widely spread in both time and location. We're working on the theory that the criminals are travelling to different towns, committing high-value robberies, then leaving and selling the stolen goods in a distant market. Sydney or elsewhere in Australia would be ideal."

"That would fit with a travelling salesman from Australia," Grace said. "Thornton, the shoe salesman, or Vaughan, the camera salesman. Or Barlow, travelling under the cover of purchasing bird specimens."

"Or the Smith brothers, operating in both Australia and New Zealand," Charlie said. "And we cannot entirely rule out the envoy from the trade delegation or his secretary. Unfortunately, they are off-limits to the investigation, because of their status as foreign government officials. Wallace has been told that investigating them would cause a diplomatic incident. The police are not even allowed to step foot inside the Grand Hotel to speak to the trade delegation."

"They may not be the robbers, but the envoy and secretary might be carrying measles," Grace said. "We must investigate them, regardless of their protected status."

"Never trust government officials or the asinine rules they make," Anne said. "My advice is to find a way around the official ban on contact, by whatever means necessary. Your Aunt Lily used to work at the Grand Hotel, didn't she, Charlie? Perhaps you could use Lily's contacts there to gain entrance to the delegation's rooms."

"I'm shocked that you would suggest such a thing, Auntie," Grace replied, at the same time as Charlie said, "Excellent idea, Mrs Macmillan."

"I'll go on my own, Grace," Charlie added. "I wouldn't want you to do anything illegal."

"And you'd better not make any plans that don't include me," Grace retorted.

"Perhaps you two could argue the finer points later," Anne said. "Be off with you. I won't be able to sleep at night until you check every single one of those first-class passengers for measles."

Charlie rose from the table. "I want to catch Mr Vaughan at his hotel, before he goes about his business for the day."

Wains Hotel was only a short walk down the hill. The desk clerk was reluctant to share any information about a guest until Charlie showed him the letter of authorisation to conduct a health inspection. Mr John Vaughan, according to the clerk, was an exemplary guest – quiet, sober and polite. Vaughan had dined either in his room or in the hotel dining room every night since his arrival. He had been in and out a great deal during the daytime, attending to business, but always with a pleasant word to the hotel staff.

The night clerk, who was about to leave, confirmed that Vaughan had not been out at night, as far as he was aware, although he noted it was impossible to keep track of guests all the time.

The desk clerk put a call through on the internal telephone system. Mr Vaughan was not only in, but willing to see them, with no break-and-enter required.

Vaughan left the door to his room open for them. At Charlie's knock, the camera salesman put down the notes he had been writing and came over to welcome them in. Business must be good, because Vaughan had taken a suite, with a generous sitting room and a separate bedroom. Unfortunately, the door to the latter was closed.

As the ship's head steward had indicated, Vaughan and Thornton were superficially similar, but very different in personality. Where the shoe salesman had launched into a flood of sales patter within seconds of meeting Charlie, the camera salesman merely smiled, invited them to take a seat, and asked how he might be of assistance. Vaughan was a fine-looking gentleman, neatly turned out, but with none of the swagger of Thornton. He was of average height and build, with dark brown hair, a face tanned by the Australian sun, and smile lines etched around his eyes.

Grace explained the situation regarding measles. Charlie took the opportunity to scan the room, while Vaughan's attention was on Grace.

Vaughan listened intently. "I would hate to think the passengers off our ship were responsible for spreading a deadly disease, Miss Penrose. I must admit that I was surprised to be released early from quarantine, although grateful to go about my business."

Mr Vaughan appeared to be healthy, but Grace needed to be certain. "As part of our health inspection, Mr Vaughan, I am required to ask if you have suffered any of the symptoms I mentioned. I will also have to inspect your arms and lower legs, as the rash leaves the extremities last."

She had expected him to be difficult, but he rolled up his shirtsleeves and raised his trouser leg without any fuss. Indeed, he did not so much as comment or make a jest about the absurdity of a female doctor. His limbs showed not a single trace of a residual rash or peeling skin.

“I have had a slight sniffle from the cold weather, Miss Penrose,” Vaughan said, “but no cough or rash. The folks of Dunedin must be hardy indeed, compared to the people of Sydney.”

“Thank you for your cooperation, sir,” Grace replied. “I can see you are well. However, it is possible for measles to have a long incubation period. A person may be infectious prior to being ill. Therefore, I must take a list of all the places you have visited since arrival. I realise that is a great deal to ask of you, given that you have now been here for a week and a half.”

“I will make a list as soon as I have a spare moment and leave it at the front desk for you,” Vaughan said. “I know nobody in Dunedin. I have been busy with my business interests during the day, and have dined alone, in this hotel each night. Early to bed, early to rise, is my motto. After being forced to spend a week in quarantine, I have been working hard to get back on schedule. First there was the matter of finding an agent for my cameras. And now my focus is on selling the camera stock I brought with me. The next two days are set aside for demonstrations, before I leave on Friday evening.”

Vaughan rose from his seat and went to a large pile of merchandise stacked in the corner of the room, returning with several boxes. From the first box, he withdrew a square object covered in black leather. It was not until he flipped the front cover open to reveal a brass fitting with an aperture in the middle, that Grace realised it must be a camera. Her only experience with photography involved a device set on a tripod, with a camera larger than a man’s head. This camera was small enough to hold in one hand.

She heard a sharp intake of breath from Charlie over her shoulder. He sat down beside her and leaned forward eagerly.

“This little beauty is one of the cameras I sell,” Vaughan said. “I specialise in the latest in hand-held cameras, popularly known as ‘detective cameras’ because of their small size and the candid nature of the photography. With this amazing device, one can take pictures anywhere, without the subject even being aware of your interest.”

Charlie let out the faintest of whimpers, but enough to alert the salesman to his desire to possess a detective camera.

Vaughan held out the camera for Charlie to inspect. "It comes preloaded with a roll of film, which takes one hundred photographs. Simply point the lens at the subject and click the shutter to achieve images of exceptional quality. For no more than a few weeks' wages, one has a camera for a lifetime. Think of it! Every special family occasion, the progress of your children through life – every joyful memory recorded for posterity."

Charlie put the camera down, crossing his arms in a show of deliberate restraint. "A truly marvellous invention, Mr Vaughan. If I was a man of means, I would be sorely tempted."

"Many of my customers are in your situation, Mr Pyke. Believe me, I understand, having made my own way in the world through hard work and perseverance. That being so, I do everything in my power to make the purchase affordable. For instance, I offer a unique opportunity to purchase the camera in exchange for unwanted, but valuable small items, such as gold watches or jewellery. Perhaps a present you disliked, but were reluctant to sell?"

Vaughan paused only briefly before opening another box. "You would be astounded at the range of detective cameras available. The waistcoat camera has proved exceedingly popular. As you can see, it is wide but flat, designed to sit underneath the waistcoat. The lens is this pin. The shutter is set by turning the top button in the waistcoat and discharged by means of rubber tubing, connected to a bulb in the trouser pocket. It contains six plates and takes portraits at a distance of two to three feet. The subject will never realise you are taking the photograph and thus you can achieve a very natural effect."

Charlie feigned the mildest of interest, while ogling the camera with lust in his eyes.

Vaughan was undeterred. "In my opinion, the waistcoat camera is little more than an amusing fancy, which lacks true photographic quality. To my mind, the best quality at an affordable price is this marvel." He extracted another hand-held camera out of a box. "A simple device, with six plates. Simply pull the string to set the next plate and take the photograph. All that is needed is a steady hand and adequate light."

Grace saw an opportunity to purchase the perfect present to mark their engagement, but she was still wary of being talked into more than she could afford. "May I inquire as to the price?"

Vaughan scribbled a number on a piece of paper. Not cheap, but a fraction of the more expensive model. The camera man sized Grace up, no doubt spotting an easy mark. "I would like to offer you a special deal, Miss Penrose. I have been taking a variety of photographs since my arrival, to demonstrate the marvellous images that any ordinary person might achieve. What I lack is a truly memorable picture of a young couple in love. Showing the audience at my demonstrations such compelling images is the key to selling these cameras. Unfortunately, some of the photographs I brought with me from Australia were damaged during the voyage. If you two would consent to have your photograph taken and used in my display, I would be pleased to offer you a splendid deal on the camera."

He crossed out the number of the piece of paper and inserted a new figure, less than half the first. "I'll take it," Grace said.

"Excellent. Come with me." Vaughan took them to a corner of the sitting room, which had been set up with chairs and lights, as well as a full-sized camera on a tripod, such as a studio photographer would use. "I use the studio camera as a prop in my demonstrations, so the audience can see how compact my cameras are."

The contrast in size between the studio camera and the detective camera was certainly stark. Grace sat in a chair, while Charlie stood behind her, with one hand on her shoulder. They both automatically assumed the classic photographic pose – ramrod straight, unsmiling, staring straight into the lens.

"No, no, that won't do at all," Vaughan said. "The point of the hand-held camera is to capture the candid beauty of life. Mr Pyke, sit beside Miss Penrose and hold her hand. Ignore the camera. Look into each other's eyes and recall a joyous memory – perhaps the first time you met."

Grace could hardly forget the unusual circumstances of their first encounter. Charlie looked into her eyes and smiled as he too recalled the memory of bumping heads over a corpse. It was no effort to hold the pose as Vaughan clicked the shutter several times in the background.

"Lovely," Vaughan said. "Exactly what I was seeking. Come along to my demonstration later this afternoon and I will have a copy of the photograph to present to you. I must rush this to my agent, so the photographs can be developed in time."

Vaughan returned to the sitting area and boxed up the camera Grace wanted to buy, adding a leaflet advertising the time and location of the camera demonstration. "Take the camera with you, Miss Penrose. I trust you to bring the purchase price later. Was there anything else you wished to know?"

"May I ask where you found an agent for such new technology?" Charlie said.

"It was not easy, I'll admit," Vaughan replied. "Photographic studios generally refuse to engage with me as they fear the competition. No more need for dull studio portraits, once people have these new hand-held cameras. I have found it best to approach the type of business owners who seek to expand their enterprise into an exciting new field. Opticians, clockmakers, printers, and purveyors of the latest electrical devices often have the required skills and interest. I spent my first week in Dunedin visiting such establishments until I finally found the perfect agent. Rather a tragic story as it happens."

"How so?" Charlie queried.

"One of the gentlemen I called upon was able to give me the crucial lead. He was a jeweller and clockmaker by the name of Emerson. I read in the newspaper that the poor man was murdered during a robbery on Sunday night. A great shock to me, having met the man briefly the previous week."

"A terrible tragedy," Charlie agreed.

"Mr Emerson was of great service to me. Although he had no interest in cameras himself, he was kind enough to direct me to Mackay's photographic studio. The elder Mr Mackay has recently passed away and his son has not the talent or interest for studio portraits. A perfect solution, as he has the skills in photography and photographic development, as well as the acumen to make a new direction succeed. We struck a deal, which means that this week I can turn my attention to selling cameras. Rather a passion of mine, as you have witnessed. Such is the interest, I have been honoured with an invitation to a prestigious trade reception. The senior trade envoy himself has agreed to open my camera demonstration this afternoon."

"You must be an accomplished photographer yourself, Mr Vaughan," Grace said. "Did you perchance take any photographs of your fellow passengers on board the SS *Australis*? We are eager to examine them all for measles, and one or two are proving difficult to trace."

"You are in luck, Miss Penrose. I had Mr Mackay prove his skills by developing the most recent photographs from my personal camera. I believe several of them feature my fellow passengers. I know I took at least two photographs of Miss Elsie Walsh to show my wife. She was quite taken with Miss Walsh when she saw a performance in Sydney. My wife will be astounded to hear that I voyaged with the lady and performed a duet with her aboard the ship."

Vaughan went into his bedroom. Charlie followed him. Although Vaughan was no doubt discomfited by this breech of privacy, he made no mention of it. He gathered the photographs from a drawer and returned to the sitting room. There were no less than four images of Miss Elsie Walsh, each showing a lady who was basking in the attention. The understudy, Miss Lucy Labelle, did not merit a single image.

"We believe that at least one of the male passengers had measles," Grace said, in the interests of moving the conversation along from the famous diva. "Were you aware of any of the other passengers being ill? Have you seen any of them since disembarking?"

Vaughan paused for thought. "I believe I spied Mr Thornton about town last week, but I did not speak to him, as I was in a hurry and he was engaged in conversation with a young lady. He appeared in good health, as well he might in such elegant company. That man could charm the crest off a cockatoo."

The camera salesman shuffled through the photographs, laying one in front of them. "That's Thornton with Mrs Quinn." The sea was clearly visible in the background. Thornton had been captured leaning forward, talking to Mrs Quinn, who appeared startled by the attention. The pictures were certainly far more candid than a studio portrait.

Charlie handed the picture back. "We are especially eager to find Mr Barlow and the Smith brothers."

Vaughan found two more photographs. The first was of a man sitting in a deck chair with his head propped between his hands. It may have been the angle of the shot or the man's pose, but he appeared thin and unwell. While the image might be of interest hung in an art gallery with the title "Descent Into Despair", it was not much use for identification purposes.

The morose Mr Barlow, Charlie guessed. "Did Mr Barlow give you any indication of where he might be or what he might be doing after his arrival in Dunedin?"

"I tried to call on him," Vaughan said, "but Barlow was not at his hotel. I confess, I was concerned about him, as he had been unwell during the last days of quarantine and seemed in very poor spirits, as you can tell from this photograph. I felt I should visit to make amends for not taking the time to inquire after his health on the ship."

"Do you have a sense of what troubled or ailed him?" Charlie asked.

"Not specifically. Money, I presumed, as far as his low spirits were concerned. One doesn't care to pry, but Barlow did drop a few hints he was strapped for funds. As for his illness, I assumed it to be a chill. I fear I did not pay him much attention on the voyage. I tried to talk to him about cameras, but he did not share his interests with me."

The second photograph showed two men in high spirits, raising their glasses to the camera. They were similar enough to be brothers. One was broader across the shoulders, the other slimmer and shorter, but by no means fine boned.

"The Smith brothers," Vaughan said, tapping the photograph. "Lively company aboard ship, but not men I would care to be more closely acquainted with. I believe they were visiting their sick mother. They talked of working in the sugarcane industry in Queensland. Good money, if they are to be believed, but a rough life, if you ask me."

"Do you recall if the family lived in Dunedin?" Charlie asked. "The Smiths gave an address for a hotel near the railway station, which suggests they might have intended onward travel."

"Now you mention it, Mr Pyke, I cannot recall whether the brothers accompanied the rest of us on the train from Port Chalmers into Dunedin, once we left quarantine. Perhaps they travelled in the other direction, to the north? I honestly couldn't say, as I was busy assisting Miss Walsh to find enough porters for her extensive assortment of luggage."

"You have been most helpful, Mr Vaughan," Charlie said. "Might I keep these photographs?"

"By all means, Mr Pyke. Anything I can do to help, you have only to ask. I had a policeman here yesterday, asking about my visit to Mr Emerson's shop. I confess that I never imagined that Dunedin would be such a centre of crime and disease. I only wish I could have been of assistance to the police. Mr Emerson was a kindly old man."

When they had left the hotel, Grace handed the camera box to Charlie. "An engagement present for you. I could not bear to see the longing in your eyes go unfulfilled."

"You should not have, Grace, especially when I have no ring to give you." But Charlie's protest was half-hearted, as he grasped the camera eagerly.

"We will find the ring. If you do not wish to have the camera as an engagement present, consider it a vital piece of equipment for your detective business."

"Thank you, Grace. It is the perfect gift," Charlie said. "Mr Vaughan is a consummate salesman, is he not? Judging from the huge stack of boxes, he must sell a great many cameras. I take it he showed no signs of measles?"

"None at all," Grace replied. "What did you spot in his rooms?"

"With the brief glimpse I had, I could not see any crocodile skin boots, as expected. However, he did have a black scarf and overcoat of good quality draped over a chair in his bedroom. Similar to those worn by the killer, although also the type of items owned by most men of means. The maid had not yet been to make his bed. Either Vaughan is a restless sleeper, or two heads lay on the pillows last night. The lacy undergarment poking out from underneath one pillow rather suggests the latter."

"But Vaughan is a married man! A gentleman."

"Not all gentlemen are well behaved behind closed bedroom doors, Grace, especially away from home."

"I know that, Charlie, but he seemed such a decent sort of man. Perhaps he carries an article from his wife on his travels, to feel close to her when they are apart? Although, I admit I did detect a hint of a feminine perfume about his rooms and noted an apparent hurried attempt to tidy up before we arrived at his door."

"Regardless of his morals," Charlie said, "we have no evidence to link Vaughan to either the robbery or measles. He was open about visiting Emerson, and apparently genuine in his desire to help us. On the other hand, Vaughan could be as accomplished as a liar as he is at selling cameras. The camera business arguably provides a good cover story for visiting jewellery shops. And he must be experienced in valuing expensive items if he is offering to sell his cameras in exchange for unwanted jewellery and watches. As we both know, the most successful of criminals may present a pleasant face to the world."

"If Vaughan was involved, he was the killer, not the accomplice, as he has neither measles nor crocodile skin boots. Which means his accomplice must also have been on the ship, presumably travelling separately to avoid suspicion. Quinn and Thornton didn't have measles either, but Barlow or the Smiths might."

"Quite so," Charlie agreed. "All of them remain on the suspect list until we find the persons responsible for Mr Emerson's death. I need to take these photographs to the police straight away, as the Smith brothers and Barlow still seem the most obvious suspects."

Grand Encounter

After they left Vaughan, Charlie went straight to the police station to give Detective Sergeant Elliot the photographs of Barlow and the Smith brothers. He memorised their faces and sketch the men in his notebook before handing the photographs over. Grace went to check in with the Measles Response Team at the medical school.

Elliot was so pleased to get the photographs, he agreed to sit down with Charlie to go over what each of them had found out so far on the Emerson murder and robbery.

Charlie shared the results of his investigations, while Elliot made notes and asked questions, ending with his lack of progress on the prime suspects. "I hope you've had more success than me, Detective Sergeant Elliot."

"I've had every available constable out hunting down the Smith brothers and Barlow," Elliot replied, "and an army of volunteers supplied by Doctor Osborne. Not a single hotel or boarding house in Dunedin admits to sheltering them. No Smith brothers, no pairs of men matching their description. Any number of single men, but none named Barlow. Thank goodness you've come up with these photographs. Somebody must have seen them."

"You've achieved a great deal in a short time. I suppose they must be staying with family or friends." Charlie knew it wasn't helpful, but he didn't know what else to say in the face of Elliot's fierce determination to find these men.

"Or one of the dozens of private residences taking in guests to pay the bills," Elliot said. "I have one lead on Barlow. After hearing he was collecting bird specimens, I arranged a local constable to visit a well-known taxidermist in South Dunedin. Barlow had been there all right, on Monday. He bought a bag of bird skins. Left on bad terms after an argument over specimens he wanted, which the taxidermist had already sold to another buyer."

Charlie thought he must have misheard. "Bird skins?"

Elliot shrugged. "Beats me why anyone would want such a thing, but apparently museums and collectors pay high prices for rare birds and they're easier to transport as a dried skin with the feathers intact. I'd say there's little doubt Barlow is the man who went to the brothel with a smelly canvas bag."

"The man with measles." Charlie hesitated to ask the obvious question, knowing Elliot would have led with it if he had an answer.

Elliot read Charlie's mind. "The taxidermist didn't ask where Barlow was staying, because Barlow didn't ask for anything to be delivered. At least we know Barlow is still in Dunedin." Elliot pushed his chair aside and paced the room, his wrinkles forming deep furrows on his forehead. "We have to find Barlow and the Smith brothers. I've a newborn great-granddaughter to protect."

So that was it. Charlie ought to have realised. Everyone had loved ones at risk of measles. Elliot had a great-granddaughter, Wallace had a young grandson, Declan Kelly had two young children, Grace's friend Molly was pregnant. No generation was untouched by the threat.

Charlie didn't wish to sound heartless, but he also wanted to know if there were any new leads on the murder and robbery. "Anything else of interest on the Emerson case?"

Elliot flopped into the chair again. "I have constables out looking for witnesses and DC Weston has been verifying statements. Nobody saw the robbers enter or leave Emerson & Son's on Sunday night. Hardly surprising, when law-abiding citizens would be tucked up in their homes so late at night on their day of rest. None of the items stolen has been sold to any of the usual dealers in stolen goods. Not a whisper on the street."

That tallied with what Charlie had found from his own sources. "Did Weston find any inconsistencies in the witness statements?"

Elliot grunted a half-hearted maybe. "Most of the statements were corroborated. Mr Jasper Newton arrived in Dunedin after the robbery, according to his father. The shipping company confirmed that Miss Walsh did change the date of departure on the tickets issued to her and the other singer, Miss Labelle, which means the women passengers are not a measles risk. Vaughan was not seen leaving Wains Hotel on Sunday evening. The same for the trade delegation at the Grand Hotel, who are still refusing to cooperate with police inquiries."

"Not that I trust any of them entirely," Elliot continued. "Weston said that the night staff at the hotels protested a little too much when asked if there was any chance they had fallen asleep during the night shift. Aside from that, there were only two minor discrepancies in the witness statements. Miss Davenport's lady's maid did a poor job of lying when she assured Weston her mistress was home on Sunday night. And Mr Quinn's secretary believed his employer had come into the office between Saturday afternoon and Monday morning, when Quinn himself says that he was at home during that period. Not much to go on, but slow and steady is the way these cases are solved."

Charlie murmured his agreement, but privately he worried that the Australian suspects would be gone long before "slow and steady" solved the case. He got up to go. "Thank you for sharing your information. I'll let you know if I hear anything new."

"Godspeed, Pyke. Don't be taking it into your head to talk to the trade delegation. Wallace has been ordered not to go within spitting distance of them."

"I cannot promise to avoid them entirely," Charlie replied, "as an acquaintance has invited me to a reception for the delegation on Thursday evening. Good luck with your inquiries, Detective Sergeant Elliot."

As Charlie passed out of the gloomy police station into spring sunshine, he reflected on the significant influence that the trade envoy must wield at high levels for the government to accord him protection from the police investigation, given the seriousness of the crime.

Elliot had warned Charlie not to attempt to talk to the trade envoy or his secretary, but there was more to detective work than talking. Anne Macmillan's suggestion of breaking into the envoy's hotel suite had merit, although Charlie preferred not to resort to illegal activities if he could avoid it. However, his interest was roused by the fact that the shoe salesman, Thornton, had sold the trade secretary a pair of the distinctive boots.

Charlie had plenty of time to spare before the camera demonstration began later that afternoon. By happy coincidence, he had to pass by the Grand Hotel as he walked down Princes Street. He hadn't been to the hotel in a while. Surely the police could not raise an objection if he had a quick look inside? Before he could decide exactly what his intentions were, he had rounded the corner and was standing in front of the large glass doors.

The doorman opened the door for him and inquired how he might be of assistance.

"I understand the Australian Trade Delegation is staying here," Charlie said, in his most officious voice. "I have a message for the trade envoy, Mr ..." darn it, what was the man's name? "Mr Nicholas Applegate, or his secretary, Mr Geoffrey Farley."

"They are meeting with government officials in the writing room, sir," the doorman replied. "It has been impressed upon all hotel staff that the gentlemen are not to be disturbed. You may leave your message with the clerk at the front desk, who will see that it is conveyed to Mr Applegate."

Charlie thanked the doorman and ventured into the ornate vestibule, with its beautiful mosaic floor and decorated glass dome. He sauntered across the expanse, trying not to be intimidated by the luxurious surroundings. The Grand certainly lived up to its reputation as the best hotel in the Southern Hemisphere, as well it should for the eye-watering build cost of £40,000.

Ignoring a look of inquiry from the uniformed attendant, Charlie took a seat and scribbled a note saying, "I look forward to meeting you at the reception on Thursday evening," adding an illegible signature.

He approached the front desk and handed the message over, watching to see what pigeonhole the note was put in. First floor, Suite 101. Charlie nodded politely to the desk clerk and strolled across to the impressive stairway, as if he belonged in the splendour of the Grand Hotel. When the door to the Otis Elevator pinged open, Charlie gave in to temptation. He had travelled in an elevator only once before, and the thrill still lingered in his memory. The first time, he had been squashed in beside Grace Penrose, shortly after meeting her. Not an encounter he would forget in a hurry.

The elevator rattled and jerked, but delivered him safely, with no effort to his leg muscles. Fortunately, the first-floor corridor was empty. He listened at the door to the envoy's suite, not expecting to hear any activity. The desk clerk had confirmed that Mr Applegate was in a meeting, with strict instructions not to be disturbed.

After another glance down the corridor, Charlie slipped his lock picks out of an inner pocket and inserted them in the lock. Without any need, as it turned out. At the pressure of his touch, the door yielded slightly. He pushed it open slowly, cringing as the hinges squeaked ever so slightly.

Charlie froze, but nobody came to the door. He stepped inside. Silence. He moved forward, into the room.

Suddenly, he caught a flash of movement in the corner of his eye. He lurched sideways and whirled to face the person, pulse racing, ready for fight or flight.

"My apologies. Must have the wrong suite," Charlie stammered, at the same moment as he recognised the figure as a chambermaid with a disconcertingly familiar face.

"Are you going to shut the door, Charlie, or do you plan to stand there all day?"

"Grace?" Charlie was about to ask what she was doing there, dressed as a maid, but the question was redundant. He closed the door. "You stole a maid's uniform and broke into a gentleman's suite? A man who could be a murderer? What in the name of Hades do you think you are doing?"

Grace gave him her best glare, which he had long ago grown immune to. "I did not steal the uniform. I borrowed it from a friend of your aunt's. And, unlike you, Charlie Pyke, I did not break in. I am here to tidy the room. In fact, I have just tidied away a nice new pair of crocodile skin boots, in the smaller of the two bedrooms. Perhaps you would care to see them, when you are quite done with being cross."

"I am not cross. I am merely recovering from a heart seizure, brought on by you pouncing on me when I believed the room was empty."

"I did not pounce," Grace retorted, "and I can tell you are cross, because the gold flecks in your eyes are glowing."

"If I am cross," Charlie said, keeping his response calm and logical, "it is because I do not want you to risk your reputation, not to mention your life, by engaging in illegal activities, however useful those activities are to our investigation."

"Charlie, I appreciate your concern, but you are not being logical. As a maid, I am legitimately in the room. Whereas if you are caught, you could be charged with breaking and entering. Therefore, unless you are willing to don this maid's uniform – which I would pay good money to witness – the only sensible option was for me to search the trade delegation's suite."

Silence followed, as Charlie concluded that Grace had a fair point, whether he liked it or not.

Grace went over to the third of three doors off the palatial sitting room. "The boots are over there. While you are looking at them, perhaps you could decide whether you want to have a wife who will work alongside you or a wife who will stay at home and tend to 'women's work'. Because if the latter is what you want, the marriage is off."

Charlie pulled them both into the bedroom and closed the door. "Of course I want us to work together, Grace, with the emphasis on together. Is it too much to ask that you consider how much I worry about you, before you charge off alone, without warning me what you are up to?"

He paused, realising she could well say the same thing about him. The fact that it was different for him, as a man and a professional detective, would land on unwilling ears, should he be reckless enough to say it out loud. Besides, he didn't want Grace to change. Not in any way, least of all this way.

"Grace, why are you screwing your eyes up like that? Please don't cry."

Grace turned intense blue eyes on him, with not a trace of tears. "If you must know, I closed my eyes because you look so irresistibly attractive when you worry about me."

The distance between them vanished in a rush of movement. Charlie was aware only of the crush of her lips against his own. Grace pulled away sharply seconds later. "Shh. Someone opened the door to the suite."

Charlie didn't wait to see if she was right. He hurled himself to the floor and scrambled under the bed. He froze as hurried footsteps crossed the sitting room.

Trade Negotiations

Charlie breathed in and out as quietly as he could manage, his chest pushing up against the underside of the bed with every breath. He hoped the guest wasn't about to take an afternoon nap, especially as Charlie's new camera had tumbled from his hands and landed beside the bed.

Grace hastened to straighten her uniform and cap. The door to the adjacent room opened, then closed again a few seconds later. Grace nudged the camera box under the edge of the bed with her foot. Charlie lay still as he heard the whisper of shoes approaching across the plush carpet. The door to the room they were in opened.

"What the devil?" A man's voice, high-pitched. A document case dropped to the floor, spilling papers right beside Charlie's head, where the camera had been sitting seconds ago. "Excuse me, Miss. You startled me."

"Please, allow me, sir." Grace reached down to gather the papers.

"I thought the maid attended to the rooms earlier, while we were breaking our fast." The man's voice again, suspicious this time. "Where is your cleaning equipment?"

"I am the under-housekeeper, in training, sir," Grace said. "My role requires me to inspect each room to ensure that the chambermaids have completed their work to perfection." She patted the corner of the sheet straighter. "We at the Grand Hotel pride ourselves on an exemplary standard of service. I do apologise for startling you, sir."

"Very commendable, I'm sure. I only came to pick up these documents."

The man crossed to the dresser. Charlie wished he could see more than the man's shoes, but he trusted Grace to act the part. He marvelled at her ability to spin a cover story at a moment's notice. A handy skill for a detective, but not such a desirable skill for a wife. Again, she probably thought the same about him.

It was one of many subjects to be discussed before they embarked on a life together. Charlie smiled as he imagined the negotiations to come. Agree to stretch the truth when interviewing suspects, but never to lie to each other. No weapons to be concealed about the person when they are alone together, especially in the bedroom. Inform their spouse before approaching a homicidal maniac alone.

And those were only the first topics that jumped to Charlie's mind, as the man rifled through the dresser drawers. Charlie wondered what normal couples talked of once they had decided on the pattern for their dinnerware and how much pin money the husband would give to his wife.

The man suddenly succumbed to a bout of coughing. Charlie jerked from his musings, hitting his head on the bed frame.

Grace was quick on the uptake, pretending to have knocked her boot against the bed leg to cover the noise. "That's a nasty cough you have, sir. Quite startled me, it did."

The man mumbled an apology.

"If you will excuse the impertinence, sir," Grace said, "I can see that your wrists are red from scratching that rash. I have some experience with such matters, from my previous training as a nursemaid. If you will wait one moment, I have something in my housekeeper's bag that will soothe the itch."

The man moved tentatively towards the door, then stopped. No doubt he didn't know how to act in the face of this highly irregular trainee under-housekeeper. In any event, the man was facing away, so Charlie took the risk of a glimpse. The man was rather delicate physically, of below average height, with thin wrists. He fitted the description of Mr Geoffrey Farley, secretary to the trade envoy.

Grace returned promptly. "If I might be permitted, sir." Grace dabbed a little of the cream on Farley's wrist, pushing up his sleeve in what must have been a complete violation of hotel rules, let alone the accepted rules of polite society. Charlie doubted real maids and housekeepers were allowed within touching distance of guests under normal circumstances, but adherence to rules would not get Grace a look at the rash on the man's arm.

Charlie had to applaud her dedication to the task, though he wished she might hurry. Fluff from under the bed had crept into his nostrils, and he couldn't raise a finger to stop the approaching sneeze.

Farley was far too astonished to stop Grace's outrageous familiarity with his person. "Th-thank you. I must say, that does feel a little less itchy already. So soothing to the skin."

Grace curtseyed. "All part of the exceptional service we offer at the Grand Hotel, sir. I shall leave the cream on your dresser, sir, with our compliments."

"Yes, well, er, marvellous. I must be getting back to my meeting. Wouldn't do to be late."

The door to the suite banged open. "Farley, what are you up to?" The man's voice smashed across the quiet room with the subtlety of a sledgehammer.

"I'm here, Mr Applegate," Farley replied. "Merely a minor delay finding the dossier."

Footsteps stomped towards them. "And if I ever hear you use the word 'compromise' again in one of my meetings, I will have you horse-whipped. Honestly, I am not paid nearly enough to deal with this incompetence. If their Minister of Agriculture and Trade rejects our demands one more time, I'm walking out of these damned negotiations and retiring to my country estate. Come on, man. We need that document now, not tomorrow. Time is running out."

Mr Nicholas Applegate, the trade envoy, was less a diplomat than a tyrant. Charlie used the tirade to sneeze as delicately as he could manage.

"I had the dossier a second ago, sir." Farley replied, his naturally high voice edging higher with each reprimand from his superior.

Applegate stopped outside the bedroom. A few more steps and he would see Grace. "Damnation, Farley. This is not a croquet match at a ladies' tea party. We cannot go home without the prize. We need that freezer ship design, by fair means or foul."

Grace retrieved the document case from the dresser, where Farley had left it, and hurried to the bedroom door. "I beg your pardon, sir. This gentleman was most clear in his instructions not to move any papers, but I'm afraid I forgot, sir. I was dusting you see –"

Applegate cut her off. "Well, well, never you mind your pretty little head. No harm done, eh." The tyrant had switched back to the voice of a cultured diplomat in an instant. "Don't you worry, Miss, I promise not to complain to the hotel manager about you." The trade envoy let loose a hearty chuckle. "A man of my considerable influence cannot afford to express such sentiments, or half the maids in the Southern Hemisphere would find themselves out of a job."

"Yes, sir. Thank you, sir," Grace said.

Charlie imagined Grace curtseying and grovelling to this odious man, after taking the blame for the mislaid dossier herself, to save Farley from further abuse. If Charlie hadn't been stuck under the bed, he would have let the trade envoy know what he thought of him.

Fortunately, the door closed. He and Grace were alone again.

Grace came back into the bedroom and slumped into the bedside chair. "You can come out now, Charlie."

He heaved the bed up and wriggled his way out. "You were magnificent, Grace."

"I nearly kneed Applegate in the groin. The rotten scoundrel actually had the nerve to pinch my bottom."

"Just as well I was stuck under the bed," Charlie replied. "I'm the only one allowed to touch your very attractive posterior."

Grace lounged back in the chair. "Strictly speaking, Mr Pyke, you ought not to touch any part of my anatomy other than my hand or arm, until I have a ring on my finger and a signature on a marriage certificate." She shot him a wicked smile. "Not that I object."

All other thoughts fled Charlie's mind at that smile. But now was not the moment for such agreeable diversions. "I'll keep that in mind for later, Miss Penrose. We had better make a thorough search before they come back." He offered his hand to help her from the chair. "You had Farley eating out of your hand. Was his rash from measles?"

"No. Eczema, I think," Grace replied. "Farley appeared to be wearing some type of cosmetic powder or cream on his face to cover it, but his lower arm was red and flaking."

"I doubt Mr Emerson's son could distinguish one type of rash from another in the dim light, especially when he was half-blindfolded and under enormous stress. Farley could well be our robbery accomplice, with the vile Applegate as the ringleader."

"Surely a trade envoy – a government official – would not stoop to robbery?"

"You heard the man, Grace. Applegate feels he is underpaid and undervalued, while Farley will do what he is told. What better cover than to travel to another country with government-approved immunity? A nice little side-earner." Charlie rifled through the bedside drawers as he spoke. "What did Applegate look like, in case I meet him again?"

"Self-important, brown hair, hazel eyes, barrel chest, medium height, jutting chin and patrician forehead. No more than forty years of age. Clothes from an expensive and capable tailor. Applegate cut quite the figure, outwardly." Grace moved to the dresser and continued her search. "I detest men such as him, who abuse their underlings when nobody is listening, then switch to acting the gentleman for an audience. Farley is terrified of him. By the way, Farley wears a rather feminine eau-de-cologne, like the robbery accomplice."

"I noticed. This bedroom reeks of it." Charlie retrieved an Emerson box from a bedside drawer. A watch box, confirming that Farley was the man from the ship who had had his pocket watch stolen and who had replaced it at Emerson's shop last week. Or had he used the theft story as a cover to inspect the security arrangements at the jewellery shop? "Are you sure you don't mind continuing the search after your close encounter, Grace?"

"It'll be quicker with two," Grace replied. She flicked him a glance. "As long as my fiancé doesn't distract me."

Charlie blew her a kiss and continued his search. The suite was luxurious by hotel standards, featuring two large bedrooms, a small study and a private bathroom, in addition to the sitting room. But there were few places where a shop's worth of jewellery and watches could be stashed. And none of them contained so much as a garnet brooch, let alone a sapphire and diamond ring.

Charlie was seated at the desk in the study when Grace found him again. Her expression told him she hadn't had any success, either.

"Find anything?" she asked.

"Nothing."

"Disappointing," Grace said. "I would have enjoyed watching you arrest Applegate. I shall have a bruise on my derrière where he assaulted me."

"All is not lost. Applegate and Farley would probably be too smart to store the stolen jewels in their own suite, even though they believe themselves immune from police scrutiny. They could have a trunk in the hotel's luggage storeroom. We'd have to find unequivocal evidence of their involvement to get the police to conduct a full search. Or catch them boarding their ship."

"Do you know when they leave?"

Charlie waved the leather-bound diary he was holding. "I'm about to check their movements."

The diary disclosed a busy schedule of meetings, visits to factories and farms, and formal receptions, including the one tomorrow night at the Davenport residence. The Sunday night of the robbery was the only blank space in the twelve days of their visit. The delegation was due to leave Dunedin on Friday evening, the day after the Davenport reception. Only two days away. Charlie didn't need the reminder that time was running short to find Mr Emerson's killer before the suspects steamed off into the Australian sunset.

Grace leaned over his shoulder. "Pity they didn't write 'Rob jewels from Emerson & Son' in the diary on Sunday night. I thought all criminals were supposed to be stupid."

"Only the ones who get caught," Charlie replied. "Maybe they are what they pretend to be – trade officials doing their duty to their country with honour and dignity."

"I'd sooner believe that kangaroos might fly," Grace said. "Applegate as good as admitted the trade mission was straying to the wrong side of the law when he said, 'We cannot go home without the prize. We need that freezer ship design, by fair means or foul.' I wonder what they are up to?" She reached over to flip back the diary pages. "They were in Sydney before they left, having a series of meetings with meat industry leaders and shipping companies."

"Don't you think our investigation is complex enough, Grace, with measles and a murder-robbery to deal with? Not to mention Lady Detective making my life difficult?" But Charlie was already riffling through the documents on the desk and in the drawers. He had the same feeling as Grace, that something was not quite right about this trade delegation.

The main focus of trade discussions seemed to be summed up by the title on a thick wad of papers: "Opportunities for Greater Cooperation between Australia and New Zealand in the Primary Industries Trade with Great Britain". Judging from the heavy scrawl of blue ink across the typed document, Greater Cooperation was proving difficult to achieve.

Scarcely a single sentence was left untouched by minor changes of wording or wholesale redrafting. Whole paragraphs had been crossed out and others added. The same hand that wrote the diary had written in bold block capitals, with exclamation marks, on the paper several times. MERINO WOOL NON-NEGOTIABLE! FROZEN MEAT EXPORTS CRITICAL! THREATEN WITH SUGAR TARIFFS IF NO SOLUTION TO CHEESE ISSUE!

Imagining the trade delegates, stuck at a table all day negotiating the minutiae of trade deals made Charlie glad to work as a detective. He could well believe that frustration had driven Applegate to crime, if only to finance an early retirement. Unfortunately, finding out what the delegation was up to would take more time than they could spare. The thick piles of paper on the desk would take hours to read and may not make sense even then.

Grace picked up the document and flipped through the pages until a paragraph caught her eye. "How about this? Paragraph 417a: 'Dairy quota concession in exchange for freezer ship design'."

Charlie gaped at her. "How the dickens did you spot that so quickly?"

"Years of studying for my medical degree. Learning to read at speed is the only way to survive." Grace put the document down in front of Charlie. "Look. They've scrawled, 'must have full access to freezer design plans' next to the paragraph. And the whole paragraph has been crossed out, so the two sides clearly haven't agreed."

"To be honest, it doesn't mean much to me, Grace. Uncompromising negotiation is hardly a crime. Unless they intend to steal the freezer design if they cannot get it by fair means."

"We could take the information to Caroline Davenport's fiancé," Grace suggested. "Jasper Newton is part of the New Zealand trade team, isn't he?"

"Good idea, Grace. Passing along the problem suits me fine. We've enough to worry about." Charlie looked at his pocket watch. "Time to go. We'll be caught if we stay here much longer."

"We have time to have something to eat before we go to Vaughan's camera demonstration. Mrs Brown said to tell you she is making your favourite soup today."

Charlie felt a rush of saliva at the thought. Breakfast was a distant memory to his rumbling stomach. "I can't take advantage of Mrs Macmillan's generous hospitality two days in a row."

Grace brushed dust and fluff off the back of his coat. "You'd better get used to it, Charlie. It's going to be our home soon."

Our home. It sounded both odd and enthralling to Charlie's ear, as if he had fallen down a rabbit hole into a strange and wonderful new world.

A Lively Demonstration

Grace heard shouting even before they reached the entrance to the hall Mr Vaughan had hired for his camera demonstration. Charlie held her back from entering the room, to listen without being seen. Two things were evident – the men who were supposed to be helping Vaughan set up the room were not working fast enough and Vaughan had a terrible temper when angry.

When there was a lull in the argument, Grace and Charlie entered the hall, conversing with each other as if nothing had happened. The camera salesman had left the room, leaving a woman to direct the two workmen, who were busy shifting display boards. The woman, who was around Grace's age, achieved the job with calm efficiency. The men were sullen, but hard at work.

Mr Vaughan reappeared from a side room off the hall. "Mr Pyke, Miss Penrose, I am glad you came. However, the demonstration does not start for another twenty minutes and we are rather busy. Everything has been behind schedule, with the week wasted in quarantine and now these useless men."

"Your assistant appears to have the situation under control," Grace said. The woman was busy unpacking a box of framed photographs and attaching them to the display boards.

"Miss Greenway has been a blessing," Vaughan replied. "A local girl I hired. Always helps sales if I engage a pretty girl to assist in the demonstration. Lends the proceedings a certain grace that we gentlemen cannot emulate."

The young woman was demurely dressed in a ruffled shirtwaist, tied high at the neck with a mauve chiffon bow. The chiffon fell in soft waves across her chest to cover every square inch that was not already covered by a well-tailored jacket. Her full skirt in a soft dove-grey wool looked well on her trim figure. The avid readers of the fashion pages of the *Dunedin Ladies' Journal* would both admire and approve this combination of style and decorum. Vaughan had aimed for the pretty girl-next-door in his assistant, rather than the alluring beauty.

Probably a wise move, as many customers would be family people. Grace knew that a certain element of society viewed amateur photography as a route to moral corruption. Instances had already been noted in the local newspapers of young rascals abusing the discreet detective-style cameras in pursuit of photographs that were rather too candid, without the consent of the subject.

Charlie wanted to speak to Vaughan, so Grace offered to help the young woman set up the photographic display. A newly hired local woman might give Grace a clearer picture of the true character of Mr Vaughan. Today's flare of temper and the possibility of a lover suggested hidden layers beneath the charming surface of the camera salesman.

"Oh, you are the lady from the photograph," the woman said, as she unpacked a box and laid out a row of framed photographs. "I'm Beth Greenway. Mr Vaughan took ever such a lovely photograph of you and your husband." She glanced over at Vaughan with a look bordering on reverence. "Mr Vaughan called it a 'vision of devotion'. He reckons it'll sell his cameras by the dozen. He's enlarged the photograph so it can be on a display board all by itself at the front of the hall. It's so fresh from being developed he hasn't even had a chance to frame it."

Grace felt a sinking feeling in the pit of her stomach.

"No need to look so worried," Miss Greenway said. "You'll simply adore the photograph. Mr Vaughan has made copies for you to keep. He's exceptionally thoughtful that way."

Despite Miss Greenway's assurance – and she did have a lovely, reassuring voice and a beguiling smile – Grace was regretting the impulsive decision to sit for the photograph. Would it be considered unseemly to have their photograph on public display for a commercial enterprise? And what did Beth Greenway mean by a "vision of devotion"? Would she and Charlie be a laughingstock?

Grace realised Miss Greenway was waiting for her to respond. "Nice to meet you, Miss Greenway. I'm Grace Penrose." She picked up a box and started to unpack it. "Tell me, how did you come to be Mr Vaughan's assistant?"

"Do call me Beth. Despite the fancy clothes he makes me wear, I am not a lady like you. Last week, I was nothing but a shop girl, selling cheap trinkets. Monday afternoon, Mr Vaughan came in when the owner reprimanding me over a silly little error I'd made. Honestly, there was no need for the owner to let me go with no notice. Mr Vaughan was kind enough to offer me this job. I'll make enough from these demonstrations to pay my train fare back to my family. I'm ever so grateful to him."

Grace wasn't sure what to make of Beth Greenway. Her clothes and sweet manner were at odds with her rather excessive use of face powder and rouge, which veered close to, if not beyond, the boundary of what a respectable lady would wear. Grace decided that Beth was probably attempting to appear older and more worldly, to catch the eye of John Vaughan, who was an attractive and successful man. Grace worried whether the girl's naivety was being exploited by the camera salesman, especially in light of Charlie's observation that Vaughan might have entertained a woman in his bed.

"What is Mr Vaughan like to work for?" Grace asked.

Beth flashed a proprietorial glance at the camera salesman, confirming Grace's fears. "He's a proper gentleman and a wonderful photographer. We'd best be hurrying to get these photographs set up. The crowds will be gathering soon."

Grace picked up a photograph and followed Beth's lead in attaching it to the display board. She wasn't about to let Beth be misled. "It must be a lonely life for Mr Vaughan, travelling all the way from Australia, leaving his wife at home alone."

Beth lost her grip on the picture in her hands, but grabbed it again just before it hit the floor. "I expect you are right, Miss Penrose. May I leave you to finish this display, while I attend to the other?"

The assistant hurried away, but not before Grace noted that the news of Vaughan's marital status had pinched Beth's full lips into a thin line. Although Grace felt unkind mentioning his wife, Beth was better off knowing the truth. At least she wouldn't have any expectations now, if indeed she ever had. Grace struggled to see her as a woman who would share a man's bed on so short an acquaintance, whether she admired him or not.

The photographs were soon mounted on the display boards, which had hooks already affixed. Meanwhile, the two workmen, with Charlie's help, had set out a table at the front of the room and rows of chairs the length of the hall, suggesting that a large audience was expected. Mr Vaughan was finishing the display at the front. Not a moment too soon, as the first visitors were coming through the doors at the rear of the hall.

Beth Greenway hurried to greet them, offering each arrival a warm welcome and a sales brochure. She directed them to view the photographs displayed around the walls before the demonstration commenced.

Vaughan acknowledged his assistant with a wink. He circulated through the growing crowd, pointing out that every photograph was taken on a hand-held camera by an amateur photographer and noting how the images captured the subjects in a way no studio could emulate. A sales pitch he had obviously given many times, but projected with apparently undiminished enthusiasm.

Charlie joined Grace in a slow circuit of the room. The photographs made for impressive viewing. Not only for the surprising quality of the images, but for the freshness and liveliness of the subjects compared to the usual stiff studio portraits. Family picnics, children at play, courting couples strolling along a promenade, grandparents proudly showing off their grandchildren, and a couple of portrait shots of ladies in low-cut gowns. Nothing unseemly, but perhaps with the tiniest hint of a saucy smile, aimed at whatever fortunate gentleman was behind the camera. In other words, a subtle sales pitch to encompass all varieties of potential amateur photographer, from the proud father to the avid gentleman admirer.

A cluster of visitors formed around the display at the front of the hall, giving Grace another tingle of trepidation. She took the opportunity to pay Mr Vaughan for the camera, in case she wanted to flee the scene after seeing their portrait on display.

Vaughan had moved to the table at the front of the room, standing ready beside a stack of boxes. The studio camera on its tripod was set up at the side of the stage behind him, to demonstrate the laughable difference in size compared to the hand-held cameras on a table beside it.

Grace approached, with her offer of a brooch at the ready.

Vaughan wavered. "Miss Penrose, I feel guilty for taking your valuables. To be honest, the wonderful photograph I took of you and Mr Pyke is worth more to me than the cost of the camera."

"I insist, Mr Vaughan." Grace handed over the brooch, which was not particularly valuable. "In truth, you are doing me a favour. The brooch was a gift that I was unable to refuse from an unwanted admirer."

Mr Vaughan took a large envelope from the table and gave it to her. "I had Mr Mackay make several copies for you. I knew as soon as I saw the photograph developed that you would want to share it with your families. I shall certainly use it for every display I mount." He looked around with a satisfied nod at the gathering crowd. "It will be a good sales day today. I feel it in my bones. I invited most of the first-class passengers from the ship, by the way, as several expressed an interest in attending."

Customers were gathering around the table now, eager to purchase the cameras even before the demonstration had started.

The crowd around the front display thinned, allowing Grace a glimpse of a large photographic portrait of her and Charlie. Caroline Davenport was standing in front of it, scribbling in her notebook. From the sardonic twist of her smile, Grace assumed there would be trouble on their horizon, in the shape of a *Dunedin Ladies' Journal* article about the Dashing Detective's latest dalliance.

Grace started towards Caroline, intending to have stern words with her, but a man got to her first. A handsome man, who looked vaguely familiar. His hand was on Caroline's back with possessive familiarity, as he guided her to a quiet corner. Caroline's stiff deportment melted at his touch. Grace turned away, leaving the lovers in peace. How nice to see that Caroline had a softer side. If only it might be transmitted to her pen to soften the sharp words she spewed into the world.

Charlie wandered over. Grace pulled him aside into a quiet corner, where she tore the envelope open. Vaughan had given them copies of their photograph in various sizes. The picture captured them at the instant they recalled their first meeting, looking at each other with laughter and love in their eyes, as if the camera had reached inside them and captured their souls. Any pretence that they were merely work colleagues, as they had told Caroline Davenport, was utterly dispelled.

Grace could not deny the superb quality of the photograph, but having it on public display was another matter entirely. "We must leave, Charlie. I feel … laid bare … in front of strangers. Caroline Davenport is here. She's sure to use it to her advantage in the next edition of the Lady Detective."

Charlie's rapt attention moved from the photograph to Grace. "Why should we care, Grace? The picture is wonderful and not at all unseemly. Personally, I couldn't be happier that the ladies of Dunedin will know I am in love with the finest of them all. Besides, Vaughan has invited all the first-class passengers from the ship to the camera demonstration, which will give us a chance to meet them again."

"Speak of the devil," Grace said. "The man who has just arrived is the trade envoy, Applegate. The smaller man, walking a step behind him, is the secretary, Farley. I hope they don't recognise me out of the maid's uniform."

Vaughan chose that moment to call for everyone to take a seat, as the demonstration was about to begin. Charlie clasped Grace's arm to prevent her from sitting, whispering that he wanted a good view of everything that happened.

When the crowd was seated and quiet, Applegate strode up the aisle between the rows of chairs, with the air of a royal personage on parade. Farley stayed by the door, holding Applegate's overcoat, hat, gloves and document case. A human hatstand, and a surly one at that.

The trade envoy greeted Vaughan as one would an old acquaintance, with a vigorous handshake and a wide smile. Grace noticed that this apparently spontaneous bonhomie was captured for posterity by Miss Greenway, who had obviously been waiting with a camera for the moment. Furthermore, the two men had angled themselves perfectly, so the moment was not only captured on film, but was witnessed by the two newspaper reporters seated in the front row. Caroline Davenport was scribbling furiously in the row behind.

Vaughan swept his hands into an arc, giving the audience a glimpse of his dazzling red waistcoat, lavishly embroidered with gold thread. "Ladies and gentlemen, I welcome you to a demonstration of the latest in modern inventions. We are honoured to have the leader of the Australian Trade Delegation here today to open proceedings. I give you – Mr Nicholas Applegate."

The audience clapped and cheered, although Grace could not imagine why, other than in response to the sheer showmanship of John Vaughan.

Applegate bobbed his perfectly coiffed head and adjusted his perfectly tied cravat. He paused for a fraction of a second, milking the anticipation. "Thank you, Mr Vaughan. And welcome, ladies and gentlemen. Our two countries have always been great friends, positioned as we are so far from the rest of the civilised world. We seek to share the fruits of our labour from our respective lands, as well as the marvels of man's capacity for invention. This fact was brought home to me by the voyage to your shores. Amongst the few travellers aboard our ship, the diversity of our trade with New

Zealand was astounding. Mr Quinn, bringing tropical fruits and sugar from Queensland. Mr Thornton, with shoes made from unique Australian leathers. Miss Elsie Walsh, sharing the culture of our lands with her divine singing. And of course, the estimable Mr Vaughan, who brings the wonders of photography into the hands of ordinary men. With no further ado, let the show begin!"

Charlie nudged Grace and bent to whisper in her ear. "Fine words from a man whose sole aim seems to be to negotiate as many concessions out of the trade agreement as he can get, by fair means or foul."

"And he forgot to mention the friendly gesture of bringing a deadly disease to our shores," Grace replied.

After the honeyed words of introduction, the show began. John Vaughan vaulted up onto the stage with practiced ease and proceeded to extol the simplicity and joys of amateur photography. Beth Greenway played the perfect assistant – handing him equipment on cue, laughing at his jokes, smiling as she posed for his photographs. Beth demonstrated every conceivable pose, starting with the traditional seated pose and the stiffest of smiles, and ending with a pirouette and a coquettish grin over her shoulder. Grace thought Beth might well take to a career on the stage, if her days as a shop girl were over.

"As pretty as a picture, wouldn't you agree, ladies and gentlemen?" Vaughan said. "But what if your lady is shy?" Beth turned away from the camera and flipped open a fan to hide her face from the eyes down.

"The camera lens can be a daunting prospect, don't you agree?" Vaughan placed the hand-held camera on a small table at the side of the stage, next to the ungainly studio camera. He flourished his hands to show they were empty. "Come now, my dear. The camera is gone. Will you not give us a sweet smile?"

Beth flicked the fan aside and favoured him with a radiant smile. From the perspective of the audience, the pale powder and bright rouge on her cheeks gave her the appearance of a blushing innocent gazing at her love. Grace realised that every aspect of the demonstration had been carefully orchestrated for showmanship, down to the cosmetics and costume.

"What man in love would not wish to capture that adoring moment?" Vaughan said. He unbuttoned his red waistcoat, to reveal a round object underneath. "And behold! The moment has been captured! Ladies and gentlemen, I give you the extraordinary waistcoat camera!!"

Gasps, cheers and laughter rippled through the audience, followed by rapturous applause. Miss Beth Greenway curtseyed and swanned off the stage, reappearing a moment later by the sales table, ready to sell cameras.

"But wait! The show is not over!" Vaughan moved to the side of the stage and took up his camera again. The stage curtain began to open, to murmurs of excitement from the audience. "Those amongst us fortunate enough to have children will know that it is impossible to get them to stand still for a formal photograph. But now, you do not need to bother!"

Vaughan waved a hand, and a small troupe of lithe boys in glittering costumes tumbled and cartwheeled across the stage. The camera salesman wandered amongst them, pretending to take photographs as they stood on their hands, flipped in circles and formed a pyramid with their bodies.

As a dazzling finale, two silky lengths of scarlet material descended to the stage from above, followed by the figure of a slim woman, who slid down in a series of twists and twirls. She landed on the back of the topmost pair of boys in the pyramid and raised her hands into the air.

Vaughan took his final photograph amid a deluge of applause. "Ladies and gentlemen, I give you the marvellous acrobats of the Wirth Brothers' Mammoth Circus, who are performing here in Dunedin this week! Don't miss their extraordinary show, folks, featuring the dazzling Miss Gloriana!"

The woman somersaulted off the pyramid, landing on her feet without so much as a wobble. The boys followed her lead, before bowing and tumbling off the stage in a blaze of shimmering colour and movement. Miss Gloriana flipped head over heels twice, stopping by Vaughan's side as the curtain closed behind her. There, the dazzling lady acrobat posed on one leg, her arms stretched wide, as Vaughan and the audience applauded her.

Grace thought the two of them were sharing rather an intimate smile. Perhaps Beth Greenway was not the object of Vaughan's attentions after all. Grace felt a pang of pity for Beth, who looked positively dowdy next to the female acrobat. Beth kept her head down, rearranging the cameras on the sales table.

Miss Gloriana curtseyed, back-flipped twice and vanished behind the curtain. Vaughan waited until the applause died, before introducing his agent in Dunedin, Mr Mackay of Mackay's Photography, for the future purchase of cameras and development of photographs.

"However, those fortunate enough to be present here today," Vaughan continued, "are offered a once in a lifetime opportunity to purchase one of these marvellous cameras for a third off the usual price. Ladies and gentlemen, I thank you for your attention and invite you to inspect my marvellous wares."

Vaughan vaulted to the floor of the hall, next to the sales table, where he and Beth were besieged by eager buyers. Beth's shop-girl skills were put to the test as the thrill of the show overcame the audience's reluctance to open their pocketbooks.

Passion Play

Grace had been holding her breath during the acrobatic display. She let it out in one long puff. "What a performance. I was expecting an interesting lecture on photography, not a spectacle. I'm glad I don't have to join that long queue to buy your camera."

"Vaughan is quite the showman, as well as a consummate salesman," Charlie agreed. "No wonder he can afford to stay in a suite at Wains Hotel."

Grace spotted a familiar face amongst the waiting customers. "Charlie, the woman in the queue wearing the chestnut brown dress is Mrs Quinn, from the ship. That's her husband beside her."

Charlie peered over the heads. "Mrs Quinn, the Sunday School teacher who thought she was ill, until you told her she was with child? She looks well today."

"Positively radiant. Her husband appears very solicitous of her."

"The proud father-to-be. Mr and Mrs Quinn live in Dunedin, don't they?"

Grace nodded. "Mr Quinn imports tropical goods, such as sugar and melons, into New Zealand. He bought his wife a pair of the crocodile skin boots, but they're not likely suspects. He says he hasn't given the boots to her yet and Mrs Quinn didn't have measles after all. Besides which, they seem to be an ordinary married couple, not a pair of callous criminals."

Charlie moved towards Mr and Mrs Quinn. "Can you introduce me? We cannot afford to rule anyone out, however improbable. Especially as Thornton only sold three pairs of the boots to his shipmates – to Mr Quinn, one of the Smith brothers and the envoy's secretary, Farley. Aside from Thornton himself, those three and

Caroline Davenport are the only people to have had a pair before the night of the robbery, as far as we know."

Fortunately, Mrs Quinn recognised Grace as the medical student who had given her the good news about her pregnancy. Mr Quinn did not recall meeting Grace, which was perhaps just as well. Quinn was in an expansive mood, radiating pride at his impending fatherhood. They were here to buy a camera to document their son's progress through life. Grace refrained from pointing out that a daughter's life might be worthy of a few photographs too. Nor did she ask whether he had recovered the bags of sugar missing from his shipment, so as not to spoil his good humour.

"Mr Vaughan mentioned that several of your fellow passengers might attend today," Charlie said.

"A fine fellow, Vaughan," Mr Quinn said. "Decent of him to invite the Australian envoy to sing the praises of our businesses. Impressive man, Mr Applegate. I'm pleased to know that our governments are working in the grand spirit of cooperation to progress trade between the countries. Personally, I have always found myself on the back foot with the Australians, who seem to have little concern for a small market like New Zealand."

"Quite so," Charlie said. "I was hoping to meet Mr Barlow and the Smith brothers."

"I cannot imagine why," Mr Quinn said. "I paid them such scant regard on the voyage, I can't say I would recognise them if I saw them again. Appalling the people they allow in first class these days. Money does not equate to breeding, you know."

But Mrs Quinn was craning her neck to scan the crowd. "They're not here. The only fellow passenger I can see is Mr Thornton." She fluttered a lace handkerchief. "Over there, with that pretty lady in the glorious gown. Rather an eye for the ladies, that man."

Grace followed her line of sight to where Caroline Devenport was standing with the man Grace had noticed earlier. From the intimacy of their meeting, Grace had assumed the man was her fiancé, Mr Jasper Newton, not Mr Thornton from the ship. The man caught sight of the fluttering handkerchief, excused himself to Caroline, and came over.

Mr Thornton flashed dazzling white teeth at Mrs Quinn. He stood a fraction closer to her than was respectable and touched her arm as he greeted her, causing her cheeks to redden. “Mrs Quinn, how delightful to meet you again.” The shoe salesman bobbed his head to Mr Quinn. “And you, Mr Quinn.” His gaze moved around to Charlie, a slight frown touching his forehead.

“Mr Pyke, from the Measles Response Team,” Charlie reminded him.

“Ah, yes, thought I had met you before,” Thornton said. “And this must be your lovely wife, Mrs Pyke. I hazard a guess that you two are newly married, from your charming photographic portrait. There are few things quite so delightful as young love.”

Grace instinctively stepped out of touching distance.

Charlie stepped forward at the same instant, putting himself between Thornton and Grace. “Mr Thornton, may I introduce my fiancée, Miss Penrose. I see you already know Miss Davenport, one of our delightful society ladies.”

Grace caught the tiny flick of Charlie’s head in Caroline’s direction. She excused herself from the group, leaving Thornton explaining he had only met Miss Davenport once, in relation to his business, when her opinion was being sought over the superiority of his footwear. Grace was happy to leave the shoe salesman behind. A ladies’ man he might be, but his superficial charms held no appeal to her. She had met plenty of men like him before. More than a few of them had left abandoned women in their wakes at Lavender House, the women’s refuge Grace volunteered at.

She preferred a man whose character matched his exterior charms. Which was rather ironic, considering Charlie spent much of his life as a detective using a variety of subterfuges to gather information. Was that so different from Applegate, with his words of friendship, when deception was his aim? Or Vaughan, with his performance today, aimed at separating the audience from their earnings? Perhaps it was a matter of perspective.

Caroline Davenport was now conversing with another gentleman. Unlike Thornton, this man appeared to be a true gentleman, born and bred, judging by his exquisite posture and tailoring. Not more than average height, but a man with presence, and handsome too. He had his hands clasped behind his back and was standing at an appropriate distance from the lady.

Grace hesitated to interrupt what was clearly a private conversation. She glanced back at Charlie to find him coming towards her. Mr and Mrs Quinn had reached the head of the camera queue and Thornton had disappeared.

Charlie came up beside her. "Do you know the man with Caroline Davenport, Grace?"

"I'm assuming he is her fiancé, Mr Jasper Newton. I hope, for her sake, that Mr Newton did not see Caroline conversing so intimately with Mr Thornton before the demonstration began."

Caroline Davenport saw them approach. A superior smirk greeted them. "Why, if it isn't Mr Pyke and Miss Penrose, the silent stars of the display. That photograph of you two demonstrates rather more than fine photographic technique. Your intimacy is so apparent to all and sundry, I shouldn't be surprised if Miss Penrose's father comes after you with a shotgun, Mr Pyke."

Grace was not about to be intimidated by a woman who hid her sly gossip behind a nom de plume. "We are engaged to be married, Miss Davenport. Not that it is any of your business."

Caroline flicked a finger at Grace's left hand. It happened to be the finger decorated by her own large diamond. "Could your beau not afford a ring, Miss Penrose? He should be more careful about the clients he takes on."

The man by her side cut in. "Caroline, dearest. Sometimes your behaviour is not fit for a lady of your class. I do apologise for my betrothed. Rather a fast bowler, my Caroline, with a wicked spin at the stumps. Still, better to have her on my team than face her at the crease, eh what?" He held out his hand to Charlie. "Mr Jasper Newton, at your service. Am I to understand that you are a private detective, Mr Pyke? How intriguing."

"I am," Charlie replied. "Our meeting is most fortuitous. I have information for you of a confidential nature, Mr Newton."

Newton wavered. "Can it wait, Mr Pyke? I am here to escort the Australian trade envoy and he appears to be about to leave."

"I ask only a few minutes of your time, on a matter of urgency," Charlie replied. "I have important information about your negotiations with the Australians."

Jasper Newton called another man over, despatching him to accompany Applegate and Farley. With a quick apology to Caroline for leaving her, Jasper and Charlie disappeared out another door, presumably to find somewhere quiet to conduct business.

Caroline watched on with slitted eyes. "What does Mr Pyke want with Jasper?"

"Feeling guilty about something, Miss Davenport?" Grace asked. "Perhaps you are worried that my fiancé will bowl you out for a duck?"

Caroline rolled her eyes. "Please, I beg of you, Miss Penrose, do not assail me with yet more reminders of cricket. Is it not enough that I have pledged my life to a fanatical adherent of that tedious sport? And, for the record, I am not the sort of woman who is likely to be bowled out before putting any runs on the scoreboard. Mr Pyke would do well to remember that."

"Have no fear, Miss Davenport. Their discussion does not concern you in the least. Mr Pyke came across information relevant to Mr Newton's sphere of work. Your fiancé's reputation stands to gain if the information proves correct."

Caroline arched a disdainful eyebrow. "In the business of peddling information now, is he, your Mr Pyke?"

Grace didn't bother to hide her annoyance. "He is passing on information of national importance because it is the right thing to do, not for financial gain. Not everyone sees life through the lens of their own self-interest, Miss Davenport."

Caroline's superior sneer vanished in an instant. "My apologies, Miss Penrose. My comments were uncalled for. I do hope you and

Mr Pyke will come to the reception tomorrow evening at my father's house. I have informed my family that there was not a shred of truth in the *Ladies' Journal* article, so Mr Pyke needn't fear being thrown out. Indeed, I insist you attend. I will need somebody to liven up a dull gathering of trade negotiators. You must promise to rescue me when Jasper recounts the story of the Ashes cricket test match yet again."

"I expect the Australian delegation will be delighted to hear it," Grace said.

"No doubt. As for me, I heartily wish that Australia had never beaten the Mother Country at her own sport. Fortunately, it is never likely to happen again, so I hear. Now, you must excuse me. There is somewhere I have to be." Caroline slipped into the crowd and was lost from sight.

Grace was left standing alone, musing on the contradictions in Miss Davenport's character. As two independent, strong-minded women, Grace felt they could be friends, if only Caroline was not so acerbic and class conscious. Jasper Newton seemed too stiff and formal for the mischievous Caroline, who had been far more animated in the presence of the rakish Thornton than with her future husband.

Out of the corner of her eye, Grace saw Caroline re-emerge from the crowd, look around, and slip into a side room off the hall. Her furtiveness suggested she was up to mischief again. Probably meeting a source to secretly gather more gossip, as Grace was sure Caroline was the writer of the Lady Detective column. Curiosity got the better of Grace. She headed for the side room too.

When she got close to the door, Grace heard a groan. Worried that Caroline was being attacked (perhaps having been cornered by a furious victim of one of her columns), Grace dashed to the rescue. It took her less than a second to realise that Caroline was a willing participant in the attack. She was locked in an extremely passionate embrace with a man, in a room filled with spare chairs and stage props.

The couple broke apart at Grace's involuntary gasp. The man was Thornton, and he was definitely not trying to sell Caroline a nice pair of shoes. From what Grace could see, Caroline's feet were the only part of her anatomy Thornton was not intimately concerned with. Indeed, if Grace wasn't mistaken, the couple only remained upright with the support of the rear end of a papier mâché pantomime cow.

Propriety dictated a speedy exit. "Oh, excuse me, I'm terribly sorry," Grace gabbled, turning away.

"Don't leave," Caroline commanded.

Grace wasn't sure what to do, but Thornton solved the dilemma. He whispered a few words in Caroline's ear, then he pushed past Grace, tucking in his flapping shirttail as he made a dash for the door.

Fortunately, Grace had excellent hearing. Thornton had whispered something about diamonds and being ready for him on tomorrow evening. The words might be completely innocent. After all, Thornton was invited to the reception tomorrow evening, and he knew – as did all invitees – that the Davenport diamonds would be on display. On the other hand, the exchange had more than a touch of furtiveness about it.

When in doubt, take the offensive. After all, it wasn't Grace who was in the wrong here, no matter how acute her embarrassment. "Are you eloping with Mr Thornton on Thursday night, Miss Davenport?"

"How dare you?"

"Taking the famous set of Davenport diamonds with you, perhaps?" Grace continued, throwing caution to the wind. "The real diamonds, I mean, not the paste replicas that are on display. My, won't that cause a commotion. Your father and Mr Newton will not be pleased. The Lady Detective really will have something to write about in the Saturday edition, if she hasn't disappeared on a ship to Australia by then."

Caroline straightened her bodice with a sharp tug. "You think yourself clever, Miss Penrose, but you know nothing. Mr Thornton was merely saying that he would see me on Thursday evening at the reception. He is looking forward to viewing the display of diamonds and the other items my father has in his collections. As you know, my father has insisted we show these Australians that we are people of substance. They do tend to look down upon us."

"Forgive me, Miss Davenport, if I express doubts as to the innocence of the exchange I just witnessed."

"Miss Penrose, whatever you thought you saw happen here," Caroline said, as she straightened the rest of her gown, "I can assure you that you were mistaken. I cannot imagine why you jumped to the conclusion that I would be eloping."

"Perhaps it was the way Mr Thornton's hands were grasping your posterior so possessively, Miss Davenport, and the way your own hands were –"

Caroline puffed up and took a step closer to Grace, who tried not to cringe in the expectation of a furious tirade. Suddenly, Caroline's indignation drained away into a rueful shrug. "All right, all right, I concede defeat. There's no need for any more of your impertinence, Miss Penrose. What concern is it of yours if I wish to experience a moment of passion before I enter a dull marriage? Having seen that photograph of you and Mr Pyke, I find it hard to imagine that passion is an unfamiliar concept to you."

"True, but then I am marrying Mr Pyke, not somebody else. I don't understand you, Miss Davenport. Why not marry a man you love? Wealth and position are not everything."

Caroline turned away to touch up her flushed face with powder, using a small compact and mirror from her reticule. "Miss Penrose, you may be content to work your fingers to the bone and live in a shabby little cottage with a man of dubious repute and uncertain pedigree, but that is not the life for me."

Grace's hand rose to give Caroline the slap she deserved. Sheer will-power – and the realisation that her loss of control might come back to haunt her on the printed page – lowered her hand again.

"How ironic that you have the gall to cast aspersions on Mr Pyke's reputation and ancestry, when I found you locked in a passionate embrace with a man who is not your own fiancé."

If Caroline was concerned about the potential damage to her own reputation, she did not show it in the least. She straightened her dishevelled hair calmly. Only when her hair was restored, did she deign to speak. "Do calm yourself, Miss Penrose. You would be wise to consider that I can do far more damage to your future husband's reputation through my articles than you can do to my reputation by spreading unfounded gossip. For instance, I happen to know Mr Pyke was arrested, resulting in the loss of his position in the police force. How do you think his attempt to establish himself as a private detective would survive that information being published?"

"Publishing anything of the sort would be libel. I warn you, if you print any more baseless lies about Charlie Pyke, I will –"

Caroline cut her off with a sniff. "Or what? You'll slap me?"

"I will sue you. Mr Kenneth Drummond, the famous barrister, is a close friend of my family. Regardless of whether we win the libel case, your name will be dragged through the mud. I doubt Mr Jasper Newton could afford such adverse publicity in his diplomatic career. Even Mr Thornton might quail at such scandal."

Caroline's cheeks flamed. Her fingers crept to her long sleeves and scratched nervously. "Put away your claws, Miss Penrose, and let us agree to a truce. We would make better allies than enemies. I do love Jasper, notwithstanding the brief flirtation you just witnessed. Our families have known each other for years. Jasper is a fine man. With me beside him, he could be a great man."

"I won't say anything about your brief liaison with Thornton," Grace said, "if you don't print anything about Charlie Pyke." Her gaze was fixed on Caroline's sleeve, which had ridden up with her scratching to reveal reddened skin. "Do you have a rash on your arm, Miss Davenport? It appears to be rather itchy."

Grace moved quickly, but Caroline snatched her arm away and stopped scratching. "It is nothing to concern you. I suffer from hives when under stress. It is high time I returned to the hall to find my companions, who will be worried about my absence."

As well they might, Grace thought, given Caroline's propensity to cause trouble. Grace watched Caroline prepare to leave, taking a moment to gather herself into a semblance of such innocence and faultless deportment that anyone who had not witnessed the events of the last few minutes would never believe Grace's word, if she chose to speak of it.

Caroline's private life did not concern Grace. What did concern her was that she and Charlie had been seeking a person with a rash on their skin ever since the robbery, and now they had found two such persons – Caroline Davenport and the secretary of the trade delegation, Mr Farley – both of whom also owned the type of boot seen at the robbery. Not for the first time, Grace wondered how far Caroline Davenport would go to get a good story … from fabricating a theft to actually committing one?

"One more question, Miss Davenport. Where were you last Sunday night?"

Caroline's head jerked sharply in Grace's direction. "I was alone in my bedchamber. I always write my articles on Sunday night, while the gossip from Saturday night soirées is fresh in my mind."

"I don't believe you," Grace said.

Caroline swept towards the door, with a rigid back and chin held high.

"Wait." Grace hurried after her. "Your buttons are undone."

"What?" Caroline reached over her shoulder, feeling the flap of her gown at the back. "How the devil did he do that?"

"Practice, I expect." Grace fastened the buttons at the back of Caroline's gown and straightened a telltale rumple of fabric around her bottom. "All ready to face society, Miss Davenport."

Caroline turned with a rueful half-smile. "Thank you, Grace. I am truly sorry for what I said about your fiancé. I fear that I have wielded a poisoned pen for so long, it has begun to poison me. I promise to be keep my sharp tongue in check in the future. Do come to the reception tomorrow night, please."

"We wouldn't miss it for the world, Caroline."

"Grace, why were you asking about Sunday night?"

Caroline appeared genuinely puzzled, but, even so, Grace hesitated at revealing her suspicions. However, nothing short of a direct challenge would elicit an answer. "We are ascertaining the whereabouts of everyone on the night Mr Emerson was murdered."

Bafflement turned to horror. "You cannot think I had anything to do with Mr Emerson's death!"

When Grace didn't answer, Caroline capitulated. "I had a rendezvous with Mr Thornton on Sunday night. We met last week at a footwear shop and our mutual attraction was instant. I had to see him again, to experience passion for once in my life. I assure you I did nothing more than what you saw just now, never leaving the grounds of my home, with my lady's maid within calling distance. Please believe me – Jasper will have me as his own in all the ways that count."

Grace nodded, although she was still unsure whether she had heard the truth or only a partial version of the truth. Caroline gave her one last pleading glance, then left. Grace watched the door close with a soft click, leaving her alone and tired of subterfuge. Time to find Charlie and retreat to the sanctuary of home.

Brothers Smith

On Thursday morning, Charlie walked down the hill to the city with a spring in his step. The sun had not yet risen over the houses on the opposite side of the street, but the day promised to be fine. Even if the weather had been miserable, Charlie knew he would still be floating on a cloud of euphoria, still not quite believing that Grace had not only accepted his marriage proposal, but wanted to marry sooner rather than later.

He forced himself to focus on the steady beat of his boots on the pavement until he could wrest his thoughts back to the other important matters at hand.

Finally, they were making progress. No known local cases of measles so far. And two pairs of potential robbers with suspicious rashes, crocodile skin boots, and weak alibis for the Sunday night of the robbery. Neither Farley and Applegate, nor Caroline Davenport and Thornton, struck Charlie as likely suspects. On the other hand, members of a trade delegation were no more exempt from the lust for riches than so-called lesser folks. And a travelling shoe salesman would need to procure wealth, if he hoped to elope with a bored and unscrupulous society lady.

Predictably, Detective Inspector Wallace had not been pleased, when Charlie had briefed him and DS Elliot late yesterday afternoon. Elliot pointed out the lack of hard evidence and Charlie's failure to uncover a stash of stolen jewellery. Wallace reminded Charlie that the trade delegation was untouchable.

All three men had agreed that the most likely criminals were still the dubious Smith brothers and the morose Mr Barlow, who were the only first-class passengers they had failed to find so far. Charlie had a hunch that today would be the day they would get the clue they needed.

If not, he had the strong sense that matters would come to a head tonight, at Mr Davenport's reception for the trade delegation. Charlie planned to make the most of the gathering of suspects under one roof. If luck was on their side, the elusive Mr Barlow might attend, along with the other passengers from the quarantined ship. Charlie had spent the previous evening making arrangements to set a trap to expose the robbers, by enticing them to commit another theft. With the fabulous Davenport diamonds on display at the reception, surely the robbers would be unable to resist, not knowing the diamonds were paste replicas.

Charlie had one significant advantage on his side. Because he had visited the suspects as part of the Measles Response Team, the robbers likely had no idea they were close to being apprehended. They would be getting overconfident, letting their guard down.

There was yet another reason for his good humour. To round off a memorable day yesterday, Miss Davenport's fiancé, Jasper Newton, had been grateful for the information about Applegate's desire to get the freezer ship design by fair means or foul. Indeed, grateful was an understatement. Newton had been positively triumphant when presented with the evidence of a possible case of industrial espionage. Newton explained to Charlie that New Zealand had gained a major advantage in exporting frozen meat to Britain. With a superior design for a coal-powered freezing plant, which kept meat frozen throughout the long voyage across the globe to Britain, New Zealand's meat export trade was thriving, while Australia's trade was struggling.

Charlie hadn't realised the implications until Newton told him how much the new developments in frozen meat export were worth in terms of total earnings to the country. The proceeds of a jewellery robbery paled into insignificance alongside the potential value of the freezer design, if the Australians got their hands on it. As Jasper Newton had emphasised with the inevitable allusion to cheating at sport, stealing the design was "akin to bowling underarm – it's just not cricket".

The main complication was that the reception would be the last opportunity for the Australian trade delegation to get their hands on the design, as well as the last chance to gather the suspects for the Emerson murder and robbery. Which meant Charlie, the police and the New Zealand delegation would have to have eyes in the back of their heads to keep track of all the potential suspects this evening.

Even so, Charlie approached the police station that morning feeling quietly confident about the day ahead and his plan for the reception.

Detective Inspector Wallace was at his desk, despite the early hour. His considerable bulk hunched behind his desk, with bushy grey eyebrows forming thunderclouds over glowering eyes. His reservations about the plan could not have been made clearer if he had taken out an advertisement in the *Otago Daily Times*.

Charlie understood Wallace's concerns all too well. None of them was relishing the prospect of conducting a police operation amidst a large gathering of influential people from near and far, particularly when the reception would be hosted by one of the wealthiest men in Dunedin, with the man's daughter as a possible suspect.

"All set?" Wallace growled.

"All set," Charlie confirmed. "I acknowledge the difficulties, sir, but we have a chance to catch the robbers red-handed at the reception tonight."

Wallace drummed his fingers on the desk. "You're assuming they will be foolish enough to attend the reception."

"With the lure of the Davenport diamonds, there is every chance that the robbers will be unable to resist. What have we got to lose, sir? Even if nothing happens, Mr Davenport will be grateful to have Dunedin's finest policemen guarding his valuables, and the government officials will be grateful that we brought the possible misappropriation of trade secrets to their attention."

DI Wallace was far sharper than he looked. Charlie knew his formidable brain was ticking through the possibilities. The gratitude of powerful men was not to be sneezed at, but Wallace would want to arrest Mr Emerson's murderer far more than he wanted a pat on the back from his superiors.

"I still think the Smith brothers and Barlow are more likely suspects in the Emerson case than trade officials and a society lady," Wallace grumbled. "I expect you want DC Kelly there this evening. DS Elliott and DS Weston will have to be there too. I'll make the necessary arrangements."

"Yes, sir." Charlie wasn't about to argue with one of the most respected officers in the police force. He'd worked for Wallace for a short time and had the utmost respect for his capabilities. If anything went wrong at the reception tonight, it would not be because of Wallace.

Without further ado, he and Wallace discussed the details of what would be required at the reception.

A knock at the door, some ten minutes later, startled them both. A fresh-faced uniformed constable peered around the door frame, looking terrified at interrupting Wallace when his eyebrows were locked together under a frown.

"What is it, Constable Harrison?" Wallace barked, not helping the constable's nerves.

"I couldn't find DS Elliot, sir, so I thought I should come to you."

"Elliot and Weston are chasing down a lead on the Emerson robbery," Wallace said. "A group of messenger boys who run errands for Emerson. Several of the lads come from the wrong side of the tracks, according to Elliot."

Johnny Todd and his team, Charlie presumed. Elliot was wide of the mark with them. Wrong side of the tracks or not, they were good lads, making an honest living as best they could within the constraints of their meagre resources and lack of education.

"This photograph, sir," the constable continued, holding up the picture of the Smith brothers and shuffling from foot to foot. "I recognise them, sir. Them's Lester and Lionel Ingram, from Port Chalmers, where I grew up."

Wallace perked up. This was what he wanted to hear. A couple of suspects who sounded disreputable, if not outright criminal, not an untouchable envoy and a society lady. "Good work, Constable. What do you know of them?"

"Right pair of Jack the lads, sir. All the Ingram brothers are dockworkers and thorns in the side of the local constabulary. Lester and Lionel were two of the worst. Nothing serious for the most part. You know the sort, sir – petty pilfering and disturbing the peace, mostly. Quicker with their fists than their brains. One night, Lester and Lionel got drunk and got it into their thick skulls to rob the mail coach. That little caper went spectacularly wrong when the coachman recognised them. Never seen again, the pair of them. Rumour has it they signed on as deckhands to Australia the same night, under false names."

Wallace rubbed his hands together. "Better and better."

"They came back to Dunedin to see their ailing mother," Charlie added, "according to what they told their fellow passengers on the ship. They work in the sugar cane industry in Queensland."

"Travelling first class, under a false name," Wallace said. "I'd wager they don't make their money cutting sugarcane in the fields for a daily pittance. It seems the Ingrams have become successful criminals in their exile. Mind you, it's a bit of a risk coming back to Dunedin to rob a jewellery shop."

"Perhaps that is why they've proved so hard to find," Charlie said. "The jewellery taken from Emerson's shop was unique and expensive. One robbery like that would pay for their trip and keep them in a lavish lifestyle when they return to Australia. Their mother might really be ill too. Even hardened criminals can love their mother, after all."

"Right," Wallace barked. "Harrison, draft in another constable and wait in the foyer. Is DC Kelly about?"

"Out at Port Chalmers already, sir," Harrison said. "Investigating a lead on the customs inquiry. An importer reported part of his cargo of sugar missing."

Charlie recognised the lead as the one he had passed on from Mr Quinn. He hoped that, if Kelly could crack the customs case, he would be rewarded with the detective sergeant role, as Elliot would soon be retiring. "The sugar was being imported from Queensland. Perhaps the Ingram brothers are making their newfound wealth in both directions. Stealing sugar using their connections at the docks at Port Chalmers, then returning with stolen jewellery to sell in Australia."

"Very efficient," Wallace said. "The Ingrams might be smarter than they look."

"I could go with the constables," Charlie suggested. "We'll find Kelly before we tackle the Ingram brothers." He saw Wallace was wavering. "I want them as much as you do, sir, if they killed Mr Emerson. There's still the chance that one or both of them has measles too."

Wallace grunted. "Then what are you waiting for, Pyke? Go."

When Charlie arrived at the railway station with the two constables, his heart skipped a beat at the sight of Grace waiting for him on the platform, ready to board the train. How had she known where he would be, before he knew himself?

Grace swung around at his approach. "Charlie, what are you doing here?" Rather than being pleased to see him, she couldn't even raise a smile.

"A lead on the whereabouts of the Smith brothers in Port Chalmers. Their real names are Lionel and Lester Ingram. What are you doing here, Grace?"

She pointed to three men. Charlie recognised Doctors Osborne, Carrington and Harvey from meetings with the Measles Response Team. "A local child has been reported with measles in Port

Chalmers. We're going there to see how far measles have spread and to put a plan in place. If necessary, Doctor Osborne will order the community to isolate. Nobody will be able to leave the area until the outbreak can be contained. If it is not already too late."

"I'm sorry to hear it, Grace. Perhaps our paths have crossed again. The Smith-Ingrams may be the source of the measles."

"I hope so, Charlie. It would certainly make our job easier if we can track the source case quickly." Grace gripped his arm. "I may be out at Port Chalmers for some time, if we find the disease has spread. Not only caring for the afflicted, but trying to track their movements and contacts. I'm sorry, Charlie. I hope you can manage the Emerson case on your own."

"Of course, Grace. You must do what's best." Charlie helped Grace up into the carriage, taking the seat behind the medical trio. "I hope Port Chalmers isn't put into isolation. DI Wallace won't be pleased if we cannot arrest the Ingram brothers and bring them back to Dunedin for questioning."

"That will not be a problem, Charlie. If the Ingrams contracted measles on the ship, they will have passed the infectious stage and pose no further risk. I'm more worried about the children in the town."

"Your team has acted promptly. I'm sure you will succeed at stopping the spread of the disease." Charlie hoped he was right, but he shared Grace's doubts. From all that he had heard of the infectiousness of measles, it would be a miracle if Port Chalmers was spared, and Dunedin too.

Grace didn't bother to respond to his hollow reassurance. "We need to be sure we have identified the source. I'll come with you to examine the Ingram brothers."

Charlie put his hand over hers and felt warm fingers entwine with his. "Grace, I know what to look for. Perhaps it might be better if you concentrate on the children, while I check the Ingram brothers to confirm whether they are the source of the outbreak."

“That does sound more efficient. Thank you for understanding, my love. Send us word at the local doctor’s surgery as soon as you have examined them.” Grace untwined her fingers and went to sit with the doctors, to apprise them of the Ingram situation.

Although Charlie hadn’t mentioned it, he was glad Grace wasn’t coming with them. The Ingrams sounded like a bad lot. He went to sit with the constables, so they could make their own plan.

Clan Ingram

Charlie helped Grace off the train at Port Chalmers. The two groups went separate ways. Grace and the doctors went to the local surgery, while Charlie and the two constables went to track down Detective Constable Kelly in a warehouse by the wharves.

The warehouse was stacked to the rafters with goods from ports across the globe. Tea from Ceylon, silk from China, sugar from Australia, and every manner of item from the so-called "Mother Country", Britain. Three of Charlie's grandparents had been born in Britain, but he thought of it with no more attachment than the homeland of his fourth grandparent, China. Charlie's allegiance was firmly with his own country of birth, New Zealand.

They found Declan Kelly within the maze of the tall stacks of imported goods by the simple expedient of bellowing his name. Kelly's booming voice responded from beyond a pile of sugar sacks.

"Any luck on the missing sugar shipment, Declan?" Charlie called.

Declan Kelly squeezed out between two rows of sacks. "The dockworkers aren't admitting anything, but I have my suspicions. There's a group of brothers working here who know more than they're telling. The youngest one incriminated himself when he said he'd 'never seen no rum'. I never mentioned rum, only sugar."

"Bringing in contraband rum, you reckon? Wouldn't be the Ingram brothers by any chance?"

"Got it in one," Declan said. "They're breeding like rats around here. Lenny, Lucas, Laurie, Lance and Lee Ingram. What was their mother thinking?"

"Their poor dear mama probably didn't have time to work her way through the alphabet," Charlie said, "with so many little tearaways to fend for."

“Poor dear Mrs Lorna Ingram is the worst of the lot, according to the local constable,” Declan replied. “The father, Lenny Senior, is currently residing at the pleasure of Her Majesty, serving a year for assault. And how was it, Charlie, that you knew it was the Ingram boys I meant?”

“We’ve come to Port Chalmers to look for Lionel and Lester Ingram, who are potential suspects in the Emerson robbery and murder. The brothers arrived on the quarantined ship, along with this shipment of sugar. Left Dunedin in a hurry a few years back, after a failed attempt to rob a mail coach. The Ingram boys work in the sugarcane industry in Australia.”

“Can’t be a coincidence,” Declan said. “Rum is made from fermenting and distilling sugarcane. Importing it illegally and selling it tax-free would be a nice little earner for the Ingram clan.”

“Lionel and Lester Ingram are partial to a drop of rum,” Charlie added. “Pouring it down their throats like water on the ship, by all accounts. The head steward was not amused. Said it was a strong brew called Bundle-something.”

“Would that be Bundaberg rum?” Another man joined them, wearing a grimy Customs uniform. “There’s a new rum producer in Queensland, the Bundaberg Distilling Company. Only opened four years ago, but they make a potent drop from the waste molasses. Top quality rum, worth a pretty penny on the black market.”

Kelly rubbed his hands together in gleeful anticipation of a pair of criminals worthy of his time. “I’m thinking the Australian-based Ingram brothers used Mr Quinn’s shipment of sugar to hide the rum in, leaving him short-weighted in sugar when the dockworker brothers removed the rum at this end of the voyage.”

“A clever ruse, if we can find the rum to prove it,” the customs agent agreed. “Mr Quinn has been down at the docks most days calling for heads to roll over his underweight shipment. He must know he has only himself to blame for not checking the consignment when it was loaded. Between you and me, rumour has it that Quinn’s business is on shaky ground. He cannot afford any further losses.”

“High time we paid a visit to the Ingram homestead,” Kelly said.

With the customs agent, Declan Kelly and two constables to hand, Charlie was sure that they had the manpower to deal with however many of the Ingram brothers were lurking at home.

He hadn’t reckoned on their elderly mother, Lorna Ingram, and her double-barrelled shotgun.

Evidently, the old lady wasn’t a woman to waste time with words or threats. As soon as Declan called a cheery “hello” to the woman sitting on the veranda, she discharged both barrels from the comfort of her chair. Charlie and Declan threw themselves behind a fence and a tree, respectively, as shotgun pellets peppered the air around them. They hadn’t even made it through the gate.

“Be off, the both o’ ya,” she yelled, “and stay off my land. Don’t think I can’t smell coppers a mile off.”

A man barged through the front door of the house, balancing a tray of tea and scones in one hand and another shotgun in the other. “What’s happening, ma?”

“Get yerself back indoors, Lester,” she commanded. “Put me tea down first, numbskull. An old lady gets thirsty defending her home.”

“Yes, ma.” Lester put the tea tray down on the small table beside her. He took the time to lay a fresh napkin on her lap and pour her tea. He also reloaded her shotgun. “Anything else you need, ma? Not too cold? Would you like me to get you a blanket?”

She waved him off. Lester Ingram went back inside, but Charlie could see his shape through the net curtains covering the window, shotgun at the ready. Another shape appeared at the adjacent window, equally well armed.

“We only want to talk to you, Mrs Ingram,” Kelly called, from the shelter of the tree.

“I ain’t got nothing to say to the likes of you, copper,” she replied, through a mouthful of scone.

Fortunately, Declan Kelly had gained an appreciation for the finer points of Ingram manners via his earlier interviews with the dockworkers. He had directed the two constables to stay out of sight and move around to the back of the house. The customs agent was scouting the rest of the property for hidden brothers and illicit rum. Which meant that Declan and Charlie were now sitting ducks as the designated diversion.

More specifically, Charlie was the diversion, while Declan was the frontal assault.

At a nod from his friend, Charlie crawled to the opposite end of the fence and showed himself, with palms upturned to demonstrate his lack of weaponry. "No need for alarm, ma'am. I'm not a policeman. It's your boys, Lionel and Lester, I need to talk to. Their health might be at risk from measles, because they were let out of quarantine too early. Not their fault, Mrs Ingram. Administrative error – you know how it is with officials. Anyways, ma'am, it won't take more than a minute. No more than a quick look at their skin and I'll be gone. May I come in, please?"

Charlie kept his hands in the air, waving them as he spoke to keep her attention on him. Out of the corner of his eye, he caught glimpses of Declan moving stealthily along the fence in the other direction, keeping his head below the bushes.

Up on the veranda, Lorna Ingram was watching Charlie ramble on, alternating with glances at the tree Declan had been behind, and bites of scone. It wasn't exactly an invitation, but it was better than another blast from the shotgun.

"My boys is fighting fit, so you can take your sorry arse off my property and leave my boys alone." Lorna Ingram put her scone down, so that she could hold the shotgun on Charlie with a steadier aim. A blob of jam dropped from her lips onto the stock. She licked it off.

"I am authorised to examine them," Charlie said. He had his eye on her trigger finger and saw it tighten. He threw himself face down behind the fence, as another blast of shotgun pellets gave him his marching orders. Mrs Ingram clearly had as little respect for health authorities as she did for the police force.

While Lorna Ingram was reloading, Declan hurdled the fence and blew a blast on his whistle. The back door to the house crashed open. The two constables had made their move. Declan charged the old lady before she could click the barrel shut. Charlie zig-zagged towards her from the other direction, acutely aware of the shadows behind the net curtains. He hoped the constables were quick on their feet.

Declan grabbed the shotgun and flung it into the bushes, muzzle first. Charlie locked his hands around a pair of thin wrists. The old woman's wiry strength shocked him, but even the age-toughened Mrs Ingram was no match for Charlie and Declan combined. The two young constables came out on the veranda with grins on their faces and the two Ingram brothers in handcuffs. A clean sweep.

The customs officer sauntered around the side of the house with a bottle of Bundaberg rum in his hand. "Would either of you two lads care to tell me how six dozen crates of rum got into your back shed, without the requisite customs stamp to show you've paid duty? Not to mention the two empty crates."

"They've never seen it before in their lives," Lorna Ingram snarled. "My boys are good lads. Your lot musta planted them crates."

"Ma's right," Lester said. "We only came home to see her, now she's getting old and frail."

Frail? Charlie could think of many descriptions worthy of the Ingram matriarch, but frail was not one of them. He'd have sooner applied the term to her boys, and Lester and Lionel were by no means delicate lads. One was on the lean and rangy side, while the other was of a more solid build, but both of them looked like they could sling a sack of sugar or a crate of rum with one hand tied behind their back.

"Hold tight, Constables," Charlie ordered. "I need to examine these fine specimens." To his frustration, neither brother showed the least trace of a fading measles rash or peeling skin. Could the rash have faded so fast?

"Where were you on Sunday night?" Charlie asked, not expecting a straight answer.

"At home, with ma and half the town," Lester answered. "Ask anyone around here, copper. If the neighbours weren't at the shindig, they sure heard it. A few of the lads had a bit much Bundy to drink. Local coppers had to arrest Lionel here and a few others. All on record."

"Drunk on Bundy, were they?" the customs agent said. "Would that be the Bundaberg rum you've never seen before in your life? The two dozen empty bottles sitting beside the back door?"

"Coppers planted it there," Lorna Ingram groused, but her heart wasn't in the lie. She was smart enough to know when the game was up, no doubt from long experience.

Lester wasn't about to give up. "The rum ain't ours. A man by the name of Quinn got talking to us on the ship and asked if we would store some crates for him for a fee."

"Save your tall tales for the magistrate," the customs agent replied. "You're under arrest."

Charlie and Kelly left the other officers to deal with the formalities of arresting Lester and Lionel Ingram, while they went inside to turn the house, and the outhouses, upside down.

Although they found a pair of the crocodile skin boots, untouched in their original box, there was no sign that the brothers owned an expensive black overcoat, black cashmere scarf and dark cloth hat. Indeed, the entire household seemed to have an overwhelming preference for brown. Brown tweed caps, brown cotton dungarees, brown wool overcoats, and brown homespun scarves. Mrs Ingram had as little imagination when it came to clothes as she did in choosing names for her brood.

Nor was there a stash of jewellery. Not even a measly watch or trinket worth having. The only clock in the entire house had stopped at two twenty-five one day and ticked no more. An enterprising spider had made a web between the hands. Whatever schemes the Ingram clan ran, it hadn't made them rich.

"Darn it," Charlie grumbled. "The Ingram brothers were our most plausible suspects for the Emerson murder and robbery."

Declan slapped Charlie on the back. "Never mind, my friend. You've helped me crack the illegal alcohol importation case. Might even get me that promotion to detective sergeant."

"I hope so, Declan. You deserve it," Charlie replied. "Do you mind if I leave you to it? I want to tell the Measles Response Team that the Ingrams are definitely not the source of measles. Then I'd better get back and tell Wallace the bad news, that we've no evidence of the Smith-Ingrams being involved with the robbery. Your boss will not be pleased."

"Good luck with that, Charlie." Declan grinned at him. "Before you go – aren't you forgetting something important?"

Charlie patted his pockets and racked his brain. "Not that I know of."

"You haven't told me what Grace said. Did she take leave of her senses and agree to marry a lowly policeman turned private detective?"

Now it was Charlie's turn to grin. "Of course she did, Declan. How could you doubt it? Grace is a smart woman. I'll be asking Alistair Stewart to be my best man, but I would be honoured if you would be my groomsman."

The two men dispensed with back-slaps and went straight for a manly embrace.

Charlie knew Declan was only teasing him, but the truth was that Charlie hardly believed it himself. No matter how strong their relationship, he had always wondered if Grace would eventually come to her senses and cast him aside, in favour of one of the eager queue of gentlemen with more to offer. A passing moment of youthful passion, before Grace settled into a dull but secure marriage, like Caroline Davenport.

Despite his failure to find the robber with the measles rash, Charlie left the Ingram house whistling a jaunty sea shanty about barrels of rum and pretty wenches. He may even have added a little jig to his step, when he was sure no one was watching.

Old Samuel

The medical team alighted from the train in Port Chalmers and went straight to the local doctor, Doctor Kemp. He had reported the measles case by telegram early that morning.

Grace's intestines were in knots again at the prospect of their first case of community transmission of measles. A single case did not sound serious to a layman, but that was all it took for the disease to take hold, if they failed to contain the spread. Carrington's map could soon transform from a single yellow-tagged pin into a spreading tide of yellow and black.

One additional worry was causing her heartburn. Grace's friend Molly had been sent out of Dunedin city to reduce the risk of her contracting measles while pregnant. Her uncle was a fisherman in one of the small villages out past Port Chalmers. Grace remembered Molly telling her how beautiful it was out there, between bush and sea. Fate would be cruel indeed if it left Molly close to an outbreak.

"I'm afraid you're too late, gentleman," Doctor Kemp said, as soon as they walked through the door. "A neighbour notified me about the boy. She said Young Samuel was in a bad way. After I sent the telegram to warn you, I went out to examine the lad for myself. Unfortunately, he had already died. I examined his body and came straight back here to meet you."

"How sure are you that it was measles, Doctor Kemp?" Doctor Osborne asked.

"Positive," Kemp replied. "I'm old enough to remember the last outbreak. Not something I'll ever forget. Nor would I care to relive it. Whatever I can do to help, you have only to ask." Kemp passed over an envelope. "I've made a copy of my medical examination notes and the details I'll be putting on his death certificate. Samuel Wick, known as Young Samuel, aged seven or thereabouts. No birth record or other documentation of his life, as far as I am aware. Born in the same cottage he died in."

Osborne took the documents. The tension in his shoulders had eased a little at the local man's willingness to help. "We'll visit the school first. I'm afraid we may have to isolate the children and their families. Perhaps even the entire community. The locals will be up in arms about it, but we won't have any choice."

"Therein lies the good news, Doctor Osborne," Kemp said. "Young Samuel Wick never went to school a day in his life. Lives out beyond Careys Bay, just him and his grandfather since his mother passed away. I'd never heard of him until the neighbour came in. The cottage is out of the way, you understand, and the neighbour only visited because she hadn't seen the lad for a few days. The grandfather – Old Samuel Wick – never brought him to see a doctor in his life. Reckoned sea air and sun would cure far more ills than any doctor could. Poor wee mite never stood a chance. He died of dehydration from the fever."

The three doctors couldn't scrape a word together between them. "Poor wee mite" was an understatement.

Grace's heart had contracted at hearing the words "out beyond Careys Bay". Surely her friend Molly could not have been so unlucky as to have sought refuge in the worst possible place? Grace prayed that her friend had had no contact with the sick boy.

"May he rest in peace," Osborne said, after the silence had stretched to breaking point. "Did you find out whether Young Samuel Wick had any contact with other people, aside from his grandfather?"

"Old Samuel wouldn't talk to me. Mrs Dover, the neighbour, told me he keeps to himself and doesn't trust anyone in authority."

Dover! That was the surname of Molly's uncle and aunt. Grace tried to focus on Doctor Kemp, who was still talking, but panic turned his words to echoes in her head.

"Mrs Dover said Old Samuel has barely exchanged a word with her since his daughter died last year, although he nods to her in passing. Mrs Dover insists there's no harm in the man, for all that he looks like a tramp. He has an order from the grocer once a month. Apart from that, Old Samuel and his grandson survive on what they produce in their orchard and garden, along with fish and whatever livestock he has." Doctor Kemp shrugged. "I know what you're thinking. How did Young Samuel get the measles when he had no contact with other people? I'm afraid that I have no answer. Old Samuel was not about to share any information with me. I can only suppose that the lad got it from a local fisherman."

Osborne paced the narrow room, evaluating the situation. "A tragedy, but we may be fortunate if the disease hasn't had a chance to spread. We'll still need to check the local children, in case Young Samuel was in contact with any of them. The fishermen's children especially. And we must at least try to talk to Old Samuel, to find out where his grandson became infected."

"Do either of the Wicks have contact with the Ingram family?" Doctor Harvey asked. "They're dockworkers here in Port Chalmers."

"I know the Ingram family," Kemp replied. "Many's the stitch I've put in their thick heads over the years. If there's a bar fight or an incident at the docks, it'll be one of them, for sure. But, to answer your question, the fishing folk from Careys Bay have nowt to do with the dockers. Nowt but the occasional brawl, that is. The sun would rise in the west before Samuel Wick passed the time of day with an Ingram."

"Perhaps the fishermen visited Quarantine Island," Carrington suggested.

"I doubt it," Kemp said. "Aside from the fact that their living is made at sea, they are a superstitious bunch. As soon as the yellow flag goes up on a ship, anyone with any sense stays well away from Quarantine Island."

Grace knew there had to be a measles source case out there. They had to find a way to get Old Samuel to cooperate with their inquiry. If he refused to talk to men in authority, perhaps there was another way. "How old was Old Samuel's daughter?"

Kemp sized her up with dawning understanding. “I imagine about your age, Miss. The neighbour told me the daughter gave birth when she was nowt but a child herself. The girl never said who the father was.”

“May I suggest that I go to see Old Samuel?” Grace said.

“I’m really not sure that would be –” Osborne began.

Doctor Harvey cut in. “Excellent idea, Grace. I’ll come too. Not even Old Samuel could take offence at a visit from a pleasant young woman and an elderly man. All we need to do is pay our respects and find out where the lad got measles.”

“We can visit the fishermen’s families while we are there too,” Grace said. “How far is Careys Bay, Doctor Kemp?”

“Fifteen or twenty minutes along the coast from here,” Kemp replied. “I’ve drawn you a map. Wick Cottage is further around than Careys Bay, but not far. However, I must warn you, Miss Penrose, Old Samuel and his cottage are not for the faint-hearted. Few men would have the stomach for it, let alone a young lady like yourself.”

“Your warning is well intended, I am sure, Doctor Kemp,” Harvey replied, “but Miss Penrose is no wilting violet. She has worked with her great-aunt at Lavender House, in the heart of the Devil’s Half Acre, for several years. She is also employed as an assistant to the police surgeon.”

Kemp pushed his spectacles up his nose to examine this odd girl more closely. “Well, well. In that case, Miss Penrose might be exactly the right lass for the job. You may take my pony and trap, which I left standing ready in the back garden.”

It was a pleasant day for a drive by pony and trap, although far from comfortable. The track was rough, and the trap lacked springs and padded seats. Once they left the township of Port Chalmers, Grace and Doctor Harvey were treated to a splendid view of Otago Harbour.

Not that Grace spared much thought for the natural beauty of the surrounds. She tried to ignore a rising dread at the possibility of the pregnant Molly Ravenwood being exposed to measles, by concentrating on how best to gather the necessary information from the fearsome sounding Old Samuel.

At Careys Bay, a scattering of mooring buoys bobbed on deep-blue water, suggesting a small but thriving fishing industry. The tranquil scene was marred by the smell of fish offal. Hardly the "fresh sea air" of Old Samuel's failed measles cure.

They continued around the point, close up against the sea on one side and the bush on the other. The Dover's house was as Doctor Kemp described, right beside the road, well within hearing range of the soothing lap of waves on the shore. It would be a wild place in a storm.

Mrs Dover was out in the garden, thinning carrots.

Grace jumped down from the trap and hurried to the fence. "Morning, Mrs Dover. You're Molly Ravenwood's aunt, aren't you? I'm Molly's friend, Grace Penrose."

Mrs Dover stuck her fork into the ground and came over, brushing dirt from calloused hands. "Good morning to you, Miss Penrose. I'm afraid you have had a wasted journey. Our Molly got as far as the station at Port Chalmers, then turned around and went home. She sent me a note. Couldn't bear to be away from her husband, she said. Newly wedded bliss is a fine thing, is it not?"

"It certainly is, Mrs Dover," Grace said, with heartfelt agreement. Molly had always impressed Grace with her loyalty and determination, no matter the odds, but Grace had never been more grateful for it than today. "A fortunate escape, as it turns out."

Grace gave her the sad news about Young Samuel Wick's death and explained their mission. Although sympathetic, Mrs Dover could add little further information. According to her, Young Samuel never played with the local lads, who were few in number and put to work at a young age. Despite his youth, Young Samuel helped his grandfather with his work, tended the garden, and went out on the fishing boats when they needed an extra hand. The only visitors to the house were herself, the grocer's boy (whose last delivery had been three weeks ago), and a couple of fishermen, who had fished these waters since Old Samuel was a lad.

"You'll not understand," Mrs Dover said, "a well-to-do young lady like you. The Wicks are odd folk, even by local standards. The boy was born on the wrong side of the blankets, o' course. His mother were a fey lass. There's them as says no man would go near her and the devil must have put her with child. Only fifteen, she were. And then there's Old Samuel's work, you see. Ordinary folk find it … well, *unnatural*. But I never mind 'em. The Wicks may keep to themselves, but there ain't no harm in 'em."

"Unnatural" was an odd word to apply to work, unless Samuel dabbled in the dark arts. The misgivings Grace harboured at volunteering to visit Old Samuel swelled into a deeper foreboding, but it was too late to back out now. "What type of work does Old Samuel do?"

Mrs Dover wrinkled her nose. "Oh, you'll find out soon enough, lass. Come to think of it, another man does visit from time to time with a cart, to pick up his handiwork." She opened the gate and cut a handful of the daffodils planted in front of the fence. "Take some daffs, love. Old Samuel's daughter, Flora, did love 'em. You'll find the cottage up a short track, if you take the turning by the old milk churn, half a mile down the road. Tell Old Samuel I'll bring him around a bit of stew for his dinner."

Grace thanked her and bade her farewell.

Mrs Dover leaned on the gate. "Give my love to Molly when you see her next. Tell her I've finished knitting the baby booties. Oh, I don't suppose … could you take 'em to Molly?" She trotted back to the house and reappeared a moment later.

The baby booties looked impossibly tiny and delicate in the palm of Grace's hand. She had to fight past a lump in her throat to thank Mrs Dover. "How lovely. Molly will be so pleased."

Doctor Harvey helped Grace back into the trap without speaking. He flicked the reins.

A subtle change in the air warned them of Wick's cottage before they saw it. Dilapidated was the first word that came to Grace's mind, followed in short order by wild and unwelcoming. Instead of the tiny, squat fishing cottage she had imagined, the cottage rose tall and broad beyond the cluster of twisted ngaio trees that sheltered it from the sea.

Grace helped the elderly Doctor Harvey down from the trap and tied the pony to the broken fence, knee high in rank grass. Was it her imagination, or did the pony give her a "rather you than me" look as they made their way towards the overgrown path?

Old Samuel must have heard the creak of the gate, because he met them before they got as far as the house. He crossed his massive arms across a barrel chest and glared at them. Eyes of sea glass, lank hair, full beard, rotten teeth, skin as tanned as the ancient mariner. Grace had no trouble seeing why folks left him alone, quite apart from his ominous silence and pungent aroma.

She gathered her courage and stepped forward. "Good morning, Mr Wick. My name is Grace Penrose. I have brought these daffodils for Flora's grave. And for her son too, if you will allow it."

Grace extended the bouquet and smiled, not moving a muscle as she waited for Old Samuel to yell at her to leave him alone.

Instead, Old Samuel stared at the flowers and extended his hand to take them. Her hand was white and soft next to his weathered skin. His fingers were surprisingly long and agile, although criss-crossed with scars. He withdrew his hand before it reached the daffodils. Instead, his eyes met hers and his head tipped ever so slightly to the side, gesturing at her to follow. He turned and walked around to the far side of the house.

Here, the wilderness at the front of the house gave way to an abundant garden and small orchard, set within a swath of wildflowers. Grace and Doctor Harvey followed Old Samuel, in silent procession, as appropriate for a funeral. And funeral it was. At the far end of the property, high enough up the slope for a view of the sea, a spade protruded from freshly dug soil, mounded over what must have been Young Samuel's body. The grave next to it was an older plot, grown over, but neatly trimmed. A simple wooden cross had been erected, engraved with a single word: "Flora".

Grace ignored her misgivings at the unofficial burial and held out the flowers to Old Samuel again. He gestured for her to place them on the graves.

"May we say a few words, sir?" Doctor Harvey asked.

Old Samuel gave no answer, but he sunk to his knees, with his hands steepled in front of him and his head bowed. Grace and Doctor Harvey followed suit.

The doctor cleared his throat. "Young Samuel Wick has been laid here today, beside his loving mother, in sight of the sea and surrounded by flowers. Who could ask for more than that, in this life or the next? Taken too soon from his beloved grandfather, but now lying at peace. God bless his soul."

Harvey finished with the Lord's Prayer, which Old Samuel mouthed silently along with him. When he finished, Grace rose and placed the daffodils on the two graves. She kneeled beside the old man again, her hand on top of his. Eventually, Old Samuel got up and walked back to the house. When he reached the back door, he turned and looked at them. Grace took it as an invitation. To what, she was not quite sure.

She took off her boots in the porch, placing them down beside one small pair of boots and one large pair. The finality of death always hit Grace hardest when she was faced with tangible reminders, such as those child-sized boots that would never be worn again. It brought back raw memories of creeping into her sister's bed after she had died from measles. The cold emptiness of the sheets and the favourite rag doll lying abandoned on the pillow had convinced her of her sister's death, where words could not.

To Grace's relief, the inside of the house was not as bad as she had imagined. The hall was warm, if rather dusty and gloomy. Grace followed the sound of Old Samuel's stockinged feet padding down the hall.

The strange odour intensified as Grace neared the end of the hall. Outside, in the fresh air, she had quickly acclimatised to the smell, but inside it was overpowering. With sudden clarity, she realised it reminded her of the mortuary, a smell she knew well, but not a smell she cared to associate with a home.

The sight that met her eyes in the sitting room sent her reeling. Whatever she had expected, it was not this.

The high ceiling was hung with seabirds caught in mid-flight – dead but astonishingly lifelike. The rafters must have been sturdy indeed, for amongst the darting storm-petrels and shearwaters, truly mammoth birds soared the non-existent breeze. The largest was at least ten feet in wingspan, possibly more. A royal albatross, Grace realised. Around the walls, stuffed birds perched and preened. Glossy black tui with white bibs, long-beaked waders, waddling little blue penguins, and a giant albatross at rest.

The far end of the room housed the workshop. A fresh specimen was laid out on the bench, amidst bottles of formalin and alcohol, rows of implements, and sacks of straw and stuffing. If Grace hadn't had years of training with the police surgeon, the wafting smell would have left her stomach heaving.

Behind her, Doctor Harvey caught his breath. "Oh, my giddy saints."

Grace was revolted and fascinated in equal measure. She much preferred to see living fauna, and shared the concern of many people that men like Samuel Wick would rob the country of its entire bird life, if the greed of bird collectors was not stopped. However, she could not fault Wick's superb taxidermy skills. And, suddenly, the measles infection made sense.

Samuel was watching her closely, presumably expecting her to either faint or turn tail and flee. Grace wandered around the room, examining specimens, before returning to stand in front of their host. "Incredible. Your skills do you proud, sir."

The skin around Samuel's eyes crinkled, amidst an abundance of deep wrinkles. She had won his approval.

A kettle whistled on the fire. Samuel poured the water into a charred teapot and got out three cups. The only three cups on the shelf. Grace looked at the cup in front of her and knew immediately that it was the one Flora had used. Samuel saw her look and pushed the cup closer to Grace. She smiled at him and thanked him. He nodded and poured the tea. No milk, which was a blessing.

Still not a word uttered by their mute host.

Grace sat at the table and sipped the tea. Finest Ceylon it was not, but that was of little consequence. "Mr Wick, you have extraordinary skill as a taxidermist. I have seen nothing like it in all my life."

"Nor I," Harvey added, "And I am nearing my four score."

"Do you make your living by selling these magnificent specimens?" Grace asked.

"Aye," Wick replied. The single word was a low growl, but a welcome break from stony silence, nevertheless.

"Do the local fishermen bring the seabirds to you?" Grace knew the royal albatrosses nested at the head of the harbour, on the far side of the harbour mouth.

"Aye."

Grace sipped more of the tea. "Mr Wick, your grandson died of measles. It passes from one person to another easily and quickly, especially amongst young children. I am here to prevent other children from dying like Samuel." She paused for Old Samuel to nod. "May I ask if you have been unwell? Any rash or cough?"

"Nay."

Grace moved on to the second critical question, hoping she was right. "May I ask to whom you sell the birds?"

Wick rose and took a box from the mantelpiece. He extracted a calling card and placed it in front of Grace. "My cousin. Takes the lot." The card was inscribed with "Robert Wick, Collection Agent, Specialist Services to Museums and Avian Collectors Worldwide."

Grace made a note of the address. "Did you or your grandson have any direct contact with your cousin or any bird collectors during the past two weeks, especially a man named Barlow?"

Old Samuel nodded. "Aye. Barlow. Robert sent him here. Barlow wanted to choose his own specimens."

Hallelujah, Grace uttered, silently. If the source was Barlow, who had arrived on the measles-infected ship, there was still a chance that the disease had not yet spread in the community. "How many days ago was this?"

"At the new moon." Samuel thought for a moment. "Twelve days past."

Barlow must have come here the day he left Quarantine Island, presumably having arranged the appointment in advance through the agent. He must have been determined to make up for the time lost to quarantine.

"Unfortunately, Mr Barlow came off the ship that was carrying measles," Grace said. "Did Young Samuel meet him?"

"Aye. Samuel went with Barlow back to the port to help him unload the specimens. Took him more time than expected. Barlow was feeling poorly, so Samuel went into town to get him supplies. Barlow paid him extra." Old Samuel's face crumpled at the memory of his grandson's fatal good deed. "'Twas Barlow what did for our Samuel then?"

"Mr Barlow wouldn't have known at that point that he had the disease himself." Grace wanted to weep for the poor boy, but now was not the time. For a child who had grown up in almost complete isolation, measles would have taken hold in his body with remorseless speed. The poor wee mite really hadn't stood a chance.

"Mr Wick, do you know where Barlow was staying?" Doctor Harvey asked.

Samuel took a second business card out of the box, inscribed with "Tobias Barlow, Wildlife Artist and Avian Collectors' Agent", with a Sydney address on it. Wick turned it over, pointing to another address in pencil on the back. "Barlow rented a crib near the port. He needed space for the birds."

Grace took a deep breath and asked her final, critical question. "Did Young Samuel have any contact with anyone other than you over the past week?"

Wick's voice cracked as he answered. "Nary a soul. Nor me neither."

"Thank you, Mr Wick," Grace said. "I'm deeply sorry for your loss, but you should know that what you have told me today might save the lives of many other children. We'll take our leave now. Doctor Kemp in Port Chalmers knows how to contact me, if you would like me to visit again."

Sorrowful eyes of sea-polished blue met hers for a moment, then Old Samuel pushed Barlow's card across the table to her and retrieved the cups. The interview was over.

Last Man

Charlie arrived at Doctor Kemp's surgery in Port Chalmers to find Doctors Kemp, Osborne and Carrington knocking back a shot of malt whisky. The hands on the mantelpiece clock had moved past midday, but not by much.

"Celebrating, gentlemen?" Charlie asked, "Or drowning your sorrows?"

"A tentative celebration, Mr Pyke, tempered with sadness," Osborne replied. "The lad with measles passed away this morning. Fortunately, he didn't go to school. We checked the local children and there was no sign of measles spreading in the community. Miss Penrose and Doctor Harvey have gone up the coast to interview the grandfather of the measles victim."

A cart rattled by in the alley outside. "That will be them now," Kemp said. "I'll get my lad to see to the pony."

Sure enough, Grace was soon sitting beside Charlie, draining a glass of water. Outwardly, she was a picture of serenity, but Charlie knew her too well to be fooled by appearances. Grace had clearly been through the wringer.

Grace set the glass down. "Excellent news, gentlemen. Neither Samuel nor his grandfather has had any contact with other people since he became infected. We also found the source of measles. It's Tobias Barlow, the bird collector, who was on the quarantined ship. What's more, he has rented a cottage in Port Chalmers, so we may be able to catch him today."

"I cannot believe you persuaded Old Samuel to talk," Doctor Kemp said. "I counted myself fortunate to have convinced the man to allow me to see his grandson's body. He spoke not a word to me. If glowering was a sport, he'd be polishing the champion's trophy."

Doctor Harvey chuckled. "Old Samuel was no match for the charms of Miss Penrose and a bunch of daffodils."

Charlie could well believe it. "I have good news too. The other possible source, the Ingram brothers, showed no sign of measles. We've examined everyone else from the quarantined ship now, so Barlow is the only remaining suspect from the ship who could be the robber with a measles rash."

"If it was a measles rash and not eczema or hives," Grace added. "We need to find Barlow either way, to establish who else he has been in contact with since he was released from quarantine."

Charlie stood up and offered his arm to Grace. "Miss Penrose and I will deal with Barlow. We'll report back to you at the medical school later this afternoon."

Less than a quarter hour later, with the help of friendly locals, Charlie and Grace found the right place. Barlow had rented a small cottage, tucked behind trees in a quiet spot well away from the main road, to the south of the port. A perfect location to avoid prying eyes. The only sounds were the twittering of silvereyes and the rhythmic swoosh of waves breaking on a nearby shore.

They circled the building, but the drawn curtains prevented them from seeing inside. Only one window was open, high up, above a closed window at head height.

Charlie tried both the back door and the front door, but both were locked. He bent down to examine the keyhole and the crack between the door and the jamb. "The key is on the inside, so Barlow must be here. Looks like the door is bolted as well, so I won't be able to use my lock picks even if I could dislodge the key."

"Barlow might be ill or dead, Charlie." Grace squinted through a crack in the curtains. "No signs of life, but I cannot see much."

Charlie pounded on the door. No reply. He tried again, with no success. "We'll have to break in." He cast a dubious glance at the solid door.

“No need to batter the door down,” Grace said. “If you boost me up to the open window, I can wiggle my way in and open it from the inside.”

They returned to the rear of the cottage. Charlie positioned himself under the window, with Grace in front of him. Now he faced the problem of how best to lift her without breeching the dictates of good manners. Using his hands as a stirrup for her foot would be the most socially acceptable method, but also hazardous, especially if she fell through the glass. Clasping her around the thighs would be safer, but grossly inappropriate. Arguably, the rules of etiquette were the least of their concerns, as they were about to commit a crime by breaking into a house, but still …

Suddenly, the absurdity of his thoughts struck home. When Grace became his wife in three months’ time, touching her legs would no longer be an outrageous intimacy, whether through a thick wool skirt or otherwise.

Grace turned her piercingly intelligent eyes in his direction. “I could feel your smirk through the back of my head, Charlie Pyke. You wouldn’t be thinking of taking a peek at my legs, would you?”

“Now why would I want to do that, Miss Penrose?” Charlie replied, wiping the smirk from his lips. “I was thinking it would be best to look before you leap. Barlow could be a killer, after all. I’ll lift you up, but only so you can put your hand in the open window and pull the curtain aside, so we can see what’s inside before we go in.”

Charlie grasped her thighs, noting (silently) that the steep hills of Dunedin had done a fine job of sculpting a shapely musculature. “Ready? Go.” He hoisted her up, waiting only long enough for Grace to push a gap in the curtains and peer inside, before he let her down again.

She landed awkwardly, giving him the glimpse of her legs she had denied him. He helped her up, keeping a straight face with difficulty.

Grace brushed herself down. “Barlow’s in there. Asleep by the look of it.”

“Not dead?” Charlie asked.

“No. I saw him twitch. Drunk, I suspect. There is an empty bottle beside him. Charlie, why are you looking at me like that? Surely a brief glimpse of a woman’s leg is not worthy of such astonishment. Should I pack a bottle of smelling salts for our wedding night?”

“Grace, my dearest sweetheart, it was not your shapely calves that shocked me, diverting as they were. I couldn’t help but notice that you have a weapon strapped to your ankle. I trust you have not taken to carrying a scalpel to attack me with?”

“Technically speaking, it is a bistoury, not a scalpel.” Grace unclipped it and swung the knife open, revealing a slender, curved blade with a sharp point. “Useful for the surgical removal of organs and for striking fear into the heart of attackers, without the weight of most knives. I thought it prudent to have some means of defending myself, as I do not have your muscular physique to rely on.”

Charlie gaped at her, seemingly incapable of forming the words he wished to unleash.

“Consorting with you does present certain dangers, as you well know,” Grace said primly. “Your glare will not work on me, Charlie. You don’t know what intimidation is until you have survived ward rounds with the senior medical consultant.”

Grace slotted the bistoury back in its strap-on pouch. “Anyway, you weren’t supposed to be looking at my legs.”

Charlie recovered his powers of speech, but did not waste words protesting at Grace carrying a lethal weapon. “I cannot imagine why you wish to hide your legs from me, Grace. They appear to be perfectly nice specimens, as far as my limited experience can judge. You did get to see mine in a kilt, so it’s only fair.”

“Perhaps I ought to warn you that I also carry another form of defence.” Grace pulled a small sachet out of the waistband of her skirt. “Cayenne pepper. Highly effective as a deterrent when thrown in the eyes of impertinent males.”

Charlie clamped his hand over her wrist to prevent her from demonstrating its effect. "I hope my attentions are not unwanted?"

"Quite the opposite. Your attentions are a serious distraction." Grace ran a finger from her free hand softly down his face and neck, trailing down his arm until she got to the hand that gripped hers. Suddenly, she grasped his wrist and twisted sharply, releasing his hold. She waved her freed hand in his face, but did not let loose the pepper. "The sooner we're married, the better."

"Grace Penrose, you are the most terrifying woman I have ever met. And utterly irresistible." Charlie encircled her with his arms, trapping her hands behind her. "If I had my way, I'd get a special license and marry you tomorrow, while I am still in one piece."

Grace slipped out of his clutches. "Patience is a virtue, Pyke. I have a week's worth of lectures to catch up on tomorrow. Now, stop being disreputable and boost me up to that window. In case you have forgotten, there is a suspect in there who may need medical attention."

"Of course, my dearest, whatever you say."

Charlie thrust her up as high as he could and watched her wriggle and tumble through the narrow window. The kitchen bench arrested her fall on the other side. He winced, but she rolled off the bench and opened the back door for him, limping only slightly. By the time Charlie was inside, Grace was examining her patient, who was alert enough to recognise their presence, but not quick-witted enough to question it.

Grace reeled off her findings in her medical voice. "Alive. Measles confirmed. Post-infectious. Dehydrated. Malnourished. Reeking of alcohol. Charlie, see if there is a bath or a bucket. No need to worry about hot water."

Charlie found a rusty hip-bath in the outside laundry. He brought it into the cottage and filled it with water from a tank by the back door. "Ready for the sobering up procedure, Doctor Penrose."

"Strip him off and dunk him," Grace ordered. "I'll search the place while you administer the treatment."

Charlie did as he was told. Not the most pleasant of tasks, as his patient's clothes and body hadn't parted company in far too long and his pores oozed gin. Mr Tobias Barlow was a lamb until he hit the freezing water. The shock made him lash out, but he was in no condition to match Charlie's strength.

"Looks like Barlow has been sleeping on the sofa," Grace reported. She opened his valise and rifled through the contents. "Not many personal belongings. Nothing suspicious."

The rest of the sitting room yielded no further evidence. Grace disappeared into the other room, as Charlie applied a bucket of water to their suspect's head. Barlow spluttered and removed a leaf from his mouth. The man was skin and bones. Not a big man to start with, being less than average height and a slim build, with thin wrists, like the robber's accomplice described by Mr Emerson's son. The rash on his skin was fading and flaky, but still clearly discernible. The odds were good that they had found their man.

"Barlow really is quite the artist," Grace called. "The bedroom is filled with dead birds and packing materials. Looks like he is preparing to ship out. It'll take a while to search this lot."

"Make an initial search, while I dry our man off." Charlie grabbed a threadbare towel from the bench, dislodging a cluster of flies from their rest. He hoisted Barlow from the bath and rubbed him down.

Their suspect was sufficiently alert now to stumble over to the sofa and don a set of fresh clothes. His hands were shaking so much, it took him a while to dress, but he appeared better for the feel of fresh clothes on clean skin. Charlie found an ancient mug, black with tannin, and filled it with water. He plucked out a fragment of bark and a cicada skeleton, before handing it to Barlow.

"Drink it slowly, Mr Barlow. You'll feel better."

Barlow tipped the water down in a series of gulps. Charlie was ready with the bucket, but the water stayed down and Barlow seemed marginally improved. He sank onto the sofa and glanced up at Charlie with scarlet-veined eyes. "Has the Devil not tormented me enough, without sending a demon to finish me off?"

Charlie placed a rickety ladder-back chair in front of their suspect. "Charlie Pyke, at your service. No need to thank me for rescuing you, Mr Barlow. I must say, we've had the devil's own job tracking you down. You listed your address as the New Provincial Hotel."

"I meant to stay there," Barlow said. "Had a change of plan when your government imprisoned us on a desolate island for a week. I did ask Miss Walsh to notify the hotel, but I expect she neither listened nor cared." He held the cup out for Charlie to refill.

"Go easy on your stomach, Mr Barlow," Charlie warned, "you're in poor shape. When is the last time you ate?"

Barlow shrugged. "I've been sick. Shouldn't have drunk that gin. Not much of a drinker normally, but sometimes oblivion is the better option."

The pantry shelves offered little in the way of hangover cures. Charlie prised open a tin of biscuits and offered it as a token gesture.

Barlow nibbled on a biscuit, then took another and another. "Why are you here?" he mumbled, spilling crumbs from his biscuit-crammed mouth.

"Miss Penrose and I are part of the team following up on a measles outbreak. The first-class passengers from your ship were let out of quarantine too early."

Barlow swallowed. "Mr Applegate, the trade envoy, insisted on being released. I came down with a measles rash within two days of moving into this cottage. God is punishing me."

Grace must have overheard, because she appeared in the doorway and came to join them. "You knew you had measles, Mr Barlow?"

"I know measles when I see it, though I wish I didn't." Barlow dropped his head into his hands and let out a low moan. His eyes sparkled with tears when he looked up again. "My baby daughter got measles a few months ago, when I was away on my last trip. She died within hours of my return."

"Our sincere condolences for your loss, Mr Barlow," Grace said.

"It was dreadful." Barlow's eyes met theirs, pleading for understanding. Words followed in a staccato gush. "My wife told me about every last agonising minute of our daughter's suffering. I should have been there for her. My wife has left me. Gone back to her parents. I couldn't bear to be away again, but I needed the money to win my wife back. The entire trip has been a disaster. The worst of it is that I have lost my daughter's silver christening bracelet, which is all I have left of her. If only I could have made a proper living as an artist, I wouldn't have had to travel and my baby girl might have lived."

Grace moved to the sofa, placing her hand on Barlow's arm. "After suffering such a tragedy yourself, you will understand how important it is that I ask who you have been in contact with since you left quarantine. We need to know in order to prevent measles from spreading to Dunedin's children."

Barlow looked at her hand as if a human touch was a foreign concept to him. "I exposed nobody to measles, I swear it. I met with a taxidermist and his grandson the day I landed at Port Chalmers, but that was the day before I got the measles rash. As soon as I got the rash, I knew. I didn't leave this cottage until the fever passed. A whole week I was here, entirely alone."

"The fever must have passed within a few days," Charlie said. "You would have been able to leave by the following Saturday, or perhaps Sunday." The Sunday of the robbery.

"I didn't go out until Monday," Barlow assured them, "to be absolutely certain I would not spread the disease. The taxidermist's grandson had brought me some food, and I had little appetite anyway. I only went out on Monday because I had an appointment in South Dunedin to pick up more specimens."

Charlie watched Grace think through her next words. He knew what Barlow clearly didn't know – that the infectious phase started before the rash appeared. He hoped Grace would go easy on the man over Young Samuel's death, after all that Barlow had been through.

“You made exactly the right choice, Mr Barlow,” Grace said. “By isolating in this cottage, at considerable inconvenience and suffering to yourself, you have saved the local population from a terrible fate. Your actions have more than atoned for whatever unwarranted guilt you feel for your absence when your daughter was sick. I thank you.”

Barlow allowed tears to flow freely, while his body trembled with repressed emotion. The trembling turned to shaking. Barlow reached for the bucket and emptied his stomach contents. Grace took the bucket from his hands and handed it to Charlie. He emptied it outside, while Grace washed Barlow’s face with a cool, damp cloth. Barlow whispered his thanks. He closed his eyes and lay back on the sofa until the trembling died away.

He was a pitiable sight. For all his misfortunes, Charlie couldn’t picture Barlow as one of the robbers – even the accomplice, much less the murderer. In his experience, men who had suffered at the hands of fate reacted in ways true to their character. The self-righteous railed at their situation and fought back, using any means possible to regain what they “deserved”, whether by violence, deceit or force of will. The moral man accepted that fate could deal out fortune and misfortune with an uneven hand. He worked to remedy the situation and fix any wrong for those who followed in his footsteps. And then there were those who fell into despair, who numbed the pain with gin, rather than fixing the problem.

Grace stood up and jerked her head towards the other room.

Charlie rose and followed. “Thank heavens Barlow had the sense to isolate himself when he became ill.”

“We’ve been fortunate, as far as the spread of measles is concerned.” Grace pulled Charlie into the room and closed the door. “I feel sorry for Barlow, after his series of misfortunes. No wonder his shipmates described him as morose. He must be the man who visited Fanny at the brothel on Monday night. Seeking human contact wherever he could find it, I expect.”

“It cannot have helped his melancholy state of mind to be thrown back out on the street – unwelcome even at a brothel.”

“We cannot allow our pity for him to cloud our judgement, Charlie. He matches the description of the robber’s accomplice.”

“I don’t think Barlow is capable of being one of the robbers, Grace.”

“No? Then you’d better see what I found.”

Birds

The bedroom was an extraordinary sight. Charlie had never seen so many stuffed birds in one place, incongruously perched on the bed and floor. An enormous royal albatross stared at him with beady eyes, surrounded by a bizarre mix of penguins, kiwi, tui, and other birds. In one corner, Barlow had set up an easel, with a half-finished painting of an albatross staring out from the canvas. As Grace had said, Barlow was a skilled artist.

The dresser held a large canvas bag, filled with dried bird skins. Their pungent smell recalled the words of Fanny Snoot, who had told Grace that her customer had a musty canvas bag with him. Charlie inspected the skins and found them labelled with the name of a taxidermist in South Dunedin, which fitted with what they knew of Barlow's movements.

Charlie turned his attention back to Grace. "What did you find?"

She pointed at a box, which was poking out from underneath the bed.

Charlie's heart leapt. The box did not contain the hoard of jewels he hoped for, but it did contain a pair of the crocodile skin boots and a black cloth cap. Inside the cap, wrapped in a black cashmere scarf, were a couple of loose items and half a dozen small items of jewellery in Emerson & Son boxes. Two pocket watches, a garnet brooch, a silver locket, and several rings set with small stones. Nothing expensive, and no precious sapphire and diamond ring, but compelling evidence, nevertheless.

As he examined the items, Charlie realised that one of the loose items was not new. A gold pocket watch, engraved on the back, "To my son, Geoffrey Farley". Barlow must have either been desperate for money or an incorrigible thief to have stolen from the only man who had befriended him on the voyage. However desperate Barlow had been to buy back his wife's favour, there could be no excuse for his crimes.

The final piece of evidence was the most damning of all. The sales register stolen from the Emersons' shop lay on the bottom of the box. Perhaps Barlow had intended to steal jewellery from the customer addresses listed in the register, but had been forced to lie low after Emerson's death.

The evidence that Barlow was linked to the Emerson robbery could hardly be clearer, aside from the fact that these items represented a tiny fraction of the robbery proceeds. Charlie cursed himself for mis-reading Barlow's character. People always managed to surprise, just when you think you have them in a neatly labelled box.

Had one of his fellow passengers learned of Barlow's financial plight and convinced him of the rewards of becoming an accomplice to the robbery? If so, the payment had been paltry. Unless …

Charlie went to the enormous albatross, peering closely for signs of loose stitching. "Do you think Barlow might have hidden the rest of the jewels inside his specimens? I'm wondering if his work as an agent for bird collectors might be no more than a clever cover story to smuggle the valuables back to Sydney."

Grace picked up a penguin and shook it. "I did find a letter from a collector in Sydney, specifying exactly what specimens he wanted Barlow to purchase on his behalf. Could have been faked, of course. I haven't had time for more than a cursory search. Barlow could have hidden the rest of the jewels under a floorboard or outside."

"He still had to get them back to Sydney. Hiding them inside a stuffed bird would be a brilliant method. No customs officer would think to cut open a valuable collector's specimen. Time to interview our man."

"I'll keep searching in here," Grace said, "and then I'll have a look around outside. Remember that the reception at the Davenports' house is this evening, Charlie. We cannot afford to spend much longer here. There is still the mastermind of this robbery to catch – the man who murdered Mr Emerson."

"I'd like to get Barlow's version of events before we deliver him to the police station." Charlie took a last look inside the box, in case he had missed a sapphire ring.

The evidence didn't sit right, to his mind. The foolishness of Barlow keeping the clothes he had worn during the robbery, for one thing, and the fact that the robber's scarf and boots were far more expensive than his other clothes. But then, it was a disguise, possibly supplied by the mastermind of the robbery. Besides, everything about Barlow verged towards the bizarre.

Charlie picked up the crocodile skin boots, which were a small size. He checked the boots against Barlow's shoes, confirming that they were the same size, suggesting that the boots were indeed Barlow's. Charlie told himself he was looking for complications where none existed, attempting to find reasons to justify his poor judgement of the man's character. Based on the evidence, Barlow had to be their man.

Grace had her head down in a box of straw, which was standing ready by the bed for packing the bird specimens. Charlie returned to the sitting room. Barlow still had his eyes closed, but the colour had come back to his face and he was sitting more or less upright.

Charlie shook him gently. "I need to ask you a few questions, Mr Barlow. I know you collect birds. You purchased some fine specimens from Samuel Wick, I understand."

"A maestro of taxidermy," Barlow confirmed. He still spoke in the delicate manner of a man with a thumping headache, but his voice quavered less than before. He sipped more water, slowly this time. "The agent in Dunedin was supposed to introduce me, but time was short and I found it more convenient to visit myself, especially after I rented this cottage to be near the port. Always better to choose one's own specimens. There are many rogues in the business. A man in South Dunedin promised me prime specimens, but he'd sold them before I could get there, after I was stuck in quarantine for a week.

Came all the way from Sydney to get a pair of huia and the scoundrel cheated me. Fobbed me off with some bird skins."

"You must have a passion for bird collecting to come all this way," Charlie said.

"Dead birds! I hate them!" Barlow shook his head vigorously, then instantly regretted it. He closed his eyes and groaned, but the dizziness passed without need of the bowl. "My passion is painting living birds in the wild, free from the chains of human greed. But I need the income, so I buy from taxidermists on my artistic travels and sell them to collectors back home in Australia. I could only afford to come to New Zealand because a prominent collector paid for my journey and supplied the funds to purchase the specimens he wanted. Rare specimens go for ridiculous sums – more than an honest man can make in a year. He desired a pair of huia above all else."

"Why a pair of huia?" Charlie had never seen one himself or heard others speak of seeing one.

"They have become fashionable as a depiction of family values, as the male and female birds must work in harmony using their very different beaks. But they are dashed hard to find these days. Even with the royal albatross and penguins, I'll struggle to make a profit. I know it's a poor excuse for taking solace in a bottle of gin."

"I need to ask a personal question, Mr Barlow," Charlie said, "for which I beg your understanding. Did you also take solace in a visit to a house of ill repute, after the agent in South Dunedin let you down over the huia pair? Monday evening, that is."

Barlow dropped his head to hide his embarrassment, muttering, "How the devil did you know that?"

"We put out a warning for the local populace to be on the lookout for possible cases of measles."

"Oh. That is why she … never mind. I admit it. My life was at a low point …"

"There's no need to explain, Mr Barlow," Charlie said. "I only wanted to be certain there was not another man with measles to account for."

"I haven't been out again since Monday night, except into Port Chalmers to arrange for the delivery of packing boxes and straw. All I want to do is to go home again. If I can just get back to Sydney, my luck will turn – I know it will."

Not much chance of that, Charlie thought. "Are you going to the reception for the trade delegation this evening?"

"What reception? I haven't seen Mr Applegate since we left quarantine, and I doubt he'd want the likes of me at his fancy reception, anyway. I did not like the envoy at all and the feeling was mutual. I'm leaving tomorrow night. Now that you have all the information you need, I must ask you to take your leave. I have a great deal of packing to do."

Charlie didn't budge. "That will not be possible, Mr Barlow. You have another matter to answer to."

"What matter? I really must protest at your continued intrusion when I have answered all your questions."

"I am authorised to ask you questions on a police matter." Charlie showed Barlow the authorisation letter that DI Wallace had written. "Items of jewellery have been reported missing."

Barlow crossed his arms and thrust out his lower lip, the picture of a man wronged. "I am no pickpocket, sir, and I resent the implication. I may be poor, but I am honourable."

Charlie had been hoping to trap him into disclosing inside knowledge. *I never went near Emerson's shop* would have been ideal. He tried again. "The items were stolen from a jewellery shop."

"I didn't even know there was such a shop in Port Chalmers," Barlow protested. "I certainly did not pilfer any items from them."

Barlow must have been more sober than he appeared to sound so plausible, unless he was telling the truth. Charlie tried another tack. "The items were taken during a robbery in Dunedin city. The proprietor was killed during the commission of the crime."

That news rattled Barlow. "I … I deny any part in such an appalling crime."

"Then how do you explain the fact that items from the robbery have been found in a box underneath your bed? Items wrapped in clothes similar to those worn by the robber?"

"What? That cannot be true! I have no knowledge of such items. Please, you must believe me, I had no part in any robbery and I could never bring myself to hurt anyone, much less kill them."

"And yet the items are here and you have already told me you have had no visitors."

Barlow merely gaped at Charlie, stricken with astonishment and growing fear. If he was bluffing, he ought to receive an accolade for acting skills. "I don't know how they came to be here, I swear. I'm innocent."

Charlie hesitated. A guilty man would have dredged up the name of somebody else to lay the blame upon, such as a visitor he had forgotten to mention. "There were two robbers. If you tell me who the second man is, it will be taken into account at your sentencing."

"Sentencing?" Barlow was close to collapse now. "No, don't do this to me. I know nothing – nothing at all. I only want to go home."

"Mr Barlow, the evidence is sufficient to warrant your arrest and further questioning by the police in Dunedin. I suggest you come with me quietly."

The Trap

Grace and Charlie parted company at the railway station in Dunedin. Barlow was a broken man, struggling to hold himself upright as Charlie took him away to the police station. Despite the weight of evidence against Barlow, Grace couldn't help but feel a pang of pity at seeing a man brought so low.

Grace stopped off briefly at the medical school on her way home, to report the good news about Barlow's decision to isolate while he had measles. The team gave a weary cheer, from around a table-full of reports and checklists. Doctor Osborne confirmed there had been no other cases reported, from Port Chalmers or elsewhere.

With luck, the city would be spared an epidemic – this time, at least. Grace whispered a silent prayer of thanks as she headed home. The people of Dunedin would never know how much they owed to a small but dedicated group, who had swung into action so effectively. Doctor Osborne and the medical team had worked tirelessly, but so had Anne Macmillan and her band of door-knockers, along with Johnny and his messengers, and many others in the community. Even so, the team might have failed, had it not been for Mr Barlow's willingness to isolate himself while ill, and the sheer luck that the two Samuel Wicks lived a sheltered life.

Grace arrived home to find Anne in the drawing room with Molly Ravenwood, who was bright-eyed but exceedingly round of belly.

"Molly! How lovely to see you." Grace opened the window and took a chair at the far side of the room. "I won't hug you, as there is a small chance I've been exposed to measles. You look in fine fettle, but I have to ask – are you sure you are only six months gone?"

Molly brushed her wayward curls from glowing cheeks. "I'm afraid so. I will be the size of a barn by the time this little one is born. Rory was so worried about measles affecting our baby that he tried to send me away to my aunt's house, but I couldn't bear to be away from him."

"A wise decision, as it happens." Grace rummaged in her satchel for the booties. "By the worst possible coincidence, your aunt lives close to a boy who died of measles this morning. Mrs Dover sends you her love and these baby booties."

Anne's cup rattled against its saucer. "The sick boy died?"

"I'm afraid so, Auntie, although you will be relieved to hear that the boy had no contact with other people during the infectious period. We've identified the source of his infection too – the missing man from the ship, Barlow." Grace glanced at the mantlepiece clock. "I can't stop to talk, I'm sorry to say. Charlie and I have a murderer to catch this evening, and I'm late already."

Anne rose, with only a trace of stiffness. "I'll make sure your clothes are ready, while you say goodbye to Molly. Only your best gown will do, if the reception is at the Davenport residence."

Molly knew Grace and Charlie too well to be shocked by talk of a murderer. "Is that man of yours leading you astray again, Grace?" Molly asked, with mock seriousness. "Can't you find yourself a nice, boring gentleman to look after you without putting you at risk from wicked criminals?"

"What a fine idea, Molly," Grace replied. "However, my new fiancé might not approve of me consorting with another man, however boring he might be."

"You're engaged!" Molly flung herself at her friend, completely ignoring Grace's warning about the risk of measles in her excitement, giving her as tight an embrace as she could manage over the baby bulge. "Wonderful news, dearest Grace. Has Charlie given you a ring?"

Grace hastened to step back. "My ring is in the clutches of a robber at present. It's a long story. I'd love you to be by my side at the wedding, Molly, but I fear that you might not be able to squeeze through the church vestibule by January."

"I'll be there, even if I have to roll down the aisle," Molly assured her. "I can hear Mrs Macmillan calling. You must tell me all about it another day, after you have caught the murderer."

Grace saw Molly out. Upstairs, the maid had Grace's evening gown ready and a basin of warm water on hand. Grace sloshed a sponge around her body and threw on her gown in record time, with the help of both the maid and Anne. She added a splash of perfume to offset any lingering smell of dead birds. Anne denied being able to smell anything untoward, but Grace could not seem to rid her nostrils of the odour.

When they were done, Anne embraced Grace with unexpected fervour. "Don't do anything rash this evening, Grace. I would prefer it if you didn't have to announce your engagement from a hospital bed with a bullet in your vital organs. No knife scars on your face before the wedding either, or you'll have both me and your mother to answer to. Not even a black eye, if you can help it."

Grace felt she ought to protest, but the truth was, she didn't have the best record when it came to such things. "I'll do my best, Auntie."

Anne was pinning Grace's hair into the simplest acceptable style when the bell at the front door rang. Charlie must have deposited Barlow in a police cell with minimal delay. Detective Inspector Wallace would soon get the poor man talking. Hopefully, Wallace wouldn't miss the reception, in favour of interrogating the prime suspect.

Grace waited for her great-aunt to place the final hair pins. She offered her arm to Anne, who waved her away. Grace hoisted her hem and raced down the stairs to find Charlie waiting at the bottom, looking exceedingly attractive in his formal evening attire.

"You look beautiful, Grace," Charlie murmured in her ear.

"Not half so handsome as you," Grace whispered back. "I hope our children take after their father."

Charlie's roving hands went still on her waist. "What if they take after my grandfather?"

“I’m counting on it, Charlie.” Grace ran her hands through his hair. “If they don’t have silky black hair, gorgeous green eyes, and a sweet temper, they’re going back to where they came from.” She felt a warm rush of air on her cheek as Charlie released a pent-up breath. The prejudice he had been subjected to throughout his life must run deep indeed, if he still feared she would reject him for his Chinese ancestry.

“What if I want feisty, blue-eyed children who prefer stethoscopes to dolls?” Charlie teased.

Grace smoothed his rumpled hair. “In that case, you’re in charge of discipline.”

“Speaking of which, I hope you have left the knife behind this evening, Grace.”

“I have. I doubt I will need a lethal weapon at a formal reception, surrounded by police officers.” Grace reached into her bodice and withdrew a twist of paper. “But I have kept the cayenne pepper. One never knows when one will have to defend one’s honour against roving hands.”

Charlie withdrew his hands from her waist. “I trust you will not have need of either weapon.”

“I used the knife today, in fact, while you were interviewing Barlow. The bistoury was the perfect instrument to slit open the rear end of the royal albatross. I can confirm that the jewels were not concealed within.”

The growing smirk on Charlie’s face dissolved into outright laughter. “I wish you had told me. I would have given up a week’s food rations to witness such a spectacle. How fortunate that Miss Davenport wasn’t present. Even the threat of you revealing her affair with Thornton would not have stopped her from commissioning a sketch of you with your hand up a giant seabird’s rear end.”

Grace joined in with a chuckle of her own. She had glimpsed herself in the bedroom mirror, arm-deep in the bird’s nether regions, and it had looked ludicrous. The things a woman must do for the love of a detective, not to mention the prospect of retrieving her engagement ring.

"In all seriousness," Charlie said, when he had recovered his wits, "we ought to keep an eye on Caroline Davenport and Thornton, and the other potential suspects. Even with the evidence against Barlow, I struggle to see him as the robber's accomplice. His clothes were worn and mended, whereas the robbers were well-dressed, and Barlow could hardly be described as pleasantly fragrant."

"Barlow's mental and physical state argues against a bold robbery too," Grace said. "But how else to explain the items from the robbery in his cottage, when nobody knew where he was staying?"

Charlie handed Grace her favourite red silk shawl, his first present to her. "Let's not dwell on it now. We must get to the reception. There is still a trap to set. Mr Davenport has agreed to our plan to lure the murdering jewel thief with the diamonds. He confirmed that the paste diamonds would be on display, while the real Davenport diamonds are secure in his safe. Wallace wasn't prepared to risk the complication of the robber making off with a fortune, if the trap fails."

Grace secured the shawl with a brooch, while Charlie watched her in the hall mirror. She wished they could be visiting friends tonight, to announce their engagement, but that would have to wait. "Has Jasper Newton shared our concerns about the Australian trade delegates' intentions?" she asked.

"He has. DI Wallace has been ordered to make it his top priority. I only hope Wallace has brought enough men to cover all the possibilities."

"We may have an interesting evening's entertainment," Grace said. "I cannot believe it is only four days since I told my great-aunt I couldn't think of anything worse than attending a reception for frozen meat devotees."

Charlie had a hansom cab waiting outside. They arrived at the Davenport residence less than a quarter of an hour later, with enough time to put their plan in place.

Caroline Davenport was waiting for them near the door. She introduced them to her father, who was hosting the reception, and Jasper Newton's father. Mr Newton owned the refrigeration business that had developed the innovative machinery powering the frozen meat export trade, while Mr Davenport supplied the meat to export. Thus, both men had a compelling reason to keep the freezer ship design out of foreign hands.

Detective Inspector Wallace and Detective Constable Kelly were already present, hovering in the background, attempting to look inconspicuous. To Grace's mind, they looked as comfortable in their evening suits as a couple of bulls restrained by straitjackets. Whereas Charlie wore his suit with elegance, despite his muscular frame testing the seams.

Jasper Newton, Caroline Davenport's fiancé, took them aside. Charlie beckoned Wallace and Kelly over and made the introductions.

"The Minister of Agriculture and Trade has been briefed on the Australian delegation's desire to get the freezer ship plans," Newton said. "Aside from my father and Mr Davenport, I have told nobody else, as you requested, Mr Pyke. We cancelled the tour of the refrigeration plant today, so Mr Applegate has had no chance to view the machinery. If he wants to get his hands on the design, it will have to be from somebody here tonight. I'll hang up my wicket-keeper's gloves if we don't have Applegate run out before the innings is over."

Caroline rolled her eyes at Grace, who tried not to laugh. There were far worse passions for a fiancé to have than cricket, after all.

"The Minister has requested that I handle the Australian delegation personally, Mr Newton," Wallace said. "DC Kelly and I will keep watch on the trade envoy, Mr Applegate, and the secretary, Mr Farley, at all times. You need only point them out to us, along with anyone who has access to the design."

Jasper Newton bowed his thanks. "Ah, here is the Minister of Agriculture and Trade now. The other fellow is his senior aide. I am his junior aide. Excuse me, I must greet them. Can't keep the captain waiting when the team is about to take the field, especially when the wicket is sticky."

Wallace watched with a wry smile as Newton hurried away. "Mr Jasper Newton is rather fond of sports, I take it. Seems a solid fellow, though. Mr Davenport was eager to have us here to look after his interests, both with regard to the Australian delegation and the matter of the Emerson robbery and murder. Naturally, Mr Davenport wishes us to catch the robbers without causing any disruption to his reception or risking any of his valuable possessions."

Charlie nodded, even though he thought it unlikely the culprits would give in without a tussle.

"DS Elliot and DC Weston will arrive shortly," Wallace continued. "Hopefully, they will have prised a name for the other robber from Barlow, which will make the arrest of his partner a simple business. So far, Barlow has done nothing but deny all knowledge of his crimes. He is either very loyal or very stupid."

"Or innocent," Grace suggested.

"By the way, Charlie," Declan Kelly said, "The Port Chalmers constable confirmed that all the Ingram brothers were either warned or arrested for creating a disturbance with their drunken antics on the Sunday night of the robbery."

"Thank goodness we can rule out two of our robbery suspects," Charlie said. "Leaving Applegate, Farley, Thornton, Vaughan and Quinn to keep an eye on this evening and Barlow safe in custody. How do you want to divvy up the suspects, sir?"

"You know these men better than us, Pyke," Wallace said. "Best you keep a constant watch on the room where the paste diamonds are on display. That's where you are setting your trap, I take it?"

"Yes, sir," Charlie replied. "The main complication is the shoe salesman, Thornton. He is close to Miss Davenport and may try to encourage her to elope with him. It's unlikely, I agree, but if those two are working together, then the real diamonds may be at risk, as

Miss Davenport will know the real diamonds are in the safe, not the display case."

Wallace grunted. "I'd be booted out of the police force if we allow the real Davenport diamonds to be stolen. I'll order DS Elliot to stick to Thornton like glue and keep an eye on Miss Davenport as well. DC Weston will stay in the reception room, keeping track of Vaughan and Quinn, unless Elliot needs him. Kelly and I will watch the trade envoy and his secretary. Let's hope they all show their faces tonight."

"All the suspects have been invited. If the famous Davenport diamonds don't get our robber licking his chops, I don't know what will." Charlie spotted a familiar face in the foyer. "If you'll excuse me, I see Mr Emerson has arrived. We have a trap to set."

Wallace and Kelly drifted away, so as not to draw attention to the son of the murdered jeweller.

Daniel Emerson headed towards Charlie with a carpetbag in one hand and the other hand outstretched. "Mr Pyke, good to see you again. I have what you requested."

Charlie shook his hand. "Thank you, Mr Emerson. May I introduce Miss Grace Penrose, my fiancée?"

Emerson broke into a smile. "Wonderful news. Congratulations, Miss Penrose. I look forward to seeing an Emerson & Son ring on your finger as soon as possible. Speaking of which, shall we put the plan into action?"

The three of them walked across the large reception room to the small sitting room, where the Davenport diamonds were on display. The paste replicas of the famous set of diamonds sparkled seductively in the display case, looking for all the world like the real jewels.

Emerson and Charlie got straight to work. The carpetbag held a mantelpiece clock, packed in a stout wooden box. Daniel Emerson had removed the inner workings of the Delander clock from his father's bedroom, which had previously held the key to the safe. The broad base of the clock had been modified to take the hand-held camera that Grace had purchased the previous day. Only the lens showed at the front, cleverly disguised within the ornate bodywork. The back of the camera protruded from the clock, but Charlie hid it in amongst a row of other items. A pair of lacquered Chinese boxes, three other clocks, a pretty music box, and several other items of similar size.

Charlie had visited the house the previous evening to secure Mr Davenport's support for his plan and to prepare the display room. Fortunately, the room faced west for maximum light. The diamond display case sat in front of a set of shelves, where the camera could be put at the correct height, hidden amongst the other items on display. The reception started at six o'clock in the evening, giving them two hours of light before the sun set.

Charlie glanced up from his work on the display case. "Grace, could you stand outside the doors please, to stop people coming in."

Grace didn't want to miss the setting of the trap, but she accepted they needed complete privacy.

No sooner was she outside than Mr Farley came into view. The secretary to the trade delegation was early for the reception and heading straight for her. Grace smiled at him before she realised the implications. She had only met Farley in her disguise as a hotel housekeeper. He ought not to have recognised her and she definitely should not have let him know she recognised him.

Farley

Grace's pulse pounded as she blocked the entrance to the display room. Whatever Mr Farley wanted, she could not allow him into the room while Charlie was still setting the trap. With his eczema rash and crocodile skin boots, Farley could not be discounted a suspect. Not in her mind anyway, because she still felt that Barlow was not their man, despite the undeniable evidence against him. Grace couldn't quite put her finger on why she felt this and hoped it wasn't simply out of pity for Barlow.

Besides, this evening was about catching the robber who killed Mr Emerson Senior, which might be any of the men. Barlow and Farley had been friendly on the voyage, so they might conceivably have committed the crime together.

Farley was approaching quickly. Grace tried to appear unruffled.

Farley bowed. "Miss Penrose. Charming to meet you again, albeit in a lovely evening gown instead of a maid's uniform." He paused to gauge her reaction, allowing a flicker of satisfaction to cross his face at her ill-concealed dismay. "No cause for alarm. I mean no harm."

Grace stretched her lips into what she hoped was a bland smile. "Mr Farley. Good evening."

"It is always difficult to place a person when you see them out of context, isn't it? I wouldn't have recognised you as the under-housekeeper from the hotel, if it hadn't been for the superb photograph of you and Mr Pyke at Mr Vaughan's camera demonstration. The ladies clustered around the portrait mentioned that Mr Pyke was a well-known local detective. I did not have to be a genius to put together the implications."

Grace thought fast. "I must apologise for the subterfuge. Mr Pyke and I have been engaged to investigate cases of measles from the ship you arrived on. Mr Applegate refused to cooperate with the New Zealand health authorities, so we were forced to adopt unorthodox measures."

"Unorthodox, Miss Penrose? I could think of a more appropriate word for illegally entering a person's room."

"The Quarantine Act gives us significant powers to search and detain, Mr Farley."

"And does it give you the right to search through diplomatic documents?"

Grace had no reply. They had been caught, fair and square. Any chance they had of catching Applegate in the act of bribery had flown the coop. Worse still, Applegate might insist on raising the matter at the highest diplomatic levels. In short, she and Charlie had landed themselves in a colossal mess. Even after the furore had died down, Wallace might be banned from ever working with Charlie again.

Farley smiled. "As a matter of fact, you have done me a favour, Miss Penrose. Two favours, in fact. The first being that marvellous cream you gave me. My skin has never known such relief from eczema. No small joy, I assure you, for which I am extremely grateful. Indeed, I was hoping to see you again, to find out where I might purchase more of it."

"The skin cream is made by an acquaintance of mine." Grace took out a calling card and wrote Mr Ormsby's contact details on the reverse. She was not at all sure what Farley was up to, but she was glad to have an opportunity to distract him, while Charlie completed his preparations. "Mr Ormsby will be delighted to know that you found the cream so efficacious. In fact, he is planning to export the product to Australia, so you may soon be able to buy it locally."

Farley contemplated the card, before slipping it into his pocket. "Is he indeed? Well, that is interesting. You see, I will soon be out of a job. I was planning to join my brother in his photographic studio, but I must say I rather fancy the prospects of becoming an agent for the skin cream in Australia."

"Out of a job?" Grace queried.

"I am an honest man, Miss Penrose. I serve my country with pride, but I draw the line at using dishonest means to advance our success. That is the second favour you have done for me. Your search of our hotel suite made me see that exposure was imminent. I wish to make a statement to the New Zealand authorities."

Whatever Grace had expected from Farley, it was not this. Nevertheless, it would serve their cause admirably. She told Farley to wait, while she went to inform Jasper Newton. Newton gathered his entire entourage, including his father, the Minister, the senior aide and the policemen. Together, they converged on the diamond display room. Grace only had enough time to knock before they entered.

Charlie stepped back from the display case with the speed of a boy being found with his hand in the sweet jar. Fortunately, he and Mr Emerson had finished their work. Daniel Emerson departed with a bow and a satisfied smile.

Once the door was closed, Mr Farley calmly admitted that the Australian trade delegation had arranged for the design of the meat freezing plant to be handed over this evening, for the payment of a substantial sum. He did not ask for immunity from the consequences, but he was given that reassurance, regardless.

"Which person is responsible for this outrage?" the Minister demanded.

Farley turned to the senior aide. "Do you wish to confess, sir?"

The senior aide flicked a glance at the door, but DC Kelly stood there with his arms crossed over his broad chest. The aide lifted his head and looked the Minister in the eye. "It is true, sir. Applegate offered a great deal of money. I'm ashamed to say I have made several unfortunate wagers lately, which have left me in an embarrassing financial predicament. But that is no excuse. I can only tender my profound apologies, sir, along with my immediate resignation. I beg you to consider the effect of a criminal prosecution on my reputation and that of our country."

Mr Newton's father, whose company stood to lose the most from the duplicity, had turned a deep purple. "Throw this man in a cell, Inspector, before I do something I might regret."

Wallace stepped to the aide's side and addressed his remarks to the Minister of Agriculture and Trade. "Might it not be best if the Australian trade envoy is caught in the act of bribing a trade official, sir? That is, if this man can be trusted to play his role without giving the game away."

"I'll do anything, sir," the senior aide pleaded.

"Agreed," the Minister said, with unabashed glee. "If you play your cards honourably and Applegate is caught, I will not press for your prosecution. There is a far greater goal at stake. Catching Applegate in the act will prove excellent leverage for negotiating an exceptional agricultural trade deal with Australia. Newton, I'll want you by my side as the new senior aide."

"Yes, sir," Jasper said. "You can rely on me to step up to the crease and put on a good score, sir."

And thus, a new game was afoot.

When the room cleared of people, Grace realised that Farley had stayed behind, near the display case. He had a way of remaining inconspicuous. Perhaps it was in the nature of a secretary, to be there when needed, while remaining unseen.

"We owe you a debt, Mr Farley," Charlie said. "Perhaps I might partially repay it by returning your watch, which we discovered during our investigations."

Farley stared with stunned disbelief at the gold pocket watch in Charlie's hand, before he took it with both hands. "I'm not sure I would care to know where you found this, but I thank you, with my deepest gratitude. My father gave me this watch shortly before he died. Having it back means more to me than any number of concessions on frozen lamb export quotas."

"Our pleasure," Charlie said. "And now, I must ask you to leave, Mr Farley, as we have other business to attend to."

"If you are trying to set a trap with that camera," Farley said, "I would suggest that you alter the angle of the fishing line you have attached to the display case. You'll need better lighting too, if you are to get a decent photograph. Here, allow me."

Charlie was stumped for a reply, so Farley made adjustments to the set-up. When he was satisfied, he went over to the window and pulled the drapes fully to the sides, tying their sashes tightly, to let in more light.

"My brother is a photographer, you see," Farley said. "You cannot take a good photograph without the right light and careful set-up. Don't listen to that charlatan, Mr Vaughan. Well-designed hand-held cameras have their place for capturing people out of doors, but the quality of the images is inferior to a professional's camera, especially indoors. As for his pantomime of photographing acrobats in action – laughable, totally laughable."

"But the photographs at Vaughan's camera demonstration were wonderful," Charlie said.

"They were indeed," Farley agreed, "and I would wager my last shilling that Vaughan took most or all of those photographs with a studio camera. We've had problems in Australia with travelling salesmen hawking the lower quality types of cameras and disappearing with the proceeds before the complaints roll in. You should keep an eye on Vaughan. I believe his charming manner hides a deep vein of deception. I'm fairly certain he was cheating at cards on the ship, a sure sign of an unscrupulous character, in my opinion."

"Thank you for your advice," Charlie said, "and for your honesty."

Farley dipped his head in acknowledgement.

"May I ask you one more question before you go?" Charlie said. "Do you know where one of your fellow passengers is staying? Mr Barlow."

“I don’t,” Farley replied. “Barlow was not much of a talker, although I tried to engage him in conversation from time to time. He spoke about birds and painting, mostly. Pointed out some rather splendid species while we were stuck on the island. Birdwatching has never been of the slightest interest to me before, but I must say he made it sound fascinating. Barlow might lack social graces, but he is a decent fellow in his own way. Not the type of man who would cheat at cards, despite his obvious financial need.”

Farley left the room, looking happier with the confession off his conscience and his watch tucked safely in his waistcoat pocket.

Grace was feeling a fool, now that she realised Vaughan had taken the marvellous portrait photograph of them with the full-sized studio camera he had set up in advance, not the hand-held camera. No wonder he had them look at each other, rather than the camera. Grace had no cause for complaint, as she had bought the hand-held camera at a low price and received several lovely photographs into the bargain. But she still felt annoyed at his deception, especially as Vaughan would now be using their image at every port of call to sell more of his cameras.

“Let that be a lesson to us,” Charlie said. “Never trust a charming salesman. Although I did think the photographs Vaughan took on board the ship were of impressive quality. Farley might be judging Vaughan’s products harshly, in light of his brother’s interests in professional photography. Farley’s poor assessment of Vaughan’s character was interesting, though, don’t you think?”

“Honestly, Charlie, after this case, I feel like I cannot trust anyone, except you.”

“And Wallace, Kelly, all our friends and family, and the vast majority of our fellow citizens. Even Farley was on the side of right and honour, in the end. Don’t look so dejected, Grace. It is time for us to hunt a killer. At least we can rule out Applegate as the mastermind of the robbery, assuming he would not be stupid enough to commit two different crimes in one trip.”

“Does that mean you have ruled out Farley as a robber, too?” Grace asked.

"Not entirely. Farley strikes me as a much cleverer man than he appears at first glance. I have to question his motives for revealing Applegate's plot to secure the freezer design. Was it purely out of honour? Or is Farley intending to use the diversion of Applegate's capture this evening as a cover for his other activities? Securing himself a small fortune in jewellery to compensate for losing his job, perhaps. If so, we are sunk, as Farley knows we are setting a trap."

"Farley was the one man who was friendly with Barlow on the voyage," Grace said. "If we concede that the evidence points to Barlow as the accomplice, Farley could still be the murderer."

"I agree, even if I don't think it is likely," Charlie said. "Farley appeared to be telling the truth about not knowing where Barlow was staying, and I cannot see either man as a cold-blooded killer. However, we cannot afford to make a mistake. Can you wait here, Grace, while I find Declan? I want to warn him to keep a close eye on the meek secretary."

As soon as Charlie opened the door, a stream of guests drifted into the display room to view the famous Davenport diamonds. Charlie had set up furniture as a barrier to prevent anyone accessing the rear side of the display case, so the trip-wire would not be visible or prematurely tripped.

Grace sat on a chair to observe the throng of elegantly dressed guests. After a busy day, she had no need to feign her desire to take the weight off her feet.

The first of the first-class passengers to enter the room was Mr Quinn, the sugar importer. To Grace's surprise, Mr Quinn was not escorting his wife, but a woman who looked vaguely familiar. Grace churned the woman's face through her memory until she found a match. As Mr Farley had rightly said, it was difficult to recognise a person out of context, especially in very different clothes. In fact, her whole demeanour had transformed.

The woman with Quinn was Beth Greenway, Vaughan's assistant at the camera demonstration. Beth had swapped the demure clothes she'd worn at the demonstration for a stunning evening gown. Indeed, the former shop girl looked every inch the lady, in emerald green silk and a sparkling necklace, with her hair piled atop her pretty head. Gone was the theatrical powder and rouge, replaced by a layer of a more natural colour, which subtly enhanced her features. Miss Greenway wore the gown, the jewels, and the attention of her admirer with the self-assurance of a woman who felt she deserved no less.

Who was this woman who had passed herself off as a local shop-girl? And why was she on such intimate terms with Mr Quinn, a married man? The adoring way Quinn looked at her eliminated the possibility of Beth Greenway being a casual acquaintance.

Grace waited until Beth and Quinn had their fill of gazing at the diamonds. She followed the pair as they left, passing Charlie on his way back into the room. Grace hurried to catch up. "Good evening, Mr Quinn. May I talk to your companion for a moment?"

Quinn relinquished his companion's arm with a bow. He wandered away, stopping to talk to Mr Thornton. Mrs Quinn was sitting alone at the far side of the large reception room, watching her husband's movements with narrowed eyes and a resentful pout.

Grace took Beth's arm and led her to a quieter spot. "Miss Greenway, I did not expect to see you here, least of all in the company of Mr Quinn."

Beth jerked when Grace said her name, presumably because she did not expect to be recognised as the camera assistant. Her eyes never stopped moving around the crowded reception room, but she avoided Grace's gaze. "A shop girl has to make the best of her opportunities, Miss Penrose. If you will excuse me, I have to go."

Grace grabbed her wrist to prevent her from leaving, but Beth jerked her arm free and hurried across the room towards the exit. Or perhaps towards Mr Vaughan, who had just entered the room.

Mr Quinn intercepted Beth before she reached her goal. From their gestures, Quinn was trying to convince her of something and Beth was reluctant to comply. Grace was too far away to overhear what they were discussing, and she doubted Beth would talk in front of her, anyway. Indeed, Grace had the feeling that if she attempted to approach her again, Beth would flee. She tried to catch the eye of

Declan Kelly, who was standing by the door, but he failed to see her wave.

Grace wasn't completely sure what was going on, but her suspicions were running rampant. She had taken a closer look at Beth's face while they had exchanged words and was fairly certain that her face powder had been laid on thick to conceal as well as to enhance. Between Beth's high neckline, long sleeves and gloves, there had been no opportunity to see any other part of her skin. Until Grace had grabbed her wrist and pulled her glove down, exposing a glimpse of blotchy, peeling skin – the last remnants of a measles rash.

Before Grace could decide what to do, a surge of new arrivals hid Beth Greenway and Mr Quinn from Grace's view. The reception room was filling fast, creating a rainbow swirl of ladies amidst the black and white of the gentlemen. Bland-faced servants circulated, carrying trays laden with crystal glasses. The drinks were snapped up by eager hands, the alcohol lubricating the swell of chatter until Grace struggled to hear herself think.

Not wanting to lose track of the persons of interest, Grace carved a path through the throng, dodging trays of canapés. She spotted the charming shoe salesman, Thornton, who stood close to Mrs Quinn, causing her to titter and blush behind her fan. The camera salesman, Vaughan, was chatting amiably with Caroline Davenport and Jasper Newton. The trade secretary, Farley, was keeping a low profile, talking to an unknown person behind a potted palm, studiously avoiding his boss, Applegate, who was pontificating to Mr Davenport. The senior aide to the Minister stood nearby, doing a poor impression of a man at ease. The Minister and Mr Newton Senior watched on, knocking back whisky without talking.

When Grace found Beth Greenway again, she was still being cajoled by Mr Quinn, with Mr Thornton and Caroline Davenport now supporting him. Beth nodded her head, albeit reluctantly. Thornton clapped his hands and called for silence, allowing Caroline to announce that there would be a musical interlude, before the speeches commenced.

Mr Quinn guided his companion with a firm hand to the piano, while Beth's gaze darted around the room, as if looking for an escape route. Quinn sat at the piano and began to play. As soon as the first chord was struck, Beth's reluctance vanished. With a gracious curtsy to the audience, Beth puffed up her lungs and launched into song, captured by the spell of music.

Grace cursed her blindness for not making the connection before, even though she had thought that Beth Greenway had done an exceptional job at the camera demonstration, for a shopgirl who had supposedly only been hired two days previously. Grace had even reflected that Beth ought to be on stage. Now, as her lovely voice melded perfectly with Quinn's, Grace knew they had sung this song together before. Yet Beth Greenway did not match the photos Mr Vaughan had taken of the ship's acknowledged diva, Miss Elsie Walsh.

Mrs Quinn was glaring at the singers. When Grace took the seat beside her, she vented her anger. "That girl had her eyes on my husband ever since she boarded the ship. Mr Quinn does love his music, and he is a fool for a pretty face. If he took as much interest in his business, it wouldn't be failing. He thinks I don't know that he bought the little hussy those expensive boots, but I'm no fool. Made from crocodile skin – vulgar, just like her."

"What is the girl's name, Mrs Quinn?" Grace asked, although she was sure she knew the answer.

"Lucy Labelle is what she calls herself, but I very much doubt it is the name she was born with. A fancy name for a cheap strumpet, if you ask me. She was the one who allowed that third-class brat onto the first-class deck. Serve her right if she got measles. She had no right to expose the rest of us to disease."

"I was told that Lucy Labelle had gone back to Australia with Elsie Walsh." Grace knew that Charlie, ever suspicious, had made sure the police checked with the shipping company. They had been told that Miss Walsh had changed both women's tickets to an earlier return voyage. Evidently, Lucy Labelle had deserted the marvellous Elsie Walsh at the last minute.

Mrs Quinn sniffed. "That's what I heard too. Miss Walsh was a proper lady with genuine talent. I cannot believe the Labelle girl abandoned her mistress to travel alone, much less had the gall to show her painted face here this evening."

Mrs Quinn clearly hadn't recognised her as Beth Greenway, the assistant from the camera demonstration. Who would, with her radical change in appearance? The question was, which of the men was she really in partnership with, and for what purpose? Her temporary employer, Mr Vaughan? The attractive but rakish Mr Thornton? Or her wealthy admirer, Mr Quinn? Although Quinn was probably not as wealthy as he made out, if his business was failing. Any of them might be greedy enough to steal from Mr Emerson, to feather their nests.

Grace excused herself and hurried over to Charlie, who was now standing at the door to the room where the diamonds were on display. One glance inside showed why. The display room was empty. Every guest was captivated by the singing.

"Charlie, we have a new suspect," Grace whispered. "The woman singing is Lucy Labelle from the ship. She's had measles – I've seen the rash – and she is the same woman who passed herself off as Beth Greenway, the assistant to Vaughan at the camera demonstration."

Charlie let out a long breath. "Brilliant work, Grace. With Barlow pegged as the most likely accomplice, I thought Vaughan must have been the mastermind of the robbery. But now, Miss Labelle could be the accomplice with the measles rash, working for Vaughan."

"There's more, Charlie. Mr Quinn is enamoured with Lucy Labelle and gave her a pair of the crocodile skin boots, which he told me he had bought for his wife. According to Mrs Quinn, her husband's business is failing, which gives him motive to commit robbery."

"Thornton sang the praises of Lucy Labelle's singing on the ship too," Charlie said. "His dealings with Caroline Davenport suggest he cares little for a lady's reputation. Perhaps I have underestimated him too. I thought Thornton was only after Caroline's wealth, which was a much easier and less risky path to success than robbery."

Grace looked around the room, searching for the mixing and mingling suspects. "It's like one of those country dances where one is continuously being spun around and finding oneself faced with a new partner. Talking of which, where are Miss Davenport and Mr Thornton?"

Charlie used his superior height to scan the room. "They were here a minute ago and now they're gone. Curse it, they've used the singing as a diversion to escape. Grace, stay here by the door. Alert one of the policemen if any of our suspects goes for the diamond display. Shout for help if you need to."

Charlie sprinted for the stairs, leaving Grace to face a possible murderer on her own. She should never have left her knife at home.

Descent Into Chaos

Charlie was reluctant to leave Grace alone to guard the diamond display, with so many potential suspects circulating in the reception room. However, he had promised Wallace that he would keep the real diamonds safe. Mr Davenport would rain fire and fury on the police force if their operation resulted in the loss of such an expensive heirloom, let alone if his daughter eloped with the diamonds and a persuasive shoe salesman.

As Charlie reached the top of the stairs, he heard voices in a room further down the corridor. He stopped outside the door to eavesdrop.

"I don't care about the diamonds, my love," Thornton pleaded. "Elope with me – that's all I desire. My ship leaves tomorrow night. We can start a new life together in Sydney."

"Bernard, darling." Caroline Davenport's voice. "Our time together has been a fleeting moment of joy, but I have no wish to elope with you. My future lies here."

DS Elliot panted up behind Charlie and pushed past him through the doorway. He dashed across the room, seizing Thornton's arm. "Mr Thornton, raise your arms so I can search you." Elliot patted him down. "If you have stolen the Davenport diamonds, I advise you to surrender them immediately."

Thornton stared at him. "What are you talking about? I am no thief. Caroline, tell him."

"The diamonds are safely locked away in my father's safe, Sergeant Elliot," Caroline confirmed. "What possessed you to burst in upon us in such an outrageous manner? I was conducting a private conversation with this gentleman."

"This gentleman has some explaining to do," Elliot snapped. "And you too, Miss Davenport. Starting with what you were really up to last Sunday night."

"You have no right to ask about my private life –" Caroline began.

After overhearing the conversation between Thornton and Caroline, Charlie doubted they had more on their minds than their brief affair. He ran the many other possibilities through his mind frantically, then barged into the room. "Thornton, as quick as you can, tell me who tried on your crocodile skin boots on the ship. Not the people who bought pairs, the ones who tried but didn't buy."

Elliot put himself between Charlie and Thornton. "What's the meaning of this, Pyke? I'm trying to interview a suspect."

Charlie side-stepped. If someone had set up Barlow to take the blame for the robbery, then they wouldn't have risked leaving the boots as evidence, unless they knew what size Barlow took. "Please, let the man answer this one question, then I will leave you to your interview."

Thornton looked from one to the other in confusion. "Smith bought a pair first. Then Miss Labelle wanted to try them on, because she needed a pair of comfortable boots for walking. Mr Quinn was there with her. When Miss Labelle said she couldn't afford them, Mr Barlow tried them on. Oddly enough, he and Miss Labelle had the same sized feet. Barlow couldn't afford them either. Mr Quinn came back later that day to buy the boots for his wife. A couple of days later, Farley bought a pair, in a larger size. That's all."

Charlie sprinted for the stairs. Downstairs, a sudden flare of angry voices cut through the final bars of the music. Quinn hit a jarring wrong note on the piano and stopped playing. The sound of the argument was muffled, as it was coming from another room, but it was clear that Applegate was yelling abuse at the senior aide for tricking him.

As Charlie pounded down the stairs, a door flew open and Applegate burst out, with Declan Kelly hot on his heels. Applegate ducked sideways to avoid Declan's grasp and ploughed on at speed, running straight into Grace. Charlie sped down the last steps, his eyes on Grace, as she fell to the floor.

The reception room was in an uproar. Men converged on Applegate from all sides. In the middle of the melee, Grace curled up on the floor with her arms shielding her head. Applegate stood over Grace, oblivious to her presence, shouting with undiplomatic belligerence at the cluster of New Zealand trade officials and policemen, demanding his right to immunity as an official of a foreign government.

Declan Kelly tried to clear the fracas so he could help Grace, but Applegate swung a roundhouse, catching Declan square in the stomach. Wallace threw a muscular arm around the trade envoy's neck and dragged him backwards, knocking Charlie over. Ignoring everything else, Charlie crawled forward and shielded Grace with his body until the crowd parted, before hoisting her to her feet.

Grace brushed at the creases in her gown. "I'm fine, Charlie. Not even a black eye. Just had the wind knocked out of me by Applegate. He used the musical interlude to make his move to bribe the senior aide to hand over the freezer design."

Charlie resisted the urge to gather her up and take her away. If Grace said she was fine, then she was fine. The hubbub had subsided now that Applegate was under control.

Charlie scanned the room, ticking off suspects. Farley was cowering behind an armchair in the corner. Thornton was at the top of the stairs, arguing about guilt and innocence with DS Elliot, while Caroline and her fiancé, Jasper Newton, were halfway down the stairs, with their arms around each other. Mr and Mrs Quinn watched from across the room, their mouths hanging open at the chaos around them. Only John Vaughan and Lucy Labelle were missing.

Charlie forced his way through the onlookers to the display room, with Grace right behind him. The door was locked from the inside, but the latch didn't stand a chance under the raw power of Charlie's shoulder-charge.

As the door slammed open against the wall, Vaughan froze in place by the open window. The lock on the display cabinet had been forced – the paste diamonds were missing.

Vaughan teetered between hurling himself out the window and staying to brazen it out, giving his guilt away by the momentary hesitation and flicker of panic in his eyes. Charlie was across the room in an instant, grabbing Vaughan's arm before he could escape.

"Let me go," Vaughan ordered. "The thief is getting away."

Charlie hauled Vaughan off the sill and thrust his head out the window, in time to see a flash of emerald green disappearing into the trees alongside the driveway. "Grace, tell Kelly to go after Lucy Labelle. She's escaping down the driveway with the diamonds. If Kelly can't catch up with her, tell him she'll probably head for their room at Wains Hotel."

Detective Constable Weston dashed into the room, passing Grace on the way out. "I saw you break down the door, Mr Pyke. Is this the thief?"

Vaughan jerked his arm out of Charlie's grasp. "I am no thief. Mr Pyke has made an unfortunate mistake. I came into this room to escape the chaos and saw that the diamonds had been stolen."

"Detective Constable Weston," Charlie said, "I suggest you detain Mr Vaughan on suspicion of theft of the Davenport diamonds."

"Has he got the diamonds on him?" Weston asked.

"His partner has escaped with them, I believe. I have sent DC Kelly after Miss Labelle." In case he was wrong, Charlie made a thorough search of Vaughan. The camera salesman submitted without a struggle, although Charlie's use of his partner's name had clearly rattled him. The diamonds were nowhere about his person.

Charlie turned back to Weston. "He hasn't got the diamonds, but I found him in a locked room, about to go out the window."

Vaughan took the chance to move away from Charlie to the far wall. He smoothed down his immaculate black evening coat, plucking a fragment of fluff off the sleeve, a picture of innocence.

"You have it all wrong, Mr Pyke. I locked the door in case the thief was hiding in the room, but then I saw the window was open. I was about to give chase when you burst in and grabbed me, letting the thief escape with a fortune in diamonds."

"Paste diamonds, in fact, Mr Vaughan." Charlie noted the momentary widening of the camera salesman's eyes. "You and your accomplice have exposed your criminal activities for nothing more than replica diamonds. Arrest him, DC Weston."

Weston took a pair of handcuffs from his pocket, dangling the cuffs from one finger, unsure what to do next.

"This is outrageous. I have committed no crime," Vaughan protested. "I merely happened to be first on the scene after the theft. I ought to be commended for trying to catch the thief, not arrested on the whim of a health inspector."

"I'm a private detective, Mr Vaughan," Charlie said, "hired by Mr Daniel Emerson to find the pair of lowlifes who robbed his jewellery shop and killed his father."

Vaughan's mask of outraged innocence slipped a little further at this news. Beads of sweat formed on his forehead, as he plotted his next move. "You have no evidence against me – none at all."

"Is that so?" Charlie replied. "A shame for you that I rigged up one of your own cameras to capture the diamond theft for posterity. Wonderful inventions, these hand-held cameras. Simply pull the cord and the photograph is taken." Charlie lifted the lid of the display case. They all heard the faint click of the shutter, when the fishing line attached to the lid tripped the camera release. "I believe that is called being 'hoisted by your own petard', Mr Vaughan."

Vaughan wouldn't have heard the shutter click the first time because of the commotion outside, but he heard it now. His confidence drained away. His eyes searched the room for the hidden camera, which was obscured from his view in his present position. "Are you attempting to play parlour games with me, Mr Pyke? I see no camera."

Charlie waved at the line of assorted clocks, boxes, and ornaments on the shelf behind the display case. “It’s in the Delander clock.”

Vaughan darted across the room and reached for the correct mantlepiece clock.

Charlie was quicker. His hand grasped Vaughan’s before he could pull the camera out. “I don’t think so, Mr Vaughan. Can’t have you opening the camera and destroying the photographic evidence of your theft.”

Vaughan backed away. “I only wished to look at it. You forget I sell these cameras, Mr Pyke. As an amateur, I doubt you had the skill to achieve a clear image of the real thief.”

“I had expert help to set the trap, as it happens, Mr Vaughan. Besides, you have incriminated yourself. You may be a camera expert, but you had no knowledge of Delander clocks, until Mr Emerson directed you to that very clock, right before you killed him and took the safe key. His son, Mr Daniel Emerson, designed the clever mechanism you see before you. Shall I call him in?”

“I’m already here.” Daniel Emerson stood in the doorway, grasping his carpetbag with white knuckles as he confronted his father’s killer. “Now I see him again, I recognise the shape of his eyes and forehead. Without a doubt, that’s the evil brute who murdered my father. I will swear to it in court.”

Emerson’s furious certainty caused Vaughan’s faltering composure to collapse completely. For an instant, he froze, then his eyes flicked to the window.

Charlie saw Vaughan’s muscles tense, ready to run. He lunged for the window. Vaughan feinted left, but plunged right, towards the door.

Daniel Emerson swung the carpetbag at Vaughan. The combined force of Emerson’s fury and the heavy clock box within the bag knocked the killer off his feet. Vaughan landed on a Persian rug with the grace of a sack of bones.

Weston stepped in, twirling the handcuffs around his finger. "Mr Vaughan, camera salesman from Sydney, you're under arrest for murder, robbery, and theft."

Daniel Emerson glared at the grovelling figure on the floor, rocking on his toes as if he was about to unleash another blow. Instead, he turned his back on his father's killer. Emerson took a deep breath and straightened his spine. "I cannot thank you enough, Mr Pyke. I had every confidence you would fulfil your promise to catch the culprit."

Charlie shook his client's hand. "We did it together, Mr Emerson. Your father would be proud of you."

"I hope so, Mr Pyke. As promised, I will repay you with an engagement ring worthy of your betrothed, even if you do not recover your sapphire and diamond ring."

"I have every hope that we will get all the stolen jewellery back, Mr Emerson. Mr Vaughan is not going anywhere other than into a cell. He'll soon see that it is in his best interests to tell us where he hid the stolen items." Assuming Vaughan's partner in crime does not get to them first, Charlie amended, silently. He could only hope that Declan Kelly had been quick enough to catch the fleeing Lucy Labelle.

DC Kelly strolled into the room. "Did I miss all the fun while I was dealing with Mr Applegate?"

"What are you doing here, Declan?" Charlie cried. "Didn't Grace find you, to tell you to go after Lucy Labelle?"

Declan's smile vanished. "I haven't seen Grace."

Shock mingled with several pointless questions in Charlie's mind, before settling on the only question that mattered. "Where's Grace Penrose?" he bellowed.

Diamonds Are Forever

Grace hadn't been able to find Declan Kelly or any of the other policemen in the crowded reception room. The minor fracas caused by Applegate had not dented the festive mood of the guests for long. The room buzzed with chatter, fuelled by replenished glasses and fresh platters of hors d'oeuvres.

By resorting to a frantic wave, Grace caught the eye of Caroline Davenport, who was at the centre of a lively group. Caroline pushed her way through the crowd and told Grace the policemen were busy with the trade delegation incident in another room. They were not to be disturbed under any circumstances.

Time was slipping by. Grace did not want Lucy Labelle to escape, even if it meant running after the singing thief in her best gown.

Grace hoisted her hem and sprinted for the exit, trying to figure out Lucy Labelle's next move. Lucy didn't know she had been spotted, so she wouldn't panic, at least until she realised that John Vaughan hadn't followed her out the window. Even then, Lucy would think Vaughan was safe from arrest, if she had the Davenport diamonds. As far as Lucy knew, there was no evidence to link her and Vaughan to the Emerson robbery. Charlie was right – she would likely head to their hotel room and prepare to leave as soon as her partner arrived.

Grace ran down the front steps of the Davenports' house, hoping she could convince one of the waiting coachmen to take her to the hotel. She was pleading with the driver of a lightweight gig, when she heard the crunch of gravel and a commanding voice behind her.

“We need the gig now, Hopkirk. Stand aside, man.” Caroline Davenport vaulted into the gig – an impressive feat in an evening gown – and took up the reins. “Are you coming or not, Grace?”

Grace had barely jumped onto the stepping plate when Caroline urged the horse into a lively trot. Grace scrambled up and twisted her rear onto the seat. “Wains Hotel, and don’t spare the horse.”

“May I ask why you are so desperate to leave, Grace?” Caroline inquired.

“Lucy Labelle has escaped with the paste diamonds from the display case.”

Caroline jerked the reins, causing the horse to stumble. “I forgot about the jewel thieves with all the fuss around the Australian trade envoy. Lucy Labelle, you say? Isn’t she the pretty singer in the emerald green dress? But she had such a sweet face and a delightful voice. I thought she was an acquaintance of Mr Quinn.”

Grace glanced at her companion, noting that Caroline’s eyes were bright with excitement. “It’s not a lark, Caroline. Labelle is a criminal. The fact that she can hold a tune is irrelevant.” Grace should not have snapped at her helper, but Caroline was treating this as an amusing diversion, probably with the aim of retelling the tale under her Lady Detective nom de plume. “Please, Caroline, I beg you. When we get to the hotel, let me down, then immediately return to tell the police officers where I am.”

Caroline concentrated on manoeuvring the little gig at speed through the streets, with the light fading as the sun dipped towards the hills. Fortunately, there were few other carriages on the road at this hour on a Thursday evening. “You cannot face this woman alone, Grace, if she really is a thief.”

“I need you to go to the police,” Grace repeated firmly. “Don’t worry about me, Caroline. I will do no more than ascertain that Miss Labelle is in the hotel room. In all likelihood, she is no more than a foolish young woman who has taken up with the wrong man and become caught up in a scheme not of her making.”

The last sentence was intended to reassure Caroline, rather than because Grace believed the words to be true. Lucy Labelle might have taken up with Vaughan and been drawn into his scheme as an innocent dupe, after falling on hard times when the singing job at Marvin's Musicale had fallen through. She was a resourceful woman, who had a way with men, despite playing the mousy understudy to the great Elsie Walsh. She certainly had the besotted Mr Quinn at her beck and call.

On the other hand, Lucy could have formed a connection with Vaughan on the ship and been part of the plan from the start. With her slim build, pleasant fragrance, measles rash and crocodile skin boots, Lucy Labelle was a perfect fit to the robbery accomplice, who had not hesitated to hit Daniel Emerson on the head when he threatened her partner. Dupe she may be, but innocent she was not.

Furthermore, if Barlow was not the robbery accomplice after all, and he had only disclosed his location to Elsie Walsh, then Labelle, always by Elsie's side, was the one person in a position to set up Barlow to take the blame for the Emerson robbery.

The uppermost thought in Grace's mind was the need to find the stolen Emerson jewellery, which would conclusively prove the robbery case against Vaughan and Labelle. There was also the vital matter of finding her engagement ring. Logic told Grace that the ring was trivial in the wider scheme of events, but it loomed large in her mind as a symbol of the future she so desperately desired.

The journey was a short one. Caroline eased the sweat-lathered horse to a halt opposite Wains Hotel. The doorman opened the door to Grace with a bow. She walked directly to the stairs. With her air of belonging and a beautiful evening gown to match, she was not challenged by any of the uniformed staff of the hotel.

Upstairs, the door to Vaughan's suite was closed, but not locked. Grace eased it open a fraction of an inch. She listened for any trace of sound from within the room. Silence. Carefully, she opened the door a little further, silently praising the staff at Wains for their attention to little details, such as oiling hinges. Not a single rustle from inside.

Grace slipped inside the room, searching it for signs of life. A small table was overturned, scattering documents onto the floor. The emerald green evening dress was hanging over the edge of a chair, flung aside in haste. The coat closet stood open, its contents hanging drunkenly or pooled on the floor.

More importantly, the camera boxes lay strewn across the room. Most were untouched, but others had had the cameras removed. When Grace picked up one of the discarded cameras, the back fell open. The interior was hollow – a clever hiding place for the stolen jewellery. Grace had arrived too late. Lucy's first instinct had been to take the jewels and desert her partner in crime.

Now Grace would never know what engagement ring Charlie had chosen for her.

A few Emerson & Son boxes were still scattered on the floor or hidden within the cameras. Grace opened several of the boxes. Brooches, bracelets, a few simple rings, but nothing that spoke to her heart. She set them aside, in case one of them was the ring Charlie had chosen. After all, an inexpensive ring was a sensible choice, when they had to keep their savings for more essential purchases. She would be happy with any ring, really she would, no matter how plain, as long as it came from Charlie.

The bedroom door stood half open, revealing more chaos strewn across the bed and floor. Lucy Labelle had left most of her possessions behind, in her hurry to escape. The evidence suggested that Grace was too late … but Lucy hadn't been that far ahead of her. Was she still in the bedroom, hiding, waiting for Grace to give up and leave?

Grace waited another minute for the slightest sound to give away the presence of another person in the room.

Suddenly, the main door burst open behind her. Grace whipped around, heart pounding, but it was only Caroline Davenport. Stupid, brave, exasperating Caroline, who refused to do as she was told.

Grace didn't bother to hide her irritation. "Caroline, I asked you to get the police."

Caroline shrugged off the reproach. "I thought you might need my help, Grace. We can send a message to the police once we have finished investigating here."

Grace closed her eyes and counted to ten. If Caroline was eager to play the Lady Detective role, there was nothing Grace could do about it. She contemplated going down to the hotel reception to send a messenger to DI Wallace, but she didn't dare leave Caroline alone.

Caroline took in the scene at a glance. "Gone already! Miss Labelle didn't waste much time." Before Grace could stop her, Caroline marched into the bedroom. "Don't just stand there, Grace, let's search this place. Honestly, you call yourself a detective –"

The rest of her sentence was cut off by a strangled cry. Lucy Labelle had jumped out from behind the bedroom door, grabbing Caroline, pinning one arm and holding a knife to Caroline's pale throat. Lucy swung her captive around, putting Caroline between herself and Grace.

Grace didn't speak or move, although in her mind she was cursing Caroline's impulsiveness and regretting her own lack of a weapon. With the situation literally on a knife-edge, Grace knew she had to remain calm and rational. Lucy and Caroline watched her with wide, panicked eyes from the bedroom doorway.

Grace sat in a comfortable armchair in the sitting room, in full view of the bedroom, to show that she was neither intimidated nor a threat. She tried to ignore the sight of the knife trembling over the paper-thin skin over Caroline's jugular vein.

"May I ask a question, Miss Labelle?" Grace said, keeping her tone soft and unthreatening.

The sharp point of the knife moved slightly closer to Caroline's neck. A drop of blood welled up and dribbled down Caroline's alabaster skin towards her beautiful satin gown. Caroline whimpered.

Lucy shifted her focus to Grace. "I'm surprised you only have one question, Miss Penrose." Her voice was tight with tension, but far from hysterical. "I'll allow it, since your companion has failed to inform the police of my whereabouts."

"The only thing that matters to me is who you had contact with, between when you left the ship and when your fever subsided." Grace leaned forward slightly, her head cocked to the side to show she was genuinely interested.

Caroline uttered an outraged gurgle, but the benign question had the intended effect. Lucy's white-knuckle grip on the knife eased. She let out a throaty chuckle over her hostage's shoulder. "Seriously? After all that has happened, you are worried about whether I infected anyone else with measles? You really are too amusing, Grace Penrose."

"It is no laughing matter. The disease is extremely contagious. Dozens, if not hundreds, of children might die." Grace leaned back and crossed her ankles demurely. "Should I call you Lucy or Beth, by the way? Miss Labelle seems overly formal in the circumstances."

The blade of the knife dropped a little further from the lethal zone. "Lucy Elizabeth is my birth name. Call me what you will, for I will soon be gone from your life forever. As it happens, I am fond of children, so I will answer your question honestly. Once I knew I was infected with measles, I stayed in the hotel room, in the sole company of unbearably conceited Miss Elsie Walsh."

"Did nobody else enter your room at the New Provincial Hotel, Lucy?" Grace asked.

"The maid at the hotel, but not often or at close quarters. And Marvin, once, when he came to refuse to pay us a penny more for our trouble. After Elsie did her grand performance of a woman wronged, she checked us out of the hotel and attempted to coerce me into taking the next ship back to Sydney. I stayed here instead, where John Vaughan looked after me. I saw no one else while I was ill. John told the maid not to go into our bedroom. There. Are you satisfied that I am not a carrier of pestilence to the masses, Grace?"

"Thank you, Lucy," Grace replied. "For that, at least, I am profoundly grateful."

"Enough questions," Lucy said. "John will be here soon and I need to pack. Grace, you will follow me into the bedroom, walking slowly with your hands raised. One wrong move and dear, stupid Miss Davenport will feel the sharp edge of my knife."

With the blade against Caroline's throat, Grace had no option but to do as she was told. Lucy was far from being frightened. Indeed, after her initial panic at being discovered, she had bounced back with a sparkle of glee about her manner, which suggested she took pleasure in her wrongdoing.

Lucy backed into the bedroom, dragging Caroline with her. "I look forward to wearing your precious diamonds, Miss Davenport, when I return to Sydney."

"They're not –" Caroline began.

Grace caught Caroline's eye and shook her head. Telling Lucy the diamonds were fake was not the best idea when she was holding a knife to a vital blood vessel.

"They're not mine," Caroline muttered. "The diamonds are a family heirloom."

"Well, they're mine now," Lucy gloated. She had retreated to the far side of the bedroom, next to a radiator. "Do be a sweetheart, Grace, and get the rope from the bottom of the armoire. You will tie Miss Davenport to the radiator, nice and tight, and gag her. Don't try anything heroic. I would prefer not to harm either of you, but I shan't hesitate if the need arises."

Grace did as Lucy asked, partly because she wanted Caroline out of harm's way.

Lucy tested the knots. She gestured with the knife to a large carpetbag, which was lying on the floor, before holding the knife on Caroline again. "Put the clothes in the bag, Grace, as quick as you can. After you have done so, I will lock you in the bedroom and take my leave."

Grace tried to get the measure of Lucy Labelle as she shoved clothes into the carpetbag. Of the three parts Lucy had played – the subservient understudy, the demure camera assistant, and the self-assured diva – the latter was the one that rang true to her real character. Time to test her mettle.

"Turn yourself in, Lucy," Grace pleaded. "The police will see that John Vaughan took advantage of your youth and innocence, especially as you were left in such a vulnerable position when you lost the singing role. Vaughan was the mastermind, of course, so you can plead for a lesser sentence or maybe even go free, if you give evidence against him."

A full-throated laugh confirmed Lucy's disdain for subservient roles. "Do I look that pathetic to you, Grace? Honestly? Perhaps you would care to observe the names on the return passenger tickets, on the bedside table."

Grace picked up the tickets. Their ship was leaving tomorrow evening. The listed passenger names were Mr John Peter Vaughan and Mrs Lucy Elizabeth Vaughan, dispelling all doubts as to Lucy's culpability. The whole endeavour had been planned in advance, using Marvin's Musicale as a cover for Lucy, while she and her husband plotted the robbery in Dunedin.

If it hadn't been for Mr Emerson's glimpse of a measles rash on the robber, linking the robbers to the quarantined ship, the pair of them would have fled the country, very much richer, with nobody the wiser.

"You do not seem surprised that John Vaughan and I are married, Grace," Lucy said. "A woman of your intelligence ought to recognise another. John was struggling to make a living hawking cheap cameras when I met him. Under my guiding hand, we have achieved wealth beyond his wildest dreams."

"But not beyond your dreams, I think," Grace replied. "Greed got the better of you. If you'd laid low after the Emerson robbery, you might have gotten away with it. But the lure of the diamonds was too much to resist."

"You forget, Grace, that I *have* gotten away with it. You are too virtuous to allow Caroline to come to any harm, so I have won."

“Your husband has been arrested,” Grace pointed out. “Your own arrest is inevitable.”

A flicker of shock passed across Lucy’s face at the news of her husband’s arrest, before she regained control and let out a derisive puff of air. “Once I disappear with the stolen jewellery, I doubt there will be sufficient evidence to charge my husband with any crime. Now, get down on the floor in the corner, Grace, facing the wall. It is time for me to vanish without a trace.”

Despite Lucy’s promise to leave Grace locked in the bedroom, Grace did not believe Lucy would take any chances. As Grace huddled in the corner, listening to the whisper of footsteps coming towards her, she extracted the sachet from her bodice. As soon as Lucy was behind her, Grace swivelled and flung cayenne pepper into Lucy’s face.

Lucy shrieked and clawed at her eyes, dropping the knife and giving Grace the chance to lunge backwards, knocking the legs from under her attacker. Grace threw her to the floor and jumped on top, trying to clamp Lucy’s flailing arms and hold her thrashing body down. Caroline let out a muffled wail from across the room, rattling the radiator as she tried to get loose.

Before Lucy could fight her way free, the main door to the suite burst open with a shuddering slam against the wall.

“Grace!” Charlie yelled.

“Caroline!” Jasper Newton screamed.

Declan Kelly said nothing, but he did race into the bedroom with his handcuffs at the ready, which was far more helpful. Declan wrenched the two women apart, so he could clip on the cuffs.

Charlie swooped in, gathering Grace from her unladylike sprawl and pulling her to safety. He wrapped her in his embrace, whispering, “Grace, thank heavens you are safe,” although her safety might be open to debate, as he was squeezing the life out of her.

Declan hauled the prisoner to her feet. "Lucy Labelle, also known as Beth Greenway, you are under arrest for robbery, theft, accessory to murder, and assault with a deadly weapon."

Grace wriggled an arm free to hand the passenger ticket to Declan. "Also known as Mrs Lucy Elizabeth Vaughan."

Across the room, Jasper Newton struggled with the knots of rope, crooning soft words to his fiancée as he worked. As soon as the ropes and gag came off, Caroline clung to her man. "Jasper, darling, you saved me."

Jasper basked in the praise. "You're so brave, Caroline. I will be proud to have you as my wife. Let me take you home, my darling."

Caroline was on the verge of protesting, but the adoration in her fiancé's expression changed her mind. "Of course, my love. We must cherish the time we have together, especially as you will be busy now that you have your promotion to senior aide."

"Don't forget your paste diamonds." Grace searched Lucy, discovering a hidden pocket in her bodice. She retrieved the jewels and passed them to Jasper.

Lucy watched them go, sour with the knowledge that she had risked being caught for nothing more than replica diamonds.

Caroline wiggled the massive stone on her ring finger. "I have the only diamond I want, but thank you anyway. Jasper, darling, might I have a private moment with Miss Penrose and Mr Pyke?"

Jasper Newton left the bedroom, along with Declan Kelly and a shackled and subdued Lucy Labelle Vaughan.

Caroline closed the door. "I owe you both much more than an apology this time," she said. "I was convinced your detective work was a mix of deception and easy money. The reality, as I am now painfully aware, is that it is both dangerous and challenging. You will have a full apology in Saturday's edition of the *Dunedin Ladies' Journal*. Lady Detective will also announce my engagement to Jasper. Might she perhaps announce your engagement too?"

Grace and Charlie exchanged unspoken words. "You may," Grace said. "I would like your readers to know that Mr Charles Pyke is a fine detective and a wonderful man, as well as being unavailable to the flocks of twittering debutantes who plagued him. Perhaps your fashion column might also mention Mr Emerson's exquisite jewellery? A rush of customers might help to relieve a little of the anguish of his father's death."

"It shall be done." Caroline hesitated, with her hand on the door handle. "I have heard on good authority that this coming Saturday will be Lady Detective's last column. She has decided that there are better uses of her time than spreading gossip." Caroline didn't wait for their reply. She swept out of the bedroom.

When they were alone, Grace showed Charlie the slim box that she had spotted at the bottom of Lucy's carpetbag. Inside, several items lay on top of a small pile of banknotes. A pair of cufflinks and a locket. A pair of garish hair combs, decorated with silver peacocks, with blue-green stones forming the peacocks' tails. And a tiny silver christening bracelet. All the items Lucy's fellow first-class passengers had reported as stolen on board the ship.

Charlie picked up the silver bracelet, which looked impossibly small in his broad palm. "It would appear that Lucy Vaughan is a kleptomaniac. She must have planted the watch she stole from Farley in Barlow's cottage, along with the incriminating items from the robbery. I'll see that Declan returns these items to Mr and Mrs Quinn, Elsie Walsh and Barlow."

"Barlow will be delighted to get his daughter's christening bracelet back. He deserves a little good news, after being set up by the Vaughans to take the blame." Grace looked Charlie squarely in the eyes. "Is it my imagination, or do I recall Barlow saying he lost a sum of money in banknotes as well as the bracelet?"

Charlie smiled. "You must have better hearing than me, Grace. I'll inform DC Kelly of that fact, when I ask him to release Barlow in time for the first train to Port Chalmers tomorrow morning. Barlow will be eager to catch his ship tomorrow evening back to Australia."

"Little chance of him making his sailing. After a night in the police cells, Barlow won't have time to pack up his bird specimens before the ship departs."

"That will not present a problem," Charlie said. "I've already sent Johnny Todd and his lads out to Port Chalmers to pack for him and tidy up the cottage. Barlow will make his ship, knowing that good things happen in this country, as well as bad."

Grace reached up to reward her fiancé with a kiss. "Charlie Pyke, you are the best of men. You never believed Barlow to be guilty then?"

"Evidence can be planted. Character cannot. I was convinced that he had no knowledge of the robbery when I talked to him." Charlie placed the christening bracelet gently back in the box. "Yet, it had to be Barlow, unless someone else had set him up. The only person who knew where he was staying had returned to Australia – or so we thought until you uncovered Lucy Labelle's identity. The boots were a problem too, as they were the correct size. But Thornton told me that Lucy Labelle knew Barlow took the same size as her. Barlow seemed the perfect suspect until we had all the pieces of the puzzle."

Charlie and Grace went into the sitting room to present their evidence. Declan scribbled everything they had to say in his notebook, while Lucy sat scowling beside him.

Grace ended her evidence with a warning. "Lucy Vaughan is the mastermind, Declan. Don't let her attempt to play the innocent young woman. Remember, she is a professional stage performer."

"It'd take more than fluttering eyelashes to deter me from my job, Grace." Declan snapped his notebook closed. "Right, if that's the lot, I'll be off. I'll take Mrs Vaughan into custody at the police station and return later to collect the stolen jewels from the Emerson robbery." He paused to give Charlie a theatrical wink. "Might take me a while to return. Make sure you lock the room when you leave."

Charlie slapped his friend on the back. "Thanks, Declan."

Declan punched him on the shoulder. "It's me who ought to be thanking you two. Wallace has assured me I'll get my promotion to detective sergeant, after cracking the rum smuggling case. DS Elliot ought to be thanking you too, as he will retire in glory, after you insisted on giving him the credit for solving the Emerson case. Even Wallace admitted he was in your debt. The Minister of Agriculture and Trade was lavish with his thanks for preventing the freezer ship design from getting into Australian hands. Not a bad week's work for a private detective agency. I do hope you reap some reward from your success."

"Achieving justice for Mr Emerson is enough reward for me," Charlie replied. "Most of all, I am thankful measles are not spreading amongst the children of Dunedin. We have many people to thank for that."

Declan departed with his prisoner, leaving Charlie and Grace alone in the suite. Alone, apart from a stash of jewellery.

"Nice of Declan to give us a chance to find the engagement ring before the stolen items get taken into police custody," Grace said.

Charlie waved a hand at the scattered boxes in the corner. "I see Lucy got in ahead of us to search the camera boxes. I always thought Vaughan must be an optimist to bring so many cameras over from Australia with him."

It didn't take long to find the bag hidden behind an armchair, conveniently near the door to the hotel corridor. Lucy had draped her overcoat over it, ready for a rapid exit.

Charlie caught Grace's arm. "Grace, why don't you check the rest of the camera boxes. If you find any ring boxes, don't open them. I want to give the ring to you."

"Agreed. I shall try to look surprised, when you ask me to marry you." Grace said the words calmly, despite the horde of butterflies flittering inside her body.

Charlie merely smiled and started unpacking the bag. Grace forced herself to leave him to it, although she ached with anticipation. She kept herself busy by shaking camera boxes and setting aside any that rattled, until Charlie let out a heartfelt whoop.

Charlie led Grace to a chair and kneeled in front of her. "Grace Penrose. You are the love of my life. Will you marry me?" He opened the ring box.

"Oh!" Grace gaped at the sapphire and diamond ring for several seconds. She withdrew it from its box with trembling fingers. She turned it in the light, examining it from all angles, shedding a tear or three. It was perfect. Utterly and completely perfect. How had Charlie known? Had she told him how much she had always loved her grandmother's sapphire and diamond necklace?

"Er, Grace, I think you're supposed to say something about now. 'Yes' would be nice."

Grace wrenched her eyes from the beautiful ring. "Yes, Charlie. With all my heart, yes. Nothing would make me happier than to marry you."

Charlie took the ring and slipped it on her finger. "Does this mean you will agree to love, honour and obey me, as long as we both shall live?"

Grace stretched out her left hand and rocked it back and forth, admiring the sparkle of the diamonds and the inky depths of the sapphire. "Might we amend that to love, honour and work together by mutual agreement?"

Charlie scooped her into his arms. "Even better. Would it be mutually agreeable if I kissed you now, my darling?"

Grace didn't waste time replying with words. This was one request she was delighted to obey, now and forever.

Read on

Coming in time for Christmas, Penrose and Pyke Book 5.5, a novella. In ***Tinsel and Trickery***, Penrose and Pyke's quiet Christmas with Grace's family is disrupted by dubious dealings affecting the local home for orphans. Charlie soon learns that being a detective is a walk in the park compared to negotiating the festive season in the Penrose household.

In Book 6, ***Murder Ignited***, Grace and Charlie's wedding is thrown into disarray, after an out-of-control protest at Lavender House ends in a tragic death.

Thank You

Thank you for reading this story. If you enjoyed it, I would be very grateful if you would leave a rating or review to help other readers discover it.

Find out about other books and sign up for notifications of new releases at https://RosePascoe.com

Historical Notes

Although this story and its characters are fictional, the broader themes were inspired by the real social conditions and health issues of the era.

From the earliest European settlement of the isolated island nation of Aotearoa/New Zealand, ships were put into quarantine to stop infectious diseases entering the country. Smallpox and plague were perhaps the most feared, but measles, scarlet fever, cholera, influenza, and other diseases were a terrifying prospect in a world without modern medicines and vaccines.

In the major ports, quarantine stations were set up on islands, including Quarantine Island in Otago Harbour. Nine thousand immigrants from forty-one ships spent time there, of whom at least seventy-two died there. The island can still be visited today (https://quarantineisland.org.nz).

Measles is a dreadful disease, as it has a high death rate amongst young children and is extremely contagious (several times more infectious than the coronavirus that caused a worldwide epidemic from 2020). One of the most infamous ships quarantined in Otago Harbour, the SS *Mongol*, suffered sixty-seven cases of measles and twenty-one cases of scarlet fever, with a dozen deaths occurring on the voyage from Plymouth in 1873-74, amongst fewer than three hundred assisted immigrants (including 108 children). Despite being quarantined, further cases were detected in the community, sparking considerable concern and a long-lasting fear of further outbreaks.

The 1874-75 measles epidemic had the highest death rate amongst the European population of all the outbreaks in New Zealand, with 80% of deaths being children under five. Another outbreak in 1893 (the year after this story is set) had the highest number of deaths in one year. The death rate for the indigenous population is not recorded, but measles and other infectious diseases have inflicted terrible devastation on Māori since the arrival of Europeans.

Information on the public health issues of the era came from *Challenge for Health: a History of Public Health in New Zealand* (F. S. Maclean, 1964, Government Printer, Wellington, NZ) and online sources.

The development of a vaccination in the 1960s led to the virtual elimination of measles in many countries, saving the lives of countless children. Unfortunately, success has bred complacency. With vaccination rates declining, there have been further outbreaks of measles in recent years, in New Zealand and elsewhere, with tragic results.

The 'Doctor Osborne' character is a tribute to Doctor Frank Ogston, who was a public health and medical jurisprudence lecturer at the medical school during the period the story was set. Ogston was later the first District Health Officer in Dunedin. His role, character and actions in the story are entirely fictional.

In the late 1880s, the invention of hand-held cameras brought photography out of the studio and into the hands of amateur photographers. The classic camera of the era was George Eastman's Kodak box camera, but the fad for taking candid shots also prompted manufacturers to develop "detective cameras" in the shape of everyday items. Advertisements in the Dunedin newspapers noted various types, especially necktie cameras, but there were also cameras in waistcoats, binoculars, pocket watches, and bags. Camera clubs flourished and articles in the newspapers discussed the use of such cameras. Inevitably, concerns were raised about their nefarious potential, taking images unbeknownst to the subject. Perfect timing for Dunedin's (fictional) first detective agency.

The *Dunedin Ladies' Journal* in this story is fictional, but there were ladies' journals published in the era. For example, *New Zealand Graphic and Ladies' Journal* (published 1890-1908) was an illustrated weekly journal containing a variety of literature, special features, society gossip and fashion notes (but no “Lady Detective”).

Shipments of frozen meat may sound unexciting as a source of espionage, but they were absolutely critical to New Zealand’s economic success, due to the distance between the country and its markets in far distant Britain. Australia had an earlier first shipment of frozen meat (1879) than New Zealand (1882), but technical and quality problems beset the fledgling Australian industry, while the New Zealand industry flourished. The story is fictional, but the rivalry between Australia and New Zealand is very real, especially when it comes to the sports field.

Bird collecting was a passion amongst the Victorians. In 1888, a single London dealer was reported to have sold two million small birds alone. The exotic nature of New Zealand’s avian fauna drew many eager hunters and collectors to our shores, contributing to the extinction of several species, including the huia. Pairs of huia were especially prized, as they were used as a moral example of male and female working together (the sexes having beaks adapted for different tasks). Huia were already rare by the 1890s, with the last confirmed sighting in 1907.

For more information and images, visit my website: https://RosePascoe.com.

Acknowledgements

A huge thank you to my fabulous beta readers – Mary, Jenny, Kathy and Ross – whose dedication is very much appreciated. Thanks also to my family and friends for their encouragement and to my readers for their ongoing support.

This novel is dedicated to all the brave people who risk their own lives during disease outbreaks, in order to protect the lives of our most vulnerable citizens.

About The Author

Rose Pascoe writes historical mysteries with a dash of romance, when she isn't plotting real-life adventures. She lives in beautiful New Zealand, land of beaches and mountains, where long walks provide the perfect conditions for dreaming up plots and fickle weather provides the incentive to sit down and actually write the darn things. After a career in health, justice and social research, her passion is for stories set against a backdrop of social revolution. Her heroines are ordinary women, who meet the challenges thrown at them with determination, ingenuity, courage, and humour.

Visit her at: https://RosePascoe.com

Printed in Great Britain
by Amazon

55938593R00154